DISTURB

and others

JA Konrath

Edition: March 2010

CONTENTS

Disturb 1

A Medical Thriller Novel

Author Afterword 219

Short Stories

The Big Guys 223

Flash fiction, winner of the Derringer Award.

A Fistful of Cozy 227

A satire of the mystery cozy genre.

Cleansing 233

An ancient crime of biblical proportions

Lying Eyes 239

Solve it yourself, given the clues.

Perfect Plan 245

Another solve it yourself. Don't you remember One Minute Mysteries and Encyclopedia Brown? 245

Piece of Cake 251

Another solve it yourself, originally featured in Woman's World. 251

Animal Attraction 257

Solve it yourself.

Urgent Reply Needed 263

A cautionary tale about dealing with spammers.

Blaine's Deal 271

A parody of hardboiled noir.

Light Drizzle 275

A light-hearted send-up of hitman stories.

An Archaeologist's Story 331

How digging up old bones leads to fresh corpses.

Don't Press That Button! 285

An essay about the gadgets in the James Bond universe, and which you need to buy.

Piranha Pool 297

A writer seeking criticism pays the ultimate price.

A Newbie's Guide to Thrillerfest 309

Never been to a mystery conference? Here's the in-depth dirt.

Inspector Oxnard 317

He's either brilliant, or too stupid to breathe.

One Night Only 321

A sports fan ends up in jail, all for the love of the game.

Could Stephanie Plum Really Get Car Insurance? 339

An essay about Janet Evanovich's famous character.

Cozies or Hardboiled? 349

Take the test to find out which type of book you're reading.

Addiction - 353

What's the worst drug you can get hung up on?

Weigh To Go 359

A humor column about health clubs.

The world, it seems, does not possess even those of us who are adults completely, but only up to two thirds; one third of us is still quite unborn. Every time we wake in the morning, it is like a new birth.

—Sigmund Freud

Sleep is the only medicine that gives ease.

—Sophocles

Prologue

"I'm going to kill somebody. Soon."

David leaned back on the mattress, fingers laced behind his blond head. His overdeveloped biceps strained the fabric of his T-shirt sleeves. He flexed his pecs, and his chest trembled like a bull shaking off horseflies.

Manny muted the television, sighing loudly enough for David to hear him. This was a familiar dialog.

"No, you won't. You don't want to get in trouble again."

David grunted. He stared at the ceiling, imagining that this was a real apartment with people living above and below. But it wasn't real; it was a cage, pure and simple. The fake scenery outside the window and the phone that only dialed out to one number made it even more ludicrous.

"I'd rather go back to prison than stay here."

"You know that isn't true. This is better for us, David. We can get through this. Look at all we've been through together."

Manny was right. They'd been through hell. But the future only promised extra helpings, with no end in sight.

"I can't take it."

"You have to."

David clenched his teeth. The hate buzzed around in his head like a hornet's nest, desperately trying to get out. He made his decision.

"I want you to kill me."

Manny turned away, shaking his head.

"No. That's not an option."

"Anyone can take a life, Manny. All you need is the proper motivation. What if I took that fire ax in the hallway and chopped up your little girlfriend? Does it have to come to that?"

"I hate it when you talk like this." Manny stood up and went to the kitchenette. He got a glass of water, staring at David's reflection in the framed Dali poster hanging above the sink. His stomach fluttered. David was older, bigger, and had a vein of mean running through him. A rich vein, that seemed to be growing. "I'm sure they're listening."

David laughed, a sound like a large dog growling.

"Of course they're listening. We signed our privacy away. It's lost, just like our freedom. Our minds are next."

Manny finished the water and sat on the edge of the bed. He tried to sound soothing. "We're a team, David. We have to see it though. That was the deal."

"To hell with the deal."

"David..."

"How can you handle it, Manny? How can you handle the dreams?"

Manny thought about the question. He suppressed a chill.

"I handle them."

"Well, I can't. I have to get out. And if I leave, you know that a lot of people are going to die. I can't control myself, Manny. It's like a thirst."

"It'll get easier. You'll see."

David pressed his hands to his face, as if he were trying to keep his skull from exploding.

"At least you're the prize show dog. I'm the big mistake, kept in the shadows. Science gone wrong. Kill me."

"No."

David reached out and grabbed Manny by the hand, imploring.

"Just do it. Stick a knife in my ribs."

"I can't."

David's grip tightened. Manny tried to pull away, but couldn't. A shadow settled behind David's face.

"I can hurt you. I can hurt you real bad."

"Please... David..."

With a quick snap, David bent Manny's pinkie backwards. The pain was instant and nauseating.

Manny yanked his hand free. His little finger jutted out at an odd angle. The blood leeched from his head, leaving his face ghost-white. He tried to stand, but his knees were spaghetti.

David's eyes got big. He put a hand on Manny's shoulder.

"Manny, Jesus, I'm sorry."

Manny pulled back.

"Get away from me."

"I didn't mean it. I swear. You see how I get? I can't control it."

Manny managed to get to the bathroom. He ran cold water over his hand, but it didn't numb the pain.

"Did I break it again?"

"Go to hell."

"I think it's just dislocated. I can pop it back."

He gently tugged Manny's wrist away from the sink. Manny began to shake.

"Please, go away."

"This'll just take a second."

David got a good grip on the dislocated finger. Manny felt the bile rise.

"No, please..."

For the longest moment, Manny was convinced that David wanted to twist it backwards even farther, wrench the finger until it came off. But David simply gave it a quick tug and the pinkie snapped back into place. He stared at Manny, eyebrows knitted.

“I'll stick with it, Manny. For you. But promise me that if I hurt anyone else, you end it for me. I know you could do it. You're not as squeaky clean as they think.”

The pain was subsiding, and Manny's stomach began to settle.

“I'll think about it.”

“Sure. You do that. We have plenty of time.” David grinned. “And plenty of fingers.”

David left, and Manny locked the bathroom door. The situation was getting worse, and the mandatory shrink visits didn't help at all. He thought about telling one of the research team, but that would ruin everything they’d worked so hard for.

Manny stared into the mirror, searching himself for an answer.

Maybe murder was the only alternative.

But could he actually kill him? Could he actually kill his own brother?

Manny looked down at his swollen finger and wondered if he could.

Chapter 1

"What would you give for an extra thirty years of life?"

The big man was no longer at the podium. He circulated among the tables, his grandiose voice having no need for a microphone. A neatly trimmed beard, the color of a black bear, extended along his jaw line and connected with a shock of matching wiry hair. Except for some busboys hustling empty plates, all the eyes in the banquet room, over a hundred sets, were on him.

"Think of it. More time to spend with your family. More time to get all the things done that need to get done. More time to enjoy life to the fullest. Time is money. Time is precious. But most of all, time is a resource, like oil or natural gas. How much is it worth to you?"

He paused, eyes twinkling. Dr. William May had seen this speech once before, but was no less impressed. Unlike other scientists Bill had met in his career, Dr. Nikos Stefanopolous had magnetism to match his brilliance. The barrel chested Greek could have hawked cooking utensils on late night TV with equal aplomb.

"We sleep one third of our lives. Thirty years. We don't have any say in the matter. But what if we did? What if we could take a simple pill that could replace a full night's sleep? Think of it."

The audience did think of it, Bill included. An impressive feat, if possible.

"You would feel just as refreshed, just as fit, just as rested, as if you'd spent eight hours in bed. But instead of eight hours, this pill would do the same amount of work in just twenty minutes. Senator, I'm sure a pill like this would do wonders for your filibusters."

The room laughed, and Senator Donner acknowledged with a nod and a grin.

"Such a pill is the culmination of twenty years of research into sleep. My daughter, Dr. Theena Boone, and myself have dedicated a good portion of our lives to the study of sleep, and its effects on the body. What does sleep actually do? What is its purpose? What chemical changes occur in the body during sleep? And most of all—can it be synthesized? At this point I'd like to introduce Mr. Emmanuel Tibbets."

Dr. Nikos rallied some applause. Bill sat up, craning his neck to see over the table in front of him. This was new.

A large man got up from the head table and walked to the empty podium. Like Dr. Nikos, he was in a tuxedo. But his fit better, every cut and pleat hinting at the chiseled physique underneath. He had dirty blonde hair, cut in a military style, and his features were hard and angular, like a child's action figure.

"Thank you, Dr. Nikos. I would like everyone in the audience to think about the last time you've been up all night. We've all experienced the symptoms; being lethargic, grumpy, unable to concentrate or focus. We look, and feel, terrible, and that's from missing only one night's sleep. How many of you have been awake for more than twenty-four hours?"

There was a show of hands, over half of the audience.

"How about forty-eight hours?"

Most of the hands dropped.

"And seventy-two hours?"

Only a few remained raised.

"After seventy-two hours, your judgment becomes extremely impaired. You drive with the same skill as someone with a blood alcohol level of zero point two. You'd be constantly falling asleep, taking micro-naps for minutes at a time, without being aware of it—even if staying awake was a matter of life and death."

Bill could relate. He'd had his share of sleepless nights. Especially in the last year.

"After seventy-two hours without sleep, you begin to hallucinate. You become paranoid, delusional, unable to function. Isn't it true, Dr. Nikos, that an EEG done on a person without three days of sleep is identical to someone suffering from acute schizophrenia?"

"True, Manny."

"How was my last EEG?"

"Perfectly normal."

"I ask the audience, do I seem to be experiencing any symptoms of sleep deprivation? Would you believe me if I told you I've been without sleep for seventy-two hours? How about ninety-six hours? A hundred and twenty? Dr. Nikos, do you have the time?"

The doctor made a show of rolling up his sleeve and looking at his watch.

"It just turned nine o'clock."

"Nine o'clock. Which means I've been awake now for nine hundred and eleven straight hours."

The audience was stunned to silence. After a moment, a single person began to applaud. It snowballed into a roaring ovation. Bill joined in.

Dr. Nikos joined Manny on the stage, eyes twinkling. He patted the larger man on the shoulder, then held out his palm to quell the clapping.

"Manny is part of the final phase of our project, the clinical test subject. Our drug, Nonsomnambulox—N-Som for short, has already passed the Chemistry and Pharmacological reviews of the Food and Drug Administration. Manny has taken one pill every day for the last thirty-eight days, which was the last time he's had a conventional night of sleep."

The applause began to build again. Dr. Nikos talked above it.

"The R & D is nearing an end, and pending Medical approval, we're ready to go into production. Needless to say, what this drug could do for the economy, for the efficiency of the human race, for the quality of life of every person on this planet—it staggers the imagination. We can take some questions."

Hands went up throughout the room, lawyers and politicians and businessmen; a who's who of status and influence in the Midwest.

"Is the pill expensive?"

"We plan on introducing N-Som to the market at fifteen dollars a dose. Are eight hours of your life worth fifteen dollars?"

"What about side effects?"

"I'll let Manny field that one."

Manny grinned, showing perfect teeth.

"Since taking N-Som, I've lost fifteen pounds in fat and gained eight pounds in muscle mass. My immune system and healing abilities have increased dramatically. I also don't get tired. In fact, three days ago I was on a treadmill for eighteen hours."

The audience murmured its disbelief. Dr. Nikos beamed.

"We were even more amazed by this than you folks are, but we've found a reasonable scientific explanation. N-Som stimulates the pituitary gland, increasing production of human growth hormone. Manny may be the most fit human being on the face of the earth."

A woman at a far table spoke.

"What about dreams? I, for one, wouldn't give up my dreams for anything."

Someone else chimed in. "I love my dreams, too."

There were many nods of agreement, Bill one of them. On most days his dream life was better than his real one.

"The dreams." Manny's eyes got a faraway look, and his smile was beatific. "They're the most vivid dreams you'll ever have. Even though they only last a few minutes, they seem to go on for hours. And you remember them, every detail, from beginning to end."

"And when does the stock go public?"

General laughter. Dr. Nikos joined in.

"That depends on the FDA. And actually, the CDER agent responsible for N-Som's approval is sitting among us. Bill, please come up here."

Bill shook off the momentary surprise and was beckoned up to the podium. This was unexpected. Though getting in front of groups was part of his job, he liked to be prepared first.

He walked to the stage and Dr. Nikos shook his hand warmly. Manny offered his hand next; his grip was like slamming your fingers in a car door. Bill disengaged himself and Dr. Nikos put an arm around his shoulders.

"May I introduce Dr. William May, from the Center for Drug Evaluation and Research. We shall continue to extend our fullest cooperation to the Food and Drug Administration, and I'm sure once our data is examined, N-Som will be judged even safer than aspirin."

More applause. Bill felt a tad queasy; he wasn't sure if his stomach was balking at the crème brulee, or if he was afraid he'd be asked to say a few words. Thankfully, Dr. Nikos wrapped up his speech and escorted Bill back to the head table amid a standing ovation.

"Dr. May, let me introduce my daughter, Dr. Theena Boone."

Dr. Boone was around Bill's age, in her mid-thirties, dark and shapely. She had a smaller version of her father's Greek nose and enough hair on her head for several women. The soft black curls rested on her bare shoulders, and the neckline of her dress made eye-contact an effort.

"A pleasure, Dr. May."

Bill took her hand and responded in kind.

"Please sit, Dr. May." Dr. Nikos pulled out a chair for Bill. "I have to be social for a little bit."

Dr. Nikos and Manny blended into the gathering crowd. Bill sat and faced the woman. He'd neatly slid from one uncomfortable situation into another. Small talk wasn't one of his strengths.

"Your father is an excellent speaker."

To Theena's credit, she seemed completely at ease. As if suddenly being forced into conversation with a complete stranger was normal for her.

"He believes all Greeks should be outspoken; the result of seeing Zorba too many times."

Unlike her father, Theena didn't have the slightest trace of an accent. Her voice was low, but soft in an undeniably feminine way.

"He does remind me a bit of Anthony Quinn."

"Don't let him hear you say that; he'd be insufferable. I'm to understand that you'll begin your investigation tomorrow?"

Bill nodded. "It's not an investigation, really. All I do is review your testing and give a preliminary report to the committee."

"But you have the power to stop the process before it gets to that, correct?"

"Yes."

She took a sip of wine, leaving the tiniest trace of red lipstick on the glass. The rim had a complete circle of half moons around it, like a deliberate design. Bill thought of his own wine, back at the other table. A nice Merlot would take off the edge.

"I've seen Dr. Nikos lecture before, but this was the first time he introduced Manny. It's incredible."

"Yes, we're all terribly excited. Manny especially. This drug has done wonders for him."

"Was he the first human test subject?"

Theena's demure expression flickered.

"Actually, no. There was someone else who began the program at the same time as Manny. But there were... complications."

"Something to do with the drug?"

"No, nothing like that. It was a personal matter. The N-Som worked fine." Theena smiled. "I hope you aren't ignoring Mrs. May to be sitting here with me."

Bill automatically looked at his wedding band.

"She... died last year."

"I'm so sorry. Was it sudden?"

Bill almost blurted out a yes. He caught himself in time.

"She was sick for a long time." The image of Kristen, lying in the hospital bed, filled his mind. "And you? Is Mr. Boone off mingling?"

Theena wiggled her large diamond ring. It caught the light and winked.

"Last I heard he was in Texas. I kept the name because anything is preferable to Stefanopolous. So, how does one get a job at the FDA?"

Bill thought about the long, boring version. After completing his studies at the University of Chicago and his internship at Rush-Presbyterian, Bill was undecided between a residency or private practice. He'd known from a young age that he'd be an M.D., but when the day finally came he realized that he enjoyed learning about medicine more than actually practicing it.

Congress made the decision for him. The year was 1992, and they'd just passed PDUFA—the Prescription Drug User Fee Act, which authorized the FDA to charge drug sponsors for their services, expediting the approval process. Suddenly CDER, which had been impossible to break into, had hundreds of openings for reviewers. Bill had leapt at the chance.

"I was just in the right place at the right time. How about you? You're a chemist, right?"

"Actually, I'm a pathologist, like my father. Specializing in neuropathology, of course."

Bill's confidence slipped another notch. Beautiful, and a brain surgeon.

"Exciting work?"

Theena laughed, a rich, warm sound.

"I think I've developed a permanent squint from looking in the microscope so often. No, it's not what I would call exciting. But it's not without rewards, either. What time shall we expect you at DruTech tomorrow?"

"Whenever is convenient."

"Anytime is fine. Research continues around the clock. Your predecessor preferred to work during the night shift."

Bill raised an eyebrow. "My predecessor?"

"The prior CDER agent. Did you ever find out what happened to him?" Theena studied Bill's face. "You have no idea what I'm talking about, do you? He was sent by the FDA last month to review some preliminary research, worked with us for a week, and then left without a word. A Dr. Bitner?"

Bill knew Michael Bitner. They'd golfed on several occasions. He'd have to give him a call, find out what had happened.

"Someone call the police!"

The cry came from the other side of the banquet room, followed by shouts for a doctor. Bill hurried through the crowd, Theena on his heels. The activity was centered around the Men's Room. Bill had to shove gawkers out of his way to get in.

"I'm a doctor! Give me some room!"

At first, all Bill saw was blood. It took his brain a second to register that under all that blood was Dr. Nikos.

Theena screamed.

Bill knelt down, soaking his pants leg. He automatically reached for the carotid artery, then stopped his hand when he saw the gash in the doctor's throat, deep enough to expose the esophagus. Dr. Nikos was gone, long beyond anyone's help.

"Over here! There's another!"

Bill was ushered over to a second pool of blood. In the center of it was Manny. His tuxedo shirt was shredded, over half a dozen wounds covering his abdomen and chest. A scalpel handle protruded from his sternum.

"Tried... tried to save... da..."

Manny coughed, spitting red. Bill tilted Manny's face to the side so the blood didn't run down his throat. His pulse was strong, but when Bill tore off Manny's shirt he didn't hold out much hope. The guy looked like a lasagna.

Bill left the scalpel embedded, concerned that removal would cause more bleeding. He enlisted four guys with cloth napkins to keep pressure on Manny's many wounds. He also put Manny's feet up on a chair to stave off shock.

The paramedics arrived shortly thereafter, intubing Manny and carting him away.

Bill looked around the room, trying to spot Theena. He went back into the banquet hall, the crowd parting for him when they noticed his bloody clothing. He checked her table, the hotel lobby, and finally the parking lot.

She was gone.

Chapter 2

Bill was in the shower when the phone rang. He let the machine pick it up, holding the curtain partially open to hear who it was.

"Bill, this is Theena Boone..."

Bill grabbed a towel and hurried out of the bathroom. The fact that Theena was attractive and single wasn't lost on him, but Bill tried to rise above that and convince himself his concern was professional. She'd just lost her father.

"Theena?"

"Bill. Hello. I... was wondering what time you were stopping by DruTech today."

The question caught him completely by surprise.

"I wasn't planning to, actually. I figured, because of yesterday—how are you holding up?"

"I'm strong, Bill. Dad raised me that way. He also wouldn't want this to interfere with our work. N-Som was his dream. Now that he's gone, it's even more important that I finish what he began."

Tough lady. Bill wondered how much of it was genuine, and how much was bravado.

"How's Manny?"

"Surprisingly well, for fifteen stab wounds. Collapsed lung, perforated small intestine, internal bleeding. He needed over sixty stitches, but is listed as stable."

"Have the police found anything?"

"Manny said there were two attackers, both with ski masks on. No leads yet. Are you coming?"

Bill glanced at the clock on the nightstand. "I can be there by ten, if that's okay."

"That's fine. I'll meet you in the lobby."

Theena hung up. Bill dried off and went into the bedroom. He noticed a spring in his step that hadn't been there a few minutes ago. Being honest with himself was a trait Bill nurtured, and he knew he was excited to be seeing Theena again so soon.

Admitting it brought guilt. He glanced at his wife's side of the closet, full of clothes. Kristen's presence was still there; her plants that Bill carefully maintained, their wedding pictures on the walls, the Hummel figurines she collected. The casual observer couldn't have guessed that the condo had been occupied by a single man for more than a year.

Bill dressed in his best suit, a dark blue Armani pinstripe. He could tie a Windsor knot with one hand in complete darkness, but he still preferred the solace of a mirror. There was a tinge of red in his blue eyes; something he hadn't been able to get rid of since Kristen got ill. He used some Visine, then combed his light brown hair and noted that he'd need a trim soon. After a quick electric shave he was in his Audi and on the way to DruTech Industries.

The weather was unusually tame by Chicago standards, especially this late in the fall. At every crosswalk there was at least one person in shorts, and the few jackets Bill saw were draped over shoulders rather than being worn. The sun felt good on his face for a while, but he eventually pulled down the visor when the glare became too much.

He played stop and go, eventually reaching I-90 and the path to the suburbs. Traffic was hellish, made even worse by the omnipresent construction, which had closed one lane off with orange cones. Bill had lived in the Windy City his entire life, and he'd never been on the Kennedy

Expressway without suffering some kind of delay. The trip took seventy minutes, ten of which were spent on the off ramp to Schaumburg.

DruTech occupied an impressive five story building off a frontage road parallel to the expressway. It was sandwiched between a water reclamation plant and an AM radio station. Bill parked in a lot that was nearly empty. The front entrance was located between two water sculptures, marble and cascading, vaguely Roman in theme.

The lobby was expansive, the size of a small movie theater. It continued the motif, with polished terrazzo floors, white columns, and a front desk located under an arch. There were two elevators next to a small cafe, which was dark and quiet. In fact, Bill didn't see any people anywhere, other than the security guard.

He was sitting behind the desk, dressed in a gray uniform which fit a little too tightly. Before Bill had a chance to say a word the guard had a black phone in his hand.

"Good morning, Dr. May. I'll tell Dr. Boone you've arrived."

"Thank you."

Bill busied himself with wrinkle patrol, the trip having done cruel things to his suit. He was checking his hair in a chrome garbage can when Theena arrived.

Her white lab coat ended several inches above her knees, under which the hem of a short black skirt was barely visible. The doctor's face was carefully made up, her lipstick a more conservative shade than the previous night's. She didn't seem bereaved in the slightest.

"Hello, Bill. Thank you for coming."

A handshake led to an awkward, but welcome, hug.

"If there's anything I can do."

She pulled back and smiled. "Welcome to DruTech. Let me show you around."

She took Bill by the arm and led him through the empty lobby. He commented on the dearth of people.

"Oh, that's Albert's doing—Albert Rothchilde. He insisted everyone take the day off due to yesterday's tragedy. Just a security guard and us today."

"I've met Albert. Cheerful guy."

"When the stock is up, yes. How much do you know about DruTech?"

"A bit. DruTech is a subsidiary of American Products. They make dish soap."

Bill, like millions of other Americans, had a box of it at home.

"Correct. They lead the industry in environmentally conscious cleaning agents. Soaps, cleansers, whiteners, stain removers. A.P. also has a large share of the waste disposal market; biodegradable plastic garbage bags and such. DruTech was bought out by A.P. ten years ago, based on the strength of one of my father's patents."

"Pain-Away."

She flashed Bill an appreciative smile.

"A skin absorbing analgesic. Doing a great business with athletes and the elderly. Albert is President of A.P., and is also the supervisory head of DruTech."

"He runs both, personally?"

"I know, he seems too young. After his parents died, he did away with the committees. He's very hands-on, and both companies are flourishing under him."

They stepped into a chrome elevator and Theena removed a plastic card from her coat pocket. She stuck it in a slot under the call buttons, and a green light flashed. The lift descended.

"Upstairs is all corporate office work. It's downstairs where we have all the fun."

She winked. Was she flirting with him, the day after her father was killed? Bill wondered if this was her coping mechanism. He cleared his throat.

“Is N-Som the only drug you have in development?”

“There are others; an experimental burn cream, a decongestant—but N-Som is the main focus.”

“How many people are working on it?”

“Six, plus Manny.” Her smiled faltered. “Five, now.”

There was an uncomfortable silence.

“It feels better, to talk about it. Grieving is a process that takes time.”

“Grief?” Theena's face was caught between a smile and a snarl. “My father was a brilliant scientist, and the world will mourn his loss. I have a mixed opinion. He... he did things.”

Before Bill could ask what she meant, the doors opened and she was walking briskly down the hallway. He followed, her words hanging in his head like a crooked picture.

The decor had changed drastically, all antiseptic white tile and harsh neon lights. It reminded Bill of a modern hospital.

“There are over a dozen rooms down here.” Theena spoke without facing him, her demeanor no longer playful. “Labs, offices, the computer center, two gyms, more medical equipment than an urban emergency room. And this.”

She opened a solid white door and held it for Bill. Inside, rather than an office...

“It looks like an apartment.”

Bill took in his surroundings. It was a fully furnished studio, complete with kitchen, den, and dining area. A stereo, cluttered with CD cases, and a pizza box on the TV gave the impression it was in use.

“Manny's room. This allows us to closely monitor him, while also giving him a semblance of normalcy. My father's idea; allow the N-Som test subject to go about daily life while taking the drug.”

Bill looked at a window. The sun peeked through the curtains, which was impossible.

“Fake view. It's a television monitor, can simulate all kinds of weather.”

She picked up a remote control and pointed it at the window. She switched from morning to night, a soft crescent moon replacing the sun. Another switch and it was day again, but overcast and drizzling.

“That's impressive.”

“I can also switch it to play movies, cable, pay per view. Even porn. Do you enjoy pornography, doctor?”

Bill faced her. Theena was unreadable—he couldn't tell if she was amused or sardonic.

“I don't have much of an opinion on the subject.”

Theena moved closer, into his personal space. Her breath was warm and smelled of mint.

“I've studied the neurological effects pornography has on the human brain. You've heard the old story, that men are turned on visually, while women are stimulated emotionally? Not according to my research. I've found that men and women get equally excited, mentally that is, while viewing pornography.”

“Interesting.” Bill felt his collar get a little tighter, and he fought the urge to pull at his tie.

“No one else seemed to think so, and I lost my funding. I think this country places too much importance on sex. It's a natural, necessary, biological process, but we keep it behind closed doors. No good comes from repression, don't you agree?”

Her smile sent a shock through him.

“I, uh, agree. Repression isn't a good thing.”

“It's different in Europe. More relaxed. There is no shame in a naked body. No shame in being open about your sexuality. Have you been with a woman since your wife died?”

Bill blushed. He was at a loss for an answer. The truth was he hadn't had sex in over a year, but that wasn't any of Theena's business. She may have been born in Europe, but Bill hadn't had that luxury. Her bluntness made him uncomfortable, and if that was an indication of his own repression, so be it.

Still, he was flattered to be hit on. If, indeed, that's what she was doing.

Theena touched his hand. Bill's ears burned.

"Would you like to see Manny's bedroom?"

He fought the urge to take a step back.

"Dr. Boone—Theena, I find you very attractive, but I don't think this is the right time."

"Do strong willed women scare you, Bill?"

"No. But I wouldn't want to take advantage of your situation."

She moved closer, her hand touching his hip, her long curly hair brushing against his neck.

"But I'm the one in control, Bill. How could you be taking advantage of me?"

Damn good question.

"Your father just died. You're confused."

"He really wanted N-Som to be approved."

Bill pushed her at arm's length.

"Is that what this is about? Theena, my job here is to review your research and based on that..."

Theena began to laugh. Her abrupt change of character was shocking.

"What's funny?"

"Sorry, Bill. I was just messing around with you."

"Excuse me?"

"I wanted to see how you'd react, that's all. It's strange to find any gentlemen left in this profession."

Bill blinked. He blinked again.

"This—this was a put on?"

"You're cute." Theena touched him on the end of the nose. "But I'm not that easy. And my father did just die yesterday. Call it an integrity check. You passed. Come on, I'll show you the other rooms."

Theena took his hand and led him out of the pseudo apartment. Bill felt as if he'd just been subjected to a battery of psych tests. He had to remind himself she was mourning, and people did crazy things while mourning.

But had it really been a gag? Bill was positive, if he'd wanted, he could have had her right there. Was he that easily fooled? Or was she that good?

Or was he that needy?

"We call this the Sweat Room. Treadmill, Nautilus Machines, Stairmaster, free weights. One of our testing criteria is to judge N-Som's effects on motor skills and muscle fatigue. Lack of sleep makes a person physically tired. Before Manny was put on the drug, we did a series of control scores. Prior to N-Som, he could stay on a Stairmaster for three hours before collapsing from exhaustion."

Bill studied Theena. She was acting like a professional again. Part of him was disappointed.

"And while he was on N-Som?"

"We had to quit at nine hours because the machine blew a gear."

She took him to a room across the hallway. Bill recognized several machines, including an EEG and an oscilloscope. Both were in operation, the electroencephalogram drawing a jagged polygraph line on an endless ream of paper.

"Is someone being tested right now?"

"Those are Manny's. He has remote sensors surgically implanted in his scalp, and they send the signal here. It's the only way to be sure he never sleeps, since it is almost impossible to watch him twenty-four hours a day."

Bill was familiar enough to interpret the data. The frequency of the peaks and troughs indicated beta waves. Manny was awake and aware. Curiosity made Bill flip through the pile of folded pages, all with the same, continuous pattern.

He looked for a variation which would indicate unconsciousness. Delta, theta, or spindle waves were obvious signs of sleep; the frequency would slow and the voltage would increase, making bigger and wider peaks. But he couldn't even find alpha waves.

“Doesn't he ever close his eyes?”

“Amazing, isn't it? Normally closed eyes slow down electrical activity, because the brain isn't being visually stimulated. Manny's brain remains in beta, even when he keeps his eyes closed for hours.”

“Shouldn't this show when he was put under for his operation last night?”

“Manny didn't go under. He insisted on a local anesthetic.”

“To repair a collapsed lung?”

“He didn't want to jeopardize the experiment.”

Bill thought about invasive surgery while being conscious. He shuddered. The guy was either very committed, or out of his mind.

The EEG needle began to move faster, the small peaks and troughs so close together it was hard to see the cycles between them.

“What's happening now?”

Theena looked closely at the readouts and frowned.

“Beta 2 waves. I've seen this before, usually when he's very irritated, or having an argument. But the police have a guard on him, and no one is allowed into his hospital room.”

“Maybe some reaction to medication.”

“No. He's not on any medication.”

“Not even antibiotics?”

“He doesn't need them. His immune system is incredible.” Theena pursed her lips. “No, he's definitely arguing with somebody. I wonder who?”

Chapter 3

"How did you get in here?"

Manny's voice was high pitched, frantic. The flimsy hospital gown he wore made him feel even more vulnerable.

David smiled at him.

"Your armed guard is taking a nap outside. Remember naps, Manny? Don't you miss them?"

Manny tried to rise out of the hospital bed, but David put a hand on his shoulder.

"Don't bother getting up. I won't stay long. Pity about Dr. Nikos, isn't it? You know what I saw in his eyes when I slit his throat? Not fear. Not pain. Just disappointment. It was delicious. How's your chest?"

David lifted up Manny's gown and peeked.

"Looks nasty. What is that tube?"

Manny tried to melt into his mattress.

"A drain."

"Does it hurt?"

David prodded at the protruding plastic, pinching it between his fingers. Manny forced courage.

"What do you want, David? Did you come back to finish the job?"

"I wasn't after you, Manny. You know that. But you tried to get in the way. Don't you see the only way we can be free is if the experiment ends?"

"I told the cops."

David grinned, patting his brother on the cheek.

"No, you didn't. You lied to them. I know you did. Now—who should we kill next?"

"Please..."

"How about the computer geek, Dr. Townsend? All those ridiculous graphs and charts, as if he could reduce us to just statistics. Or Dr. O'Neil? Aren't you sick of his fumbling attempts at taking serum samples? Maybe Dr. Fletcher. He tries to poke around in our heads with all the subtlety of a linebacker. Or Theena...?"

Manny's eyes got wide.

"Maybe I should pick up your Theena." David rubbed his face, as if mulling it over. "We could have some fun together. I bet she's a real tiger."

Manny tried to raise his arm, but it was taped to the rail so the saline drip IV wouldn't pull out. This greatly amused David.

"Yes, I think Theena it is. Unless you'd prefer someone else. Who should I kill instead of Theena? I'll let you pick."

Manny stared at his brother with tortured eyes. This was worse than being attacked. David was going to kill someone, and there was nothing he could do to stop it.

But at least he could save Theena...

"Townsend."

David's smile was ghastly.

"The computer geek. Excellent. I'll come back later with the details. Maybe even some pictures. See you, bro."

David left. Manny looked at the phone. He had to talk to Jim Townsend, warn him what was coming.

He called DruTech and got the number from Barry, the head security guard. Barry attempted to wish him well, but Manny hung up on him, anxious to make the call.

Townsend wasn't home. His machine picked up. Manny left a message.

"Dr. Townsend. This is Manny. Your life is in danger. The same people that killed Dr. Nikos are going after you."

Manny squeezed his eyes shut at the lie. How could he still be protecting David, after all he'd done? He swallowed hard, and continued.

"You have to go away for a while. Don't tell anyone where you're going. These people—they can't be stopped. They're maniacs. Please believe me. I don't want anyone else to get hurt."

He gently set the receiver in its cradle and laid back down. Outside, clouds had covered the sun, turning everything gray.

Manny closed his eyes and wished, for the thousandth time, that he could just go to sleep.

Chapter 4

Dr. Jim Townsend hated days off. The call from Rothchilde's secretary came while he was in the car and already halfway to work. He'd briefly argued with her, insisting on coming in anyway, but she told him security had been informed not to let anyone in.

Irritating.

He was essential to the project. Without his organizational skills the experiment would be all over the place, untamed. Townsend had been the one to lay out the plans, run the schedule, catalog the results. His conclusions dictated what would be tested next. Though he didn't invent N-Som, it would never be ready for FDA approval if he wasn't on the team. The Nobel Prize people had better be aware of that when the time came.

Faced with the ugly prospect of nothing to do, Townsend pulled the Hundai into a supermarket parking lot and weighed options. A frown creased his doughy face. He scratched at a spot on his glasses, pushed the comb-over back on his balding head, and tried to think of something to kill time until tomorrow.

Movies, and all forms of media entertainment, bored him. There was nothing to do back at the apartment; the little amount of time he spent there was for sleeping, dressing, and washing. Eating was a joyless necessity, usually something quick and convenient. His burgeoning stomach was a testament to this, but exercise bored Townsend as much as anything else.

The library? He needed to catch up on his reading; many of his subscriptions had run out, and prestigious scientific journals didn't send you a little card to fill out as a reminder.

A search of his wallet revealed his library card was expired. To get a renewal meant lines and hassles. The library was out.

Museums? It seemed a chore to go into the city, search for parking, fight the crowds of school children.

He thought, enviously, of his computer at work. When the strain became too great, he'd play a chess program to help ease his mind. It was somewhat banal, and he never lost, but it was the closest thing to entertainment that he pursued.

Though efficient on many different operating systems, Townsend had never gotten around to owning his own computer. The ones he worked on were always vastly superior to home versions. But he knew that modern models had a tremendous amount of speed and memory, quadruple that of only a year ago. Was it time to join the personal computer revolution?

"Why the heck not?"

Computer stores seemed to be everywhere in the suburbs, and Townsend located one of the larger chains and went inside.

Four different salespeople approached him, and each time he shooed them away, annoyed at the interruption. He finally did require assistance after deciding on a model, and of course it took forever to find help. Such a burden, shopping.

After rebuffing pitch after pitch for accessories, Townsend allowed himself to be talked into two chess programs, each claiming to have beaten grand masters. He even felt a tinge of excitement, driving home with his purchases in the back seat. It wasn't nearly as fulfilling as work, but these boxes represented a slight promise of challenge, something he hadn't felt in a long time.

It took three trips to bring everything up to his third floor apartment. Badly out of breath, he needed a rest and a glass of orange juice before setting up his new system. His answering machine was blinking, but he was too preoccupied to notice.

Assembly was easy, and he didn't bother with the instructions. The system had dutifully included a CD for free internet hours, but he decided to put that off until later. Townsend installed the first chess program, somewhat surprised by his new computer's speed, and after familiarizing himself with the controls he began to play.

Within forty minutes, the computer was up a piece.

Townsend had to grin at the move. It was a brilliant one, a pin that forced him to give up his rook to save his queen. Townsend made the computer go back several moves, not to cheat, but to see if he could have prevented it. He couldn't have. The program had planned it at least six moves in advance.

"Wonderful."

He hunkered down and continued play, trying to be wary but thrilled at the possibility of being beaten.

It was only when Townsend began to squint at the keyboard that he realized the sun had gone down. He checked the clock and was surprised to see he'd been playing for seven hours.

The computer had beaten him three games out of six. They were tied in this seventh game, and Townsend was preparing a sacrifice that would lead to checkmate if the computer didn't see it. The odds were slim; the computer saw just about everything. Unlike the chess program at work, this one could think several hundred moves ahead, and understood the concept of sacrifice for the sake of position.

He paused the game on his turn and ordered some Chinese food to be delivered. After a bathroom break and a splash of water on his face to keep him focused, he returned to the computer and made his move.

The computer didn't take the bait.

"I figured you'd see it. Good one."

A knock at the door. Townsend was so involved with the game that he never bothered to question the obvious fact that his food couldn't have been there so quickly.

The man in the hallway was wearing jeans and a leather jacket. He wasn't delivering sweet and sour pork or any other food. Most irritating of all, it was someone that Townsend knew, and happened to dislike.

"What are you doing here?"

"Hello doctor." David grinned, his pleasure genuine. "I came here to kill you."

When he saw the scalpel, Townsend's annoyance puddled into fear. He took several steps back.

"This... this is a mistake. You'll jeopardize the project."

"That's the point. Manny and I are sick of being guinea pigs. I think it's made us somewhat unhinged."

"Manny and I? What do—"

Townsend saw the slash, saw the blood, but didn't feel a thing. He tried to speak and it came out in a gurgle.

David appraised the wound.

"The first cut is the deepest."

When Townsend coughed, it was through the gash in his neck rather than his mouth. Things became blurry, and he fell over.

David closed the door behind him. He inspected the apartment, giving an empty monitor box a small kick.

"New computer? Nice."

Townsend crawled over to his desk, reaching for the phone. He came up short and pulled his keyboard down on top of him.

"Careful, Dr. Townsend. You'll void the warranty if you bleed all over it."

Townsend began to pass out. He knew that if he did, he'd never wake up. He had to get the phone, had to get help.

"Do you want the phone?" David laughed. "What are you gonna do with the phone, Dr. Townsend? Your tongue is hanging out your neck. Maybe I can help."

David knelt down next to him. Townsend felt his consciousness ebbing, the darkness closing in.

He was almost dead when David began to work on him with the scalpel.

Almost.

Chapter 5

The sheer amount of collected data impressed Bill, but not nearly as much as the content. Each document he read was more fascinating than the last. He got up from his sofa and stretched, his back crackling like a bag of chips. He took a sip of coffee. Cold.

The clock told him it was coming up on one in the morning, but Bill wasn't ready to turn in yet. He plodded into the kitchen for another cup. He used three spoonfuls of instant, extra strong, and popped it in the microwave. The deluxe espresso maker stared at him from the counter, dejected.

The machine was Italian, a top end model. It had been their first purchase together, after moving into the condo. Kristen loved making lattes, and double cappuccinos, and espresso so thick you could eat it with a fork.

Bill turned away from it. The microwave dinged and he stirred some sugar into his coffee and went back to the sofa.

The log he was currently reviewing detailed experiments with rhesus monkeys. An early version of N-Som had kept a test animal awake for almost eight months. Bill wanted to find out how the experiment ended.

Day 236—Sam continues to act strangely, refusing his usual morning fruit. Vitals are normal, though his eyes seem a bit glassy. After discussing the situation with Theena, I order for a complete blood work up.

Bill reached for the next page, but there were no more in file.

He looked by his feet, to see if it any had fallen under the table. Coming up empty, he sifted through the previous pages, then the pages of several other folders.

Nothing.

Bill frowned. The guy in charge of organizing everything, Dr. Townsend, had done an amazing job putting every relevant bit of information about the project into coherent, chronological order. Previous experiments had ended with a calculation of results and Dr. Nikos's notes and conclusions. There were none to be found in this case.

Bill yawned. “Maybe back at DruTech.”

He took another sip of coffee and peeled off his socks, balling them up and taking them into the bedroom. As he undressed, he thought about the unlimited potential for this drug. Revolutionary didn't begin to describe it.

A world without sleep. Where commerce existed twenty-four hours a day, and brilliant thinkers never became fatigued. There would be more time for work, to get things done, to make more money. And more time for play, to be with friends, to spend extra hours with loved ones. How much were those extra hours worth?

Bill knew. He knew more than anyone.

He yawned again, and glanced down at his coffee.

“You're not doing your job.”

It was late, anyway. Tired as he was, he might actually sleep well tonight. Bill was just sticking his toothbrush in his mouth when the phone rang.

Theena?

She hadn't come on to him again, after the scene in Manny's bedroom, and had remained strictly business for the remainder of the tour. Their meeting ended with a brusque handshake. Had her flirting really been an act? Or did she really find him as attractive as he found her?

Bill picked up the phone.

“Dr. May?”

It wasn't Theena. The voice was male, Midwestern, deep and cold.

“Yes? Who is this?”

“There's a package for you in the hall.”

A click, and then Bill was left listening to the dial tone. He walked, warily, to the door. The peephole showed an empty hallway.

Keeping a firm grip on the knob, he unlocked the dead bolt and eased it open a crack.

There was a thick manila envelope sitting on his doormat.

Bill again peered down the hall, then snatched the envelope and locked his door.

It was unmarked, unsealed. Inside was a VHS videotape without any label.

Bill searched his mind for a friend or coworker that might pull a stunt like this, but he came up empty. No one he knew would do this. Especially this late at night.

He shivered.

Part of him didn't want to play it, to put it away until the sun was out, until he had other people around him.

But curiosity overcame his trepidation. Bill popped the tape into his VCR.

After several seconds of black, a dimly lit room came on screen. It had concrete floors and walls. Possibly a basement. Bill could tell by the quality that it was home video.

“Come over here.”

The voice was off screen. Then two men walked into frame from the left. One had on a ski mask, and he was holding a gun to the back of the other man.

Michael Bitner.

Bill's golf friend, the doctor who had been assigned to the N-Som case before him.

“Kneel down.”

Mike had some blood in the corner of his mouth, and his right eye was swollen almost shut. He looked terrified. His captor forced him to his knees.

"N-Som will get FDA approval."

Mike whimpered. "Yes. I promise it will."

"I wasn't talking to you."

The shot made Bill bite the inside of his cheek. Mike flopped sideways, twitched twice, then was still.

The tape ended.

Bill double checked to make sure the door was locked.

Then he called the police.

Chapter 6

“How could he be gone? There was a cop outside the door.”

Captain Halloran scratched his graying mustache and shifted his bulk in the chair, which was small for him and seemed too low to the ground. He shouldn't have taken the seat when offered. It hurt his back, his knees, and made him seem fatter, older and less important that he actually was. Halloran knew Rothchilde had bought that chair for those very reasons—his own was higher and wider, with armrests that ended in polished mahogany knobs, like a throne.

He didn't like Albert Rothchilde. The man was whiny, arrogant, and spoiled. Whereas Halloran earned his rank by busting his ass for twenty plus years, Rothchilde was simply born into the right family. Halloran knew the guy wouldn't last two minutes on the street.

But this wasn't the street. This was Rothchilde's twenty-two room house, the one that was featured in People Magazine. Halloran glanced at some stupid painting hanging behind Rothchilde's desk. Rothchilde had casually mentioned its worth during a previous meeting, and then chuckled saying he'd bought the Mayor for less.

To make matters more uncomfortable, Rothchilde was completely right. Halloran's men had screwed up. All Halloran could do was grit his teeth and bare the storm.

“The Officer said he'd gone to get a cup of coffee. When he came back, Manny was gone.”

“Coffee?” Rothchilde smiled, but his beady eyes showed no trace of amusement. He was a thin man, almost skinny, with soft hands and slender fingers that were always carefully manicured. His hair was black, parted on the side, and his hawkish nose and slight overbite reminded Halloran of a rat.

"This man is worth over a billion dollars to me, and you lost him for a fifty cent cup of coffee."

"The guy just had surgery. Who would have thought he'd get up and leave?"

"How do we know he left? How do we know he wasn't taken?"

Halloran tried to sound like the authority his title represented. "Couldn't have happened. Patient in the room across the hall saw Manny steal some clothes from a drawer. He called the nurse, but too late."

Rothchilde let out a slow breath. Truth be told, Halloran was afraid of him. It didn't matter that he could break Rothchilde's skinny little canned-tan body over his knee like a broomstick. Rothchilde's power was greater than physical. The President of the United States took his calls. So did the capos of the biggest families on both coasts.

"We need him found, Captain." Rothchilde used the rank as if it tasted foul in his mouth. "Whoever killed Dr. Nikos obviously wanted Manny dead too. We can't let that happen. It would cause an unforgivable delay."

"We'll find him."

"Then why is your fat ass still sitting here?"

Halloran ground his teeth. The extra money wasn't worth it. He should tell this bozo off right here and now.

Instead, he left the office and went to check on the search for Manny.

Albert Rothchilde watched him go. Insulting Halloran was normally a fun activity, but there was no joy in it today. There was too much at stake.

Rothchilde swiveled around in his leather chair and stared up at his Miró. He found the use of color garish, and didn't think the composition was correctly balanced. But it was a Miró, and status couldn't be much more symbolic than that.

If things went according to plan, he'd be able to plaster every wall of his mansion with Mirós. That was frivolous yet lofty enough to make people talk about him. He could make his home the largest Miró museum in the world.

But that was only the beginning. Art was a hobby. Rothchilde wanted power. He wanted American Products to expand, for his corporate empire to grow.

And grow it shall. Perhaps he would become big enough to take over Microsoft. Or Disney. General Motors might be fun to run. He imagined launching a new sports car, calling it the Rothchilde GT.

"Maybe I'll buy it all."

Rothchilde had his people come up with projected sales figures for N-Som. It staggered him, and he'd been around money all his life. With a conservative estimate of only ten percent of the US population taking the drug, Rothchilde would be making nine billion dollars a month. Of course, more than ten percent would take it. Within five years, half the population of the world would be taking it. And that didn't even include the proposed military contract, which would make him richer than the combined fortunes of the next seven runners-up.

Rothchilde idly wondered if France was for sale. He'd have his secretary make a few calls.

But first things first.

Someone was trying to sabotage the N-Som project, and Rothchilde needed to find out who.

There was a chance, however slight, that Dr. Nikos's murder had nothing to do with N-Som. Perhaps the doctor had personal enemies. Or perhaps it was just some unfortunate random lunatic. Rothchilde hoped that was the case, but he had to plan for the worst.

Besides the CPD, Rothchilde had enlisted his friends in the government for help. He also sent feelers out to all of the families he supported, to see if anyone in the underworld had issues with him. So far, nothing had come up.

"Could be anyone. Anyone at all."

In his more creative moments, sipping hundred year old port and snorting coke off a call girl's welted backside, Rothchilde imagined he was being challenged by another pharmaceutical company. Sleeping pills were a billion dollar industry. Perhaps the manufacturer of Dalmane or Halcion was trying to keep their bread and butter.

It could even be the Sealy Mattress company, afraid of losing long-term sales. Soon, the bedroom would be a thing of the past. The same with pajamas, hotels, night lights, caffeinated beverages, and a slew of other products related to the sleep/wake cycle.

Rothchilde delegated it to the back of his mind. All the wheels were in motion. Manny would be found, and his attacker would be dealt with. The important thing now was Dr. Bill May and FDA approval.

He opened a side drawer in his desk and took out Bill's file. The doctor had been a medical officer with CDER for over ten years. During that time, he'd overseen clinical trials on forty-eight different drugs. Only eight of these had gone on to receive FDA approval. Bill was responsible for killing the other forty.

Like most governmental offices, the FDA worked by committee. Besides the clinical review, new drugs must submit to Toxicology and Chemistry panels. Rothchilde had been able to pass these already—the chemistry reviewer had children. It was easy to coerce her into approval without having to reveal the secret manufacturing process. As far as pharmacology went, N-Som wasn't toxic. The way it was made didn't negate the fact that it worked, and worked well.

Unfortunately, the previous clinical reviewer asked too many questions. Rothchilde stared at Bill's file and hoped this wouldn't end up the same way. The doctor's history showed him to be smart, ethical, and stubborn. Three times in the past, companies had attempted to bribe him. Those companies were no longer in business. Even if Rothchilde threw an obscene amount of money at him, he knew Bill wouldn't take it.

Especially after the unfortunate occurrence with Bill's wife.

Perhaps there was a way to work that angle. It warranted some thought. Unfortunately, there was no other person in Bill's life that they could use to squeeze him.

Rothchilde wondered if the video tape was having its desired effect. Was Bill terrified and eager to please?

Doubtful. But that wasn't Rothchilde's plan. He hoped to unhinge Bill just enough to keep his full concentration off the review process. A scared man might miss the things his predecessor had uncovered.

Rothchilde predicted Bill's course of action. He'd call the police, who wouldn't help—Halloran would see to that. Bill might look closer at N-Som to find out its secret, but Rothchilde had disposed of all the risky paperwork. Another threat or two, maybe an actual physical encounter, and Bill would have no evidence that N-Som was dangerous, but every incentive in the world to approve it.

In a way, it was lucky that Dr. Nikos was murdered. He would have had to be dealt with sooner or later. The same as his daughter, and the rest of the team.

The grandfather clock in the corner of the den chimed four times. Rothchilde smiled. He was fully awake and alert, and would be for another eighteen hours. And the total cost? Only eighty cents a pill.

“I'm going to be the wealthiest man in the world.”

Rothchilde's mirth disappeared when he remembered how N-Som was made. He couldn't get the antacids out of his pocket quick enough.

“Chemicals. That's all. Nothing more than chemicals.”

But it took the whole roll to calm his stomach down.

Chapter 7

Manny looked around Townsend's apartment. The first thing he saw was a heap of bloody clothing, stacked in the middle of the living room carpet.

Upon closer examination, he realized it wasn't clothing at all.

Manny turned quickly to get out of there, slipping on a wet spot. He fell forward, covering himself in gore. The scream grew in his lungs, and Manny squeezed his eyes shut and clamped a hand over his mouth to squelch it.

Don't attract attention, he thought. *Stay calm.*

He forced himself to carefully get off the floor. His clothes were soaked. He needed to change. Townsend's clothes? Doubtful. The man was half his size. Maybe he had a large sweater, but pants would be impossible.

After a focused search he found the laundry room behind some double closet doors. Manny quickly stripped and threw his bloody clothes into the machine, adding half a box of detergent. He left red hand prints on the lid and the knob.

There was some underwear folded neatly on top of the dryer. Manny took them and wiped the entire surface of the washer. Careful not to touch anything else, he walked naked through the condo, looking for the bathroom.

"Hello, Manny."

Manny yelped.

David was stretched out in the bathtub, the water a bright pink. He frowned at Manny. "Quit acting like a baby, and see if there's another bar of soap in that cabinet."

Manny couldn't move his feet. He stared down at his brother, who was picking bits of something out of his fingernails.

"Did you hear me, bro? Soap!"

Manny recoiled at the shout. He tore open the vanity and found a bar of soap.

"Thank you." David unwrapped the bar and rubbed it onto a rag, making red bubbles. "Want to come in? Water's fine."

Manny took a breath and found his voice. "Do you... do you feel better now?"

"Now? You mean, now that I've killed?" David thought it over, eventually grinning. "Yeah. Yeah, I do."

"You're a monster."

"Sure I am. We both are. Created in a lab, just like Frankenstein. It's the N-Som, Manny. You know it as much as I do. I don't see how you can stand the dreams without cracking."

Manny bit his knuckle, drew blood.

"They're only dreams, David."

"Sure they are. Here."

David searched through the bath water and came up with a scalpel. He held it out to Manny.

"I don't want it."

"You promised. You promised if I killed again, you'd end it for me."

Manny stepped back.

"I can't, David."

"Kill me, Manny."

Manny shook his head.

"Kill me, or I'll skin you like I did Townsend."

Manny reached behind him, trying to find the door knob. David stood up, bloody water cascading off his naked body.

"It was hard, Manny. Like pulling the upholstery off a couch. You really have to put some muscle into it."

David climbed out of the tub. He held the blade in front of him.

“I'll hurt you, Manny.”

“Please, David. I don't want to kill you.”

David frowned. The scalpel caught the light and glinted.

“Too bad. Well, I guess I don't have any choice then. You broke your promise, and I have to punish you.”

Manny began to cry.

The cries quickly became screams.

Chapter 8

The phone was ringing when Bill walked in the door. He was exhausted and scared, but his prevailing emotion was anger. This was insane.

Six hours at the police station had provided no help. The tape was clear evidence of a murder, and the fact that it was given to Bill was a threat that even a three-year-old could see. But the cops seemed to wallow in skepticism and ennui. The case was given to an overworked duty officer who thought it was a prank, and Bill was told they'd get back to him after their so-called investigation.

Bill answered the phone, half-hoping it was the asshole who gave him the tape. He wanted to vent.

“Bill? It's Theena. I've been trying to call all night.”

Bill sat on the couch and rubbed his face. It had occurred to him that Theena could be involved. He had her down as a bit flaky. But the hundred grand question was; did that extend to murder?

“I was at the police station.”

“Are you okay?” Her concern sounded genuine. “What happened?”

“It... I got a death threat. It has to do with approving N-Som.”

“My God. Was it Manny?”

“Manny? No, why?”

“He's been missing from the hospital since last night. I have no idea where he is. I think the people who killed my father took him.”

Bill tried to make sense of the news. “He could have left on his own.”

“Maybe. But he was in bad shape.”

"Have you checked..." Bill began, wondering if she'd checked Manny's remote EEG.

"Yes." Theena had anticipated him. "Manny's still alive. I'm at DruTech right now. He's in distress, running Beta 2 waves. It's been going on for a few hours. Are you okay, Bill?"

Her voice was soft, genuine.

"I'm fine. Someone sent me a video tape of Mike Bitner being killed."

Bill got no reply.

"Theena? Are you there?"

"I... I don't believe it. He's actually dead? This is, this is just horrible. What are you going to do?"

"Do you think your boss could do something like that?"

"Albert Rothchilde? I don't like the man, to be honest, but he's not the killer type."

Bill had only met the man once, and didn't like him either. He rubbed his eyes and tried to think.

"Is American Products doing well?"

"Extremely well. Stock is way up. I can't believe this is happening."

"What do you know about the other investors?"

"Albert has a controlling share. But there are dozens of other stakeholders. Politicians, businessmen..."

"The mob?"

Theena's silence told him more than if she'd answered.

"Look, Theena, I'm going to the Feds. They have an organized crime bureau. Maybe they can help."

As he said it, Bill realized he'd left the tape at the police station. Maybe he could get it back somehow.

"I'm scared, Bill."

"You'll be safe at DruTech. It has security. I'll give you my cell phone number if you need to talk."

“I'm sorry. I feel like I'm the one who got you into this.”

“I'll be by in a few hours.”

“Thanks, Bill.”

Bill hit the disconnect button, then dialed his office at the FDA in Maryland, hoping that someone was there early. Luckily, a secretary picked up.

“Hello, Dr. May. How's the sleep research?”

“Exhausting. Laura, can you look up Mike Bitner's number and address for me?”

“Sure, just a sec.”

“Have you heard from Dr. Bitner lately?”

“No, not for a while. Here it is.”

Bill memorized the information and thanked her. When he called, he got Mike's answering machine. There were at least ten seconds of beeps, indicating unheard messages. Bill hung up.

“The police have to investigate.” Bill said it to reassure himself, but it didn't help. As the duty officer had repeated over and over, “There's no crime without a body.”

Bill was positive Mike was dead, but if a video of his murder wasn't enough proof, maybe he could find more.

Bitner lived in Roscoe Village, only fifteen minutes away. Bill took a cold shower to wake himself up. After dressing in chinos, a polo shirt, and an older blazer, he hit a corner store and bought a large coffee and a bottle of ma haung weight loss pills. He choked down four.

The sun was up by now and the city was opening its eyes. Bill's condo came with a garage, which he shared with three of his neighbors. He climbed in his Audi and headed north. Traffic was sparse, but there were a good number of joggers and bikers out. The caffeine and ephedrine hadn't kicked in yet, so Bill paid careful attention to his driving.

Bill took Addison to Hoyle and located Bitner's two-flat without difficulty. It was brick, slightly lighter brown than the buildings on either side of it. The porch light was on. He parked in front of a hydrant and waited until a roller blader passed.

Instead of trying the front door, Bill walked straight to the gate leading into the back yard. The rear entrance was attached to a deck, where a wooden chaise without a cushion and a somewhat rusty gas grill kept a silent vigil. Checking either side of him for witnesses, he approached a window and peered inside. It was dark, quiet.

Bill could hear his heart, pounding with a combination of fear and stimulants. He contemplated returning to his car and leaving; other than traffic violations, Bill had never broken the law in his life. Breaking and entering was a felony, right?

The police won't help you. You need more evidence. Just do it.

He took off his jacket, put it up against the pane, and hit it with the heel of his hand.

The glass cracked with the sound of a gunshot, and the falling pieces seemed to tinkle forever. He locked his knees and refused to run away. Searching for the latch to unlock the window reminded Bill of the first time he assisted in surgery as an intern, trying to find the appendix while all eyes were on him.

A dog barked, a few backyards away. Bill probed the inside of the window frame for a full minute before locating the lock. Two seconds after that, it was up and he was in.

It was the kitchen. The only light was streaming in from the opening he'd crawled through. A steady hum from the refrigerator seemed to exaggerate the silence. He stepped clear of the broken glass and made his way into the hallway.

The drapes had all been drawn, and seeing was tough. He took a minute to let his eyes adjust, and then began poking around, careful not to touch anything.

There was a stereo, hundreds of CDs organized in a rack. An entertainment center hugged the wall, flanked by two large floor plants that were going brown. The sofa and loveseat were black leather. He searched a bookshelf and found some current bestsellers, magazines, some medical texts.

Nothing in the hall closet, nothing in the bathroom. Bill located the basement stairs and flipped on the light. He descended, slowly.

The odor hit him halfway down. It was a smell he knew well, and one he always hated. Musky, putrid, clinical, final.

At the bottom of the stairs, Bill went right. A hand was over his face, and when that no longer worked, he covered his nose with his shirt bottom. The basement was unfurnished, the walls and floor bare concrete. In one corner was a washer, dryer, and an oversized utility sink. Some cardboard boxes were stacked in the center. The furnace and water heater were side by side, next to a large PVC pipe that stretched down from the ceiling and into the sump hole.

To the left of all that, a concrete wall with a door in the middle of it. Much as he hated to, he made it his destination.

When Bill pushed the door open the smell enveloped him like a dry heat. He had to take several steps back or risk vomiting.

Bill decided to examine the rest of the house first, allowing time for the death room to air out. He went up to the second floor and located the bedroom. The dresser and closet contained nothing extraordinary. The bed was unmade. A nightstand drawer revealed a remote control for the TV, some Kleenex, and a Robin Cook paperback.

Bill headed across the upstairs hall and found a study. The drawers had been pulled out of the desk, their contents strewn over the carpet. A large file cabinet had been similarly disturbed, files and papers littering the floor. Bill didn't think poking through it would provide any answers. It was doubtful that whoever made the mess left anything important.

On a hunch, Bill went back to the bedroom. Many doctors took their work to sleep with them. He looked under the bed, behind the nightstand, and eventually found the file wedged between the nightstand and the bed. The tab on the manila folder read N-SOM. It was thick, held closed by a large rubber band. Bill tucked it under his arm and went into the adjoining bathroom.

In the closet was an old tube of Ben Gay. He dabbed some on his upper lip. It burned, but it was a small price to pay to smell menthol rather than rot. Then he pushed aside his trepidation and walked back down to the basement.

The door was waiting for him. Bill approached without enthusiasm, knowing what was in there, knowing he had to look anyway. When he pushed it open, the stench surrounded him like a tropical breeze. He pulled the cord on a hanging bulb.

The tarpaulin-covered bundle in the middle of the floor was the source of the odor, and the shape left no doubt as to its contents. Bill still had to be sure, and holding his breath he pulled back the canvas.

Mike Bitner's eyes were open, two white marbles stuck in a pink, bloated face. Bill looked lower, saw the exit wound in the chest. The amount of dried blood staining the floor around him left no doubt that this was where he died. They'd videotaped Bitner's murder in his own basement.

Bill left the room and tried to think it through. He had to get the authorities to see this, without them knowing he'd been here. Maybe he could leave an anonymous tip. Pretend he was a neighbor, complain about a smell coming from the house. Or even say he heard shots, or saw someone breaking in.

Once the police found the body, they'd have to protect him.

Bill walked over to the stairs, planning the call in his head. The creak took him by surprise.

It had come from the floor above. Bill stopped, and heard it again, louder this time.

There was someone upstairs.

Chapter 9

“That window could have got broken weeks ago.”

Franco came up next to Carlos, the broken glass crunching underfoot. Carlos shook his head and scratched at his graying goatee. He had a dark face, all sharp angles, and it suited his personality.

“Floor's dry. It rained two, three days ago. This is recent.”

Franco shrugged, but he took out his weapon just the same, a laughably large Coonan 357 Magnum with a six inch barrel. Carlos's Colt Model 38 was already in hand, a reliable gun that never jammed like Franco's cannon.

“So you want to search the place?”

Carlos thought it over. If someone had been here, that someone might be coming back with heat. He didn't want to waste any time.

“No. Let's do it and get the hell out of here. Just be careful.”

Franco laughed at the warning, a girlish giggle that didn't fit with such a large, muscular body. He bore the badges of pro boxing; scar tissue around the eyes and a grossly misshapen cauliflower ear. Nothing frightened Franco. But Carlos had been in the business a lot longer, and you could get dead even if you weren't scared.

“Jesus, you smell that stink?”

Carlos didn't. He'd come prepared. The suit he wore was throw away, and he'd cut a menthol cigarette filter in half and shoved a piece high up in each nostril. The method was so old hat that his speech was barely affected.

Franco led the way into the basement. Carlos stayed a few steps behind, taking in everything. When he saw the light on in the corner room an alarm went off in his mind. Carlos was sure he'd turned it off.

The larger man walked in without a care, grumbling about the smell. Carlos stood at the bottom of the stairs and scanned his surroundings. There were some boxes. A large sink. A water heater. Several places a person could hide. He thumbed back the hammer on his gun and walked towards the boxes.

"I thought we wasn't searching."

"Real quick. I wanna be sure."

"Hurry up. I stay down here long, I'll deliver a street pizza."

There was no one behind the boxes, or in the big sink. That left the water heater. He approached it and brought his gun around in a firm, two handed grip.

No one was there.

"You sure are cautious, for an older guy."

"That's how I got to be an older guy."

Carlos walked over to the room to help with the body removal. He didn't hear the small expulsion of breath come from beneath the cover of the sump pit.

Bill knew he wouldn't have been able to do anything if they'd found him. He was on his knees in the sinkhole, curled up. It was a tight fit, made even tighter by the discharge pipe pressing into his back. He'd unplugged the sump pump before climbing in, and since it wasn't running and his head was bent forward he was practically drinking the foul water. If the killers had lifted the lid, it would have been like shooting a big fish in a small barrel.

When he'd heard them upstairs, Bill knew his hiding places were limited. He put the N-Som file in the dryer and was relieved beyond words that hole was large enough to hold him. Once the contorting was complete, the hard part was keeping still. As the footsteps drew nearer, Bill was sure he'd be discovered. He'd closed his eyes and begun to pray.

But the moment had passed, and it looked like he might actually live through this.

He sighed, too loudly for comfort. There was an odor, but it wasn't as bad as the death smell in the other room. Bill kept his left eye on the light coming in through the crack in the lid opening. He wanted to change position, but didn't dare for fear of making noise.

They'd come to get the body. He only had to stay there for a few more minutes, then he could get out.

Then something brushed his hand.

He flinched. It was a reflex. His head bumped against the sump lid, knocking it slightly askew.

“Did you hear that?”

Carlos cocked an ear to the side, listening.

“I didn't hear shit. Lift your end up higher.”

Carlos pulled on his end of the tarp, drawing it closer to his chest. The effort made him groan.

“Don't have a heart attack, Grandpa. I don't wanna have to lug two stiffs outta here.”

Franco laughed at his own joke. Carlos frowned. He shouldn't have been here with Franco, doing this. He was a specialist. The murder, that was worthy of him. This was grunt work. He stared at Franco, the cauliflower ear stuck to the side of his head like a fat pink pretzel. No wonder he didn't hear anything. Gino liked to joke that Franco's ears were for decoration only.

“I heard a noise in the corner.”

“You checked it already.”

Carlos nodded. There was nothing there. But he was sure he'd heard something.

“Maybe it's, whaddaycallit, senile dementia.”

Franco laughed again. Carlos pursed his lips, making a silent wish that someday Gino put a hit out on Franco. Carlos would take that contract for free.

“Lift higher. You're not doing your part.”

Carlos strained with his end. He hadn't been paying attention, and Franco had gotten to the stairs first. When the tarp began to leak, it leaked on Carlos.

Whatever had brushed against Bill was bony and covered in fur. He'd stirred it climbing in, and felt it move up along his body and breach the surface next to his cheek.

Dead rat, bloated and rotten.

Bill closed his eyes. The gorge was building in his throat, and he knew he had to do something or he'd throw up.

Carefully, he moved a hand up to the rat and took it between his fingers. He dragged it back under water, where the smell couldn't get to him.

The air was still funky, but the nausea had passed. He stared up at the lid. The crack was wider now, the cover several inches off center.

He braced for the worst, sure that they'd heard him and were on their way over. They'd pull up the lid and point their guns. The same guns that killed Mike Bitner. Bill would die curled up in foul water, clutching a dead rat, hearing the laughter of petty thugs.

But the seconds slouched by without incident. Bill heard nothing. His neck had begun to cramp, and his legs had long ago lost circulation. Slowly, gently, he straightened up his head and pushed back the cover, peering over the edge of the hole.

The basement was empty.

He climbed out, cold and shaking.

Carlos slammed the car trunk closed and wiped his gooey hands on his pants. Franco giggled.

“You look worse than the stiff.”

It was true. On the way up the stairs, the tarp came open and spilled all over. Carlos was a mess.

"I gotta go clean up."

"No shit. Ain't getting in my car like that."

Franco leaned against the hood and lit a smoke while Carlos made his way back into the house.

Bill was in the kitchen when he heard the back door open. There was nowhere to go except the bathroom. He was there in two steps, throwing the N-Som folder in the cabinet under the sink. Then he climbed into the tub and closed the shower curtain.

The shower curtain was transparent.

Carlos immediately noticed the water on the floor. He pulled out his gun and peered down the basement stairs. Dirty wet footsteps, leading up through the kitchen, and into the bathroom.

"Dr. May, right?"

Bill was pressed into the corner of the shower, shivering. The man before him was thin and angular. His hair and beard were dirty gray, and he had eyes the color of flint. He raised the gun to Bill's head.

"Answer me."

"I'm William May."

The man nodded. "Thought you looked familiar. We've got our eye on you, you know."

The man winked at him. Then he fired the gun.

Bill crumpled into a ball. The shot was so loud it hurt. He hit his head on the bathtub edge and covered his face.

But other than his new lump, there was no wound. He hadn't been shot.

He peeked through his fingers and saw the man at the sink, washing his hands with some soap.

"Consider that a warning, Dr. May. I only miss on purpose. You see the body?"

Bill didn't trust his voice to answer.

"Did you see the body, or do I have to drag you outside and shove you in the trunk for a closer look?"

"I saw it."

"Then you saw what happens when good doctors don't follow orders."

The man rubbed a rag on his face. Another man, much larger, appeared in the doorway with a gun. He aimed it at Bill, but the older man pushed his arm down.

"We don't need to kill him, Franco. He'll cooperate."

The big man squinted at Bill.

"That so?"

Bill nodded. His heart was a lump in his throat.

"Dr. May knows what's best for him. He knows he can't go to the cops, because we own the cops. That's why he didn't get any help with the video tape. He also knows he can't run, because we can follow him anywhere in the world. The only way he's gonna live through this, is he if approves the drug."

Franco leaned over the bathtub and grabbed Bill by the shirt. He pulled him close with an ease that was terrifying.

"That right, Doc? You gonna approve our drug?"

Bill had never felt so helpless.

"Yes."

Franco giggled like a woman. He gave Bill an approving slap on the cheek. It was like being hit with a board, and the stars came out.

"Good boy. Are you a medical doctor?"

Bill nodded.

Franco's face became solemn. He released Bill and unzipped his fly. Bill blanched. Revulsion and shame mixed in with his terror. He decided he had to do something, even if they killed him. When the big man dropped his pants, Bill made a fist and got ready to punch.

"What does that look like to you?"

Franco had hiked his boxer shorts over his upper thigh, and was pointing to a small brown mole.

"What?"

"Is that cancer?"

"It's... it's just a mole."

"You sure? I don't remember having it."

The smaller man laughed. "You don't remember how to count to ten without using your fingers."

"Shut up, Carlos. I want the doc's opinion."

Bill cleared his throat. "Has it gotten bigger? Or has it ever bled?"

"No."

"Then it's just a mole. Sarcoma has an irregular shape, and it grows and bleeds."

Franco seemed relieved. He pulled up his pants and walked out of the bathroom.

Carlos tossed Bill the rag and winked again.

"Be seeing you, Dr. May."

Then he was gone.

Bill sat back in the tub. He wanted to laugh and cry at the same time. He did neither.

After a few minutes, he got up and put his hands on the bathroom sink. His stomach was dancing Mambo number five, and he leaned over the toilet. Nothing came.

Bill washed up without looking at himself in the mirror. Then he sat on Mike Bitner's sofa in the living room, the N-Som folder clutched to his chest, and didn't move for almost half an hour.

The drive back to his place was a blur. Bill felt nothing, and yet he felt everything. He knew that he had almost died, and an experience like that was life-changing. He also knew that he'd done nothing to prevent it, and his cowardice made him rethink his self image.

They hadn't killed him, but they'd changed him forever. The important question; was he changed for the better, or for the worse?

When Bill pulled into his garage, he didn't notice the man hiding in the shadows.

The man with the scalpel.

Chapter 10

The blinking light indicated the call was a transfer. Special Agent Smith set down his coffee, hit the button, and picked up the receiver.

The caller was Dr. William May of the FDA.

He laid it all out for Smith, starting with the murder of Dr. Nikos.

Smith listened closely, asking the questions he was trained to ask, taking notes when appropriate. The caller went on to talk about the video tape, the lack of police involvement, and finally went into the harrowing tale of discovering the body and being caught by the two killers.

When Dr. May was finally finished, Smith reassured him that the Bureau would get some men on the case. He advised him to stay in his home, avoid strangers, and try to always have friends around him.

Smith gave Dr. May his personal cell phone number, and said he should call if anything else happened. He also told him that the FBI would keep him under protective surveillance, but they were going to stay out of sight so as not to arouse suspicion. It seemed to calm Dr. May a bit, and he thanked Smith before getting off the phone.

Smith reviewed the notes, to make sure he had the story straight in his mind. When he was satisfied that he did, he picked up the phone and called Albert Rothchilde.

Chapter 11

When he saw himself, he was someone else.

The gun was in his hand. He knew what he was going to do, and he was powerless to stop it.

His wife was asleep. He woke her up, let her look down the barrel and have one last scream before he shot her in the forehead.

The sound woke up the kids. Bobby, the youngest, began crying in his bed across the hall. His older sister Sally came into the room, eyes wide.

"Daddy! What did you do to Mommy?"

She took the bullet in the chest, and when she fell it was slow motion, almost beautiful, like a ballet dancer.

He went into Bobby's room. His son was frightened, hysterical.

"Don't be afraid. Daddy's here."

He picked him up, held him close. When Bobby began to calm down, he put the gun under the boy's chin and fired.

"Just one more."

He turned the gun around so his thumb was on the trigger and the barrel was pointed at his own chest.

"Forgive me, Lord."

Then he pulled.

Manny opened his eyes and screamed. It took him a second to realize where he was. He saw the scalpel in one bloody hand, the bottle of pills in the other.

N-Som dream.

He shivered and pulled his knees up to his chest. Bad batch. One of the worst. He wondered how many of the pills in the bottle came from the same source. Manny shook his whole body like a wet dog, trying to erase the memory from his mind.

But he couldn't, of course.

Didn't matter. It was over, and he was fully refreshed. The fatigue that had been setting in before he took the N-Som was gone. His fear was replaced with a feeling of strength and well-being.

Manny stood up. He was in Dr. May's garage. There was a car parked in Dr. May's spot, where one hadn't been earlier.

The doctor was in.

Manny was infused with a sense of purpose. He hoped he wasn't too late.

He put the scalpel and the pills in the shopping bag, on top of the Tupperware container, and eased the entry door open. It led into a hallway, beneath Bill's condo.

Manny walked fast, not wanting to be seen. The washer had faded the stains on his clothes, but the bandage on his hand was soaked with blood and would prompt questions.

The elevator took him to Dr. May's floor. He knocked on the door. Almost a minute passed. Manny knocked again, harder. His tongue tasted like pennies, and he realized he was biting it.

"Manny?"

Bill was in a bathrobe. His hair was wet and smelled of shampoo.

"Dr. May—quick! Inside where it's safe."

He stepped past the doctor and looked around the room to make sure it was empty.

"Is anyone else here?"

"I'm alone, Manny. Are you all right? What happened at the hospital?"

Manny walked to the sofa, thought about sitting down, decided against it, and paced back to Bill.

"They took me."

The lie came out weak. He wasn't sure why he was still covering for David, after all the horrible things he'd done. Fear? Devotion? Guilt?

"What happened to your hand?"

Manny stared at his fist, the gauze almost completely red.

"They cut my finger off. Can you sew it back on?"

Manny reached into the bag and removed the Tupperware container. His little finger was carefully sealed in plastic wrap and surrounded by ice.

Bill reached for the phone. "We have to get you to the hospital."

"No! He... they, they'll find me there. I have to stay here, to protect you."

"Manny, you need microsurgery to reattach a finger. I don't have that kind of equipment here."

Manny held Bill by the arm, imploring.

"You don't understand. It's not safe. The people who took me... they said that you were next."

The doctor seemed to think it over.

"Fine. Let me put on some clothes, and we'll go someplace safe."

Bill went into another room. Manny chewed his fingernails, both eyes locked on the front door. He knew David was close by. He could practically smell him.

When they were kids, Manny and David had been very close. Even when they were fighting. Even when David did bad things. And more bad things were coming, Manny was sure of it. He could feel them drawing closer.

"Are you ready?"

He jumped at the doctor's voice. Bill put a hand on his shoulder.

"It's okay. It must have been horrible, but you're safe now. Got the finger?"

Manny clutched the bag to his chest.

“Good. Let's go.”

Bill led him down the stairs and back into the garage. It was a hellish walk for Manny, expecting David to pop out behind every corner. He felt a tad safer once they were in the car and driving.

“You've lost a lot of blood. Are you light headed?'

“A little.”

The car stopped at a light. Manny checked to make sure his door was locked.

“When was the last time you took N-Som?”

“A little while ago.”

Bill nodded. “Do you think maybe you should put the experiment on hold for a little while, get some sleep?”

“NO!”

The doctor flinched at the outburst. Manny tried to tamp down his emotion.

“I mean... I can't stop now, there's too much at stake here. This was Dr. Nikos's dream. I'm okay. I really am. I'm just scared. As you said, I've been through a lot.”

A car honked behind them. Manny jerked around. Just an SUV, wanting Bill to go because the light turned green. Bill complied.

“So... what's it like? Being on N-Som?”

“Like?”

“How does it feel?”

Manny was used to questions. He was asked them every day by the team's shrink, Dr. Fletcher. The familiarity made him relax a bit.

“It feels normal. You just don't get tired. Dr. Nikos calls it ZFS—Zero Fatigue Syndrome.”

“Physically or mentally tired?”

“Neither. I can exercise for a very long time. I can also concentrate for extended periods. I never get sleepy."

"How about when the drug wears off?"

"As long as I take it every 24 hours, the effect never stops. If I miss a dose, I start feeling tired and I know it's time to take it again."

Like earlier. Manny couldn't remember when he'd last taken the drug; the visit to the hospital had interrupted his daily dose. But the fatigue had been an indicator it was time.

"Are there side effects? Does it make you jumpy? Irritable?" He looked at Manny. "Paranoid?"

"N-Som isn't a stimulant, Dr. May. I'm acting paranoid because people are really after us."

They drove in silence. It got to Manny, and after a minute he had to talk.

"Look, Doctor, this is an amazing drug. Not only does it replace sleep, it improves your health. I don't get sick anymore. Dr. Nikos and Theena have injected me with different diseases, and none have any affect. I can gain muscle mass at an amazing rate—in one week my biceps grew two inches. And healing... watch this."

Manny found the scalpel in his bag and took it out.

"What are you doing?"

He brought the blade up to his cheek and make a shallow cut from his ear to his lip.

"Manny...!"

"Calm down, Doc. I have a pretty high threshold for pain. Now look."

He lowered the visor and adjusted the vanity mirror so he could watch too.

There was bleeding, but not much. After a few seconds he wiped his cheek with his sleeve to show that it had stopped all together.

"See?" Manny put his fingers on either side of the cut and spread them open. The wound had closed.

"It's healed?"

“Not completely. My blood clots at the same rate that yours does. But both sides have knitted together already.”

“How is that possible?”

“Sleep promotes healing. While asleep, the glands manufacture chemicals.”

“The pituitary gland. It makes human growth hormone. It's responsible for building muscle, repairing damage, and a slew of other things. But an abundance of HGH is dangerous, Manny. It produces a condition known as acromegaly. The bones and organs enlarge, causing deformity and ultimately death.”

“Not in my case. N-Som fools the brain into thinking it has slept, and the brain responds by increased hormone production. But my increased metabolism compensates for it. In technical terms, N-Som overrides the superachiasmatic nucleus of the hypothalamus and the midbrain recticular formation, resulting in...”

“I know,” Bill interrupted. “I read the chemical review. N-Som is a synthetic exitatory neurotransmitter. But I didn't know it affected anything other than the Circadian Clock.”

Manny grinned, his pleasure genuine.

“Pretty amazing stuff, huh? So you understand why this experiment is so important. Once this drug is approved, not only will the productivity of the human race increase, the individual quality of life will too.”

When Bill pulled into the parking lot, Manny saw that they were at the hospital. His smile melted.

“What is this?”

“Unless you can grow your finger back, you need surgery.”

“I told you...”

“Manny, I'll be with you the whole time. We'll be safe.”

But Manny knew better. If he went in here, there would be forms to fill out, insurance information, DruTech would be called...

David would find them.

"I can't..."

"Manny, please be reasonable."

Manny looked down at his hands. He could live with nine fingers. But eight? Six? Two?

David had threatened to cut them all off if he tried to interfere. That, and worse.

"My finger doesn't matter, Doc. The Project matters. You, Theena, everyone involved is in danger. He wants to kill all of you."

"Who, Manny? Who wants to kill us?"

Manny nervously glanced in the rearview mirror. He was so shocked that he yelled.

David.

"You have to get away, Doc. Go!"

Manny pushed out of the car and ran away as fast as he could.

Chapter 12

When Bill arrived at DruTech, Theena was waiting at the front door. Her lab coat was over another short skirt, and her hair was in a loose ponytail. She hugged him, and Bill felt the tension slip away for the short time she was in his arms.

"What happened?"

Theena was appraising the mark on Bill's cheek, where Franco had slapped him.

He gave her the whole story as they made their way to the research level. When the elevator stopped, he'd just gotten to the part with Manny.

"He's okay?"

There was excitement in her voice, perhaps a bit more than Bill found comfortable.

"He says some people took him from the hospital and cut off his finger, but he got away from them. I took him back there so they could reattach it, but he ran off."

"That poor man. He must be terrified. And you too. Bill, I don't know how you managed it. You're very brave."

Theena kissed him on the cheek.

Bill tried to shrug, but it came out more like a squeak. She took his hand and they left the elevator.

"The others are here—everyone except for Jim Townsend. I left several messages, but haven't heard from him."

"Is that normal?"

"For Jim, no. I keep wondering if he had some kind of accident."

Theena ushered Bill into a conference room. It was a moderate size, the walls adorned with motivational posters with sayings like "All answers began as problems." The lighting was softer than the harsh neon of the hallways, and the air smelled faintly of tobacco. A large oval table was surrounded by a dozen chairs, only three of which were taken.

"This is Dr. Bill May, from CDER. I'm sure you all remember him from the other day. Bill, this is Dr. Mason O'Neil, our MD."

Bill shook his hand. Mason was about ten years older than him, short and stout. He had furry gray sideburns that seemed to swallow his ears, an obvious attempt to make up for the lack of hair on his head.

"Next to him is our chemist, Dr. Julia Myrnowski."

Julia was young, chubby, with short blonde hair. She smiled shyly at Bill and offered a moist, limp hand.

"And this is Dr. Robert Fletcher, our psychiatrist."

"Call me Red."

Bill couldn't imagine why—the doctor's hair was pure white. Red seemed to read Bill's mind.

"Nothing to do with my hair. I was a bookworm when I was younger. Nickname stuck."

"Nice to meet all of you." Bill glanced at Theena, unsure if he was supposed to tell the day's events. She pushed on without acknowledging him.

"I'd like everyone to state a brief overview of their work here, to give Bill an idea of how we're running this project. Can you start, Mason?"

"Of course." Mason had a school teacher voice, the friendly kind. "I'm basically Manny's doctor. I oversee all of the testing. Tissue work ups, serum samples, vitals, lab tests, that sort of thing."

"And how is his health?"

"Remarkable. Every possible stat has improved since he began using N-Som. Blood pressure, cholesterol, body fat, endurance, you name it. You're an MD yourself, correct? I'd be thrilled to go over his charts with you."

Bill had seen many of them already. Mason did thorough work.

Theena smiled, comfortable playing group leader. "Julia? Can you tell Bill about your job?"

"Well, I work in the lab a lot. Sometimes with Mason doing testing, but my specialty is NMRs and mass spec."

"Julia is the one that mapped the atomic make-up of the N-Som molecule."

"Three molecules, actually." Julia blushed. "It's a beautiful drug, on an atomic level. I've built several models."

"I'd like to see them."

"Sure."

Julia blushed. She was so shy Bill felt an urge to pat her head.

Red coughed into his hand and cleared his throat.

"And I assess Manny's mental state, along with providing needed therapy."

"Does he need therapy?"

"We all need therapy, Bill. Perhaps Manny needs a bit more than others."

Bill had gone over some of Manny's physical reports, but hadn't been privy to any of his psych evaluations other than a brief bio.

"I've read a little about his past. He grew up in a foster home."

"Yes, with his brother, David. Their mother was a drug user, neglectful. The state took over custody."

"Can you give me your personal assessment of him?"

Red smiled, apparently delighted by the question.

"Complicated man. He has a grounded sense of right and wrong, yet many times in the past he chose the wrong. Burglaries, car theft. We got him through the CIRP, you know."

Bill hadn't known that. The Correctional Institution Reform Project offered prisoners reduced sentences by allowing them opportunities to volunteer in scientific programs.

"What was he in for?"

"Assault. He started a fight in a restaurant, hit another man with a beer mug. When the police arrived, he fought with them as well."

"So he's temperamental."

"When I first got him, yes. I'd like to say that my guiding hand has made him a calmer person, but I don't think I'm the cause in this instance."

"N-Som?"

"I think so. Besides his many physical improvements, Manny has become calmer, more at ease with himself, and even a nicer person."

"Is he ever paranoid? Delusional?"

Something passed behind Red's eyes.

"Manny has some unresolved issues involving his childhood, and has resulting ego problems. I'm sure you know how hard self acceptance can be, especially if you've made some big mistakes."

Bill was taken aback. Did Red know? Was this talk of self acceptance and big mistakes a reflection on Bill's past?

"I'm not sure I understand."

"I'm sure you do. I read about you in the paper last year, Dr. May. You and your wife. But obviously, with therapy, a person recovers. You did seek professional help, right?"

Bill felt it build inside him. He tried to repress the bottled emotion.

"The topic is Manny, Red."

"Surely you can talk about it after all this time."

The memories came flooding back, and Bill couldn't stop the switch from being flipped. With them came pain, guilt, and self-hatred.

"Whether I can or I can't isn't your goddamn business."

Red stared at him without expression.

"I apologize, Dr. May. If you need an ear, I'm here. It's almost impossible to get over things like that without help."

Bill tried to swallow, couldn't. All eyes were on him, watching him while he cracked. He stood up to leave.

"If you'll excuse me." Bill fought to keep his voice even. "The last thing I want to do is tell a group of complete strangers about how I murdered my wife."

Chapter 13

Theena watched Bill storm out of the conference room, his face ablaze with pain. Against the advice of Red, she followed, somewhat surprised by the degree of her own concern.

Bill was leaning against the wall, his thumb and index finger pressing his eyes closed. Theena touched his shoulder and discovered he was trembling.

"Bill? What happened in there?"

When he took his hand away from his face, his eyes were red.

"I'm not sure I can talk about it."

"Have you ever talked about it?"

Bill said nothing. Theena waited, watching him wrestle with some inner demon. When he finally spoke it was flat and without emotion.

"My wife Kristen had an inoperable brain tumor. It didn't respond to conventional therapy. I knew there was an experimental drug that looked promising, but it was still in pre clinical development—it hadn't been tested on humans."

His mouth twisted in a sour smile.

"I pushed the application through the Investigational New Drug process, even though the sponsor wasn't prepared for clinical testing. The FDA can do that for emergency cases; allow a treatment IND even if the drug hasn't been approved.

Theena could guess where this was going. Her stomach clenched with pity.

"The tumor was slow growing, but I didn't want to waste any time. I rushed her into treatment. I can remember promising her it was going to be okay."

His red eyes glassed over. His voice was a pain-filled whisper.

"The first dose killed her."

Theena tried to touch his cheek, but Bill turned away.

"I shouldn't have pushed it through. If I had more thoroughly investigated the drug..."

"She was going to die anyway, Bill."

He laughed, a harsh expletive sound.

"The very next month, a doctor in Europe perfected a new procedure for mid-brain tumorectomy. If I'd waited a few weeks, Kristen would still be alive."

There was nothing Theena could say, but she tried.

"You did it to save her."

"I killed her. It was no different than putting a gun to her head."

Bill walked off in the direction of the elevator. Theena could imagine trying to live with that guilt, and she felt terrible for him. She also felt something else; a tenderness inside her that had been missing for a long time.

Theena followed, grabbing his sleeve.

"Don't go."

He shook his arm free. She grabbed him again, harder, yanking him around to face her. Bill's face was vulnerable, but there was also inner strength there. He was hurt, and for some reason this hurt her too. It was impossible to bring his wife back, and almost as impossible to make him forgive himself.

But maybe, for just a moment, she could help.

Before he could object, she had her fist locked around his tie and her mouth pressed to his.

Bill resisted for the briefest of moments, and then kissed her back.

It wasn't tender or tentative, as first kisses usually were. This was hard, frantic. He gripped her tight, both hands pressing into her lower back, and she wrapped her fingers in his hair and tried to pull him even closer.

It didn't take much effort to lead him to Manny's room. The passion continued to grow in Theena until it drowned out all other thoughts. Bill's wife, N-Som, her father's death, Manny's disappearance; nothing mattered except sensation, and she gave herself to it fully.

They got as far as the sofa before the clothes came off. She didn't expect Bill to last long—it had been a while for him. But he surprised her, and when the rhythm she liked began he was able to maintain it until she found release, sinking her teeth into his shoulder.

He came while she was riding the wave, and for those few precious seconds, everything in life was perfect and pleasant and real.

Theena luxuriated in the post-glow, his weight on top of her, their sweaty bodies, the feeling of his heart beating against her breast. Sex with a new man was often awkward, but this was as good a start as she could remember.

She whispered in his ear, giving it a tiny nibble and tasting salt. "I really needed that."

Bill pulled away and grinned at her. "It sure beats psychotherapy."

"Cheaper, too."

He kissed her, tenderly this time, and then maneuvered so he was sitting on the sofa. She curled up next to him, hooking one leg over his knee.

"Are you okay?"

He thought about it for a moment, and nodded.

"I've got a lot on my plate, but I'll manage."

"Can I be forward?"

Bill laughed. "I think you already were."

"My father's funeral is tomorrow. I'd like you to take me."

"Of course."

Theena had been putting off mourning. When she saw Dad in that casket, she knew she'd break down. Having Bill with her would help.

"So it's really been over a year?"

He nodded.

Theena found the remote control and aimed it at the fake window. After a few sunsets, the porno channel came on.

"After that long, I bet you have a shortened refractory period."

Her hand found him, and she proved herself correct.

They took it slower this time, now that the urgency was gone. Theena enjoyed the change of pace, almost as much as she enjoyed the change of partner.

She wondered, idly, what Manny was doing at that moment. She'd never said they were exclusive, even though the poor dope proposed marriage every time they made love. He would probably fly into a jealous rage if he found out.

But as she approached orgasm, it wasn't Manny she was thinking about. Nor was it Bill.

In her mind's eye, she saw someone completely different.

The only man she'd ever truly loved.

Chapter 14

After sitting in the conference room for several minutes, Dr. Red Fletcher knew that Theena and Bill weren't coming back. He assumed that they were in Manny's room—it was obvious they had the hots for each other, even if you weren't a trained psychoanalyst. Under the guise of testing his assumption, he bid good-bye to his colleagues and went to his office, located a few doors down.

The room was an intentional replica of the office at his practice downtown, with the same style Victorian desk, the same leather couch, many of the same books on the shelves. There was no view, naturally, but he compensated with several landscape paintings and soft track lighting. A place for thinking, a place for healing.

The main difference between his two offices was the secret place, as he liked to call it. The brown door in the corner was always locked, and Red had the only key.

Red went into the secret place and switched on the light. The Mac on the desk hummed; it was always on. The space was small, cramped, the size of a large closet. He sat down at the keyboard.

Dr. Nikos had been the only other person that knew about this place—Red had needed his permission and funding to set it up. But Nikos hadn't even known the tip of it.

Along the walls, in racks, were dozens of labeled CDRs. The computer looked like any other modest system, unless you examined the back and noticed the extra cables running to and from the CPU. Red typed a command

and the sound came up on the speakers.

Moaning and breathing, from Manny's room.

Red smiled. He'd been right. He checked to make sure it was being burned on the CD, and then turned the sound down.

Bugging Manny's room had been his idea. Red was an ethical doctor, but this was an exceptional case. Manny was his patient, yes, and he wanted to help him. But first and foremost, Manny was a guinea pig for an experimental drug. Red's job here was to evaluate the psychological effect it had on Manny, and if that meant violating his trust, so be it.

It was a good thing he did, because some of the things Red had recorded were extraordinary.

He took down a CD labeled "MANNY and DAVID #7", put it in the second disk drive, and turned up the volume.

Voices filled the small room, David and Manny in a heated argument. Red sat down and picked up his notebook, leafing through it.

"You cover for me. You always cover for me."

"I have to, David. You're my brother."

Red squinted at his handwriting, wishing it were more legible. He found the session he wanted and read. Manny had been talking about his youth, describing an instance where David killed a neighbor's dog. Manny told their foster parents. David was sent to juvenile hall, and like most kids in juvee, he'd been abused.

Manny had never gotten over the guilt of doing that to his brother. Even though Manny hadn't been the one to beat the animal to death, he felt responsible.

"Stop it, David! You're hurting me!"

Red pursed his lips, listening to the tape, wondering if he could actually hear the singeing sound of the hot iron on skin or if it was his imagination.

He questioned, yet again, if he should have attempted to stop it. True, Manny's healing abilities were accelerated, but shouldn't he have stepped in and tried to prevent him from being hurt?

"Not my job." Red said the words to reaffirm his decision. "My job is to observe and evaluate."

Dr. Nikos had never known about the friction between Manny and David. Red had planned on telling him, but had wanted to gather enough data to formulate a diagnosis first. He knew David was violent, but was unsure if his incessant mention of homicide was real or imaginary. He believed that David would never actually kill someone. It was just tough talk; bravado and swagger.

Or was it?

A sobering thought, especially in light of Dr. Nikos's murder. But Red was sure it couldn't have been David. David hadn't been there.

No, someone else killed Dr. Nikos. Red set it in his mind. It had to have been someone else.

He popped out the CD and checked on the sounds in Manny's room.

More moaning and groaning.

Red smiled. "Ah, youth."

He left it on, again telling himself it was for professional rather than prurient reasons. Theena intrigued him. As a Freudian, he was immediately aware of the complex she suffered from; it was her primary motivation for beginning the affair with Manny. Red was unsure of her motive in this instance.

It might have been the need for sex, but she seemed to have been getting enough of that already. Was she doing it with Bill out of pity?

The moans didn't sound like pity to Red.

Something else then. Romantic feelings, perhaps? Or perhaps Bill was a more appropriate substitute than Manny was.

Red switched off the sound and left the room, locking the door behind him. Fascinating as she was, Theena wasn't his patient. She had a right to her secrets.

He did, however, pocket a CD labeled MANNY and THEENA #4, to listen to later.

It was only lunch time, but with Manny still missing, Red had no reason to stay at DruTech. He pondered going into the office downtown, but everything there could wait.

Red chose to go home. Rather than track down his fellow employees to inform them he was going, he used the intercom. Units were in every room, on the wall next to the entrance. He stood next to his and pressed the speak button.

“I'm heading home. Good day, everyone.”

His voice echoed loudly over the house speakers, imbedded in all the ceilings throughout the complex. A moment later, the speakers bellowed with a feminine voice.

“GOOD-BYE, DR. RED.”

Red smiled. Julia always responded. He hardly ever talked to her professionally, but he knew her shy nature made self-reaffirmation through others a necessity. In return she always offered affirmation back in greetings and farewells.

He knew she was awaiting a response, and he gave it to her.

“Good-bye, Julia. See you tomorrow.”

“SEE YOU TOMORROW.”

“Have a nice day.”

“YOU TOO. HAVE A NICE DAY.”

He could have replied again, knowing Julia would keep this up forever. But amusing as it was, he wanted to get on his way.

Red owned a ranch house in the wealthy town of Barrington. The sun was out in full force, and in the parking lot Red paused to take some big, full breaths. Autumn was in the air, with its own special, earthy smell.

The weather was mild enough to roll down the windows halfway, and he took a route through the forest preserve to see the trees turning. Nature pleased Red, and fall colors were a special delight. The leaves reminded him of his youth, placing them under paper and rubbing them with a crayon to get impressions. Simple tactile pleasures.

The hit from behind was wholly unexpected.

Red always drove under the speed limit. Mostly for safety's sake, but he also got a secret pleasure causing road rage in the impatient.

As a result of his driving habits, he'd been rear-ended several times. It had never been his fault, and was never anything more serious than a fender bender.

This was different.

Red's head was jerked back, and his car swerved onto the shoulder. He hit the brakes, spun, and finally came to a stop facing the wrong side of the street.

When focus returned, he saw what had hit him. It was a pickup truck, full size, the chrome bumper wrinkled like a piece of tin foil.

The driver hopped out of the cab and hurried over to Red, opening his door. Red was grateful for the speedy assistance, until he looked into the driver's eyes.

"David?"

"Hiya, Doc. Beautiful day for a drive."

David reached down and unbuckled Red's seat belt. He firmly tugged the older man out of the vehicle. Red was a solid man, tall enough to have played basketball in high school. But David handled him as easily as if he were a child.

Another car slowed down beside the accident site, the driver sticking his head out the window.

"Are you guys okay?"

"I think so." David shrugged. "No one's hurt, but my wife's gonna have a fit."

"Do you want me to call the police?"

“Already did. Thanks.”

David waved, and the car sped off.

Red was still stunned, and his neck was beginning to ache, but he wasn't afraid. David had apparently followed him from DruTech, and he obviously needed to talk.

“You seem sort of edgy, David. Any idea where Manny is?”

“That cry baby? No idea.”

“I have to question your method of approach here. Wouldn't a phone call have been easier than rear-ending me?”

“Sorry, Doc. You know I'm impulsive sometimes.”

Red nodded, then winced.

“Neck hurt? Let's go sit down.”

David took Red's arm, assisting the older man with his footing on the bumpy grass. David led him down the ditch and over to a copse of trees. He leaned the psychiatrist against a massive oak.

“Thank you, David.”

“With the ditch, you can barely see the road over here. It's like we're all alone in the woods.”

Red agreed. “Private. It's nice to get away, sometimes.”

David sat next to the doctor and twirled a brown oak leaf in his fingers. Red waited. Silence was important. It was good to let patients work things out for themselves.

“I was there.”

“Where, David?”

“When Dr. Nikos died.”

Red did his best to hide his alarm.

“I didn't notice you there.”

“I came later, after the speech. I know Dr. Nikos didn't want me there. Manny's the success. I'm the failure.”

“That's not true...”

"It is true. That's why I killed him."

For the first time in his professional career, Dr. Red Fletcher felt a spike of fear. He'd had David pegged as antisocial, prone to fits of temper, but not homicidal.

His diagnosis had been wrong.

It all made sense now. And Red was in serious danger. Stupid, to have let his own ego blind him from the truth.

Red controlled his breathing, trying to treat the conversation like it was just another therapy session.

"You believe Dr. Nikos thought you were a failure."

"Of course. If anyone knew about me, do you think N-Som would get FDA approval? I know I'm a secret. That new CDER guy, Bill, doesn't even know about me, does he?"

"No."

"See? Big embarrassment."

Red chose his words carefully. He didn't want to get David riled up. They had a relationship, mentor and student. He could still control where the situation went.

"You're not an embarrassment, David. You may have some problems..."

"Problems?" David spat. "I sliced Dr. Nikos up like a pizza. And when Manny tried to stop me, I did the same to my own brother. The one person in the whole damn world that I love."

"You... you need help, David."

"No shit."

"But we'll be able to work it out. It isn't your fault that Dr. Nikos is dead. We can actually blame the drug. You can get through this, David."

David crumpled the dry leaf in his hand, the brittle flakes grabbing the air and blowing away.

"Sometimes I think I can. Sometimes I really do." His mouth formed a lopsided grin. "But it would be a lot easier if I just killed you."

David took a scalpel out of his back pocket. Red felt the sweat bead up on his forehead. He kept his voice steady.

“That's not in your best interest, David.”

“You said it yourself. I can blame the drug.”

David moved closer. Red crab walked backwards, keeping his feet between him and the advancing blade.

“I can help you, David. I can help make you well.”

“I appreciate the effort. Really, I do. But between me and you, Doc, I think psychiatry is a big load of horseshit.”

The scalpel flashed. Red tried to defend himself, tried to ward off the unrelenting slice after slice after slice. After a while he gave up and just prayed for it to end quickly.

But it didn't.

“Now it makes sense.” David laughed, digging in. “Why they call you Red.”

Chapter 15

Nathan White liked every aspect of his job except this one.

His mother thought being a courier was the same as being a pizza delivery boy. She couldn't have been more wrong. They both involved driving, and dropping things off, but the similarity ended there.

Even though he worked for a company, Nathan was technically an independent contractor—his own boss. But more than that, he was actually part of something. Many people, companies, and institutions depended on him.

Fed Ex offered next day service, but in many cases that wasn't quick enough. Sometimes it had to be the same day, or even within an hour.

Nathan had delivered contracts that saved companies from bankruptcy, organs for emergency transplants, evidence that helped convict murderers, water to disaster victims—things that helped make the world better.

He was paid well, treated with respect, and people were always happy to see him when he arrived just in the nick of time.

Kind of like Superman, Nathan thought. Except Nathan was fat with acne and no super powers.

The job had only one downside; the DruTech run. Or, as he called it, the cadavalivery.

He picked up his two-way radio and spoke to headquarters.

"Dispatch, I'm at the morgue, over."

"Roger, Nathan. Make it quick—you wouldn't want the corpsicle to thaw."

Nathan winced at the joke. He got out of the car and rang the buzzer at the rear entrance. Like always, his mind began to wander while he waited.

Once a week, for almost two years, Nathan had been coming to the morgue to pick up packages. The procedure was always the same. He'd give Sully a sealed envelope, Sully would give him an insulated box.

The boxes varied in size, some small enough to hold shoes, some large enough for a TV. They were always cold to the touch. Sometimes they steamed slightly, and the odor made Nathan gag. A year back, a package had even leaked, and the stain was so rancid Nathan had to cut it out of the upholstery, resulting in a hole in the back seat.

Nathan knew that even the big boxes were too small to hold an entire cadaver, but he had no doubt the boxes had something dead in them. After all, this was a morgue.

So his mind played tricks every time he made the DruTech run. He'd imagine the box was full of illegal third trimester abortions. Or severed limbs, which were going to be cooked and served to a secret club of corporate cannibals. Or that he was picking up different body parts each time, and a mad doctor was building a monster out of them.

One thing was certain; the weekly deal was shady. It always took place at the back entrance, which was never in use. It always involved an exchange for an envelope full of cash (Nathan never opened it, but it felt like cash). And Nathan was paid for the run off the books, in cash as well.

Nathan patted his pocket to make sure he had the envelope. He did, naturally. If there was one run he didn't want to screw up, it was this one. Nathan harbored many fears of what would happen if he'd accidentally lost the envelope. He figured he'd wind up in one of those insulated boxes, and his replacement would deliver his parts to DruTech for nefarious purposes.

The door swung open, and Nathan jumped. Sully snorted at him. Pale, hairy, a drawn out face—Sully looked exactly what a morgue attendant should look like. As usual, he wore his bloody apron. Little things were stuck to it on this occasion, and Nathan had no desire to know what they were.

“Got the envelope?”

Nathan handed it to Sully. The dour man stuck it in his back pocket, then bent down and handed Nathan a medium sized Styrofoam box, the lid sealed with tape.

It was steaming.

Nathan held it away from his body, trying not to sniff the rising fumes. Sully laughed.

“Get a move on. You don't want to have it with you when it thaws and wakes up.”

The color drained from Nathan's face, and Sully slammed the door. Sully always messed around with him like that. There couldn't be something actually alive in there.

Right?

Nathan didn't want to find out. He hurried to his car, placed the box on the roof as he opened the door, and when he went to grab the package it slid out of his hands and hit the ground.

Nathan yelled in surprise. This was the worst thing that had ever happened in his twenty-three years of life.

The package landed on its corner. The impact caused the top to pop off, flapping open like a hinge, the tape still stuck to one edge.

The steam slowly dissipated, revealing the thing inside the box.

Nathan stared down in horror. It was worse than anything he could have imagined. His mind screamed at him to run away, but his legs remained locked and his eyes couldn't tear away from the nightmare before him.

It was a human head.

The head was severed under the jaw line, packed in smoking dry ice. Two curly wires were stuck in the tear ducts of its open eyes, the other ends attached to a large lantern battery.

And it was opening and closing its mouth.

The scream was in his lungs, filling them, but he couldn't get it out of his throat. He was so terrified he couldn't exhale.

There was a soft, rhythmic *click click click* as the head's upper and lower teeth met, as if it was chewing.

Or trying to speak.

"Whoops."

Nathan turned and saw Sully standing next to him. The scream finally came out, but it was more like an asthmatic wheeze, so high-pitched only dogs could hear it.

Sully bent down and picked up the box, holding it under Nathan's face.

"See? You woke him up. Now it must feed on the blood of the living."

Nathan's bladder let loose and the blood drained from his head. He was about to pass out.

Sully snapped the lid on and put the box in the back seat.

"You okay, kid?"

"... it's... it's... still alive..."

Sully laughed and clapped Nathan on the shoulder. "It's not alive. Some doctor's going to use it for experimental research. The battery keeps a small electric charge in the brain so the tissue doesn't decay, and the jaw moving is just a reflex."

Nathan began to sob. Sully frowned, clearly embarrassed.

"Look, kid, it's no big deal. No harm done. You want to come in, get cleaned up?"

Nathan shook his head, his hand reaching into his wet jeans for his car keys. Sully took out the envelope Nathan had given him and removed a fifty dollar bill. He shoved it in Nathan's vest pocket.

"Here, have a nice dinner on me."

Nathan mumbled a thanks. It was automatic. He didn't feel thankful at all.

"If there's anything left, pick up something for our friend here. Maybe he'd like a pack of gum."

Sully opened his jaw and clicked his teeth together, doing an eerie imitation of the head.

Nathan climbed into the car, oblivious to Sulley's laughter. He drove in a daze, way over the speed limit, paying no attention to traffic signals. When he got back to headquarters Nathan quit on the spot, and demanded they remove the box from his back seat and take it to DruTech themselves.

The next day he got a job delivering pizzas.

Chapter 16

Bill had never been to a funeral where it hadn't rained.

Today was no exception. He huddled under an umbrella, Theena clutching his arm hard enough to bruise it, trying to remain calm while the minister's droning voice got lost in the wind.

There had been a wake earlier, loud and good natured, pharmaceutical people mingling with politicians, investors, family members. But it was all bad for Bill. The closed casket brought back memories of his wife's funeral, and several colleagues he hadn't seen since then felt the need to ask how he was coping.

Theena hadn't said a word since this morning, when she apologized for not putting on any make-up. Her nonstop crying since then was the reason why.

But he'd managed to stay strong through the wake, for Theena, for himself. He wasn't sure how much longer he could last. When he'd learned that the funeral was being held at St. Matthew's it took all of his will power not to walk out on Theena.

He looked to his right, again, over the rows of graves, to a barren tree on a hill a hundred yards away.

His wife was buried under that tree.

Bill hadn't visited her once since she'd been interred. The scene had been very much like this one, support people mumbling meaningless words of sympathy in the rain.

A procession had formed before Dr. Nikos's casket, mourners pulling flowers from an arrangement and setting them on top. Bill tried to ease Theena into line, but she refused to move. The people standing to their left had to walk around them.

Finally, adorned with flora, the coffin was lowered into the muddy earth. Theena wailed, a sound like a tortured ghost, and collapsed onto the ground. Bill knelt next to her, cradling her head, feeling his wife watch them from the hill.

Several people came by, including the minister, offering their assistance. Theena simply sobbed. After a while, she and Bill were the only ones left.

The wind got worse, stinging as it slapped their faces. Bill's pants were soaked to the thigh. He could imagine how cold Theena was, in a black skirt, sitting on the ground in a little ball.

"We have to get you inside."

"No."

"Theena, you'll get sick out here."

"I'm not leaving Daddy."

Bill tried to lift her by the armpits, but she fought him. He had an irrational impulse to slap her, make her get up so he could leave, and that made him feel even guiltier than he already was.

"I want to put a flower on his casket."

She allowed Bill to help her up, and they approached the grave.

The hole was already filling with water. So cold and wet and alone. Awful.

Theena picked a rose and dropped it. The flower bounced indifferently off the casket and fell alongside. Theena shook herself free of Bill's arms and ran, across the cemetery, towards the parking lot, her face in her hands.

Bill watched her go. He wanted to follow, but his feet had something else in mind. They took him in the other direction, up the hill.

Kristen's headstone was black marble. All it listed was her full name, her birth date, her death date. The carver had asked Bill if he wanted anything else, a phrase or line.

To sum up a person's life in one phrase had seemed so pathetic at the time, and Bill had passed. Now he wished he'd put something, anything there, to set it apart from all of the other nondescript graves, rows and rows of them.

"I'm sorry, Kristen. I'm so sorry."

He cried, letting it all out, sobbing with his whole body like Theena had. He was so overwhelmed with grief that he didn't notice the two men approach him from behind.

"Well, lookee here, Franco. It's the Doc's wife."

Bill spun around. It was the two thugs who'd almost killed him the day before.

"It's nice that you visit her, ain't it Franco?"

Franco put out a palm and shoved Bill backwards. Bill tripped over his wife's stone and landed hard on his butt.

"I thought we told you not to call the cops."

"Easy, Franco. Can't you see the guy is grieving here? You gonna kick his ass on top of his wife's grave? Show some respect."

The older man, Bill remembered his name was Carlos, held out his hand to help him up. Bill refused to take it.

Carlos shrugged and got down on his haunches.

"Franco is right, though. We warned you not to call the cops, and you went and called the FBI. We feel like maybe you didn't take us seriously."

"Fuck you." Bill spat in his face.

Carlos smiled. He took out a handkerchief and wiped his cheek. Then he backhanded Bill across the face.

"I'm sentimental, so I'll forgive that. But we need you to understand that no one's gonna help you, Doc. You could call the CIA, Internal Affairs, the goddamn Governor, and no one will help. But we'll hear about it. And we won't be happy."

Bill probed the inside of his mouth with his tongue, tasting blood. A tooth was wiggly. He stared up at Franco, but there was no fear. There was no pain, either. All Bill felt was a coldness inside him. He embraced it, drew strength from it. This wasn't going to be a repeat of yesterday.

He made a show of getting to his feet, looking weak and beaten. Then he made a tight fist and hit Carlos with everything he had.

Carlos went down. Franco stood there, immobile and confused. Bill lowered his head and charged the bigger man, connecting solidly with his gut. Franco grunted and doubled over, and Bill swung hard between his legs, an upper cut that he put his whole body behind.

Then he ran.

The grass was slippery, and it was hard to keep his balance. He heard the thugs yelling after him, heard a shot and felt it go over his head, but he didn't stop. Not until he reached the parking lot and found Theena sitting in his car.

Bill scrambled for the door handle, his free hand digging for the car keys in his jacket pocket.

They weren't there.

He tried his blazer pockets, vest pocket, pants pockets, patting his body all over.

No keys. They must have been lost in the scuffle.

Theena hadn't even noticed him—she was staring blankly out the window, an emotional zombie.

"Theena! We have to get out of here!"

She didn't bother looking. Bill glanced over his shoulder, saw Franco and Carlos coming down the hill.

He reached in the car and wound his fingers around Theena's long, black curls. Then he yanked.

She was jerked from her seat, the pain making her yell. Bill locked his hand around one of her flailing wrists and pulled her out the driver's side door.

“We have to go!”

There was a boom and a crash, and a spider web of cracks blossomed in the Audi's rear windshield. Theena's eyes widened, and Bill dragged her away from the car as another bullet smacked into the open door.

With her long legs, Theena had no problem keeping up with him. They ran, hand in hand, through the parking lot and onto the street. There were apartment buildings on either side, for blocks in either direction. Bill tugged her towards the nearest one, heading for the front entrance. The security door was locked. He frantically pressed buzzers, hoping someone would let him in.

“Who is it?”

Bill put his face to the intercom speaker.

“Please! Someone is trying to kill us!”

“Who is this? Lionel?”

“Open the door!”

Another thunderclap, the bullet slapping into the brick wall and peppering Bill's face with bits of wet rock.

They took off in a crouch, making a beeline for the next apartment building.

No one answered the buzzers.

“They're coming.”

Theena's voice was soft, fatalistic. Bill chanced a look. Carlos and Franco were jogging towards them, less than a hundred yards away.

Bill looked in the other direction. The street was deserted, not a vehicle in sight. They ran for it.

Halfway down the block, a car turned the corner and began to approach. Bill released Theena and waved his hands over his head, yelling for the car's attention.

The car didn't slow down, and veered slightly out of their direction as if to drive past. Frantic, Bill tried to position himself in front of it, holding out his hands, praying the driver would stop.

The driver slammed on the brakes. The tires couldn't find purchase on the wet pavement and the car hydroplaned, rushing at Bill faster than he was able to get out of the way.

It slid to a stop just a foot before impact.

Bill placed his palms on the hood. The driver was invisible behind tinted gray glass. He was probably petrified, wondering if this were a robbery or a car jack. The car was a late model Lincoln Continental, the rain beading off the many coats of wax.

Bill motioned for Theena to come over.

“We need help! Someone's after us!”

The driver's window rolled down.

“Bill May? Theena?”

It was DruTech President Albert Rothchilde.

Chapter 17

Theena glared at Rothchilde. He was in all black, except for a blood red rose pined to his lapel. He had come to the funeral late, and left early. But she had a pretty good idea why he'd stuck around.

Rothchilde returned her obvious anger with a blank stare, then focused on Bill. “Are you both all right?”

“Some people are chasing us. They have guns.”

“Guns?” Rothchilde raised an eyebrow.

Theena kept her voice even. “Open the doors, Albert.”

“Of course.”

Rothchilde hit the unlock button. Bill climbed into the back seat, Theena the front. She watched her boss try to feign concern.

“Shall we head to the police station?”

Bill shook his head. “They won't help. Just get us out of here.”

Theena noticed the faintest of smiles appear on Rothchilde's lips. “Are you sure you're okay? Who were those men? Were they trying to rob you?”

“I think they're organized crime.” Bill opened his mouth to say more, but nothing came out.

He suspects Rothchilde, Theena thought. *Maybe the guy isn't as gullible as he looks.*

“Just take us home, Albert.”

“Well, I still think we should call the authorities. Do you want to go home, Dr. May?”

Bill said nothing.

Theena could understand his trepidation. They knew where he lived.

"You can stay with me, Bill."

"Are you sure?"

Theena nodded. Rothchilde gave her a slight jab in the ribs, which she ignored.

"If I can stop at my place and pick up some things."

"Of course. Just show me the way."

Bill directed Rothchilde to his condo and told them he'd only be a minute. When he was out of the car, Theena turned to Rothchilde and slapped him.

"You asshole! They were shooting at us!"

Rothchilde's eyes twinkled.

"They missed. They're pros, Theena. They were just delivering a message to Bill. You weren't even supposed to be involved."

"You're a bastard."

He gave her knee a squeeze.

"We both have the same goal here, darling. I see you're playing your part to the hilt. How was Dr. May? It's been a while for him, I understand."

Theena refused to be baited.

"Have you found out who killed my father, yet?"

"Not yet. I've got the whole Chicago PD on it."

"Maybe they aren't looking in the right place."

"Meaning?" Rothchilde moved closer. "Oh, I understand. Maybe they should be looking in this car, right?"

Theena looked into his eyes. Beneath the amusement they were blank, dead. She wondered, not for the fist time, what she'd gotten into.

"You killed Mike Bitner, didn't you?"

"There's no way to prove that."

He did, the bastard. And he was reveling in it. Theena felt a tickle of fear spider-walk up her spine.

“How do I know you didn't kill my father, too?”

“You know I didn't. It wouldn't make sense. He was worth too much.”

“What does that matter? Maybe you had your own warped little reason. Once a killer, always a killer.”

Rothchilde pinched her cheeks and squeezed them together, making her lips pout. “And once a whore, always a whore.”

She shook out of his grip. He put his hand on her knee again, rubbing.

“I didn't kill your father, Theena.”

His caress was cold, oily. She didn't know if she believed him or not.

“How about Dr. Townsend and Dr. Fletcher?”

“What about them?”

“They weren't at the funeral.”

Rothchilde frowned. “Yes, I noticed that, too. I'll have Halloran check on them. I should probably put some men on you as well. If someone's trying to sabotage me, they may go for you next.”

Theena folded her arms.

“I can take care of myself.”

“Of course you can, dear. If the bad guy comes to your door, you can always fuck your way out of danger.”

She made a fist, intent on putting a permanent dent in his long pointed nose. But Bill was leaving the building. He'd changed into jeans and a new jacket, and was lugging an overnight bag.

Rothchilde blew her a kiss. “It's that fire in you that makes you so dynamite in the sack.”

Bill climbed into the back of the car, putting his suitcase on the seat next to him. “All set.”

Rothchilde didn't need directions to Theena's apartment, but she gave them anyway. Bill may have suspected Rothchilde, but he gave no signs that he suspected her. She wanted to keep it that way.

They drove in silence. Theena harbored so many doubts that sorting them out was difficult. She had originally aligned herself with Rothchilde because they shared a common goal. Whomever sponsored N-Som needed to have deep pockets and major clout. Theena was a large part of the reason that American Products acquired DruTech. She'd slept with him at her father's request.

But sex and murder were two entirely different things.

Theena knew men, what they wanted, and how to control them. She thought she had Albert wrapped around her finger. Now she wasn't so sure. And the stakes had gotten higher than simply getting N-Som approved.

Theena thought about Townsend, and O'Neil, and Julia and Red. She'd been working with these people for years. They were her family. Now Townsend and Red were missing, Manny had been attacked twice, and her father was dead.

Could she be next?

Theena furrowed her brow, trying to come up with a solution. Rothchilde owned the police. He had friends in both the state and federal government. He was in bed with organized crime. If Rothchilde wanted them all dead, who could she go to?

Don't panic, she told herself. Maybe he was telling the truth. Maybe it would all work out for the best.

She knew it was a lie, but she clung to it anyway.

It was all she had.

Chapter 18

Carlos was holding a napkin to his swollen lip when the car phone rang. He had a pretty good idea who it was.

“Yeah?”

“You were supposed to scare them, not shoot them.”

Carlos spat some blood out the window. He pretended it was in Rothchilde's face.

“The prick sucker punched me.”

“I thought Gino told you to follow my orders exactly. Shall I tell your boss you're having a listening problem?”

What was with this guy? They were doing him a favor. He could show a little respect. These big business types felt like the whole world should bow at their feet.

“No, Mr. Rothchilde.”

“I'm glad we understand each other. I just dropped them off at Theena's place. The situation has changed. I want them out of the picture.”

“Out of the picture?”

“Theena and Dr. May have worn out their usefulness to this organization.”

Carlos shook his head. At the first little bump in the road, Rothchilde wanted to whack everybody. And saying this on an open line, yet. Gino must have been making a real mint off of this idiot to keep him around.

“That's not a smart idea, Mr. Rothchilde. Two FDA agents dead, both on the same case, plus her father and her.”

“We had nothing to do with her father.”

“So? Cops will still look.”

“Let me handle the cops. You just clean out your wop ears and do what you're told.”

“I'm Cuban.”

Rothchilde went off on a yelling jag, and Carlos hung up. He looked at Franco, who was clutching an ice pack between his legs.

“He wants us to take out the Doc and the girl.”

Franco smiled.

“Good. I'll enjoy snuffing that guy. And the girl will make a yummy dessert.”

Carlos frowned. He didn't like the way any of this was going. He decided to call Gino.

“Whaddaya want?”

“Gino, it's Carlos.”

“No shit. You see that big bright display on your phone? It's called Caller fucking ID.”

No respect. Didn't anyone see the movie *Scarface*? Now Pacino, he had respect. Maybe it was just this generation. Carlos had worked for Gino's father, years ago. That man respected everyone who worked for him, and he got that respect back. Carlos would have taken a bullet for him. He wouldn't take a mosquito bite for Gino.

“He wants us to take the doc and the girl out.”

“Jesus. That guy. Okay, you do it, make sure it don't get back to me. I don't want it to look like a hit. Maybe a robbery. Or some crazy killer Charlie Manson thing. Messy. Franco is good at that psycho shit.”

Carlos sighed. It kept getting better and better.

“You got it, boss.”

Gino hung up.

“We gonna do it?” Franco was practically drooling.

“Yeah. We have to make it look messy.”

“I like messy. We need to stop at the store for supplies.”

Carlos kept a box of disposable latex gloves in the trunk. He also had duct tape, carving knives, and some butcher's aprons, along with his disguise. The tools of the wet trade.

“We're set.”

“You got rubbers, too?”

“Rubbers?”

“Make it messy, right?”

“Jesus, Franco.”

Maybe it was this generation. Carlos suspected MTV had a lot to do with it.

“Stop at that place on Damon. They sell the extra large kind.”

Carlos pointed the car east.

Chapter 19

Theena's apartment didn't match her personality. It was plain, with little frill or flourish. There were no photos of friends or family anywhere, and the bland painting hanging over the sofa looked like it came with the frame, probably purchased because the color scheme matched the sofa and love seat.

Neat, tidy, impersonal. *Sort of like a motel,* Bill thought. The only distinctive object in eyeshot was a potted cactus next to the front door, jutting out of its terra cotta pot like a two foot, green exclamation point.

"Are you hungry?"

"Tired, mostly."

They'd spent the previous night in Manny's room, and hadn't slept much. Bill could say without question it was the best day he'd had in over a year. It was more than just the sex. He felt connected. For a few wonderful hours, Theena had taken away his guilt and loneliness, and given him back a shred of self-worth.

But the woman Bill had been with yesterday was nowhere to be found at the moment. Today's Theena was withdrawn, distant, defeated.

"The bedroom is the second door, there."

Bill yawned. He needed a nap, but there was a lot he had to do. The N-Som folder he'd taken from Bitner's house was in his overnight bag. Among other things, Bill was anxious to see how the experiment with Sam the monkey ended.

But it was more than that. Bill didn't want to sleep because he was afraid Carlos and Franco might find him. He couldn't be caught unaware.

"I'm okay, thanks."

"You look exhausted."

"I am. But I don't think sleep is a good idea right now."

He wanted to share his doubts about Rothchilde with Theena. Bill had a solid feeling that the A.P. President was behind those two thugs, Franco and Carlos. He also believed that Rothchilde had some kind of pull with the Chicago PD, which is why Bill hadn't gotten any help.

But something held Bill back. Even with all he'd shared with Theena, there was still something he didn't completely trust about her.

Or maybe the lack of sleep was just making him paranoid.

"I have some N-Som."

"Hmm?"

"You could take a pill. Then you don't have to sleep."

"No thanks, Theena."

Theena came over to him, serious.

"Bill, I've been working with this drug for almost a decade. It's safer than taking Vitamin C."

Bill didn't answer. Any courage he might have harbored concerning unproven drugs died with his wife.

"Look." Theena dug into her purse and took out a pill bottle. "You've read up on the chemistry, right? There's nothing toxic in here, Bill. They're neurotransmitters. The body manufactures these naturally. It's an acetylcholinesterase inhibitor, which activates the aminergic drive."

"I know what it's supposed to do. But is that all it does?"

"Manny's been awake for over a thousand hours. He's fine."

"Are you sure of that?"

"This is how sure I am."

Theena popped the top off the bottle and placed a pill in her mouth, swallowing it dry.

"It takes about four minutes to be absorbed into the bloodstream—the drug has an amino acid chelate so it immediately passes through the ion channel. Then it produces a reaction similar to narcolepsy. But it isn't really sleep because the brain stays in alpha."

Theena sat down on the sofa and stretched out her legs.

"The effect lasts anywhere from ten to twenty minutes, and then you snap immediately out of it and you're completely awake and aware."

"No residual effect?"

"None. The brain counteracts the drug with an increased production of norepinepherine. You wake up refreshed."

Bill was intrigued.

"If it inhibits sleep, why do you have a narcoleptic episode for twenty minutes? Shouldn't it simply keep you awake?"

"N-Som doesn't inhibit sleep. It replaces it. The same neurotransmitters that are responsible for waking are responsible for sleeping. N-Som affects the sleep center first, causing a state we call hyper-relaxation. The brain automatically releases its own neurotransmitters to counter the effect. The result is twenty-three hours of ZFS."

"Zero Fatigue Syndrome. Manny mentioned it."

Theena laid back on the sofa and closed her eyes.

"I may toss and turn a little. It's possible to rouse a person in hyper-relaxation, but not easy—it's like trying to wake up someone in deep sleep."

"Will you dream?"

Theena nodded. "Extremely realistic dreams. You'll almost swear they're really happening. Even though they only last a few minutes, several hours can seem to go by in your head."

"Well, then. Sweet dreams."

Theena nodded. After a minute, her breathing began to slow down.

Bill sat down next to her and took her pulse. Her heart beat twenty times in fifteen seconds. That was average. He waited and tried again. It had slowed to sixteen. A minute later it went down to thirteen, and stabilized.

He opened an eyelid, and the eyeball was moving back and forth. REM. She was focusing on some unseen object. He reached for the table lamp and moved it closer, but the pupil didn't dilate.

"Theena? Can you hear me?"

Bill gave her a light shake and a tap on the cheek. She didn't respond. Her skin was noticeably cooler to the touch.

If Bill hadn't read any of the N-Som reports, he might have thought she was going into shock rather than reacting to the drug in a predicted manner.

He waited by her side for the next ten minutes, holding her hand. It brought back images of Kristen, sitting next to her hospital bed as she slept. The memory hurt, but not as much as it used to.

Perhaps he was beginning to heal after all.

Theena's hand slowly became warmer, and her breathing quickened. She opened her eyes a moment later, her face cracking in a smile.

"I was surrounded by loved ones, warm and happy. It was beautiful."

Bill couldn't deny she looked one hundred percent better. The dark bags and redness were gone from her eyes. Her face was brighter. She seemed like a new person.

"Want to try it?"

"I'm still not sure."

Tina touched his lips with her fingertip. The moodiness was completely gone, and she was back to playful and flirtatious.

"I bet you were one of those kids in college who never tried pot."

"Wrong. I had a roommate who grew the stuff in our dorm closet. He had a pair of four foot female plants, called them Laverne and Shirley."

"So what's stopping you?"

"I already told you."

"Bill, if you can't trust your own judgment, why do you stay with the FDA?"

Damn good question.

Bill sighed, relenting.

"Fine. I'll try it."

"One thing. I just had a pleasant dream. But some of the dreams in hyper-relaxation aren't pleasant. I'd say the ratio is something like ten to one. It has something to do with the refining process, we're not entirely sure yet."

"So I might have a nightmare?"

Theena nodded.

"Nightmares and I are old buddies. I can handle nightmares."

Theena handed over the pill. It was oval and the color of caramel, covered with tiny brown flecks. Like a miniature robin's egg.

Bill swallowed it without water.

"Would you like the sofa, or the bedroom?"

"The sofa is fine."

He traded places with Theena, reclining as she had. There was a tickle in his throat. He hoped this wasn't a mistake. He hoped nothing would go wrong.

Bill closed his eyes, and felt the beginning stirrings of panic.

"It's okay." Theena put her hands on his. "Nothing to be nervous about. You'll have a quick dream, and be back to full capacity in fifteen minutes. You trust me, right?"

I want to, Bill thought. *But I don't know if I can.*

Then everything went black.

Chapter 20

Carlos and Franco circled Theena's apartment building twice before finding a parking spot.

"I'm outta change. Pay the meter."

Franco giggled. "We come here to waste some people, you're worried about a traffic fine."

Carlos sighed, the weight of the world on his shoulders.

"You ever hear of the Son of Sam?"

"I saw the movie. Mass murderer guy."

"Where is he now?"

"In jail."

"You know why he's in jail? The cops traced his parking tickets to the scenes of his crimes."

Franco paid the meter.

Carlos checked the street for bystanders, then popped the trunk. In a gym bag, next to the murder kit, was a baseball cap and matching jacket, both with a Fed Ex logo. Carlos put them on and picked up a medium sized Fed Ex box and an electronic clipboard. The gizmo was key to the disguise. Only the real deal would have an expensive gadget like this, with an LCD screen that recorded your signature.

"I'll call when I'm in, be ready."

Franco was picking his teeth with his thumbnail. If he'd heard Carlos, he didn't acknowledge it.

Carlos walked to Theena's building, package under his arm, putting himself in the role. The key to any deception was believing it yourself. He was an employee for an overnight delivery service. This was his tenth delivery of the day, and he only had three more before quitting time. Before he pressed Theena's buzzer, he took the time to fill out the blank receipt taped to the package.

Then it was show time.

"Yes?"

"Federal Express delivery, for Dr. Theena Boone."

"Who is it from?"

"Albert Rothchilde, American Products."

Carlos took a step away from the door. If she were able to see him from her window, she'd see a Fed Ex guy.

Sure enough, she buzzed him in.

Carlos took the elevator to the fifth floor. He turned on the electronic clipboard, and the screen glowed faintly. His gun was in his belt, under the jacket. Carlos rehearsed his lines before approaching her door.

Knock knock. "Fed Ex."

He tried to look bored while she gave him the once over through the peephole. When the door opened, it was only a few inches. The safety chain was on.

"Dr. Theena Boone?"

She nodded. Carlos showed her the box. The Fed Ex box was too big to fit through the crack in the door. If she wanted her package, she'd have to open up.

"I need your signature, here."

He held out the clipboard, making no attempt to slip it through the door.

"Just a second."

The door closed, and he heard the chain come off.

Carlos had his gun in hand when the door reopened. He shoved it under her chin hard enough to make her teeth click.

“In the apartment, move.”

She stepped back, her face awash in surprise. Carlos took a quick look around. The doc was on the couch, snoring.

Carlos pulled Theena close, one arm around her neck. He reached back into the hallway for the dropped box, and closed the door behind him. Then he fished out his cell phone and hit the speed dial.

“I'm in.”

Chapter 21

When he opened his eyes, Franco and Carlos were standing over him.

“Good morning, Doc.”

A large hand grabbed him by the shirt.

“This is what happens when you don't play along.”

Fear coursed through him, so hot and deep it was just as palpable as the blood in his veins. He was off balance, and summarily dragged away in a half stumble, half crawl.

A gun was pressed to his head. It felt huge. He watched, unable to move, barely capable of drawing a breath, while Carlos pulled on a ski mask.

There was a camcorder resting on a nearby box.

They were going to videotape his death.

He looked around the room for a weapon. There was nothing suitable. *Do something,* he screamed in his mind. *Don't die without a fight.*

He made a fist and swung, a big loping blow aimed at Franco's chin. The large man twisted, catching the punch on his shoulder. He giggled, high pitched and horrible, and then hit back.

The hitting went on. And on.

“Quit it. We have to do this on tape.”

Franco gave him one more kick.

“Aren't you excited, Doc? Gonna star in a movie.”

The world had become pinpoints of pain. Rather than cringe, he embraced the sensation. It might very well be the last thing he ever felt.

Carlos handed Franco the camcorder.

“If it means anything, Doc, I kind of liked you. You were an okay guy.”

Franco pointed the lens.

“Action!”

The red light on the camera began to blink.

“Come over here.”

Carlos led him into the corner of the room. He couldn't get his brain around what was happening. The magnitude was so tremendous he refused to accept it.

“Kneel down.”

He tried to think of something, a reason, a point. Not just for his death, but for his life. Something, anything, to take with him into the void.

“N-Som will get FDA approval.”

A speck of hope. Was this all just another scare tactic, to make him approve that damn drug?

“Yes. I promise it will.”

“I wasn't talking to you.”

He didn't even feel the shot. The wind left his lungs, as if he'd fallen on his back. He tried to breathe, but his brain couldn't get his lungs to work. Everything got fuzzy, soft. His life leaked out the large hole in his chest.

I hope there's something else.

But he knew there wasn't.

That was his last thought, and he died.

Chapter 22

Bill's eyes sprung open and he sucked in air. He sat up, frantic. His hand felt his chest.

No hole.

N-Som dream.

Theena had said they were realistic, but he had no idea. The detail, the imagery, the tactile sensations, all making him feel as if he'd actually been there.

Mike Bitner's death.

The perspective was different than the video tape. Bill felt like he'd actually lived through his death, seeing everything happen through Bitner's eyes, feeling what he felt up until the very end.

And unlike a regular dream, this remained lodged in Bill's head like a real memory. He could close his eyes and still feel the cool concrete of the basement floor under his knees...

"Good morning, sleepy head."

Bill stood up and spun around. Carlos was standing by the front door. He had on some kind of delivery uniform. Standing next to him, a gun pressed to the back of her head, Theena was fighting not to cry.

Bill blinked and shook his head.

This was no dream.

"Sit down, Doc. Put your hands above your head."

"Where's your fat buddy?"

"He's coming. You in a hurry to get this party started?"

Bill considered his slim options. Carlos was only half a dozen feet away, the sofa between them. Going over it was faster than going around it, but either way Carlos would be able to shoot him before he got there.

He had to think of something, and fast. Once Franco arrived the odds would become much worse.

"I have a lot of money."

"Is that so?"

Bill nodded. He laced his hands behind his head and walked over, trying to look submissive.

"Two hundred and eighty thousand dollars. You let us go, you can have it."

"And you got this where, in your wallet?"

"In a CD. Two phone calls, I can pull it all out."

He stood in front of Carlos, his muscles tensing.

"And how do I get the money, once you pull it out?"

"We can go to the bank, together. Franco stays here with the girl, so I don't try anything funny."

Carlos laughed. "I like that, Doc. You're a thinking man. Wouldn't work, though. Soon as we got out in public, you'd start screaming your head off."

Bill set his jaw. He had to make a play for the gun. It would endanger Theena, but there was no other choice. They were both going to die anyway, and he wasn't going to go out like Mike Bitner did, on his knees wondering what the meaning of life was. One memory like that was enough.

"I can call my lawyer. He's got authorization on my account. He can bring the money here."

Carlos grinned. "It's getting better. But wouldn't the bank be suspicious, taking out all that money?"

Bill eyed Carlos's pistol. He hadn't ever fired a gun, but he had a basic understanding of how they worked. Carlos had a revolver, the kind that gunslingers from the old West used. Pulling the trigger caused the hammer to draw back. When the hammer fell, it would hit the bullet in the cylinder, causing the gun to fire.

Bill stood in front of Carlos, his hands out in supplication, his voice frantic.

"I'll tell him I need it for bail, for my cousin."

"Clever, Doc. You're a clever..."

Bill shot out his hand, aiming for the hammer, grabbing the gun near the back.

Carlos fired. A spark of pain shot up Bill's wrist.

Instead of falling on the bullet chamber, the hammer pinched the webbing between Bill's thumb and forefinger. The gun couldn't fire.

He tugged. Carlos refused to let go of the weapon, being pulled along with it. They fell to the floor.

Bill was bigger, and younger, but he'd never been in a real fight before. The older man snarled and kicked with ferocious energy, tearing at Bill's eyes with his free hand, trying to bite Bill's arm.

Bill strained, trying to kick Carlos away, but he received a stiff poke in the eye and the pistol was ripped from his hand.

"You son of a..."

There was a thumping sound, and a scream. Bill squinted, focusing his blurry vision.

Theena had whacked Carlos across the face with her cactus.

She dropped the pot. Half the plant was gone, a ragged break on top leaking milky fluid.

The other half was embedded in the killer's face. He wrestled with it. Some of the needles held like fish hooks, stretching his skin as he pulled. His wail was keening, a hurt puppy.

Bill scurried to his feet and picked up his overnight bag—he didn't want to lose the N-Som file. Then he grabbed Theena's wrist.

“Back door!”

She stared for a long moment at the man writhing on the floor, then ran with Bill to the apartment's rear entrance.

They hit the stairwell and bounded down two at a time. Their footsteps echoed on the concrete, and Bill couldn't be sure he didn't hear someone above, coming after them. It fueled his fear.

The cold gave Bill a shock when they stepped outside. The earlier drizzle had frozen, forming an icy sleet. Without a coat, the weather pinched at his cheeks and hands. He tugged Theena through the alley, trying to decide where to go.

He saw a cab, coming down the block. Bill chanced a look behind him. Franco, charging towards them like a bull, his head down and fists pumping.

Bill stepped in front of the cab, forcing it to stop. He and Theena practically dove inside.

“Go! Go! Go!”

The cabbie gave Bill a look of annoyance. He opened his mouth to object and then noticed Franco barreling towards his cab.

“A hundred bucks to get us out of here!”

The cab squealed tires, doing a little fishtail peel-out, leaving the overgrown thug hollering after them.

“Are you in some kind of trouble?”

Bill didn't answer. Where could they go?

“We could try the police...”

Theena shook her head. “Those were Rothchilde's men. He owns the police.”

Bill remembered he had Agent Smith's cell phone number. Carlos and Franco had known he'd called the FBI, but they could have found out by bugging his condo, or hacking into his phone records. Or the FBI could have told them. Should he take the chance?

“Does he own the FBI?”

"I don't know. It's possible."

Bill's cell phone was in his jacket, back at Theena's. He looked at the cabbie's picture, posted on his license. His name was Fasil. Bill tapped on the glass partition.

"Fasil, do you have a cell phone?"

"I'm sorry, I do not lend it to customers."

"One call. I'll give you another hundred."

Bill fished out his wallet and slipped four fifties through the opening. The cabbie handed Bill his phone.

Bill's trembling fingers refused to obey, and he dialed the wrong number three times. The fourth time, the call finally went through.

"Agent Smith."

"This is Dr. William May, I talked to you the other day."

"Yes, Dr. May. Are you in trouble?"

"Yes. You still have agents watching us, right? We need them to take us in. Too much is going on."

"Where are you right now, Doctor?"

Bill didn't sense any kind of deception. But that could have been because he wanted a way out of this so badly.

"We're in a cab, heading southbound on Foster."

"Foster and what?"

Bill squinted out the window.

"Irving Park Road."

"Okay, Doctor. I need you to park and wait there until I can contact my men. Can you do that?"

Bill instructed the cabbie to pull over. Theena shot him a panicked look.

"Okay, I did it. Now what?"

"Some agents will approach the cab. They'll show you ID. You can go with them, they'll take you to a safe house. Do you understand?"

"Yes."

The line went dead. Bill patted Theena's thigh. “It's okay. The good guys are coming.”

The cabbie swiveled around in his seat.

“You want me to park here?”

“For a few minutes. Someone is coming to pick us up.”

He put an arm around Theena and felt shivering. Bill wasn't sure if it was her or him.

A few minutes passed.

“Come on, Smith. Where are you?”

“Smith?” Theena pulled away from Bill, her eyes wide. “Gerald Smith?”

“Special Agent Smith is the Fed I talked to. I don't know his first name. Why?”

“I've overheard Albert on the phone before, talking to someone named Gerald Smith. I got the impression he was with the FBI.”

Bill chewed his lower lip. To his right, a dark sedan with tinted windows approached the cab and slowed to a stop.

“Bill, we have to get out of here!”

The doors of the sedan opened, and two men in suits got out of the car.

“Bill, please!”

“Fasil, get ready to move if I give you the signal.”

“I appreciate the money sir, but I am becoming frightened. Please get out of my cab.”

One of the men tapped on the window. He was holding up a wallet, showing Bill his ID and badge.

“Dr. May? We're the FBI. Step out of the vehicle.”

Bill was torn apart with doubt. If Smith was a good guy, this whole thing would end here. The Feds would take them in, they'd tell their story, and hopefully it would be enough to put Rothchilde away.

But if Smith were in this with Rothchilde...

"Bill, if we go with them, we'll die. Please."

Theena squeezed his arm, imploring. Bill decided he couldn't take the chance, tempting as it was.

"Fasil—please drive us away from here."

"I do not want to get involved."

"Please, Fasil. If we get out here, these men will kill us."

"Then they may kill me as well. Get out of my cab."

Bill took off his watch, a high end Movado with a diamond at the twelve o'clock mark. He held it up to the glass.

"It's worth over two grand. Just drive us away from here, and it's yours."

The FBI agent tried to open Bill's door. Theena screamed, and Bill pulled on the handle to keep it closed.

"Please, Fasil!"

There was a screech, then the cab rocketed forward. Bill turned around.

The agents had drawn their guns.

"Get down!"

The pop-pop-pop of gunfire ensued, immediately followed by the metallic twang of bullets hitting the trunk.

Fasil made a hard right, the cab skidding around the corner at such a speed Bill thought for sure they'd crash.

But even on the slick street, the tires held.

Fasil followed up the maneuver by narrowly cutting off a bus, careening into oncoming traffic, and taking a hard left into an alley.

He stood on the brakes. The cab screeched to a halt a few feet in front of a dumpster.

"We shall wait here for ten minutes, until we are sure they are gone."

"Thank you, Fasil."

Bill began to put the watch in the pay slot, but Fasil held up a hand.

"No need. I come from a country where the government oppressed me. Many people helped me to escape. I am happy to help you."

Bill put his watch back on. With his shaking fingers, it required every bit of his concentration.

Theena leaned towards Bill, snuggling against him. He put his arm around her.

"We have to go to DruTech, Bill."

"Won't they guess we'll do that?"

"It doesn't matter. There's security around the clock, and they work for me, not Rothchilde. We can be safe there, until we sort this out."

"Maybe we should just leave the state. Or the country."

"For how long? If we run, they'll be waiting when we get back. I'm not going to let these bastards chase me away from my life."

"Why don't you two go to the media?"

Theena and Bill looked at Fasil.

"I do not know what your story is, but it seems very big. If you involve the media, it will force the government to take action against those who are after you."

Bill's foot was resting on his overnight bag, which contained the N-Som file he'd gotten from Mike Bitner's place. If he could prove something crooked was going on, the media was a logical place to turn.

But was Theena involved? How deep was she in?

"Fine, we'll go to DruTech. How about the other doctors on the team?"

"I'll call them, tell them to meet us there."

Bill handed Theena the cell. "Have them pack a bag—we don't know how long we'll have to stay."

Theena dialed a number and spoke for a few minutes with Dr. Julia Myrnowski, the chemist. Then she left messages with Dr. Jim Townsend and Dr. Red Fletcher.

Bill was staring out the window, watching for the sedan, when he felt Theena jerk next to him.

"You okay?"

Theena was holding the cell phone at arm's length, staring as if she'd never seen one before.

“I just called Mason O'Neil, our MD.”

“What's wrong? Is he all right?”

She looked at Bill, terror filling her eyes. “He was screaming.”

Chapter 23

Dr. Mason O'Neil tried to judge how much blood he had left by looking at the puddle on the floor.

The outlook wasn't good.

He was down at least a pint. His blood pressure was dangerously low, hypovelemic shock just around the corner. The tingling in his extremities and his rapid heartbeat confirmed the diagnosis.

Mason tried, once again, to put some pressure on his brachial artery to staunch the bleeding. His hand was knocked away.

"Don't prolong it, Dr. O'Neil. I have other things to do today."

His tormentor paced before him, like an expectant father in a waiting room, constantly checking his watch. David. When Mason had let him into his apartment fifteen minutes ago, he couldn't have predicted this turn of events.

"I've done nothing to you. In fact, I always considered you a friend."

"You conduct experiments on all of your friends?"

Mason's mouth was dry; his tongue felt like a paper towel. It was getting harder to speak.

"You volunteered. All you had to do was say you wanted out."

David sneered. "And go back to prison. Some choice."

The doctor watched the blood run down his fingertips, still flowing freely from the deep wound on his wrist. Drip. Drip. Drip. Like sand in an hour glass, each passing second bringing him closer to death.

"So why are you still taking the drug? If you're so against the experiment, why are you still using N-Som?"

David appeared confused.

"I'm not."

"I can see the pill bottle, in your coat pocket."

David shoved the bottle father down, as if it shamed him.

"You treated us like lab rats."

"But you're not in the lab now. Your free. So why are you still taking it?"

David's face became pinched. He nervously twiddled the scalpel in his fingers.

"It's addictive."

O'Neil let out a slow, soft breath. He was getting sleepy.

"We both know it's not addictive. You're taking it because you want to. Because the experiment is important to you."

The MD gently lifted his wrist above heart level, a pathetic attempt to stave the flow. David didn't notice.

"If the experiment is so important, why am I killing everyone involved?"

Mason's thinking was becoming blurry, and he couldn't have made up a lie if he'd wanted to.

"Because you're out of your mind."

David laughed. The sound was forced, but it caught and quickly escalated into an hysterical giggle. Mason shifted, again pressing his fingers deep into his brachial artery. His pulse was rapid, weak.

"Okay, Doc. I'm crazy. I'll admit it. But you did it to me."

"I didn't know, David. No one did."

"Dr. Fletcher knew. Good old Red knew for a long time."

"He didn't tell us. If he had, we would have stopped this. No one wanted to hurt you."

David knocked his hand away. Mason groaned, the blood coursing through his arm and spurting. It sounded like a small squirt gun.

"Do I have to cut off your fingers to get you to stop that? Consider yourself lucky. I skinned Townsend, and Red is hanging by his intestines in the forest preserve. I'm letting you off easy."

Mason's head titled forward. His eyes were rheumy.

"I'm going to die."

"That's the point."

"Manny wouldn't want me to die."

David bit his knuckle. He paced away from the doctor, then back again.

"Call an ambulance." His voice was barely above a whisper. "You can still help me."

"No help!" David pointed at him, his finger accusing.

"Please, David."

"You know how N-Som is made?"

Mason knew. They all knew. The fact that Rothchilde had somehow passed the FDA's pharmacological review was amazing. The president of DruTech couldn't have done it honestly.

"You know how it's made, and you let me take it anyway."

"You volunteered."

"Not for this." David's eyes took a trip somewhere. Somewhere horrible. "I've seen things, Doc. Things no one alive has seen. Can you imagine?"

Mason couldn't imagine. Once was bad enough.

"Do you know I've died forty-three times? And I remember each time, like movies branded into my head."

"I'm... I'm sorry."

His breath was becoming fainter, and consciousness was drifting away. All of Mason's senses softened, grew fuzzy.

"Seeing things like that can really mess a person up, Doc."

Mason felt as if he was sinking in a deep, dark pool. A small part of him wanted to protest, but didn't have the energy.

"Manny... Manny..."

"Manny isn't here, Dr. O'Neil."

David cradled the doctor's head in his hands. Mason only had a vague awareness of it.

But he became fully aware when David began to pound his head against the hardwood floor, over and over, trying to crack it open like an egg.

And he was still somewhat aware when David succeeded.

Chapter 24

“Don't let anyone into the building except DruTech staff. If the police come, demand to see a warrant.”

“No problem, Dr. Boone. Everything all right?

Theena smiled thinly at the security guard. “No, Barry, it's not. Has anyone else arrived?”

“Dr. Myrnowski went down to the lab a few minutes ago. She's the only one.”

“Did the delivery come?”

“It came this morning. I signed for it, but the box looked damaged.”

A flash of fear. “Damaged?”

“Cracked on the side, top kind of messed up.”

“Was it leaking?”

“Didn't seem to be.”

“Thanks, Barry.”

Theena went into the elevator, Bill a step behind her. If something had happened to the contents of that package...

“I know this is a stupid question, but are you okay?”

Theena put her key card in the slot and looked away from Bill. He was so concerned. She felt a tinge of something in her gut, and wondered if it might be guilt.

From a very young age, Theena realized that men were the ones with the power. Her father had proven it time and again. Men controlled the money, the government, the world. They did it by threatening, bribing, blackmailing, fighting, insulting, extorting, stealing, and killing. None of these were inherent female traits.

But a woman could have power. All she had to do was learn to control men.

Theena was an expert at this. Flirting. Flattery. Seduction. Sex. They were all tools; a means to an end. Her personal taste didn't interfere with her goals—sometimes she liked the guys she slept with, sometimes she didn't.

Bill, she liked. She liked him so much it was messing up her game plan.

Theena glanced at him, his broad shoulders, the laugh lines in the corners of his eyes. For the briefest of moments, she forgot about N-Som, and power, and goals. She pretended that she was just a woman, and Bill was just a man, and they were together. No control, no betrayal, no ulterior motives. Just love.

It was a sweet little fantasy, but that was all it was. Real life conspired otherwise.

"I'm fine. This is a lot to handle."

Bill nodded. He took her hand. She hugged him, unsure if her actions were real or pretend.

"I have to check something in the lab. If you don't mind, I need to do it alone."

"Not a problem. I want to look at the N-Som file anyway."

She forced some crocodile tears and looked at him.

"With all that's happened, you think the drug can still be approved?"

"If it's safe, I'll approve it."

Theena hugged him again. The elevator stopped and Bill went off to the conference room, a folder tucked under his arm. She had a momentary spike of panic, but then she remembered that there was nothing incriminating in the N-Som file she'd given Bill—it had all been edited.

Her mind drifted to Michael Bitner. Another man she'd liked...

Dr. Julia Myrnowski was in the lab, peering through a microscope when

Theena walked in.

“Hi, Julia.”

“Hi, Theena. How are you holding up?”

“Fine. The package is here?”

“In the freezer. I haven't opened it yet.”

Theena took a white smock from her locker and removed a hair net from the side pocket. She put both on. After snapping on a pair of latex gloves, she went to the freezer.

The box was definitely cracked, and the tape on the lid looked like a repair job. This wasn't Sully's work—she paid the morgue attendant too much for him to make mistakes. The courier must have done it.

Theena made a note to change services. If they'd seen what was inside the box, she could explain it away. But dropping important material like this was inexcusable.

“I want to do the biopsy and convert right away. Can you assist?”

“Dr. O'Neil is better at it than I am.”

“Dr. O'Neil isn't here, and I could use a second set of hands.”

Julia frowned. Theena couldn't blame her. It was a pretty hairy extraction procedure. But there was no one else, and this had to get done now.

Theena placed the box on the table, next to the surgical vise. She snugged a pre-fitted plastic cover onto the clamps and turned the handle to open them wider.

Then she went to the autoclave and pulled out the sterilized instruments; enlarging burs, dura separator, skull traction tongs, cranial drill, saw blade and guide, and various retractors, curettes, forceps, and rongeurs.

After spreading out the tools on a tray, the moment of truth arrived.

Theena broke the seal on the box, letting out a breath when a wisp of carbon dioxide plumed upward. If there was still dry ice, perhaps the specimen hadn't been compromised.

She unwound the tape and lifted off the top. The smoke dissipated, allowing her to see the perfectly preserved severed head.

Theena's lower lip trembled. She pulled the wires out of its tear ducts and gently removed the head from the box.

"Daddy."

The tears came. Theena gingerly placed Dr. Nikos Stefanopolous's head in the vice, and after sniffling once, she reached for the scalpel.

Chapter 25

Bill sat in the conference room and leafed through the file he'd found at Mike Bitner's house. Almost immediately, he began to notice differences between this file and the one Theena gave him. Omissions, mostly. But also some completely different experimental results.

Some of Manny's CTs and PETs showed abnormalities, which grew as his N-Som usage continued. In the file Bill had at home, the scans were all healthy and normal.

There were also notes that Manny had been put on the antidepressant Prozac and Xanax antianxiety. The doses had continued to go up, rising to levels that Bill thought were toxic. Eventually, Dr. Red Fletcher began giving him Compazine. This was a powerful antipsychotic, given to people with serious mental problems.

Manny's mental health wasn't the only irregularity. His diet had become increasingly extreme. He once went without food for a period of six days, refusing to eat. When the fast ended, he went into a phase where he only ate marshmallows and raw meat. Last month, Dr. Nikos came into Manny's room to find him devouring a box of pencils.

Theena's story of Manny being on a Stairmaster for nine hours was true, but it didn't end because the equipment failed. It had ended because Manny began to scream, and was unable to stop screaming for several hours, until his throat began to bleed.

But Manny wasn't N-Som's only casualty. The more Bill read, the worse things became. He leafed through one disastrous animal experiment after another. Test subjects would become catatonic, or erratic. They would refuse food and sex. Some became sick, others became violent.

The worst thing that happened was to poor Sam the monkey.

Bill located the missing page, the end of the experiment. After Sam had become lethargic, he'd gone into a rage, attacking Dr. Nikos, biting Theena, and eventually...

Bill read the paragraph again.

Day 241—We found Sam this morning, dead in his cage. Cause of death was a massive hemorrhage. Sam had pulled his own eyes out.

He scanned through the autopsy report. A lesion was found in Sam's corpus callosum, extending upwards to the cerebrum. Smaller lesions were found on the cerebellum, medulla, hypothalamus, and pons.

The monkey's brain was almost twenty percent scar tissue.

Bill put down the folder and pushed away from the table. Could Theena have known how dangerous this drug was? Could all of this information have been hidden from her somehow?

He tried to make it work. He wanted her to have been deceived. Her father could have falsified data. Maybe she was kept in the dark. Maybe...

He picked up the Sam report again. The notes were in Theena's handwriting.

So she knew.

She knew N-Som was dangerous. And she tried to hide that fact.

“What else have you done?”

Bill stood up, his heart racing. Had she been lying to him about her feelings, too? Was she in league with Rothchilde? Worst of all, did she have a part in Mike Bitner's death?

He'd been deceived. Used. Played for a fool. The tenderness that had been growing inside him crumpled and blew away.

Bill collapsed in the chair, wondering what to do next. There was only one certainty. He wasn't going to approve N-Som.

There was probably another certainty as well; Rothchilde's men were going to kill him.

Bill had to make sure the truth about the drug got out, so even if he died, the drug wouldn't be released. The media was probably the best option for that.

But first...

First he had to confront Theena.

Bill headed for the lab. He had every right to be angry, but mostly he was numb. He had no idea what he was going to say to her. Accuse her? Ask for an explanation?

He opened the lab door, watched as Theena quickly tossed a cloth over whatever she'd been working on.

"Bill! I'm sorry, I'm in the middle of something. If you could wait outside..."

"I know."

She began to say something, then stopped. Her eyes changed. Bill detected sorrow in them, but sorrow wasn't good enough. Nothing would be good enough.

Julia, who was standing by Theena, saw the intensity going on between them. She excused herself and hurried out of the room.

Bill walked over and calmly pulled the sheet off the bulge on the table.

Dr. Nikos's head was in a vice. Theena had performed a craniotomy, and the skull cap was resting next to the head, upturned like a bloody, hairy bowl.

All at once, Bill knew. He knew a secret even worse than N-Som's damaging effects.

N-Som wasn't synthetic.

"You make the drug out of people's brains."

Theena said nothing. She just gave a soft nod.

"So the pill I took, where I had the nightmare about Mike Bitner's death..."

"I didn't know, Bill. My father prepared that sample. I thought Rothchilde had paid Bitner off. I swear."

Bill was barely listening. He pulled out a chair and sat down.

"That wasn't a nightmare, was it? It couldn't have been. The images were too strong for a nightmare."

"Bill..."

Bill focused on her. "I was experiencing his last thoughts, wasn't I?"

"Bill, I'm sorry."

"You grind up people's brains to get the neurotransmitters. But memory is chemical. So you're actually stealing their thoughts as well."

Theena grabbed his hand, knelt down next to him.

"Bill, I swear. I only found out about Bitner's death today. Albert told me in the car. He's after both of us now."

Bill looked at her as if she'd just sprouted horns.

"How could you? How could you do this, and still try to get the drug approved?"

"Bill..."

"Was it the money? You did it for the money?"

"It wasn't for me, Bill."

"Then who?"

Theena bit her lower lip. The tears streamed down her face.

"I did it for Nikos."

"For your father?"

"He was more than my father." Theena looked away, her face burning with emotion. "He was also my husband."

Chapter 26

Theena focused on the floor, unable to bare Bill's accusing stare. She could never make it up to him. She knew that. But at least she could offer an explanation.

"My real father had me late in life, when he was in his fifties. He died on my ninth birthday. Heart attack. It was sudden."

Theena closed her eyes, tried to remember his face. The memories were elusive. She had a vague recollection of a dark, fat man, whom she and her mother feared.

"Nikos was my cousin. My uncle's son, on my father's side. After my Dad's death, he began to see my mother. They eventually married. But there was a problem. I had a terrible crush on Nikos."

Theena swallowed. She chanced a look at Bill. His eyes were far away, but he appeared to be listening.

"Nikos was everything my father wasn't. He was my mother's age, almost twenty years younger than my father had been. He was handsome. He was a scientist. And he treated me like a princess."

Theena hadn't spoken about this in over ten years, since she went to see that psychiatrist. He'd called it an Elektra Complex. The female version of Oedipus, being in love with your father. But Nikos wasn't her father, really. He raised her, and acted like her father, but the incest taboo wasn't there. In Greece, cousins are free to marry.

"Nikos loved my mother. He loved me, too, but not in that way. And I began to hate my mother for it. Can you imagine? Being jealous of your mom? But I was. I took up an interest in medicine, just so he'd pay attention to me. I knew I could win him over. And I did."

Theena could remember the day clearly.

"I'd been terrible to him for many years. Teasing him. Leaving the door open when I showered. Walking around the house naked. Breathing in his ear when I kissed him goodnight. He always remained a perfect gentleman. Up until the day I graduated high school. That night, while my mother slept, he came into my room."

It had been Theena's first time. Recalling it still gave her shivers.

"We tried to hide it for a while, but my mother eventually found out. She left us. I begged Nikos to marry me. At first, he refused. He was becoming prominent in his field, and didn't want the scandal. I convinced him, eventually, and we had a secret ceremony. But while in public, I had to be his daughter. I took the last name Boone, just so I could wear his ring."

She smiled ironically.

"Here's the funny thing. For years, I was always competing with my mother for his attention. And then, when she's finally out of the picture, I had to compete with his work."

She stared into Nikos's eyes, wide open and dead. They looked at her with the same feeling as when he'd been alive.

"N-Som was his dream. His life. I became a neurosurgeon so I could be part of his dream. But he was never fully mine. He was married to science, not me."

Theena lost her smile.

"I'll never forget the first time he asked me to sleep with another man. A Senator, with a lot of money and power. We needed the government grant, so my father, my husband, pimped me out."

The sobs came suddenly, racking her body. She'd never allowed herself to feel the shame before. Theena had always cited love as her motivation. She slept with other men because she loved Nikos. She worked with him on

N-Som, knowing it was potentially dangerous, out of love. Love led her to betray her own mother. Love led her to bribe Mike Bitner and initiate a course that led to his death.

She hadn't lied to Bill about that. She truly thought Bitner had left the country with a suitcase full of cash. But Rothchilde had used her, just like Nikos had. Theena had never been in control. She'd been fooling herself.

Theena sat on the floor; the guilt was so heavy she could no longer stand. Her nose was running. She could feel Bill's eyes on her, burning like heat lamps. Theena wanted to run, hide someplace far away, where she could never hurt anyone again.

"I'm going to tell the media."

Bill's voice startled her. She didn't look at him, but she silently agreed.

"The authorities will get involved, Theena. There may be arrests."

She sniffled. "It's the least I deserve."

"I have one question."

Theena didn't know if she could handle it. But she nodded anyway.

"You're trying to make N-Som out of Nikos's brain. Why?"

"I think... I think Albert murdered him. This is the only way I can prove it."

"You want to see your husband's death? Feel his last thoughts?"

She found an inner reserve of strength and met his eyes.

"I have to. I have to know who killed him."

Theena could sense Bill was struggling with it, figuring things out.

"I'm sorry I got you involved with this, Bill. My motives were selfish, and now you're in danger."

Bill walked over to her. He seemed more preoccupied than upset.

"How does N-Som affect a person in long term use?"

"We're still not totally sure. Manny has become unbalanced, and there are some shadows on his CT that might be lesions. When they first appeared, I pleaded with Nikos to stop the experiment. But he and Manny insisted on continuing."

"How about short term? Taking it once and a while?"

"I've taken it almost a dozen times. Not consecutive days, but every few. My last CT was normal."

He squatted down next to her. Theena wanted, needed, for him to just hold her, but she didn't dare ask.

"Is it safe to take it now, after you just took some at your apartment a few hours ago?"

"I'm not sure. But I'm willing to try it."

Bill didn't say a word for the longest time. Theena didn't know what to expect from him. Was he going to spit in her face? Hit her? Call her names? That's what men did. And in this case, she felt as if she deserved it.

But she didn't expect him to hold out his hand. Theena took it, trying to keep her emotions in check.

"What now?"

Bill's face softened, just a bit.

"I'll help you prepare the drug. Can you make two doses?"

Theena squeezed his hand and nodded.

"Okay, then. Let's find out who killed your husband."

Chapter 27

Albert Rothchilde wanted to break something. On days when he leaned towards self-reflection, he knew that he was a tad spoiled, had a wee temper, and wicked little sadistic streak. The perfect solution would be to find a whipping boy. Someone that he could keep in a cage and beat whenever he felt lousy.

Perhaps someday in the future. When the billions started rolling in, there was very little you couldn't buy.

But for the moment, all he had was Captain Halloran. He made do.

"You fat, incompetent bastard."

Halloran's face reddened. He cleared his throat.

"You should have told us to watch your people earlier."

"You should have figured it out yourself. It's your job, you pathetic prick. You should have put my people under protection after Nikos was murdered. Have you checked on Julia?"

"She's at DruTech, with Theena and Bill. We've got men there, watching the place."

Rothchilde drummed his fingers on his desk, thinking. Halloran's men had found Dr. Townsend and Dr. O'Neil, both dead. They'd also gotten word that Dr. Fletcher had been killed near his home in Barrington.

These were people that he still could have used, alive. And the two people he needed erased, Theena and Bill, were now under this idiot's protection.

"The plan has changed. I want them dead. Theena, Bill, Julia, and

Manny, when you find him."

Halloran narrowed his eyes.

"I've done some bad things for you, Albert. But I'm not a hired gun."

"You idiot. I'm not paying you to kill them. I have people for that, people who won't fuck it up like you would. You just need to turn the other way. Do you have any sway with the Schaumburg Police?"

"I know the Chief. We're friends."

"When all hell breaks out at DruTech, the Schaumburg PD may be called. How much will you need to buy me some time with them?"

"Some people can't be bought."

"You'll convince him."

"And if I don't?"

Rothchilde smiled blandly. "While I find it amusing to see that you still have a little bit of backbone left, you're in too deep to back out now. If those people aren't killed, I'll go down. If I go down, you go down. How are cops treated in jail, Halloran? The lifers will swap you for cigarettes."

Halloran shifted his weight from one foot to the other. He was frowning.

"I'll need money."

"Name your price."

"Two hundred fifty thousand."

The number elicited a guffaw from Rothchilde.

"A quarter of a million dollars, to bribe a stupid suburban cop?"

"Captain Drury is clean. I need a big number to tempt him. It may not even be enough."

Rothchilde observed Halloran. They both knew the number was ridiculous, but was the Captain actually trying to scam him, keep some of it for himself?

Ultimately, it didn't matter. It was pocket change to what N-Som was going to bring in.

"I don't have that kind of cash here, and I assume he won't take a check.

Come back in an hour."

Halloran shuffled off.

Rothchilde swiveled around in his chair and eyeballed his Miró.

After this was over, there would be an unavoidable delay in the schedule. He needed scientists, discreet scientists, to take over the N-Som research. The FDA was going to be a washout, so the smart thing to do was take production to another country. Mexico, probably. Not nearly the same regulations there, especially if you had money.

It wouldn't be the same as selling the drug legitimately in America, but he'd still make a fortune through internet sales. It would take years before the US could ban it from importation, and by then he'd have enough money to buy the Presidency. Plus there was Europe, Asia, the world market to exploit. And of course, good old Uncle Sam.

The Army wanted twenty-four-hour soldiers. It wanted them badly, and was willing to pay for it. Rothchilde would be able to use much of the altered N-Som paperwork to close the sale, confidant that the military wouldn't care in the least about the FDA setbacks.

The only possible hurdle was the dreams—some of those N-Som dreams were pretty disturbing, and Rothchilde didn't want to think about some three star General trying out the drug and reliving someone else's violent death.

But Rothchilde had already planned for that. While it had proven impossible so far to synthesize N-Som, the source could be changed. Rather than harvest the neurotransmitters from the brains of dead people, Rothchilde planned to use aborted fetuses.

A second trimester fetus had the same brain chemicals that were needed to make N-Som, but it didn't have any memories. Dr. Nikos had given Rothchilde a sample to try, and the results were enthralling. Not only did the drug keep you awake and aware, but the N-Som dream was the most beautiful, most content, most relaxing thing Rothchilde had ever experienced. He had actually gone back to the womb. The feeling was so good, he could easily triple the price of the pill and people would still demand it.

Rothchilde stood up and pulled back the Miró. It swung away on hinges, revealing his wall safe. He dialed the combination and tugged the door open.

The current situation was a setback, but only a small one. Once the rest of the team was dead, he could rebuild.

Rothchilde took out five stacks of hundred dollar bills and set them on his desk. Then he picked up his phone.

"Yeah."

"Theena and Bill are at DruTech. So is another doctor, a chemist named Julia Myrnowski. I want her taken care of as well. The guard at the desk has a security card. You'll need it to get to the basement level. There's a slot in the elevator."

"Will the guard give it to us?"

"No. You'll have to kill him, too."

He heard Carlos sigh. "Why don't we just set the whole building on fire?"

"Don't fuck this up, Carlos. No more mistakes."

"You're asking us to walk into a public place and start wasting people."

"You won't have any trouble with the police. I've already taken care of that."

"I still don't like it."

Rothchilde frowned. He'd have to talk to Gino about this guy's attitude.

"Be ready to go in ninety minutes. You get this done, there will be a bonus."

"How much?"

"Triple."

Rothchilde could picture Carlos, adding up all that cash in his greedy little mind.

“We'll take care of it.”

“I know you will.”

He hung up. Rothchilde looked across the office to a framed photo on the wall, of his father, Albert Rothchilde Sr. He'd been a pitiless, terrible parent, but his business skills were brilliant in their ruthlessness. In one of his rare kinder moments, he'd talked to young Albert about wealth.

“The key to getting it is taking risks. The key to keeping it is avoiding risks.”

Diversification. Never put all your eggs in one basket. Which was true, and which also led to his untimely death. As the elder Rothchilde watched his son grow, he saw in him the same lust for power that he had. He'd groomed his son to be his successor, teaching him the ins and outs of corporate domination. He taught him too well, in fact.

On Rothchilde's twenty-first birthday, he got in touch with some of Chicago's disreputable element, and for a small cut they permanently ended the career of Albert Rothchilde Sr. and his wife, leaving young Albert a fortune.

Rothchilde smiled at his father’s picture. “Should have diversified.”

Then he picked up the phone and dialed Gerry Smith. If Carlos and his dumb partner failed, he would make sure the FBI seals the deal.

Chapter 28

"Dr. May, let me introduce my daughter, Dr. Theena Boone."

Dr. Nikos winked at Theena, a signal for her to turn on the charm. It was one of the few things she was good at.

"A pleasure, Dr. May."

Bill shook Theena's hand, returning the greeting.

"Please sit, Dr. May." He pulled out a chair for Bill. "I have to be social for a little bit."

Bill was in good hands, Nikos knew. She was a much better whore than her mother was.

The speech had gone as expected, the audience eating it up. He looked around for Manny, and found him shaking hands with one of the Governor's aides.

"Can I speak to you a moment?"

Manny nodded. "Sure, Dr. Nikos. If you'll excuse me."

They walked through the banquet hall, smiling and waving at people. So many wanted their ear, it became obvious that privacy was impossible. Luckily, the washroom was empty.

"Did I do okay?" Manny was nervous, agitated.

Nikos looked at himself in the mirror and fingered his beard, smoothing it out.

"You did fine. But I need you to do something else."

Manny tugged at his collar.

"I just want to get out of here. I don't know how much of this I can take.

I feel the walls closing in."

"Take it easy. It will be over soon."

"I need something, Dr. Nikos." As if cued, sweat broke out on his forehead. "I'm about ready to tear my face off."

"All I have on me is Compazine. You take one of those, you'll act like a drooling idiot. I need you sharp. Did you see the back table? With all the military men?"

Manny nodded. Nikos had to admit, the guy looked close to cracking.

"I need you to go impress them. They're the ones offering the defense contract."

"I don't know. I... I can try."

Manny went into a toilet stall and closed the door behind him. Nikos frowned. Their prize pony wasn't doing so hot. Trotting him out for the buyers might not be the smartest move.

Unfortunately, Rothchilde had insisted. Everything hinged on the military money. With unlimited funds, Nikos was sure he'd be able to develop a synthetic version of N-Som. He was morally compelled to. The experiments with fetuses were promising, but Rothchilde was already making deals with several South American countries...

The president of American Products wanted to finance baby factories; paying scores of impoverished women to get pregnant and abort. The whole thing left a bad taste in Nikos's mouth.

A moan, from Manny's stall.

"Manny? Are you okay?"

Nikos knocked on the stall. There was another moan, louder.

"Manny?" The door was locked. "Let me in."

A scream, so shrill it pierced Nikos like glass. He took a step back and kicked the door in.

Manny sat on the toilet. His tuxedo was in shreds, and there was so much blood he looked like an autopsy in progress.

In his left hand was a scalpel.

"Manny!"

Manny fixed his eyes on Dr. Nikos. His gaze was malevolent.

"No. Not Manny. I'm his brother, David."

Nikos took a step back. Manny's voice, his posture, his demeanor—all had become threatening. He wasn't acting like Manny at all. Nikos recalled the monkey experiments, and what long term N-Som use had done to their brains. He'd been deceiving himself about the drug's safety, turning a blind eye to the truth, and now the awful realization of what he'd done was staring at him like a hungry animal.

"Manny, get a hold of yourself. You aren't David. David died when you were kids."

Manny stood up. His lips peeled back, revealing bloody teeth.

"I didn't die." He tapped his temple with the scalpel handle. "I've been up here all the time."

"We need to get you to a doctor, Manny. I had no idea you were this bad."

Manny took a step forward. "The name is David."

Nikos felt fear. He was a big man, robust, but he'd seen what Manny was capable of. Manny could bench press three hundred and fifty pounds. Manny could punch through safety glass with his bare hands. And now, some internal switch had been flipped, and this unstoppable machine had become a full blown psychotic.

Nikos raised his hands in supplication.

"David is dead, Emmanuel. He committed suicide in juvenile hall. Don't you remember? You told me yourself. Please, Manny..."

"Stop calling me Manny!"

The move was so quick, Nikos couldn't even lift an arm to defend himself. All he saw was a blur, and then there was a waterfall of blood cascading down his chest.

Nikos clutched his neck, felt his fingers sink in to the trachea. He fell over.

"You killed him! You killed him!"

Nikos watched as Manny screamed at himself, turning the scalpel inwards and jabbing it over and over into his own chest. Eventually he collapsed as well.

"Dr. Nikos... I'm sorry. I couldn't stop him."

Nikos barely heard. He stared at the bathroom ceiling, knowing it was the last thing he'd ever see.

Theena's mother was right. She'd always told him that all of his hard work would kill him.

He almost laughed at the irony.

I never should have left her, he thought. One of many mistakes he'd never have a chance to fix.

And then he died.

Chapter 29

David exited Route 53 at the Schaumburg off ramp. He'd always wanted a pickup truck. When he and Manny were kids, they shared a small die-cast toy. It was the only thing that stayed with them, from foster home to foster home. Their one constant. He even remembered how they lost it.

It was nearly twenty years ago. They were walking home after school, taking a short cut through a field. Manny began throwing stones at a bird's nest, trying to hit the bleating chicks inside. David told him to stop. When Manny refused, David tossed their truck into the woods, never to be seen again.

Or was it the opposite? Had he been the one who was trying to hit the bird's nest?

He shrugged it off. He had a real truck now. Full size, with four doors, all wheel drive, and a bumping stereo system.

The only drawback was the smell. David lowered the window another three inches. The truck's former owner had voided his bowels when David stuck the scalpel in his neck, and he hadn't found a suitable place to dump him so the body was still in the back seat.

The clock read just after five, and most of the DruTech employees would be going home for the day. David knew that the N-Som team always worked late. There was a good chance Theena and Dr. Myrnowski were still there, along with the FDA guy. Once those three were taken care of, David would finally be free.

He fought the departing traffic, inching his way through the parking lot until he found a space near the front entrance. When he turned off the ignition he noticed the bandage on his hand.

David was missing a finger.

When had that happened? He knew that he'd cut off Manny's finger, to teach the coward a lesson. But had Manny somehow done the same thing to him?

The memory was hazy. He could picture himself, hacking at the joint, wiggling the scalpel to get through the knuckle. He could also remember a moment of white hot pain, but was that his pain or Manny's?

He entered the DruTech Building, unable to figure it out. The answer was so close, tantalizing him, something he was almost on the verge of remembering.

The security guard, an overweight ex-cop named Barry, offered a curt nod.

“Good evening, Manny. Glad to see you're out of the hospital.”

“I'm not Manny. I'm David.”

Barry raised an eyebrow.

“You feeling okay?”

Actually, he wasn't feeling okay. The missing finger nagged at him. It meant something important.

“Who else is here?”

“Dr. Boone and Dr. May from the FDA. Dr. Myrnowski as well.”

“I don't have my elevator pass to get down to the basement.”

“No problem, Manny. I'll take you. Let me call down to Dr. Boone.”

David put a hand on Barry's wrist, not allowing him to pick up the phone.

“I'd prefer to surprise her.”

He emphasized his point with a squeeze, feeling the wrist bones beneath Barry's flab. The guard's eyes widened.

“Sure, Manny. I'll walk you to the elevator.”

David smiled and released his grip. The chubby man led him to the lift, his gait uneasy. He used his security pass in the slot under the call buttons. The green light went on, and the doors closed.

“You have something on your shirt.”

David looked down, and wasn't surprised to see a large dried blood stain on his stomach. He had no idea whose it was. He'd killed so many people.

He touched the stain absently, and was startled to find a lump underneath. David lifted up his shirt.

Something that looked like a small plastic faucet was sticking out of a puckered hole in his belly. It protruded almost an inch. There was a fine mesh screen on the spout, leaking brown fluid.

Barry made a face.

“Ouch. A surgical drain. They put one of those in me when I had my colon operation two years ago. Keeps the swelling down after surgery. You should keep a bandage over the end so it doesn't drain into your clothes.”

David touched it. He'd seen one before, on Manny, when he'd visited him in the hospital. But why did David have one? He pinched the end and began to pull.

“You really shouldn't...”

Barry stopped talking, only able to stare. An inch of tube came out, wet and slimy, making a sucking noise like a worm crawling out of the muck. Then two inches. Four.

David continued to yank. The sensation was sublime, a soft finger moving through his insides. Almost a foot of tubing came out of his stomach before he reached the end.

He stared at the tube, curious. It was filled with foul smelling liquid the color of cola. The open end dripped onto the floor. David watched as the hole in his stomach closed like a tiny mouth.

Barry made a gagging sound. The elevator stopped and the doors opened.

“Thanks for the ride.” David smiled at Barry and handed the mute guard the drainage tube. Then he stepped out of the elevator.

The hallway was quiet, serene. Dr. Nikos sometimes piped music through the intercom speakers, but now the only sound was the hum of the neon lights.

David hated this place. It was worse than prison. Terrible as doing time was, it had a tangible ending. You could dream about getting out. Here, at DruTech, there was no end in sight. And the only dreams you had were of other people's deaths.

David went into his room and took off his shirt. Finding Theena and Bill asleep on his bed was a delicious surprise.

He changed into a sweater and sat down next to Theena.

She was really quite beautiful. He could see why Manny was in love with her. David touched her smooth cheek, then let his hand slide down her neck, past her shoulder. He cupped a breast. Squeezed.

Theena didn't wake up.

David took her pulse, watched her breathing. She was having a little N-Som siesta. Bill's pulse was also weak, his wrist cool to the touch.

So... what-to-do, what-to-do? David took the scalpel from his back pocket. Two quick slices, and they would never wake up. He touched the blade under Theena's chin. She whimpered, her eyes rolling back and forth under her lids.

Bad dream.

“Sucks, doesn't it?”

He put the scalpel back in his pocket. This wasn't the right time. David wanted her to be aware when she died. She had to know what was happening, and why.

“See you soon, sleeping beauty.”

He gave Theena a lingering kiss, forcing his tongue between her lips, licking her teeth. Then he got off the bed and left his room, on the prowl for

Dr. Myrnowski.

The hallways hummed. David moved cautiously, even though he had no need to. It made him feel like some jungle beast, stalking prey. He was the master of his domain. The top of the food chain. Unstoppable.

He found her in the kitchenette. She was sitting at the breakfast bar, nibbling a bagel. Pudgy, blonde, shy Julia Myrnowski. He hoped she was enjoying her last meal.

"Hi, Julia."

Dr. Myrnowski almost fell off her stool.

"Manny. You startled me."

Why was everyone calling him Manny? Was there some big joke going on that he didn't know about?

David sat next to her.

"Do you mind if I ask you a question?"

She nodded, but her body language didn't concur.

"You've tried N-Som, right Julia?"

The chemist shifted, leaning slightly away from him.

"Hmm? No, I've never tried it."

David sidled closer. "Why not, it's perfectly safe, right?"

Julia was visibly uncomfortable. She'd always been a real wallflower. He wondered if she were still a virgin. He wondered if he should check.

"Yes, I guess it's safe. But I'm not big on taking drugs, I guess."

"I see."

Julia offered a meek smile, then got off her stool and put the remainder of her bagel in the refrigerator.

"I'm, um, going back to the lab."

"No you're not."

Julia had no idea how to respond to that. She just stood there, stupidly, a deer in the headlights.

David was next to her in two steps. The chemist shivered, tried to make herself smaller. David fed on it like junk food.

“You're afraid of me.”

A small whimper.

“You're afraid, because you know what N-Som has done to my brain.”

“Please don't hurt me...”

David let the anger wash over him. This feeble, cringing, pathetic creature was earning her salary by torturing him to death.

He put his arms around her, sympathetic. She started to sob.

“I won't hurt you, Julia. Unless you think this hurts.”

The scalpel slid into her back, up under the shoulder blade.

Julia went rigid, and then collapsed onto herself like an old building.

A keening wail escaped her lips, and her arms flopped and twitched with a mind of their own.

“Well, I guess it hurts after all.”

David knelt next to her. He cradled her head in his arms and gave her the sweetest kiss, amused at how her lips trembled while he jammed the blade in and out.

Chapter 30

Bill woke up first. This was the second time he'd undergone another person's death, and it hadn't gotten any easier.

The experience was so much stronger than normal dreaming. While under N-Som's influence, Bill had not only relived Nikos's final thoughts, but also the man's feelings and senses. The bathroom smelled like lemon disinfectant. Nikos's voice sounded different, because he'd heard it through the ears of the man speaking it. Worst of all, Bill felt the scalpel enter his neck, the blood leaking down his throat like hot acid.

No wonder Manny was so messed up. He'd taken N-Som how many times? Add to that the organic brain damage...

Bill knew enough psychology to be familiar with Disassociative Identity Disorder—what used to be termed multiple personality. He never bought it. Supposedly, children who were abused retreated into an alternate personality within their minds as a way of escape. Bill viewed it with the same disdain as so-called Repressed Memory Syndrome. A shrink could very easily, through inadvertent suggestion, implant these beliefs in a person's head during therapy.

But Manny was something different. He'd been chowing down on brain chemicals for so long a schism had formed between his left and right hemispheres, dividing them. Through Dr. Nikos's eyes, Bill saw Manny change into someone else.

And Bill was converted into a true believer.

He glanced at Theena, lying on the bed next to him. Her face was glossy with tears. He felt a knot of pity.

Not only did she experience her husband's death, she was also privy to his thoughts about her. Thoughts that were neither loving nor pleasant.

Bill looked around the bedroom for a box of tissue. They were in Manny's pseudo-apartment, the only place in DruTech with a bed. After extracting the brain matter from Dr. Nikos's head and processing it into N-Som, they came here. Bill had almost balked at taking the drug; knowing where it came from, knowing what it did. But he wanted to learn the truth as much as Theena, and she had made trusting her impossible. So they'd taken the plunge together.

"Nikos..."

Theena opened her eyes. There was no Kleenex, but Bill found a roll of paper towels by the dresser. He tore one off and offered it.

"He thought I was a whore." Her voice was soft, small.

Bill didn't say anything. Theena had made some big mistakes, because of love. He'd been captaining that same ship for over a year.

"You saw what I saw." Theena's face flushed, and she hid behind the paper towel. "You saw what he thought of me. A man I devoted my whole life to. I was a regret. His last thought was regretting me."

Bill juggled embarrassment and compassion.

"He didn't think that. He regretted leaving your mother."

"Same thing."

"Theena..." Bill chose his words carefully. "Your husband, he wasn't a very good man."

Theena took a while to respond.

"I know. You won't believe me, but I didn't know anything about the fetal experiments. I also had no idea Manny was this bad. I showed him his CTs, tried to get him to quit. But Manny was just as obsessed as Nikos. Blind. Both of them were blind." She let out a slow breath. "Me too."

Maybe it was because he'd felt her husband's thoughts, but Bill wasn't angry at Theena anymore. He couldn't condone what she'd done, but he hadn't ever truly forgiven himself, either.

"You can make it right. We can make sure this drug is never put on the market."

"We can't go up against Albert. He's too powerful."

"He may have some friends in high places, but if we go to the media with this, the public will demand recourse."

"How about Manny?"

How about Manny? He was truly screwed up, possibly beyond any help. Bill pitied him. But he'd also seen the cold blooded way he killed Dr. Nikos.

"We have to let the authorities take care of Manny."

"It's all my fault."

"We can't handle him ourselves, Theena. He's too far gone, and too dangerous. You know what he's capable of, physically. It would be like trying to catch the Terminator."

"THEENA? BILL? YOU AWAKE?"

Bill jumped at the sound. A man's voice, coming over the intercom speakers. Mannny. But Bill knew that even though the voice matched, this wasn't Manny at all.

"YOU'VE GOT TWO WAYS OUT, THE ELEVATOR AND THE EMERGENCY STAIRS. I CAN ONLY WATCH ONE. SO HERE'S THE GAME. IF YOU CAN MAKE IT TO ONE OR THE OTHER, YOU'LL GO FREE. BUT IF I CATCH YOU... TELL THEM, JULIA."

The shriek was the most frightening thing Bill had ever heard. It went on and on, raw terror and extreme pain, like the bleat of a tortured animal.

The awful sound was cut short with a gurgle and some bubbly coughing.

"IF I CATCH YOU, YOU GET TO JOIN DR. MYRNOWSKI HERE. THE CLOCK IS TICKING. GOOD LUCK."

"Julia..."

Theena was two steps to the door when Bill caught her wrist.

“Hold it. We have to think.”

“He's killing her.”

“She's already dead, Theena. We go rushing blindly into the hall, we're next.”

Theena's face was distilled anguish. Bill could guess his expression was the same. They both fought to keep cool heads.

“Okay...” Theena's brows scrunched up. “The elevator is down the hall, to the left. The emergency stairs are to the right.”

“Where is Manny?”

“He could be anywhere. Every room has an intercom next to the door.”

Bill looked around the room, saw the phone. Theena intercepted him.

“Doesn't dial out. It's a direct line to the lab.”

He took out his cell phone, but again Theena shook her head.

“Too far underground. No signal.”

“Are there any damn phones down here?”

“No. Nikos wanted us to be isolated, shut off. No interruptions.”

“How about security?”

“The lab has a link to the security desk, but Manny knows that too.”

Bill wanted to rip out his hair. “How about a fire alarm?”

“There's a box in the kitchen. It can be pulled.”

“Then the fire department would come?”

Theena nodded, but neither of them moved. They weren't anxious to go out into the hallway. Bill scanned the ceiling for a sprinkler. There was one over the bed, but he had no way of setting it off. For this first time in his life, Bill wished he smoked.

“Maybe I can talk to him.” Theena chewed her lower lip. “Manny and I have an understanding.”

“That's not Manny.”

“I can try anyway.”

“First let's do something about this door.”

Theena helped him push the dresser up against it, snugged tight underneath the knob. For good measure they put the desk behind that. Bill gave the door a firm tug, but it didn't budge.

“That should be okay. Now what?”

Theena pressed the intercom button on the box next to the light switch.

“David? It's Theena.”

“HI, THEENA.”

“We want to help you, David. We want you to get better.”

“I'M TOUCHED.”

“I mean it. I know that this experiment hurt you. It's not your fault.”

“I'M GLAD YOU THINK SO. OPEN THE DOOR, WE'LL TALK.”

Theena threw Bill a desperate look. He joined her by the intercom.

“David? It's Dr. Bill May from the FDA.”“

“HELLO, BILL. HOW'S THE INVESTIGATION GOING?”

“It's over. N-Som won't get approval in this country.”

“TOO BAD. WE'VE ALL WORKED SO HARD. MANNY WILL BE CRUSHED.”

“Can we speak to Manny?”

“I DON'T KNOW WHERE HE IS.”

Bill took a shot. “David, you're Manny. He's inside you. You're the same person.”

No response. The silence stretched. Theena tapped Bill on the shoulder.

“Is it smart to confuse him like that?”

“As far as we know, Manny's not a killer. Only his alter ego is. Maybe a catharsis will snap him back to normal.” Bill hit the intercom button. “Manny? Are you there? Hello? Manny?”

“I JUST PICKED UP A NEW CD. WANNA HEAR IT?”

A groan came over the loudspeaker. It was feminine, undeniably sexual, and Bill could identify it from experience.

Theena looked mortified. The female voice was joined by a male one, the sounds of two people making love filling the entire underground complex.

Bill was confused. Was it a recording? How?

"I REALLY NEEDED THAT."

Theena's voice. That was what she'd said after she and Bill had sex the first time. But the voice that answered didn't belong to Bill.

"MARRY ME, THEENA."

It was Manny. Out of breath, vulnerable.

"YOU'RE SO SWEET, MANNY."

Theena blushed furiously. She lowered her head, refusing to look at Bill.

"PLEASE, THEENA. YOU'RE THE ONLY REASON I STAY HERE. THE N-SOM—SOMETIMES IT MAKES ME CRAZY."

"YOU KNOW IT'S SAFE, MANNY. DR. NIKOS AND I WOULDN'T MAKE YOU DO THIS IF THERE WERE ANY POSSIBLE DANGER."

Theena put a hand over her face. The playback ended, and the room got eerily silent.

"Nikos told me to sleep with Manny. To keep him on the project."

"Even though it was hurting him?"

Bill felt bad right after it left his mouth. They both knew what her mistakes were, and he shouldn't keep rubbing her nose in them. But hearing her with Manny stung. It was more than jealousy. Being with Theena had made Bill feel special, and he'd hoped the feeling was mutual.

She started to cry, but caught herself. Bill could sense the courage it took her to meet his gaze. "What you and I did, yesterday..."

"Theena, don't."

"I need to say it, Bill. For what it's worth, no one made me do that. I did it on my own."

They stared into each other's eyes. Maybe it was ego, maybe it was gullibility, but even after being lied to so many times, Bill believed her.

"DO YOU STILL THINK THERE'S NO POSSIBLE DANGER,

THEENA?"

Theena jerked her head up at the speaker, and then launched herself at the intercom.

"Manny, I know you can hear me. You and David are the same person. I know you're inside him, somewhere."

"IT SOUNDED LIKE HE WAS INSIDE YOU A MINUTE AGO. DID YOU ENJOY THE RECORDING? I GOT IT FROM THE LATE DR. FLETCHER. IT WAS MARKED 'MANNY AND THEENA #7'. YOU SURE KEEP BUSY."

"Dammit, Manny! You're not a killer! You're my friend, and you can fight this!"

They waited for a response. None came.

"Manny?"

Silence. Had Theena gotten through to him? Was he in some grand conflict with his other self, fighting for control.

BAM!

The knock on the door startled them both. They exchanged a frightened glance.

"Theena? Bill? It's Manny."

His tone was meek and submissive. Theena put her hip against the dresser and began to push.

"That's him. We can open the door."

Bill held her back. "He could be faking it."

"How do we know?"

Bill wished he'd paid more attention to psych class in college. He knew that all DIDs had a core personality. Manny was the core. Did the core ever know about the other identities?

Bill didn't think so. He recalled that old Sally Field movie, *Sybil.* She didn't know that people existed inside her.

But it went beyond that—Manny and David thought they were separate people.

"If that's Manny, how did he know we're in here? David knows we're in his room. But if Manny just woke up, he wouldn't know what was going on. Right?"

Another knock. "Theena? Bill? I'm okay now. Open up, I'm scared."

Theena edged the desk back into place.

"We can't, Manny. We don't know if we can believe you."

The room shook with a massive WHUMP. Bill and Theena jumped back and stared with horror at the fire ax blade poking through the door. It worked itself free, and David winked at them through the newly made hole.

"Hi, guys."

Bill spun around, frantically looking for something he could use as a weapon. He picked up a floor lamp with a heavy brass bottom, ripping the cord out of the wall.

David chopped away at the door, making fast progress. The upper half was quickly full of holes, and every whack connected more of them together. He soon had decent sized opening.

Bill moved closer, holding the lamp like a baseball bat. When David reached his arm through to push back the dresser, Bill swung.

He connected solidly with David's shoulder, the metal lamp vibrating in his hands at impact.

David howled like a kicked dog, his arm snaking back through the opening. They watched him move away from the door, out of view.

Bill's breath was coming out in pants. His whole body shook with adrenaline. Theena put her hand on his back and he jumped in surprise.

"I think he's gone."

Bill tried to open his hands, but they refused to let go of the lamp. He took a cautious step towards the opening, trying to get a better view of the hallway.

"Is he there?"

Bill couldn't see David, but he wasn't going to stick his head through the hole to be sure.

“I don't know.”

“We should make a run for it.”

“I'm not sure that's a good idea.”

“THAT WAS A NICE SHOT, DOC.”

Again, they both were startled by the intercom.

“I THINK MY SHOULDER IS DISLOCATED. IF I ASK REAL NICE, WILL YOU OPEN THE DOOR AND FIX IT FOR ME?”

Bill saw no reason to answer.

“I THOUGHT DOCTORS TOOK AN OATH TO HELP PEOPLE.”

Theena pulled a drawer from the dresser and moved to smash it against the intercom. Bill held her back.

“We may need it later.”

“I can't take his mocking.”

“I know.”

She began to tremble.

“This is my fault. This is all my fault.”

Bill managed to set the lamp down. He reached for her and they held each other.

“WHY DON'T YOU JUST OPEN UP, GET IT OVER WITH? I PROMISE I'LL MAKE IT QUICK AND PAINLESS.”

David broke out in a hysterical giggle. It was the distilled sound of homicidal madness, and scared Bill out of his wits.

“WAIT, JUST WAIT A SEC, I KNOW I CAN SAY THAT WITH A STRAIGHT FACE.”

Bill closed his eyes. This was a nightmare. No—worse than a nightmare. You could wake up from those.

“LOOK, GUYS. NO ONE IS GOING TO HELP YOU. I'VE KILLED EVERYONE ELSE. DR. FLETCHER, DR. TOWNSEND, DR. O'NEIL...

ALL DEAD. YOU'RE THE LAST ONES."

"How about Barry upstairs?" Bill was running out of ideas. "Will he check on us when we don't come up?"

Theena frowned. "Security is used to us staying down here overnight. David's right. No one can help us."

"YOU DON'T HAVE ANY FOOD, AND EVENTUALLY YOU'LL GET TIRED AND HAVE TO SLEEP. I DON'T HAVE THAT PROBLEM. JUST ACCEPT YOUR FATE." Another insane giggle.

Bill held Theena tighter.

Theena's voice was barely a whisper. "We're going to die down here, aren't we Bill?"

"No. Of course not. We'll figure something out."

But Bill had a horrifying feeling that she was right.

Chapter 31

The gun felt heavy in Captain Halloran's pocket. It was an old Smith and Wesson Rimfire, a throwaway piece, untraceable. A 22 LR wasn't his preferred weapon of choice—when Halloran walked the beat, he'd always used something with more stopping power. But at close range, it should be fine.

He was oddly at ease with himself for a man about to commit murder.

The way Halloran saw it, he had no choice. He was in over his head, much too far to back out. Rothchilde had put him in an untenable position. A man of his rank couldn't allow himself to be connected with any of these murders. Prison terrified Halloran. Cons weren't nice to cops on the inside.

So it was a matter of self preservation. Rothchilde was getting too careless, ordering murders like they were pizzas. He had to be taken down. The two hundred and fifty k wasn't the motivating factor. It was just a bonus.

At least, that's what Halloran kept telling himself.

He'd gotten into the mansion using the key Rothchilde had given him—the DruTech President didn't want his servants to know how often Halloran came and went.

Rothchilde's paranoia had served Halloran well. The icing on the cake was Rothchilde's office—afraid of being overheard, he'd had it soundproofed. The guy was practically begging for someone to shoot him.

Halloran let himself in after a one-two knock.

"How did it go with the Schaumburg police?"

Classic Rothchilde. No greetings. No pleasantries.

"Fine. Where's the money?"

Rothchilde offered one of his frequent condescending smiles. "It's in my wall safe, of course. Do you think I'm going to let you just walk out of here with a quarter of a million dollars?"

Halloran didn't like where this was going.

"How am I supposed to give it to him?"

"You don't have to. I already made arrangements."

The cop's eyes narrowed. "What do you mean?"

"I mean, I called up Schaumburg myself. Strangely, the Captain there doesn't even know you. But he was willing to look the other way for only thirty thousand."

Halloran took out the piece. "I'm through messing around, Albert. Just give me the cash."

Rothchilde continued smiling. "Frankly, Captain, I'm surprised. I didn't think you had the stones to cross me."

"The safe, Albert."

"Isn't it your intention to kill me anyway? Why should I also let you take my money?"

Halloran's face twitched. He could feel the sweat climb down the back of his neck. The moment was getting away from him. Halloran had killed a man before, in the line of duty, clear self-defense. Killing in cold blood was a horse of a different color. If he was going to do it, it had to be now, before he lost his nerve. The money wasn't the motivating factor. This was self-preservation.

Halloran thumbed off the safety.

"Before you shoot me, maybe you should know about my insurance."

Rothchilde glanced up at the corner of the room. Halloran followed his gaze.

A video camera winked down at them from the corner.

"A rich man like me needs security."

Halloran snarled. “Where's the VCR?”

“I don't think I'm going to tell you.”

It kept getting worse and worse. Halloran had spent his career talking to criminals who couldn't understand how their careful plans had gone so wrong. He was watching the same thing happen to himself.

“I could make you tell me.”

“Perhaps. Or you could continue to work for me, and I'll give you a nice bonus. Put away the gun.”

Halloran didn't move. This had gone very sour, and the very last thing he wanted to do was give Rothchilde the upper hand again. But what else could he do?

Halloran shoved the gun back into his pocket.

“Good cop. I've got your bonus in here.”

Rothchilde opened his desk drawer and stuck his hand inside. Alarm bells went off in Halloran's head. Rothchilde was moving too fast, and the expression on his face was wicked, almost bloodthirsty. Halloran dug back into his pocket, pulling at the 22, getting it caught on the fabric.

Rothchilde's hand came out holding a large 9mm. He didn't hesitate. He didn't talk. He aimed it at Halloran's face and pulled the trigger.

Maybe he's not a good shot.

That was Halloran's last thought, and it went out the back of his head with a good portion of his frontal lobe.

Rothchilde watched the cop pitch over, a fine mist of vaporized blood settling to the ground after him.

It had been like shooting skeet at the club. Aim, squeeze, score. Easier, even; a clay pigeon was small and fast, not fat, stationary, and stupid.

Rothchilde stood up and walked around the desk, surveying the damage. There was a black, gooey hole where Halloran's left eye had been. His other eye was wide open, still registering shock. It delighted Rothchilde so much that he located his Polaroid and took a picture.

When the novelty wore off, he realized that this had to be dealt with. There were stains, and as time wore on there was sure to be an odor. He picked up the phone and dialed the familiar number.

“Yeah.”

“Carlos, when you're finished at DruTech, I need you and Franco at my place.”

“I got hit with a cactus.”

“I can't say that I care. You both must come here when you're finished.”

“Okay.”

Rothchilde frowned. Didn't the man want to know why?

“I need you to dispose of something.”

“Okay. I said we'll be there.”

Rothchilde tried to quell his desire to brag. This was his first kill, a symbolic rite of passage. He proved that he had the intestinal fortitude to get his own hands dirty—wet work, the mob called it. Carlos should have sensed that, offered to share their bond and welcome him as a member of the club. Instead, Rothchilde got blind obedience.

“How long will you be?” Rothchilde had to slip it in. “This body is doing terrible things to my carpet.”

“Should be soon. We're pulling into DruTech right now.”

Was the man dense? Or was he so used to murder that it had become mundane to him?

“Fine.” Rothchilde sighed. “Keep me posted.”

He hung up, annoyed. Why did he care what Carlos thought, anyway? The man was a petty thug. Even worse, he was the hired help. Rothchilde would have to be content with keeping his victory to himself.

His spirits buoyed a bit when he noticed the hole in the far wall. Using his letter opener, he pried the slug out of the wood paneling. It was mashed on one side, like a small lead mushroom, still sticky with Halloran's blood.

Rothchilde placed it in an envelope and locked it in his wall safe. If he couldn't share the experience, at least he could keep a trophy.

Then he sat back at his desk and relived the whole scene in his head. The look on Halloran's face was priceless. He wished he could do it all over again.

Then he remembered the security camera.

Excited, Rothchilde left his office, locking the door behind him. He moved at a brisk clip, down the grand staircase, into the library, through the keypad entrance where all of the security VCRs were located. Several minutes later he was watching the correct tape on his big plasma screen, mouth frozen in a grin and eyes wide as saucers.

It was hugely disappointing.

Rothchilde's equipment was state of the art, but its purpose was to aid in security, not produce Hollywood blockbusters.

First of all, there was no sound. All of the delicious things Rothchilde had said—taunting Halloran, getting him to put away his gun, all of it was missing. And while the color was fine, the stationary downward angle didn't show either of their faces.

But the worst part was the speed. The VCRs recorded in time lapse, so an entire twenty-four hour period could fit onto one eight hour tape. It only videotaped one frame every second, so things were ridiculously speeded up. From the time Halloran entered the office, until he was dead on the floor, lasted a measly eight seconds.

Rothchilde tried to watch it using the slow motion button, but the result was still jerky and unimpressive.

A pity. He would have given a lot of money to see himself in action. Too bad there wasn't a way.

But there was a way, wasn't there?

Rothchilde stood up, heart hammering. It might not work. He'd shot Halloran in the head. Perhaps he'd damaged the part of the brain that can be made into N-Som.

But it was worth a try, wasn't it?

He bounded up the stairs, back to his office, and called Carlos. They would have to postpone the murders, until Rothchilde could force Theena to turn Halloran into N-Som.

The phone rang, and rang, and then he was connected to Carlos's voice mail.

“Damn it.”

The dumb thug had turned off his phone. He was probably very close to killing them both. If that happened, it would be weeks before Rothchilde could find replacement scientists to do the work.

If it was one thing the rich hated, it was waiting.

Rothchilde hung up and dialed his pilot.

“Fredrick? I need you to fly the chopper over to the mansion, ASAP. I have to get to DruTech as quickly as possible.”

Fredrick complied. Rothchilde rarely used the helicopter, and it cost an extraordinary amount of money to keep it always on standby, but it looked like his indulgence would pay off today. Weather permitting, he could be at DruTech in twenty minutes.

But he had something to do, first. Rothchilde went to the kitchen and quarter-filled a plastic garbage bag with ice. Then he grabbed the largest butcher knife in the rack and headed back to his office.

Chapter 32

Carlos didn't like it.

There were unwritten rules for hits. That's how he'd lasted in this business as long as he had. Bending the rules was asking to get caught—or worse.

The DruTech building was practically empty, but it was still a public place, and that went against the rules. Carlos wasn't some inner city gang-banger who got his kicks doing drive-bys. Carlos was a pro, and he wasn't being treated as such.

There were other rules being ignored as well. Never work with a partner, especially a dumb ox like Franco. Don't do contract work for the corporate sector. And most of all, never return to a crime scene. He'd broken all of these in the last two days.

It got worse. That moron Rothchilde called a little while ago, bragging he just wasted someone, wanting him for yet another garbage run. The risk of cleaning up after amateurs was incredibly high. It just wasn't right.

"You okay? Looks like you got a saggy diaper that leaks."

Franco laughed at his own idea of wit.

"Stay sharp. This one feels like it could be messy."

"I'm always sharp."

Yeah, right. Sharp like a box of dumb bells.

Carlos parked where they couldn't be seen from the front entrance, and again did the Fed Ex thing. The doors were locked, but one fat security guard was reading a paperback behind his stand in the lobby. Carlos knocked.

The guard made a show of walking over, pulling out a loaded key ring and fumbling with the lock.

“Late today.”

Carlos gave him his practiced 'average Joe' shrug. “Overnight guaranteed, even if there's nobody here.”

The guard looked him over.

“You cut yourself shaving?”

Carlos seethed beneath his bandages. He'd spent twenty minutes in front of a mirror, pulling out cactus spines with tweezers, and he didn't find it amusing.

“Yeah. I always shave my forehead.”

Carlos offered the clipboard for the guard to sign. Then he did a discreet screening of the perimeter before putting a bullet in the fat man's temple.

The sound was deafening, but this was the suburbs—they weren't used to hearing gunfire. No one would guess that's what it was.

Carlos knelt next to the guard and did a quick frisk. He took the keys, his wallet, and found the elevator card Rothchilde had described.

Franco came up behind him, and together they hauled the body into the lobby and locked the door.

“How many guards are on?”

“Just the one. We can take our time.”

The elevator had a slot beneath the call buttons, and Carlos jammed in the card key.

Franco giggled in his girl's voice. “Like James Bond.”

Carlos sighed. Maybe it was time to think about retiring. The mob didn't offer a pension, but he had a few dollars socked away. Plus he'd put money in the 401k. Not enough to live like a king, but enough to get by.

When the elevator stopped and the doors opened, Carlos sensed something was wrong. Franco picked up on his vibe.

“What is it?”

“Not sure.”

Franco sneered and walked into the hall. He was completely unprepared for the maniac with the fire ax who came careening around the corner, whooping and swinging.

Carlos managed to get his gun out. The guy chopped away at Franco like a tree, sluicing the white walls with blood, his howls mingling with Franco's wails. A scene from a slaughterhouse in hell.

Carlos had five shots in his Colt's cylinder and he fired them all.

Three of the slugs buried themselves in Franco's back, ending his misery. The other two took the psycho in the chest. At least, Carlos thought they did.

Franco dropped to his knees and slumped over, but the other guy ran back the way he came, not giving any sign that he was hurt.

Carlos stood there, stunned. The 38 Special was warm in his hand, a trail of smoke spiraling up from the barrel. Why didn't that guy go down? Carlos was positive he'd hit him.

He thumbed the extractor and emptied his brass into his hand. Without needing to look, he located his speed loader in his pocket and nudged in six more bullets. Holding his breath, he strained to hear down the hallway. The only sound was the drumming of his own heart.

“YOU CAN'T KILL ME.”

A man's voice, coming from everywhere at once. Carlos traced it to the overhead speakers.

“Come out and I'll try again!”

“LET'S PLAY HIDE AND SEEK. YOU'RE IT.”

Carlos moved cautiously, keeping both hands on the gun. A trail of blood droplets glinted on the tile floor. He followed them, hugging the far wall as he turned the corner.

The loudspeaker giggled.

“GETTING WARMER.”

Carlos stopped. He was scared. Fear was an old, familiar roommate, but he didn't show up too often.

The first time Carlos killed someone, as a green thirteen-year-old joining the Latin Kings, he was scared. Every time Gino made him deal with those crazy Colombians, with their dead eyes, he was scared. Years ago he'd gotten arrested, and some punk ass street cop, hungry for a promotion, beat Carlos with a phone book, trying to get him to squeal. He'd been scared then, too.

But this time the fear was different. Carlos felt like he was in a haunted house, waiting for some deformed monster to jump out and say boo. A bullet proof monster with an ax.

"DON'T STOP NOW. YOU'RE SO CLOSE."

Carlos knew he should turn around, take the elevator back up, and get the hell out of there. Why walk willingly into a nightmare? He could come back with more men, take care of this the right way.

Gino wouldn't stand for it. Franco was Gino's nephew. He'd trusted Carlos to take care of him. If Carlos came back without avenging him, he was dead anyway.

He began to move forward again.

"Come out! Come out, I'll finish you off!"

The hallway came to a division. Carlos looked left, and then right, searching for the blood trail. He went right.

"WARMER. WARMER. GETTING HOT."

The door up ahead was ajar, a smear of blood on the knob. Carlos tried to swallow, but his throat was too dry.

"BURNING UP! YOU'RE ON FIRE!"

He kicked the door and went in low, gun close to his body. It was a small kitchen, something large and bloody slumped on the floor in front of him.

Carlos fired three times at the figure, four times, his brain registering that this wasn't the guy, that this was some poor dead girl, but he couldn't stop firing, he was too scared to stop, and when he was out of bullets and clicking on an empty chamber he felt movement behind him.

Carlos spun, falling to the ground as the man with the ax towered over him like an immense shadow. He had a sick, happy smile on his face, and there were two bloody bullet holes in the front of his shirt.

Why was this guy still standing?

Carlos heard a horrible scream, and realized that it was coming from himself.

Then the ax fell, and the screaming stopped.

Chapter 33

“We should go now, while they're busy.”

Bill agreed. When they'd first heard the gunshots, he and Theena had held out hope for rescue. Their escape plans evaporated when they realized the two mob thugs had come to call.

But the situation had improved slightly. Close as they could figure, Carlos and David were in the kitchen. That meant the hallway to the emergency staircase was open.

Bill displaced the desk and Theena helped him drag the dresser out of the way. They had problems opening the door; the ax had done so much damage the mechanism was stuck. Bill gave the knob three solid kicks to free it up.

They pushed out into the hallway, liberated and frightened. Theena uttered a surprised gasp.

David was standing at the corner. He looked like a blood-drenched demon from hell, swinging his ax and staring at them like Satan coming to collect souls.

Bill grabbed Theena's wrist and they sprinted in the opposite direction. His feet were fueled by terror, and they made it to the fire door and up two flights of stairs before Bill had time to even take a breath.

Two more flights, and they were at the lobby door. Bill wasted precious seconds fumbling with the dead bolt, and then they were suddenly through. They ran to the front doors and pushed against the glass.

Locked.

Bill stared at the keyhole, unable to comprehend it. He rammed his shoulder against the doors but they didn't so much as shudder.

Theena came up behind him, holding a cylindrical chrome garbage can. She and Bill hefted it on their shoulders.

"Close your eyes."

They rammed it into the glass door with all they had.

There was a loud clanging sound, and the can bounced off the glass. There wasn't so much as a chip. What the hell were they making glass out of these days?

"There has to be a fire exit somewhere. Come on."

Again he grabbed Theena's wrist and they ran back behind the security desk, practically tripping over Barry's body.

Theena screamed. The security guard looked like a dropped watermelon from the neck up.

Ding.

Bill and Theena turned as one and faced the elevator.

It was coming up.

Bill had no idea what to do. The DruTech Building was big, fifteen stories and hundreds of offices. Maybe they could hide somewhere, wait for help to come.

"Barry..."

"Barry's dead, Theena."

"He has a gun."

Bill hustled back to the security guard's body. Sure enough, there was a gun in a leather holster on his waist. Bill knelt down, fumbling to unbutton the clasp.

Another ding. The elevator doors parted like a stage curtain.

David smiled at them. There was a splash of blood on his face, matting one side of his hair. His shirt and pants were streaked with gore. He was leaning on his ax like a walking cane.

“Are you guys trying to get away from me?”

Bill tugged at the gun, pulling it free. He'd never held one before, and was surprised by its weight. This was a different kind of gun that Carlos had, not a revolver, but the other kind where you loaded the bullets in the bottom. He pointed it at David with shaking hands.

“Don't come any closer!”

David stepped out of the elevator, swinging his ax.

“Are you sure you know how to fire that gun, Doc?”

Bill closed one eye, aiming at David's chest. This whole scene was surreal. Bill didn't want to kill him. The thought of killing someone scared Bill almost as much as getting hit with that ax.

“David, please.” Theena was on her knees alongside Barry. “We want to help you.”

“Sorry, Theena. I don't have a choice.”

He raised the ax up over his head.

Bill closed his eyes. This was not what it was supposed to feel like. All of those movies and books, where the hero nonchalantly blew people away by the dozens. That was garbage. This was real, and frightening, and so very final.

Worst of all, Bill knew what it felt like to kill somebody. Horrible, beyond words. He wasn't anxious to relive the feeling.

“Bill.” Theena gripped him, trembling. “You have to.”

He bit his lip and pulled the trigger.

Nothing happened.

“That's a semiautomatic, Doc. You have the safety on. It's that lever in the back.”

Bill's fingers pushed at the little lever to unlock it. His resolve was slipping away. David seemed to know it, too, and found it humorous. He'd begun to swagger.

Bill forced courage. He pointed the gun again and fired.

Click.

"Nothing in the chamber, Doc. You have to work the slide. Don't you watch TV?"

David continued towards them, grinning. He was less than five yards away, twirling the ax like a baton. Theena crouched behind Bill, her hands on his shoulders.

Bill pulled the top half of the gun back, and the mechanism loaded the round.

He fired.

The shot was wild, way over David's head, and the gun bucked so hard it almost flew out of Bill's hands. There was a jingling sound when the spent cartridge hit the terrazzo.

"Keep both eyes open, Doc. Squeeze the trigger, don't jerk it. And you have to lean into it a little. Want me to show you?"

This was too much, having make the same horrible decision over and over. Bill took a deep breath and tried to keep his hands steady. David was less than ten feet away. He couldn't afford to miss.

The ax cocked back. Theena screamed at Bill to shoot. He pulled the trigger.

The shot hit David high in the chest. He fell over, the ax skittering across the floor.

Theena cried out in relief, burying her face in Bill's neck and holding him tight. Bill let out the breath he was holding and pulled her close. He felt a wave of sickness wash over him. The implications of what he'd done began to gnaw at him. He'd taken a life.

"Look at Manny!"

Bill spun around, half expecting to see the man back on his feet, like some unkillable Halloween monster. Instead he saw Manny cough, his chest rising and falling.

Bill's hope soared. "He's still alive."

"Help him."

Bill wasn't sure that was such a hot idea. He was happy Manny wasn't dead, but if he suddenly recovered Bill didn't think he could shoot him again.

"Theena..."

"Bill, please. It's not his fault."

She was right. If ever there was a textbook case of insanity, it was Manny.

Bill went to him, felt the carotid. Pulse was weak but steady. He tore open Manny's shirt and used it to wipe away the excess blood. There were three bullet holes, one in the sternum, one just above the belly button, and one through the right nipple. Incredibly, they were no longer bleeding.

"We need to get him to a hospital. Call 911. Get the police here, too."

Theena nodded. Bill gently lifted Manny into a sitting position and examined his back. One exit wound, under the shoulder blade. The other two bullets were still in his body somewhere. Manny's breathing was raspy, shallow. He laid him back down and put an ear to his chest. Collapsed lung.

"Get something to put under his feet."

Theena finished the phone call and brought the chrome garbage can over. They placed Manny's legs on top to help improve blood flow to the brain and stave off shock. All at once, Manny started to twitch and tremble.

Bill listened to his chest again. The arrhythmia was obvious. He guessed it was ventricular tachycardia—Manny's heart had to be up near two hundred beats per minute.

"What's happening?"

"He's having a heart attack. A clot probably dislodged."

"What can we do?"

Bill didn't have an answer. In a fully stocked ER there was plenty he could do. But without drugs, all he could manage was keep CPR going until the paramedics arrived. Manny's heartbeat, though fast, wasn't effectively pumping blood through his body, and if Bill couldn't get the blood to circulate, the man would be dead within minutes.

He raised Manny's neck, opening the airway.

“Bill, there are drugs in the lab downstairs.”

“What kind of drugs?”

“Everything. We're stocked for World War III.”

“Heparin? TPA? Streptokinase?”

Theena nodded.

“How about epinephrine and beryllium?”

“I'll be right back.” Theena ran for the elevator.

“Hold on. You shouldn't go down there alone. We don't know if those two mob guys are dead.”

Theena's face was frantic. “I can't just let him die, Bill. It's my fault this is happening.”

Bill thought it over, then handed her the gun. “Don't take any chances. And don't forget the syringe.”

Theena took off. Bill stared down at Manny, watching his face contort in pain. His legs thrashed, kicking the garbage can across the lobby. He'd gone from V-Tach to V-Fib, his heart playing an erratic game of stop and go, beating without coordination. He'd also stopped breathing.

Bill raised both hands over his head and brought them down hard, giving Manny a precordial thump on the chest. The object was to restart the heart's electrical current and override the arrhythmia. A defibrillator would work better, but he doubted even Theena's well stocked lab had one handy.

He checked Manny's heartbeat and hit him again. Then he did a quick mouth sweep and tilted Manny's head up, giving him the breath of life. Bill fell into the familiar rhythm of CPR, putting one hand over the other and pressing on Manny's ribcage, feeling the heart spasm under his palms.

A sound, from outside. Bill turned to look through the doors, continuing his chest compressions.

A helicopter was landing in the parking lot.

Before Bill had a chance to laud the incredible speed of Schaumburg paramedics, Albert Rothchilde climbed out of the bird and ran to the front doors.

Bill gave Manny another breath, wondering what to do. Why was Rothchilde here? To see if his goons finished the job?

Rothchilde unlocked the front door and entered the lobby. He held a glistening black garbage bag. He approached Bill with an expression of quiet amusement.

“Dr. May. So good to see you. Is Theena still with us?”

Bill punched Manny's chest again.

“We need to get this man to a hospital. Help me with his legs, we'll use your chopper.”

“Sorry, but I don't think so. In fact, why don't you just stop trying to help him.” Rothchilde produced a gun from his pocket. “Now, please.”

Bill continued the CPR. Rothchilde might hire guys to do his dirty work, but Bill didn't think him the type to do it himself.

Rothchilde aimed and fired, putting another bullet into Manny's gut.

Bill jumped back, raising his hands. So much for his character assessment. He looked down at Manny.

Manny twitched twice, and then was still.

Rothchilde was all smiles. “Much better. Now where's Theena?”

Bill felt anger clogging his throat, making speech difficult. “You bastard.”

“Dr. May, I have no time for games. Don't make me ask you again.”

“You're going to kill me if I help you or not.”

“True. But if you don't help me, I'm going to shoot you in the kneecap. It's supposed to be excruciating. Shall we see?”

Bill mulled it over. Theena was one of the reasons he was in this ridiculous mess. Why should he suffer, especially since Rothchilde would inevitably find her anyway?

But he couldn't do it. He couldn't let this megalomaniac find her, even if it meant pain. Bill was confused about his feelings for Theena, but if he could protect her he would.

“Those thugs you hired shot Manny and took her away.”

Rothchilde squinted at him. “That doesn't make sense.”

“They said they wanted to find out what she knew. That it was worth a lot of money.”

A flash of panic swept over Rothchilde's face.

“Do you know where they took her?”

“Back to her apartment.”

“And why aren't you playing hero and trying to save her?”

Bill tried to sound cold. “I don't owe that bitch anything.”

Rothchilde smiled. “She is quite the little charmer, isn't she? Did you find out about her and daddy yet? And he's the one that sent her to me. There's enough in that relationship for a lifetime of therapy.”

Bill had to get him out of here. Theena could be coming back any second.

“You'd better go. The police are on their way.”

“No, they aren't. I've taken care of that.”

Rothchilde moved closer, his focus intense.

“Move your arm, please. I want a clear shot at your heart.”

Bill knew with absolute certainty that he was going to die. This was more than Rothchilde simply needing him out of the way. The bloodthirsty bastard actually wanted to shoot him. He was practically drooling.

Bill grasped at a straw.

“I'll take money.”

“What money?” Rothchilde laughed.

“Half a million.”

Rothchilde rolled his eyes, obviously enjoying himself. “And why would I give you half a million?”

“For the FDA to approve N-Som.”

The smile faded and Rothchilde raised an eyebrow.

“An interesting proposal. But I don't think you'll do it. You're too honest.”

“You could keep men with me until it's finished. We could have all the paperwork done by the end of the week.”

Bill watched him think it over. He could almost see the little balance scale in Rothchilde's head, weighing the pros and cons.

“You'd do it for a measly half a million?”

“Half a million, plus my life.”

Rothchilde pondered for what seemed like an eternity. Finally, he grinned.

“Deal.”

Ding.

They both looked off to the side.

The elevator was coming up.

Bill fought panic. As soon as Theena stepped out, Rothchilde was going to catch the lie and kill him.

“Ready to go?” Bill took two casual steps towards him. Rothchilde bayed him with the gun.

“Hold on. I want to see who's in the elevator.”

“It's probably Dr. Myrnowski. I asked her to bring me some medicine for Manny.”

“We'll see in a moment, won't we?”

Ding.

The doors opened. Bill tensed.

There was no one in the lift.

No... there was something crouching down. Something unbelievably bloody.

Rothchilde cocked his head, looking like a confused dog. “Carlos?”

The lump raised his arm. It ended in a gun.

Bill dove to the side when the shooting began.

Rothchilde danced back and forth, firing with insane glee, the muzzle flashes lighting up his eyes.

Carlos was a ruin, not even recognizable as human. He was barely able to hold up the weapon, let alone aim.

Bill took off. The front door was unlocked, the portal to freedom open. But Theena was still in the basement.

He headed for the emergency exit.

Bill threw a glance over his shoulder and watched Rothchilde stand over Carlos and pump round after round into his extremities, the mobster wiggling like a worm on a pin. The look on Rothchilde's face was rapturous.

Bill ducked through the doorway and took the stairs down two at a time. When he reached the lower level he screamed out Theena's name.

"Bill?"

She ducked out of the lab, her arms filled with drugs.

"The gun! Quick!"

"What about Manny?"

Bill grabbed her arm, bottles toppling to the floor. "Your boss showed up, he just killed Manny."

"Albert? I don't believe..."

There was a distant bell. The elevator was coming down.

Bill pivoted back towards the staircase, then hit the brakes.

Was Rothchilde really in the elevator? Or did he just send the elevator down to force them up the stairs, where he was waiting?

"Dammit. We have to hide. The gun."

Theena handed it over. Bill ushered Theena back into the lab. He needed a vantage point, a place where he'd have a clear shot. There were three large counters, lined up in rows, each running half the length of the room. Bill pulled Theena behind the corner of the farthest one, crouching behind the built-in sink.

"Albert really shot Manny?"

"While I was giving him CPR. Then that mob guy came up in the elevator, and Rothchilde shot him in the arms and legs."

"Why would he do that? I thought they worked for Albert."

"To be honest, I think he did it because he liked it."

Bill fumbled with the gun. He found the button that released the clip, and was shocked to see there was only one bullet left. That plus one in the chamber. Two bullets didn't seem like a whole lot.

"Should I use the intercom, try to talk to him?"

"I don't think it will help."

"So we should just wait here and shoot him when he comes in?"

Bill jammed the clip back in. "That's the idea."

He rested on one knee and kept a bead on the doorway. The adrenaline was wearing off, and Bill tried to come to grips with their situation. He was planning on killing someone. It went against everything he knew, everything he was. His education, his sheltered upbringing, his lofty morals, his profession; none of it mattered any more.

After Kristen's death, he'd made an oath to never hurt a person again.

I don't have a choice, he told himself. Rothchilde was going to kill them both. If it didn't happen today, it would happen soon enough. The man had too much to hide, and murder was his only out. Plus, the son of a bitch enjoyed it.

Self-defense, self-defense, self-defense. It echoed in Bill's head, his mantra. But he kept seeing Manny after he shot him, falling to the ground, gasping for air. Then he saw Kristen, her vitals slipping away moments after he gave her the injection that was supposed to heal her.

There was a noise in the hallway. Footsteps.

Bill no longer wanted to hold the gun. He wanted to drop it and run away.

The door opened.

Theena nudged him. Rothchilde stuck his head in the door and took a cautious look around.

Bill knew he couldn't do it. Maybe his morals were too strong. Maybe he was afraid of the guilt. Rothchilde was only ten feet away, a sitting duck, and Bill's hands shook with effort but he couldn't kill the man like this.

He fired a bullet into the ceiling instead.

Rothchilde dropped to the ground and rolled behind the opposite counter.

"We've both got guns." Bill's voice was wavering as much as his hands. "There's no way to get out of this cleanly."

"Exciting, isn't it?"

So exciting that Bill wanted to retch.

"Theena? Are you with Dr. May?"

Bill put his finger to his lips, but Theena was too angry to hold back. "You're a killer, Albert."

"I know. It's very empowering. Listen, darling, I need your help. I have a... specimen, and I need you to make some N-Som out of his brain. If you do that, I'll let you both go."

"It's over, Rothchilde!" Bill tried to sound confidant. "Just walk out of here. You have time to get out of the country before this story breaks."

"Theena, honey. Listen to me. This can't end peacefully, but I promise you'll survive. You have my word. Take Bill's gun away from him. Just take it away, sweetie. He won't fight you."

Theena grabbed the gun and pulled. Bill had been gripping the weapon loosely, and she pried it away before he could react.

He looked into her eyes, unable to speak. The depth of her betrayal left him devastated.

Theena raised the gun. Her face was so sad, the saddest thing he'd ever seen.

"Bye, Bill."

Then she sprung up over the counter and launched herself at Rothchilde's hiding place.

Bill reached out, realizing her intent too late, trying to stop her. He watched her disappear behind the next counter.

The gunshot was deafening.

Chapter 34

Albert Rothchilde felt incredible.

He thought he knew power. Rothchilde grew up ordering servants around. He was a corporate hot shot who planned hostile takeovers for the thrill of it. A wall street maverick, with long term investors from around the world following his lead time and again. A man to be feared, by his competitors, his employees, the prostitutes he beat up.

But he hadn't known true power until today.

Firing people, hurting people, crippling them financially, all of that was child's play.

Murder was the ultimate rush.

It made everything pale next to it, the feeling of taking someone's life. Better than sex and money and drugs. Better even that the billions of dollars he'd earn with N-Som.

His gun, a 9mm Sig-Sauer that he'd only previously used to shoot targets at firing ranges, felt like an extension of his body. Killing Halloran was just a taste. Shooting Manny and Carlos made him realize what an intoxicating addiction this had so quickly become.

Now, crouched behind the counter in the lab, in an actual gun fight, Rothchilde felt like a god.

He was caught completely by surprise when Theena jumped in front of him and fired.

Missing.

The bullet passed so close to his face he felt the breeze. The sound was thunderous, both terrifying and exhilarating. He sat there, transfixed, as Theena pulled the trigger again and again, the gun clicking harmlessly, her expression changing from anger, to confusion, to fear.

The smile slithered across Rothchilde's mouth like a snake.

"Out of bullets?"

Theena raised the gun to strike him with it, but she was a mere mortal. Rothchilde was a greater deity. He gave her a firm punch in the nose and she fell backwards, her black mane falling over her face when she landed.

There was blood on his knuckles. Her blood. He anointed his forehead with it, and then stood up.

"Come out, Dr. May. Or I kill her."

"Don't do it, Bill!"

Rothchilde reared his hand back to strike her. She stared at him defiantly, her jaw thrust outward, her eyebrows furrowed in anger. It turned him on a great deal.

"Okay, Rothchilde. You win."

Bill stood up from behind the counter, his hands over his head. The look on his face was pure defeat. This was a man with no hope left.

Delicious.

He wanted to feel Bill's fear, know his defeat at the hands of a superior male. A chest shot should do it. Or perhaps he should shoot his legs first, have him crawl around and beg for his life.

Rothchilde brought the gun around.

"No!"

He glanced at Theena, amused.

"Don't tell me you have a little crush on Dr. May. I didn't think you were capable of feelings."

"You kill him, I won't help you."

"I think I'll be able to convince you."

"I can't make N-Som by myself, Albert. It's a two person job."

Rothchilde hesitated. He knew nothing about the manufacturing process of drugs, and had no idea if she was lying of not. If he killed Bill now, he'd be able to relive the whole gun battle. But if Theena really needed two people...

Rothchilde stared hard at Bill. Shooting him would be so sweet. He'd heard the term 'itchy trigger finger' in countless old westerns, and fully understood what it meant.

"I can still push N-Som through CDER. You'd have approval in a few days."

The President of American Products frowned. He normally didn't deny himself pleasure, but the hassle he'd save himself if the FDA accepted N-Som was greater than his bloodlust.

"Fine." He lowered the weapon, exercising his absolute self control. "I have a head in this bag. How many doses can you extract from it?"

His little wench had gone submissive, pouting. "Ten to twelve."

That was perfect. Rothchilde could envision an N-Som cabinet next to his wine cellar, vintage Cabernets alongside the last thoughts of the dozens of people he would kill. Like a personal collection of snuff films that he alone could savor.

"Get started. I don't have all day."

He tossed the garbage bag to Theena. Her repulsion was priceless.

Rothchilde sat in a chair and kept a bored eye on the doctors while they set Halloran's head in a vice.

They were all too busy to notice the EEG machine sitting on a table in the back.

Manny's EEG machine, scribbling down a continuous jagged line of Beta waves on an endless ream of paper.

Chapter 35

Manny opened his eyes to pain.

It was an alarming experience. Not the pain—he was used to that. But the feeling of waking up. That was something he hadn't done in a long time.

He looked around and discovered he was in the lobby of the DruTech Building. There was blood all around him. When he tried to sit up, he realized the blood was his.

“You don't look so good.”

David was staring at him, reflected in a chrome garbage can that had fallen over.

It was one of those moments of instant clarity, like a fog lifting. All at once Manny understood.

He only saw David when he looked in a mirror.

Manny had seen David at Dr. O'Neil's place. He'd gone there to warn the doctor, to tell him he had to hide. But David had gotten there first. The apartment looked like a slaughterhouse. David had been sitting on the sofa, eating a box of chalk.

Manny had tasted chalk, too.

He tried to remember prior conversations with David. They all involved a mirror of some kind. Through the vanity mirror in Townsend's bathroom. In his bed back at DruTech, which faced a dresser with the oversized mirror. Was there a mirror at the hospital?

“The window, next to your bed. You could see my reflection in there.”

Manny stared at the garbage can.

“I'm you.”

“Don't act so surprised. This is news to me, too.”

“You're not really my brother. You're me.”

“We're two sides of the same coin, Manny. This is what I've been trying to tell you. This is what that drug has done to us.”

Manny closed his eyes, tight as he could. He tried to remember the night of the banquet, when David killed Dr. Nikos. But the memory didn't exist. He remembered going into the bathroom, seeing David, and then nothing else.

“That memory is mine, Manny.” When David talked, it was like a speaker emanating from the middle of Manny's head. “It's like we're two people, sharing one body. I have my thoughts, you have yours.”

Manny began to shake, the tears streaming down the sides of his head.

“How many people have we killed, David?”

“Do you want to see?”

He didn't. God help him, he didn't want to see.

“I think I can show you the memories. They're yours, too. We're of one mind.”

“Please, don't.”

The feeling was similar to deja vu, like suddenly remembering something that you'd known all along, but many times stronger. The memories flooded into his head all at once, overpowering him. He saw everything... Dr. Nikos... Dr. Townsend... Dr. Fletcher... please make it stop... Dr. O'Neil... Dr. Myrnowski... no more oh god there's more... a big man with a gun... and then a smaller man, the ax chopping and chopping...

Manny threw up. He watched David throw up as well.

“How about Theena?”

“She's in the lab, downstairs. We were going to kill her, too. But we've been shot a few times.”

Manny touched his chest and David let him see the shots, relive the experience. The small man, Dr. May, Albert Rothchilde...

"We should be dead."

David agreed. "But we're not. We can't die. Not like before. I won't die again like before."

Manny had been in gym class when the assistant principal pulled him aside, gave him the news that his older brother David had killed himself at the juvenile correctional institution. The institution he'd been sent to because Manny tattled on him.

"You're not really David. David's dead."

"His body, yes. But your memories keep him alive. Your guilt made him grow. And the N-Som—well, you know what a bad deal that turned out to be."

Manny could remember his reaction to David's death. How he became withdrawn, violent. Almost as if he was filling the void created by his brother's absence. Manny became the one who got into trouble all the time. Trouble that continued into adulthood with, arrest after arrest.

But never murder.

Manny bitterly laughed, the action causing the pain in his chest to flare.

"I should have killed you when you asked."

"It's too late now."

Manny shook his head. It wasn't too late. The next chance he got, he was ending it.

"Won't work, Manny. First of all, we don't die easily. But mostly, I won't allow it."

"You won't allow it? It's my body."

The face reflected in the garbage can changed. At one moment, Manny was looking at David's reflection. Then there was a shift, and he could sense that it was David who was looking at him.

"I'm in control now, Manny. You follow my will."

Manny experienced a feeling of isolation, darkness. He tried to cry out, but he kept getting smaller and smaller, his vision dimming. His own mind was trapping him, shielding him from his own senses. He tried to scream, but nothing came out.

A moment later, he was gone.

David sat up. He could feel Manny inside him, struggling to free himself, like a tiny fly in a web.

It was a strange experience, but an understandable one. The mind was a mysterious thing, but science was demystifying it a bit more every day. David knew enough to grasp what was happening to his.

Memory is chemical. He could remember an early lecture from Dr. Nikos, talking about experiments with flatworms. They could be taught simple stimulus/response reactions, and these reactions could be passed on from Group A to Group B by feeding Group B the brains of Group A.

In his free time, of which he had a lot, he'd read about the collective unconscious, and inherited memories known as archetypes. These were common in animals. How could horses walk minutes after birth? How did salmon know to travel upstream to spawn? It was called instinct, a genetic imprint passed on to offspring. A form of inherited memory.

But it was so much more than memory. Every thought was a chemical reaction happening in the brain. Movement, speech, emotion, motor skills; these could all be removed with a scalpel or overridden by an electric probe.

Even the personality was nothing more than a complicated exchange of neurotransmitters. Drugs can alter mood and control behavior. A blow to the head could turn a nice person into a permanent jerk, and a lobotomy could tame even the most savage psychotic.

David was simply a result of complicated chemistry and brain damage. Every time he took N-Som, a residual amount stayed in his brain—a stockpile of other people's neurotransmitters. It literally took root, changing his chemical structure, allowing Manny's violent thoughts to grow until they'd taken over the core of his personality.

A maniac is born.

David sat up, ignoring the pain. He no longer needed thoughts of revenge to compel him to kill. The compulsion existed without logic; it was an emotional response. And David's overriding emotion was hatred. He didn't question it. He just went with the flow.

David got to his feet, wobbling a bit. A coughing fit brought up quite a lot of blood. He took a few tentative steps until he was sure he could trust his legs.

His ax was waiting for him, near the security desk.

Then he headed for the emergency staircase.

"A hunting we will go."

He was just opening the front door when he saw someone walk into the lobby.

Chapter 36

Special Agent Smith didn't consider himself crooked.

He'd entered the Bureau out of college, young and full of energy. The FBI had been his dream job. The pulse-pounding training he'd gotten at Quantico promised him a career filled with thrills and shoot-outs and manhunts and TV interviews.

But real life conspired against him.

He broke his ankle tripping down a flight of stairs just one week after graduation.

Three operations later, Smith still didn't have full use of his foot. He was assigned to the Chicago office, riding a desk. Smith had become a bureaucrat, which was a fate he'd been purposely trying to avoid when he joined the Feds in the first place.

So he pushed papers for three long years, secretly jealous of the agents around him who saw action. Agents who actually got to draw their guns on the job. He debated the pros of drinking himself to death versus the cons of eating himself to death. It was during the mayor's holiday party, while Smith was attempting to do both, that he met Albert Rothchilde.

Smith knew from the start that he was being fleeced. Rothchilde was looking to buy a friend in the Bureau, and Smith was the perfect candidate; pathetic, angry, needy. The president of American Products pushed Smith's buttons with the skill of a cult guru; asking questions, listening closely, offering praise and reassurance.

Rothchilde sent him Cuban cigars, expensive wine, concert tickets, high priced call girls. He invited him to the country club, took him golfing, let him use his condo in Florida for vacation. Smith was courted by Rothchilde for almost two months before the man asked him for a tiny favor—some information on organized crime that only the FBI was privy to.

Smith provided the info. Not because he felt he owed Rothchilde for his kindness, or because he was under the spell of his Svengali-like manipulation. Smith did it for a single, selfish reason; it was exciting.

Being bribed to steal FBI documents was a thrill, like being a double agent. The extra money was nice, but Smith would have done it for free. The more outrageous Rothchilde's request, the more fun Smith had figuring out how to pull it off.

What began as simply buying information had become much more dangerous. Smith routinely sent agents out into the field to secretly run Rothchilde's errands. Only Smith knew the true reasons behind the missions, and he'd climbed high enough within the Bureau to be able to cover his own tracks.

It was like a chess game. Smith stopped drinking, lost weight, and actually began to enjoy work again.

But everything in the past paled next to that moment, the moment Smith entered the DruTech Building.

This wasn't just stealing files and sending agents on fake missions. This was the real deal. Smith was actually in the field himself. When he saw Rothchilde's chopper outside, he got even more excited. His mind filled with fantastic scenarios, saving Rothchilde in a hostage situation, neutralizing the targets, being able to actually shoot somebody.

Smith couldn't run the hundred in less than thirty seconds, but for the very first time he felt like a real Fed.

He scanned the lobby, overhead, then at eye-level, and finally sweeping the ground. His pulse broke into a rumba when he saw the guard's body. Smith moved in for a closer look, favoring his good leg. He wanted to shout

out in excitement when he saw the head wound.

This was it, what he'd waited his whole life for. Real danger. He knelt down next to the corpse and felt for its pulse, knowing he wouldn't find one, doing it anyway because that was what they always did in the movies. He could imagine telling this story later, people hanging on his every word.

"He's dead."

Smith spun, knees bent in a crouch, both hands on his weapon in a perfect Weaver stance. Just like he'd practiced a hundred times. But none of his training prepared Smith for what was standing fifteen feet away from him.

At first, he thought he was looking at a corpse. The man was caked with dried blood, which seemed to streak out of the four bullet wounds in his torso like fireworks. Any one of those wounds should have been fatal, but the guy was standing there, obviously alive, with a goofy grin on his face. And an ax.

Smith went by-the-book. "Drop the ax! Hands on your head, get down on your knees!"

The man lifted his hands above his head, but he raised the ax with them.

"Drop the ax!"

The man didn't drop the ax. He did something that Special Agent Smith wouldn't have ever expected. He held it like a lumberjack and threw it.

Smith's reflexes took over. If he were a seasoned pro with plenty of field experience, perhaps his first instinct would have been to fire the gun. But since he wasn't, Smith did what anyone would have done when an ax came at them. He put his arms over his face and ducked.

The ax handle hit him across the forearms, sending his gun flying.

Smith got up out of his crouch and was seized by an overwhelming feeling of giddy delight. He'd been absolutely sure that the ax was going to bury itself in his head. The fact that he'd escaped with only bruised elbows was amazing.

But it wasn't over yet.

The bloody man was walking towards him, his arms wide open. Like a giant bird of prey, swooping down.

Smith knew he needed to find the gun, but he couldn't take his eyes off the spectacle before him. When he returned to his senses, it was too late. All he could do was run.

But Smith and running weren't good buddies.

He took off through the lobby in a comical hobble, his bad ankle unable to fully bear the weight of his body even after all of the therapy. It was like trying to run with a ball and chain on his leg. Smith pushed past the pain of bones rubbing against each other, but it just didn't work right.

He chanced a look over his shoulder and saw the bloody man following in a brisk walk. Not even running, but quickly gaining ground. He'd picked up the ax.

Ahead of Smith was a dark hallway, doors at the end. He was sweating now, fear and pain pushing out his prior thoughts of glory and excitement.

"What's wrong with your leg?"

Smith concentrated on the doors. If he could just make it there, maybe he could lock them somehow, keep the bloody man away. It wasn't that far. Smith forced himself to move faster, ignoring the fire in his ankle, pushing himself harder than he ever had in his life.

He made it! The bloody man was only a few steps behind him now, and Smith grabbed the door handle, turning it, pushing forward with his shoulder.

Locked.

But it wasn't over yet. He still had his training. Hand to hand combat. Martial arts. He hadn't practiced regularly, because therc hadn't been a need. But he still knew enough to defend himself, even if his opponent did have an ax.

Special Agent Smith spun around, feet planted a shoulder's width apart, arms out in a defense stance.

"Keeeyaaa!" Smith's battle cry echoed down the hallway.

The echo lasted longer than he did.

Chapter 37

"Is it damaged?"

Rothchilde was referring to the thalamus, hypothalamus, corpus callosum, and other parts of the brain that were harvested to produce N-Som. In the head he'd brought, all of these parts were intact. The bullet had only done damage to the motor cortex, central and longitudal sulcus, and occipital lobe.

"It's fine."

"There's enough to make N-Som?"

Theena nodded, removing a section of the medulla oblongata. Bill raised an eyebrow at this, but kept his mouth shut. Theena was grateful for that.

They ground up the tissue with a mortar and pestle, and then began the laborious task of making it into a pill.

Theena didn't bother with precise measurements this time. She also abbreviated the suspension in the acetonitrile and eyeballed the amount of the dimethylformamide dispersant. Rothchilde didn't know any better.

Since DruTech contracted out for the actual pill manufacturing because it was a complicated process, the way to make ingestable N-Som in the lab was to simply add some hydroxypropyl methylcellulose and sodium starch glycolate, then spoon the mixture into empty gelatin capsules.

The work, although forced, had a calming effect on Theena. This day had been a trip to hell, with no end in sight. She was happy to lose her mind in a familiar chemical procedure. But as it neared the end, she began to worry about what would happen next.

“Those don't look like N-Som.” Rothchilde was eyeing the capsules suspiciously.

“We can't make tablets here. We don't have the proper equipment.”

Rothchilde pointed the gun at Bill. “Take one.”

Bill shrugged, reaching for a capsule. Theena had a terrible moment of mind-bending panic, and made her decision immediately.

She grabbed a capsule first.

Rothchilde gave her a disapproving glare. “I was talking to Dr. May.”

Theena knew she must look like hell, and she couldn't recall a moment where she'd ever felt less sexy. But she'd been manipulating men all of her life, and for the very first time her life depended on it.

Theena smiled as seductively as possible, and brushed up against Rothchilde with a smooth roll of her hips.

“You killed this man, didn't you Albert?”

Albert met her gaze, trying to look nonchalant. Theena lowered her voice, breathy and soft.

“I want to see it.”

“Really? You're a fickle one, aren't you?”

“Just because I want to be on the winning team?” Theena pouted slightly, a move that always worked for her. “You won't let me share your victory? Share your power?”

She placed a hand on Rothchilde's arm and caressed it. His face softened.

“Maybe we could try it together.”

Theena nodded, putting the capsule between her lips. She held it there, like a cigarette, teasing. Rothchilde raised a hand and plucked it out.

“Not now. Later. We have other things to do now.”

Theena struggled to hide her relief. Rothchilde turned his attention back to Bill.

“You're still interested in pushing N-Som through the FDA?”

“You're still willing to part with half a million?”

Theena eyed Bill. Had Rothchilde actually been able to bribe him? Or was Bill planning something else?

Rotchilde nodded his head. “We'll give it a try, then. Let's gather up your things. You know I'll need to hold you someplace until all the paperwork goes through.”

“I'd want assurances that I'd be released when it happens.”

“Of course. You're sure it won't bother you allowing N-Som on the market, after seeing what it did to poor Manny?”

“I'll live with myself.”

Rothchilde's mouth twisted. “Yes. You're good at that, aren't you? Gather up your things, we won't be coming back.”

Bill nodded, and as he turned, Rothchilde shot him in the back.

Chapter 38

The feeling was similar to a muscle cramp, multiplied by a hundred. It hit Bill like a pick ax in the right shoulder, the pain flaring across his back and extending down his arm.

He pitched forward, vision blurring, bouncing on the unforgiving tile floor.

“I watched your extraction procedure, Theena. You'll be able to do it yourself next time.”

Bill felt a hand on his back, directly on the wound. Theena, trying to stop the bleeding. It amplified the pain and he saw stars.

“No more killing, Albert.”

“Theena, dear, you don't think he's really going to approve our drug, do you? He's just buying time.”

Bill tired to gauge how bad the wound was, but he couldn't without seeing it. He could breathe okay, and bend his arm. His best guess was the bullet broke his shoulder blade.

“I don't want you to kill him.”

“You said you wanted to be on the winning team. I'm the winning team.”

Rothchilde held out his hand for Theena. “Come on. You can process his brain and we'll relive his death together.”

Bill knew it was over, and the thought didn't bother him too much. His quality of life hadn't ever been what it was when Kristen was still alive. He didn't like dying at the hands of a bastard like Rothchilde, but it was probably a better way to go than being hacked to death by David.

Theena met his eyes, and he nudged her, trying to get her to save herself.

She took Rothchilde's hand, got daintily to her feet, and punched him between the legs.

Rothchilde doubled over, still gripping the gun. Theena launched herself at him, both hands locking on his weapon, kicking frantically at his legs to get it away.

"I'M BACK."

The voice boomed over the intercom, unmistakable. It infused Bill with a fear that made his pain seem minor. Somehow, David was still alive.

Bill rolled over and saw Theena and Rothchilde topple to the floor, his hand entwined in her hair. Bill managed to pull himself over to them, adding his good hand to the wrestling match for the gun.

Rothchilde was thin, slight, and not much of a fighter. Theena clawed at his eyes and face, and sunk her teeth into his wrist.

He screamed out a slur and let go of the gun.

Bill grabbed it and had a momentary tug of war with Theena, who was too enraged to notice he'd joined the fight.

Rothchilde, both hands free, managed to scramble to his feet. He grabbed a handful of the N-Som Theena had produced, then ran out the door.

Theena managed to pull the gun away from Bill and she fired two wild shots after him, ready to squeeze off a third.

"Save the bullets!"

She stopped, looking at Bill with confusion, and then relief. Without thinking, she threw her arms around his neck and kissed him, causing him to yelp at the pressure.

Theena relented and hurried to a medical cabinet.

Bill managed to sit up. "David's still alive."

"First things first." She hurried back to Bill with a large metal case, and unsnapped it. Using scissors, she cut away the back of his shirt.

"I'm giving you a shot of morphine first."

"Not morphine. I need to stay alert. Do you have any Novocain?"

"How about lidocaine?"

"That'll work."

Bill felt a prick in his shoulder.

"I KNOW WHERE YOU ARE. YOU'RE IN THE LAB."

"How long will it take to numb you?"

"We don't have time to wait. Just do it."

"This is going to sting."

She emptied a bottle of alcohol on the wound, and tears squirted out of Bill's eyes.

"Here, bite this."

Theena handed Bill a roll of gauze. He'd barely gotten it in his mouth before something sharp went into the bullet hole and began to poke around.

He moaned, his nervous system lighting up like a Christmas tree. Theena dug deeper, and deeper, and then there was a small sucking sound and a tremendous feeling of relief.

"I got the slug. You need stitches."

"We have to get out of here. Dress it."

Theena slapped on some cotton pads and taped them to Bill's skin. The lidocaine hadn't completely numbed him, but it was taking the edge off the pain.

She helped Bill to his feet. He was woozy.

"Can you walk?"

"Watch me."

They were halfway to the door when David filled the entrance.

"Hi, Theena. Dr. May. You'll be happy to know that Manny and I have resolved our differences."

He swung the ax.

Chapter 39

Theena jumped back. The ax cut the air inches before her face, ripping out a few stray strands of hair that didn't move as fast as she did. Her butt hit the counter behind her, and David lifted the ax again, his eyes shining with a madness she knew all too well.

"I don't want to kill you, David!"

Her grip on the gun was tight, certain. David advanced.

She shot him in the thigh, and he folded in half and hit the floor, still clutching the ax.

"Go ahead, Bill! I'm covering him!"

Bill had a moment of uncertainty, then he stepped around David and fled the lab. Theena kept the gun and both eyes on David, following Bill's route. David's eyes tracked her every step, a cobra poised to strike. He had one hand clamped over the wound on his leg, but already the bleeding was slowing down.

"We have to get out of here."

Bill turned for the elevator. She caught his arm, holding him back.

"You need a key card." Theena fished it out of her lab coat. He eyed her strangely when she offered it to him.

"How about you?"

"I have to contain David. If we leave, so will he."

"But we'll be safe."

"He needs help, Bill. I owe him that."

The look he gave her was priceless, a cross between bewildered and resigned. He was such a good guy. Maybe when this was over...

She pushed the impulse away. Theena couldn't think about happily ever after. She knew she didn't deserve it.

Bill let out a long breath. “What do you have in mind?”

“We can tie him up. There are jump ropes in the gym.”

“Lead the way.”

They jogged down the hall and turned left. Blood was spattered over the floor and walls, and many of the overhead fluorescent tubes were smashed. The remaining lights flickered and hissed, erratic strobes throwing crazy shadows. A portion of Theena's resolve eroded with every step. Her sense of responsibility was slowly being overtaken by her fear. David seemed to be hiding in every corner, ready to leap out and mutilate all of the people that hurt him.

And she was the last one.

The gym was a decent replica of a modern health club; too bright, completely encircled with mirrors, and crammed with stacks of machines that looked like torture devices. For some insane reason, the equipment locker had a padlock on it. Theena shoved the gun in her pocket. She unclipped the overhead T-bar from a lat-press and wedged it in the latch. She twisted, her muscles bunching with effort. The lock was bending... bending... *SNAP!*

Theena tugged open the locker door and snagged five jump ropes, shoving them under her armpit.

“Theena!”

She turned at Bill's voice, followed his frightened gaze.

David was in the room with them, leaning on the ax like a cane. He grinned.

“Is the Stairmaster free?”

Theena drew the gun.

“Drop the ax, David.”

“This ax?” With a violent jerk, David thrust the ax into the mirror alongside the doorway, smashing glass with an ear-bursting crash.

He shifted and swung in the other direction, shattering a reflection of himself, droplets of his blood peppering the glinting shards that fell at his feet.

Theena took careful aim and shot him in the leg again. There was a small eruption of blood, and his knees buckled, but he somehow managed to stay on his feet.

She shot twice more, the first bullet missing, the second taking off part of David's calf.

He still didn't go down.

“Hold your fire!”

Bill threw himself at David, a fifteen pound barbell in his good hand. He connected solidly with David's chest. There an audible thump, and both men toppled over.

Theena was there in three steps, kicking away David's ax. He was flat on his back, arms and legs akimbo. His eyes were open but unfocused.

The time to act was now, but she didn't want to take the gun off of him to tie him up. Bill managed to get to his feet, wincing. Unfortunately, he wouldn't be much help in the knot-tying department with a broken shoulder blade.

“Take the gun.”

Bill hesitated, then accepted it. Theena wasted no time, winding a jump rope around David's ankles, cinching the knot so tight her arms burned.

“Theena!”

Bill's warning came too late.

David jackknifed into a sitting position and batted her across the face. She fell to the side, just as David was rolling in the opposite direction.

Towards his ax.

Her vision cleared in time to see David grip the handle, lift it back to swing at her.

"Bill!"

He fired.

The gun offered an anticlimactic *CLICK.* There were no bullets left.

The pain was as blinding as it was sudden, an explosion in her right side just above her hip. Theena stared down at the thing buried several inches in her side, unable to fathom what was happening.

An ax. She had an ax sticking out of her.

She touched it, fingers trembling, blood bubbling up and swallowing the blade.

There was a sucking sound, and suddenly the ax was out. Theena watched her life spill out of the hole in a gout of blood.

She stared at David, lying a few feet away from her, lifting the ax for another blow.

Then everything went black.

Chapter 40

"You killed her!"

Manny had been watching everything happen in mute terror, unable to stop it. He was a passenger in his own body, unable to control his muscles, his actions, his intent. David had banished him. All he could do is scream out his feeble protests to deaf ears as one atrocity after another was committed by his hands.

But when the ax hit Theena, the balance of power shifted.

Manny's rage inflamed his brain like a fever, forcing David back. He stared at the ax and willed his hands to open. They did, the ax falling to the ground.

His eyes scorched Bill, the cords in his neck bulging. He forced out the words.

"Pick... up... the... ax."

Bill remained rooted, jaw agape.

"Give it up, Manny." David's voice echoed in his head. "You can't win. I'm going to bury you so deep in our mind, you'll never come back out again."

Manny pleaded again. "The ax..."

"Look! Theena's still breathing! Why don't we crawl over there and finish the job?"

Manny rolled onto all fours against his will. But his voice was still his own.

"The ax!"

Bill bent down and took the ax in his good hand. He held it away from his body, as if it were a poisonous snake, a stricken look on his face.

"We're going to snap her neck." Manny began to crawl to Theena. Every inch was a struggle, and it was a struggle he was losing. "I'm going to let you feel the bones break beneath her soft skin while you're squeezing."

"Kill me!"

Manny's hand shook, but he couldn't hold it back. It was reaching, reaching for Theena's throat. Manny felt himself being pushed back again, back into the dark space, David muscling him down and taking over.

"PLEASE KILL ME!"

His hands reached Theena's thin neck, and began to squeeze.

THUNK!

The ax hit him in the small of the back, pinning him to the floor.

There was no pain. Just a spreading warmth that was almost pleasant.

The struggle was over. The conflict in his mind and body seemed to have ended. David's voice had lost its anger. It was quieter now, almost peaceful.

"You finally did it."

Manny saw David, in his mind, but he was a kid, no more than nine-years old. And Manny saw himself, a year younger that his older brother. They were sitting together on the porch of their house, sharing an apple. A happy time, before the State took their mother away. Before foster homes, and juvee hall, and suicide.

"I didn't want to kill you, David."

"I know. It wasn't your fault."

"It wasn't?"

"No, Manny. I shouldn't have killed those cats. It was wrong. You did the right thing to tattle on me."

"But juvenile hall..."

"I was never going to be happy, Manny. That's how it was for me. It wasn't your fault I ended it. It didn't have anything to do with you."

"I wish things turned out better."

"I know. I'm sorry."

David took something out of his pocket, handing it to Manny. It was small, yellow, and seemed to shine with its own inner light. A die-cast pickup truck.

"I love you, David."

"I love you too, Manny."

The warmth was all around him now, covering him like a blanket. It was different, so different than all of the other times he'd died taking N-Som. There was no fear, no pain, no emotional turmoil. Manny was infused with a deep and calming peace, which welcomed him into the thing he wanted most of all.

Everlasting rest.

Emmanuel Tibbets let out a gentle breath, closed his eyes, and went to sleep for the last time.

Chapter 41

"Theena."

Bill knelt down next to her, gently taking her hand off the wound.

"Bill..."

It was bad. The tear was ragged, ugly. The ax had penetrated the dermis and subcutaneous tissue, neatly severing her external obliques. There was a lot of blood. Deep inside, he caught a glimpse of liver and ascending colon.

Bill placed her hand back over the injury, keeping pressure on it. Her pulse was weak, but rapid, her skin clammy to the touch. The onset of hypovelemic shock, brought about by massive blood loss. This was turning into a repeat episode of what happened with David in the lobby.

He wouldn't fail this time. He wouldn't let her die.

"I'll be back."

"Don't go."

Bill ran out of the gym, trying to remember the direction of the lab. He found it by noticing all of the medical supplies Theena had dropped in the doorway. Bill scooped them up; streptokinase, atropine, epinephrine, beryllium, an IV drip and a bag of saline. He then entered the room and picked up the bottle of alcohol and the syringe Theena had used on him, as well as the metal first aid box.

When he arrived back in the gym, Theena was in V-Fib.

Bill hung the IV from one of the nearby exercise machines and threaded the needle into her wrist. She wasn't breathing, and her heart was in chaotic arrhythmia, shaking and trembling in her chest. Bill hit her chest as hard as he could, sending shock waves of pain through his injured shoulder. Then he titled up her head, pinched her nose, and filled her lungs with his breath.

Into her IV he injected a syringe full of epi. He began chest compressions, both arms rigid, bending her rib cage to force her heart to pump blood. He could only keep it up for thirty seconds before the ripples of agony in his back made him close to passing out. Bill forced his breath into her, and gave another thump on the chest.

Her pulse was still erratic.

"God dammit!"

Bill wouldn't let it happen. Not again. He couldn't lose her, too.

He drew a 500 milligram dose of beryllium, a powerful anti-arrhythmic, into the syringe and injected the bolus in an IV push. After another thirty seconds of CPR, he checked her heart.

A normal rhythm had returned, but it was too slow, much too slow.

"I won't let you die."

Bill administered a dose of atropine, and the effect was almost instantaneous. Her heart rate rose dramatically.

Bill checked her carotid. Pulse still weak. She didn't have enough blood in her system to raise the pressure. He had to close up that wound.

In the med kit was a box of single use Ethilon needles, pre-threaded with black monofilament. He tore open a pack and then dumped rubbing alcohol over his hands and a pair of scissors.

Theena moaned when his fingers entered her. The blood flow had slowed considerably. He tied off four veins, and then gently tucked her ascending colon back into her muscle wall. Then he sutured the subcutaneous tissue back over the oblique, and closed her up with twenty-eight stitches across the epidermis.

His back was on fire when he finished, his forehead sopping wet. Bill checked her pulse.

Strong and steady.

"Bill..."

Her eyelids fluttered. Bill felt his chest well up, emotion threatening to choke him.

"Theena."

Pain be damned, he bent down and held her. In that single moment, the only thing that mattered in the whole world was the woman in his arms. Alive and breathing.

He hadn't let her die.

Bill gave her a shot of lidocaine near the injury to help with the pain, and then located the elevator card.

They weren't completely out of the woods yet. Theena was still in critical condition, and needed to get to a hospital. Plus there was the danger of Rothchilde coming back. Bill needed to get them out of there, along with enough evidence to make sure N-Som was never approved and Rothchilde was implicated to the fullest extent of the law.

Bill took the elevator to the lobby and used the phone to dial information. He got the number for the Hoffman Estates Police Department. After several minutes of convincing them that he'd already tried the Schaumburg PD and they hadn't come, they promised to drop by. Bill reminded them to bring an ambulance.

Then he went back into the bowels of the building to find the N-Som file he'd gotten from Mike Bitner's place. It seemed like an eternity ago.

The file was where he'd left it, in the conference room. Inside was enough information to expose the truth about N-Som. Hopefully this, coupled with Theena's testimony, would be enough to put the DruTech President away for a long time.

It was the very least the bastard deserved.

Chapter 42

The only drawback to flying by helicopter was the noise. Unless Rothchilde wore one of those ridiculous radio headsets, he had to yell for his pilot, Frederick, to hear him.

The bird banked left, Rothchilde's dinner almost leaving his stomach from the maneuver. Below them, streetlights and headlights sparkled like stars, competing with the real deal overhead. The Chicago skyline could be seen in the distance, anchored by the blinking antennae of the Sears Tower and the Hancock Building.

Rothchilde decided it might be prudent to leave the country for a few weeks. He wasn't sure how this whole DruTech mess was going to resolve itself. The best scenario had Manny killing Theena and Bill, and then dying himself. But things seldom ended neatly.

The smart thing would be to send in his own troops and clean the place out—bodies, evidence, everything. Unfortunately, Rothchilde had murdered both of the people he could use to do that, Halloran and Carlos. Their bodies would be found, and Rothchilde wasn't anxious to answer persistent questions from either the police or the mob.

So he would go on vacation. Let things settle down. He'd get his lawyers on it, extricate himself from the situation, and get everything back on track. The military contract should still hold up, and he already had some places picked out in Mexico for N-Som production.

Rothchilde yawned. Before he could do anything, he had to take care of Halloran's headless corpse, decaying in his office. Messy. Rothchilde tried to think of someone he could call to assist him, someone who would ask no questions. But he didn't place his trust in many people.

His servants would to it, if ordered to. They feared him. Maybe he could have them wrap up the body, haul it someplace secluded, and then Rothchilde could kill them, too. No witnesses. The only problem was replacing them; it was so hard to find good help these days.

Rothchilde rubbed his eyes. Exhaustion seemed to settle on him like a thick blanket. Sleep now wouldn't be wise. He needed to be alert and focused to deal with everything happening.

There was N-Som back at the mansion. He hadn't taken any since the day before, so he was ready for another dose.

But he didn't have to wait until he got back home, did he?

Rothchilde stuck a hand in his pocket and pulled out the capsules Theena had made from Halloran's brain. He'd killed the captain just a few hours ago, but already the memory of the act was fading.

Maybe what he needed right now was a refresher.

He opened the onboard cooler and took out a Perrier. The pill went down easily, bubbles mixing with a pleasant tang of residual blood, and he settled back in his seat, ready to re-experience his first murder from the victim's point of view.

Rothchilde closed his eyes, a sweet smile settling on his face. The anticipation was exquisite. Better than the Christmas Eves of youth, waiting for Santa.

The first effects of N-Som were sensory. Sounds became blurry, touch was muted. Opening the eyes yielded a dark, fuzzy world, which dimmed as the drug took hold, eventually spiraling the user into blackness. Then the dreams began.

But Rothchilde felt nothing.

He waited. Normally, he'd have been under by now. Was it taking so long because the sample was fresh? Theena mentioned that she didn't have all the equipment to make pills at the lab, and so she'd given him a capsule. Did the fresh stuff take a longer time to get into the bloodstream?

Minutes passed. His smile faded. He began to wonder if the little whore had duped him.

A moment later, he realized just how duped he had been.

Albert Rothchilde had forgotten how to breathe.

He thought he was unconsciously holding his breath at first, tense because the N-Som hadn't kicked in. But when he tried to inhale, he found that he just couldn't. His lungs refused to obey.

His eyes flapped open and he tensed, the first stirrings of panic building inside him. This was impossible. A person just didn't forget how to breathe. Breathing was automatic. He opened his mouth and sucked in his stomach, trying to fill his lungs. It didn't work.

Had Rothchilde known anything about anatomy, he might have noticed that Theena hadn't harvested the parts of Halloran's brain normally used for N-Som production. Instead she'd gone deeper down, into the brain stem, and taken sections of the medulla oblongata.

These fibrous neurons housed a very primitive part of the brain; the reflex centers. They controlled a person's swallowing, sneezing, heartbeat, blood pressure, and breathing.

Just as a regular dose of N-Som overrode a person's thoughts, this refined dose was overriding Rothchilde's instinctive knowledge of how to breathe.

Rothchilde began to see red. His lungs screamed at him, begging for air, but his brain was full of reflex neurons that had frozen in death.

His heart stopped next, in mid beat. The pressure in his chest was excruciating. Every nerve cell in his body fired, sending out distress signals to the brain in the form of pain. Rothchilde's brain responded by ordering the release of adrenaline, which did nothing but heighten his awareness of his terrible situation.

Rothchilde thrashed in his chair. Every muscle in his body burned, starving for oxygen. Black spots mingled with the red in his vision. He tried to scream, but nothing came out.

The pilot, Frederick, couldn't have done anything even if he'd left the controls. All of Rothchilde's systems were crashing. The reflex center of Rothchilde's brain was convinced it was dead, and it was just following orders.

Rothchilde went rigid as he was seized by a spasm of pure agony. He voided his bowels and bladder. His vital organs began to shut down. Rothchilde was helpless, and aware that he was helpless, and the frantic struggle for breath coupled with the body-wracking pain was more than his mind could handle.

The neurons in his head all fired at once, and during that microsecond they burned into him an eternity of torture without escape.

He was no longer rational at this point, or he might have seen the irony. He had, after all, wanted to experience Halloran's death.

Frederick began emergency landing procedures, but there was no hurry.

The president of American Products was dead long before they touched the ground.

Chapter 43

"The ambulance is on the way, Theena."

Theena didn't respond. She looked terrible. Her face was pale, waxy, and her jowls seemed deflated, hanging limply on her face. But her pulse was strong, and she was awake and aware.

Bill touched her cheek. "Are you thirsty?"

She shook her head.

Eventually, Bill would have to go upstairs. He wanted to be there to greet the authorities. But he still had reservations about leaving Theena alone. He'd started her on a streptokinase drip to prevent blood clots from clogging her heart. It was a risky move, considering her injury, but that was looking surprisingly well.

"Where are we?" Her voice was hoarse, low.

"DruTech, the lower levels. In the gym."

Her eyes swept the room, coming to rest on Manny. The ax was still buried in his back.

"Manny's dead."

"I'm sorry, Theena. I didn't have any choice."

Theena's shoulders began to shake. She was too dehydrated to form tears, but she cried just the same. Bill held her, sharing some of her grief.

He hadn't wanted to kill Manny, but at the same time he knew it was the right thing to do. Not only did it save Theena, but in a strange sort of way it had saved Manny as well. Bill hoped the man was finally at peace.

"I'm going to check on the cops. Will you be okay for a few minutes?"

Theena didn't answer. She just stared at the puddle of her own blood, congealing on the floor.

Bill kissed her forehead, then got to his feet and grabbed the N-Som file. The rubber band broke, spilling papers all over the gym floor.

He bent over, the pain flaring in his shoulder, and began to gather them up. Every single sheet was important. This was more than just proof N-Som was dangerous. This was evidence of murders. Many murders.

His hand closed around one of Manny's CT scans, a three dimensional picture of his brain. It was labeled Day 45. There was so much scar tissue it was surprising he had lived up to that point.

Bill examined the picture closer, reading the handwriting on the margin. His stomach clenched.

This wasn't Manny's scan.

He searched through the papers until he found the log. Written in Dr. Nikos's hand. A day-by-day account of the second clinical test subject. Someone else, besides Manny, who'd been taking N-Som and hadn't slept in over one thousand hours. Someone else, whose brain was just as fried.

Bill heard movement behind him. He spun around, his head swimming, shocked beyond words. How could this be so? How could he have missed this? He remembered when he first met Theena, her telling him about another test subject.

"Theena..."

She stood over him, her face oddly calm. Her eyes were distant, unrecognizable.

"My name isn't Theena."

And then she hit him with the ax.

From: 23ytrd34bot@boonepharmaceuticals.com.mx
Subject: [spam] N-SOM AVAILABLE NOW!!!
Date: 2003-05-09 04:05:33 PST

N-SOM AVAILABLE ONLINE NOW!

Are you sick of getting tired?

Never have enough time in the day to get everything done?

Want more out of life?

Laboratory grade Nonsomnambulox shipped to your door overnight!

This revolutionary new drug is available exclusively through Boone Pharmaceuticals, only $299 for a thirty day supply!

This is the real deal, not some cheap imitation!

AS FEATURED IN NEWSWEEK AND TIME MAGAZINE!

ORDER ONLINE!!!

http://www.boonepharmaceuticals.com.mx/nsom.html

ALL MAJOR CREDIT CARDS ACCEPTED!

Or send a check or international money order to:

Boone Pharmaceuticals

887-4 Hacidena

Mexico City, Mexico 4758

YOU WILL NEVER NEED TO SLEEP AGAIN!!!!

Author's Afterword

The book you're now reading has never been conventionally published.

Let me backtrack a little.

In 1999 I landed a literary agent with a technothriller novel called *Origin*, about the United States government keeping Satan in an underground research facility in New Mexico.

Origin was my seventh novel, and arguably the first I'd written that was any good. The other six never got published, though they did garner me more than 400 rejections. Apparently *Origin* wasn't good enough either, because it was rejected by damn near every editor in New York.

Undaunted, I wrote another technothriller, blending in elements of science, mystery, and humor. *The List*, in my opinion, was better than *Origin.* Not only was it trendy, tying in closely to the work being done on the Human Genome Project, but it had more heart than its predecessor.

It didn't sell either.

I decided my problem was mixing genres. Since there's no *Thriller-Humor-Horror-Sci-Fi* section in bookstores, I needed to write something that fit easily within an established genre.

I chose a medical thriller, in the style of Robin Cook and Michael Palmer. No humor this time. Just a by-the-numbers, straightforward, homogenous thriller, with an everyman hero trapped in a terrible situation that quickly spirals out of control.

The book was called *Disturb.* My agent hated it, probably because it had no humor in it, and she never sent it out. So *Disturb* remains my only book that has never been rejected.

After *Disturb*, I wisely chose to put the humor back into my narratives, and wrote *Whiskey Sour*. I've been writing Jack Daniels thrillers ever since.

When I started having some success with the Jack books, I looked back on my earlier novels and decided to offer *Disturb*, *Origin,* and *The List* as free downloads on JAKonrath.com.

The reader response took me by surprise. The books have been downloaded thousands of times each. I'm humbled and flattered by the attention my failures have gotten, and have answered quite a bit of email about them. The question people most often ask is, "When will these be published?"

I still don't have an answer to that.

Origin, The List, Disturb, and my short story collection *55 Proof* aren't available in bookstores, or libraries, or anywhere other than JAKonrath.com and Amazon Kindle. They don't have ISBN numbers. They haven't been catalogued by the Library of Congress. They haven't been professionally typeset, or edited. But fans, collectors, and completests have asked for them, so here they are.

Disturb is my red-headed stepchild. While I love the main concept, and many of the scenes and ideas, there isn't much of me in the book. If anyone wondered what a JA Konrath thriller would look like stripped of its humor, this is it. Many years later, I wrote another book without any humor in it. I used the pseudonym Jack Kilborn, and the book was a horror novel called *Afraid.*

I hope you enjoyed *Disturb*, and would love to hear what you thought. I wrote this back in 2002, and recently in the news there has been talk of pharmaceutical companies working on the same thing that I postulated five years ago. Let's all hope they aren't as unethical as the scientists in *Disturb*.

Which brings us to the other stories included in this collection.

The first grown-up books I ever read, at the age of nine, were mysteries.

This had more to do with them being on my mother's bookshelf than any particular design on my part. But I fell in love with them. Spenser and Travis McGee were my first literary heroes. I really enjoyed Ed McBain's 87th Precinct, and the Remo Williams Destroyer series by Richard Sapir and Warren Murphy.

Then I got into hardboiled and noir. Mickey Spillane. Max Allan Collins. Lawrence Block. Ross MacDonald. Donald Westlake and Richard Stark. Chandler and Hammet. Andrew Vachss. Reading about cops and PIs was cool, but reading about criminals was cool too.

In my teen years, I was floored by Red Dragon and Silence of the Lambs, and that started me on a serial killer binge. I devoured John Sandford, James Patterson, Robert W. Walker, David Wiltse, and Ridley Pearson.

Which is probably why my novels are such a mishmash of different genre styles.

When I sit down to write a short story, it's for one of two reasons. First, because someone asked me for one. Second, because I have an idea that begs to be written. If I'm writing to fill an anthology slot or crack a market, I usually start with a few lines, which leads me to a premise, which leads to conflict, which leads to action. But if I already have an idea, it usually springs full blown from my head and onto the page as fast as I can type.

Often, I have story ideas that won't fit into the Jack Daniels universe. Sometimes these are horror stories, or straight humor, or sci-fi, or a combination of different styles.

Sometimes they're crime stories, many of which are included in this collection. But *crime* doesn't have to mean *serious*. If I could turn an unbiased critical eye toward my own work, I'd say the thing that makes it unique is the humor.

My standard author bio says I used to do improv comedy. In college, I wrote and starred in a comedy play called The Caravan O' Laughs, which was a collection of insane skits that had a few shows in Chicago and southern Illinois. I'm comfortable in front of an audience, and from early on I could always find the joke in any situation.

Comedy has its roots in the same part of our brain that responds to fear. We laugh at things that scare us, confuse us, and surprise us. We're wired to recognize and process millions of pieces of incoming information, and when something defies our expectations, laughter is the result. An evolutionary tension breaker to help us deal with being confused.

Most of my writing contains varying degrees of humor. I can't help it. When I'm editing, the thing I spend the most amount of time doing is cutting jokes for the sake of the story. I hate cutting jokes, and if I snip one I'll usually use it later in another tale. My work desk is scattered with little pieces of paper, each containing a joke, many of them awful.

It's a sickness, really.

Some of the following shorts use various forms of humor to varying degrees of success. There's satire, and parody, and black humor, and puns, and inappropriate humor, and one-liners, and slapstick, and a lot of irony. Out of everything I've written, the funny stories have the most of me in them. And while I'm aware that a few of these pieces can't really be called *crime* fiction, I hope you enjoy them just the same.

Joe Konrath, February 2010

The Big Guys

This was one of three stories written for Small Bites, an anthology of flash fiction to benefit horror author and editor Charles Grant, who needed assistance paying some hefty medical bills. Flash fiction is a story of 500 words or less. Strange as it sounds, writing shorter is sometimes harder than writing longer, because you have less words to fit all of the story elements in. Small Bites used three of my flash fiction shorts. This piece won a Derringer Award.

"I'm surprised you asked me here, Ralph. I didn't think you liked me."

Ralph grinned over the wheel. "Don't be silly, Jim." He cut the engines and glanced over the starboard bow. There was some chop to the sea, but the yacht had a deep keel and weathered it well.

"Well, we've been neighbors for almost ten years, and we haven't ever done anything together."

Ralph shrugged. "I work crazy hours. Not a lot of free time. But I've always considered you a good friend, Jim. Plus, our wives are close. I thought this would give us a chance to get to know each other. Belinda mentioned you like to fish."

Jim nodded. "Mostly freshwater. I haven't done much deep sea fishing.

What are we going for, anyway?"

Ralph adjusted his captain's cap.

"I was originally thinking salmon or sailfish, but it's been a while since I went for the big guys."

"Big guys?"

"Sharks, Jim. You up for it?"

"Sure. Just tell me what I need to do."

"First step is getting into the harness." Ralph picked up a large life vest, crisscrossed with straps and latches. "This clips onto the rod, so you don't lose it, and this end is attached to the boat, in case you get pulled overboard."

Jim raised an eyebrow. "Has that ever happened?"

"Not yet, but it pays to be careful. These are Great White waters, and some of those bad boys go over two thousand pounds."

Ralph helped Jim into the vest, snugging it into place.

"What next?"

"We have to make a chum slick."

"I've heard of that. Fish blood and guts, right?"

"Yep. It's a shark magnet. You want to get started while I prepare the tackle?"

"Sure."

Ralph went to the cooler and took out the plastic bucket of chum. Even refrigerated, it stank to high heaven. He handed it to Jim, with a ladle.

"Toss that shit out there. Don't be stingy with it."

Jim began to slop chum into the blue waters.

Ralph swiveled his head around, scanning the horizon. No other boats.

"So," Jim asked, "what's the bait?"

Ralph gave Jim a deep poke in the shoulder with a fillet knife, then shoved his neighbor overboard.

Jim surfaced, screaming. Ralph ladled on some guts.

"Not very neighborly of you, Jim. Screwing my wife while I was at work."

"Ralph! Please!"

Jim's hands tried to find purchase on the sides of the yacht, but they were slippery with blood. Ralph dumped more onto his head, making Jim gag.

"Keep struggling." Ralph smiled. "The big guys love a moving target."

"Don't do this, Ralph. Please. I'm begging you."

"You'd better beg fast. I see that we already have some company."

Jim stared across the open water. The dorsal fin approached at a brisk pace.

"Please! Ralph! You said you considered me a good friend!"

"Sorry...wrong choice of words. I actually meant to say I considered you a good chum."

It took a while for Ralph to stop laughing

.

A Fistful of Cozy

Satire, written for the webzine ShotsMag.uk at their request. This pokes gentle fun at the sub-genre of zero-violence cozy mysteries, with their quirky but spunky amateur sleuths.

"This is simply dreadful!"

Mrs. Agnes Victoria Mugilicuddy blanched under a thick layer of rouge. Her oversized beach hat, adorned with plastic grapes and lemons, perched askew atop her pink-hued quaff.

Barlow, her graying manservant, placed a hand on her pointy elbow to steady her.

"Indeed, Madam. I'll call the police."

"The police? Why, Barlow, think of the scandal! Imagine what Imogene Rumbottom, that busy-body who writes the Society Column, will say in her muck-raking rag when she discovers the Viscount de Pouissant dead on my foyer floor."

"I understand, Madam. Will you be solving this murder yourself, then?"

"I have no other choice, Barlow! Though I'm a simple dowager of advancing years and high social standing, my feisty determination and keen eye for detail will no doubt flush out this dastardly murderer. Where is Miss

Foo-Foo, the Mystery Cat?"

"She's in her litter box, burying some evidence."

"Miss Foo-Foo!" Agnes's voice had the pitch and timbre of an opera soprano. "Come immediately and help Mumsy solve this heinous crime!"

Miss Foo-Foo trotted into the foyer, her pendulous belly dragging along the oriental rug. Bits of smoked salmon clung to her whiskers.

"Barlow!" Agnes commanded, clapping her liver-spotted hands together.

Barlow bent down and picked up the cat. He was five years Mrs. Agnes's senior, and his back cracked liked kindling with the weight of Miss Foo-Foo.

Agnes patted the cat on the head as Barlow held it. Miss Foo-Foo purred, a sound not unlike a belch.

"We have a mystery to solve, my dearest puss-puss. If we're to catch the scoundrel, we must be quick of mind and fleet of foot. Barlow!"

"Yes, Madam?"

"Fetch the Mystery Kit!"

"Right away, Madam."

Barlow turned on his heels.

"Barlow!"

Barlow turned back.

"Yes, Madam?"

"First release Miss Foo-Foo."

"Of course, Madam."

Barlow bent at the waist, his spine making Rice Krispie sounds. Miss Foo-Foo padded over to Agnes and allowed herself to be patted on the head.

Straightening up was a painful affair, but Barlow managed without a grunt. He nodded at Mrs. Agnes and left the room.

"To think," Agnes mused, "only ten minutes ago the Viscount was sipping tawny port and regaling us with ribald tales of the gooseberry industry. Just a waste, Miss Foo-Foo."

Agnes's eyes remained dry, but she removed a handkerchief from the side pocket on her jacket and dabbed at them nonetheless.

Barlow returned lugging a satchel, its black leather cracked with age. He undid the tarnished clasps and held it open for Mrs. Agnes. She removed a large, Sherlock Holmes-style magnifying glass.

"The first order of business is to establish the cause of death." Mrs. Agnes spoke to the cat, not to Barlow. "It's merely a hunch, but I'm compelled to suggest that perhaps the lovely port the Viscount had been sipping may have been tampered with."

"An interesting hypothesis, Madam, but perhaps instead it has something to do with that letter opener?"

"The letter opener, Barlow?"

"The one sticking in the Viscount's chest, Madam."

Agnes squinted one heavily mascaraed eye and peered through the glass with the other.

"Miss Foo-Foo, your hunch proved incorrect. The poor, dear Viscount appears to be impaled through the heart with some kind of silver object. But what can it be, puss-puss?"

"A letter opener, Madam?"

"Could it be a knife, Miss Foo-Foo? Perchance some rapscallion gained entry to the den though the window, intent on robbing the rich Viscount? Perhaps a fight ensued, resulting in the bloodthirsty criminal tragically ending the Viscount's life with this vaguely Freudian symbol of male power?"

Barlow peered at the body.

"It appears to be the letter opener you bought me for my anniversary, Madam. The gift you presented to me for fifty years of loyal service."

"Miss Foo-Foo!" Agnes bent over the fallen Viscount and lightly touched the handle of the protruding object. "Why, this is no knife! It's

Barlow's letter opener! I can see the engraving."

"'How lucky you must feel to have served me for so many years.'" Barlow intoned.

"This changes everything!" Mrs. Agnes placed the magnifying glass back into the satchel, her gnarled fingers latching onto a tin of fingerprint powder. "Some heathen must have stolen Barlow's lovely gift–"

"Sterling silver plated," Barlow said.

"–with the intent to frame our loyal manservant! Barlow!"

"Yes, Madam?"

"Open this tin so I may dust the offending weapon!"

"Yes, Madam."

Mrs. Agnes used the tiny brush to liberally apply a basecoat of powder to the letter opener's handle.

"Why, look, puss-puss! There's nary a print to be found! The handle has been wiped clean!"

"Perhaps the murderer wore gloves, Madam?" Barlow reached for the powder tin with a gloved-hand.

"Or perhaps, Miss Foo-Foo, the killer wore gloves! This fiend is no mere street malcontent. This seems premeditated, the result of a careful and calculating plot. But why the Viscount?"

"Perhaps he was a witness, Madam? To another murder?"

Mrs. Agnes squinted at her manservant.

"That's daft, Barlow. Even for a lowly servant such as yourself. Do you see another victim in this room?"

"Indeed I do, Madam."

Barlow removed the cheese grater from his vest pocket, a gift from Mrs. Agnes for his forty year anniversary, and spent forty minutes grating off the old dowager's face.

The old bat still had some life left in her after that, so he worked on her a bit with his thirtieth-year-anniversary nutcracker, his twentieth-year-anniversary potato peeler, and finally the fireplace poker, which wasn't a gift, but was handy.

When she finally expired, he flipped the gory side face-down and spent a leisurely hour violating her corpse–something he couldn't have managed if she were alive and yapping. Sated, Barlow stood on creaky knees and picked up the bored Miss Foo-Foo.

"You have a date with the microwave, puss-puss. And then I'm the sole heir to Madam's fortune."

Miss Foo-Foo purred, making a sound like a belch.

Three minutes and thirteen seconds later, she made a different kind of sound. More like a pop.

Cleansing

The bible is full of crime stories. Here's one that never made the canon.

"There's a line."

A long line, too. Thirty people, maybe more.

Aaron cleared his throat and spat the result onto a rock. He could feel the desert heat rising up through the leather of his sandals. An unforgiving sun blew waves of heat into their faces.

"It seems to be moving."

Aaron squinted at Rebekah, fat and grimy. The wrap around her head was soaked with sweat and clung to her scalp in dark patches. Her eyes were submissive, dim. A bruise yellowed on her left cheek.

Looking at her, Aaron felt the urge to blacken it again.

"I cannot believe I let you drag me here."

"You promised."

"A man should not have to keep the promises he makes to his wife. In another nation, you'd be property. Worth about three goats and a swine. Perhaps less, an ugly sow such as you."

Rebekah turned away.

Aaron set his jaw. A proper wife did not turn her back on her husband.

He clutched at Rebekah's shoulder and spun her around.

"I could have you stoned for insolence, you worthless bitch."

He raised his hand, saw the fear in her eyes.

Liked it.

But Rebekah did not finch this time, did not cower.

"I will tell my father."

The words made Aaron's ears redden. Her father was a land owner, known to the Roman court. A Citizen. On his passing, Aaron would inherit his holdings.

Aaron lowered his fist. He tried to smile, but his face would not comply.

"Tell your father–what? Any husband has the right to discipline his wife."

"Shall I open my robe to show him the marks from your discipline?"

Aaron bit the inside of his cheek. This sow deserved all that and more.

"Our marriage is our business, no one else need intrude."

"And that is why we are here, Husband. I will not tell Father because you consented to this. It is the only way."

Aaron spat again, but his dry mouth yielded little. The line moved slowly, the sun baking their shadows onto the ground behind them.

As they approached the river, Aaron's throat constricted from thirst.

But this river was not fit to drink. Shallow and murky, the surface a skein of filth.

"Perhaps I should tell your father that his daughter has been seduced by a cult."

"My father knows. He was cleansed a fortnight past."

"Your father?" Aaron could not believe it. Her father had clout and status. Why would he jeopardize that by fooling around with fanatics?

Aaron stared at the river, confused. Another person waded into the center. Unclean, smelling of work and sweat, someone's servant.

The man known as the Baptist laid hands on the zealot's shoulders and plunged him underneath the scummy waves.

Then the Baptist yelled in a cracked voice, about sin and rebirth and Jehovah. A few seconds later the servant was released, gasping for air.

"He has been saved," Rebekah said. "John has cleansed his soul."

Aaron frowned. The man did not look saved. He looked muddy and disoriented.

"You are a fool, Rebekah. This talk of souls and one god is illegal and dangerous."

"It works, Aaron. I have heard the tales. Healing the lame. The sick. Purging anger and hatred from men's hearts."

"I will not let that fool dunk my head in that putrid water."

"Good day, Father."

Aaron followed her eye line, turned.

Rebekah's father Mark smiled at Aaron, clapping a hand on his shoulder.

"There is nothing to fear, Aaron. The stories are true. At my baptism, I felt as if released from bondage. I felt my soul shrug off the chains of sin and soar like a bird."

Aaron stared into Mark's twinkling, smiling eyes and calmed a bit.

"I am not afraid, Mark."

"Good. You are next."

Rebekah and her father stepped onto the bank with Aaron. The warm water lapped against his toes.

"Am I to go alone?"

"We are family," Rebekah said. "We shall all go together."

She took his hand, a gesture that she had not made since their wedding day. As a unit, they waded over to the man called John.

"Are you ready to cast aside sin and be reborn in the glorious love of your Father, Jehovah?"

Aaron looked at Rebekah's father. The older man smiled, nodded.

"Yes," Aaron said. A quick dunk and it would be over.

John put his hands upon Aaron's shoulders and shoved him downward.

The water was hot, alive against his skin. Aaron's shoulders were pressed down to the bottom and the muck parted to accept him.

He held his breath, straining to hear the words John would speak.

But John spoke nothing.

Aaron shifted, placing a hand on John's thick wrist. He gave it small squeeze, a signal to begin.

The wrist did not yield.

Aaron felt another hand upon him, and then a weight against his chest.

He grasped at it.

A foot.

Alarm coursed through Aaron. Something was wrong. He opened his eyes, peered up through the murk.

John held him firm, Rebekah hunched beside him. Her eyes were venom, and it was her foot that pinned down Aaron's chest.

Aaron tried to twist and thrash, but he had no leverage. A burst of precious air escaped his lungs, bubbling violently up through his field of vision in an endless stream.

This crazy cult was going to murder him.

He reached out his hand, grasping at Rebekah's father. He could not allow this.

Mark caught his wrist, held it tight...and pushed Aaron deeper into the mud.

Aaron screamed, sucked in a breath. The water tasted sour and burned the inside his lungs as if they'd inhaled fire instead. He pried at John's fingers with his free hand, and a moment of clarity flashed through the chaotic panic in his mind.

This was not John the Baptist. He'd seen this man before. He was a servant of Rebekah's father.

The crowd by the river. They'd all been Mark's servants.

And through the weighty distortion of the water, he could hear them cheering.

Lying Eyes

The following four stories were all written for the magazine Woman's World. Every week it publishes a 1000 word mini mystery, in the tradition of Donald Sobol. The story provides the clues to solve the crime, then the solution is explained. I wrote four of these for Woman's World before finally selling one. This one was a reject, but was later published in the magazine Twisted Tongue. Can you solve the mystery?

It was a textbook kidnapping, or so they thought...

Billionaire David Morgan didn't look anything like he did on television. His distinguished face appeared worn and tired, and his piercing blue eyes were bloodshot from lack of sleep.

"I just want her to be okay," he said, for the hundredth time.

Detective Starker patted his shoulder.

"I know, Mr. Morgan. The kidnapper said he'll call with your wife's location."

Morgan's eyes released another tear.

"Are you sure they have the money?" he asked.

"We're sure."

Starker thought back to the money drop, and his insides burned. One million dollars in unmarked bills, left in a suitcase in a parked car. The kidnapper had warned the police that any attempts to stop him or track him would result in the death of Celia Morgan, David's young wife.

Nonetheless, Starker had made sure there was a tiny transmitter in the suitcase, housed in the lining and impossible to detect.

But at the money drop, Starker had watched the kidnapper transfer the cash into a large plastic bag, leaving the suitcase and the tracking device behind in the parking garage, leaving the authorities with no way to find him.

Now Celia's only hope was that the kidnapper was a man of his word, and would reveal her location.

"What if he doesn't call?" Morgan asked, voice trembling. "When Margaret, my first wife, passed away, I never thought I'd love again. I couldn't bear..."

His words were lost to another crying spell. Starker gave the millionaire another pat on the back.

"Don't worry, Mr. Morgan. We'll get her. Let's go over your list of enemies again."

"Enemies? I told you before. I'm the CEO of one of the largest manufacturing companies on the planet. I've been in this business for forty years. I have more enemies than there are names in the Manhattan phonebook."

"Does anyone stand out? Someone who felt you wronged them? Someone wanting money from you?"

"You saw the list. Everyone on it hates me. I told you before, Detective, that line of investigation is hopeless."

"How about around your home? Fired any of the help lately? Landscapers? Maids? Chauffeurs?"

"Celia handles all of that. Wait—I did have to fire the pool cleaner a month ago. I came home from work early and found him in our living room, watching television. Fired him on the spot."

"What was his name?"

"I don't remember. Celia will know...oh dear..."

The mention of his wife's name brought fresh tears. Starker felt awful for the man.

"Where did you meet Celia, Mr. Morgan?"

"She...she was one of my house cleaners. I pretty much ignored her for the first few weeks she worked for me. But she always had a kind word, a bright thing to say. Soon, I began to linger before going to the office, chatting with her over morning coffee. I know she's barely a third of my age, but she makes me feel young."

The phone rang, startling Starker. He nodded at Morgan to pick it up.

"Hello? Is she okay? Where is she?"

Starker, listening in on an extension, wrote down the address for the storage facility where the kidnapper claimed he'd left Celia Morgan.

"Let's move," Starker told his people.

Super Value Storage was across town, but Starker arrived in record time. He led his team, and the anxious David Morgan, to storage locker 116. It was a large sized unit, used for storing furniture, and the door had a combination lock on it. One of the cops used the bolt cutters, and Starker raised the door, a chemical stinging his eyes and making him squint.

He shone his flashlight inside, revealing a terrified-looking Celia Morgan.

She sat in the dark, tied to an office chair, a gag in her pretty mouth. Behind her were two empty buckets of something called sodium bisulfate, and a large empty cardboard box that had BROMINE written on the side.

David Morgan rushed to his wife, white granules crunching under his feet.

"Mr. Morgan!" Starker shouted. "Don't touch anything until we've collected evidence!"

Starker stepped in, snapping on a pair of latex gloves, removing the gag from Celia's perfectly made-up face. She was a strong one—her mascara hadn't even run. He then used a utility knife to cut the clothesline that securely bound her, careful to leave the knots for the crime lab to analyze.

"Celia, my love!"

David Morgan embraced his wife, and she kissed his cheek.

"I'm okay, David. He didn't hurt me."

Starker motioned for his team to come in, and he reached overhead and fumbled with the bare bulb hanging overhead, burning his fingers before eventually finding the pull cord and bathing the area in light.

"Did you have a chance to see your kidnapper?" Starker asked the woman.

"No. I'm sorry. I never saw his face," she said, her clear blue eyes drilling into him. "I've been sitting here in the dark for hours."

"Hours?" Starker repeated.

"Yes."

Starker gave Morgan a final pat on the back, and then separated the married couple.

"I'm sorry, Mr. Morgan, but I'm going to have to arrest your wife...as an accomplice in her own kidnapping."

How did Starker know?

* * *

SOLUTION: Celia's make up was perfect. If she'd been in that room for hours, locked up with chemicals that made Starker's eyes sting, her own eyes would have been red she would have been crying. Plus, when Starker reached up to turn on the light, the bulb was hot, meaning it had recently been on. Thus, Celia had just gotten there, and was lying to them. Since bromine and sodium bisulfate are pool cleaning chemicals, Starker suspected Celia was in on the scheme with the pool cleaner Morgan had fired a month previously.

Perfect Plan

Another Woman's World rejection. Though these are short, fast reads, they took a bit of thought to produce. They were a fun exercise in the mystery tradition of seeding clues.

The heist was flawless, except for one large detail...

Marty had been watching them for over a month. The Richardsons were an attractive young couple, wealthy by chance—they had rich parents on both sides. Five nights a week they prowled the town, dressed in fancy clothes and expensive jewelry. Sometimes to the theater. Sometimes to a five star restaurant. But they enjoyed riverboat gambling the most.

Mrs. Richardson's weakness was hundred dollar slots. She could go through ten thousand dollars an hour. For Mr. Richardson, the allure of blackjack proved irresistible. He was what casino folks called a 'whale,' betting more money on a single hand than Marty earned in the last three years—and Marty held down two jobs and couldn't even afford a car. By day, Marty drove a school bus. At night, he cleaned casino ashtrays and emptied trash cans.

But if Marty's plan worked out, he'd never work another shift at either job.

Marty had seen the Richardsons gamble many times, reckless in the way the very rich tended to be. Mostly, they lost. But sometimes they won, and won big. When they did, they took their spoils in cash. On those big win days, the casino sent an armed escort with the Richardsons, to make sure they arrived home safely.

Marty watched, and waited, polishing slot machines and vacuuming gaudy plush carpeting. He was biding his time until the Richardsons hit it big, because the next time they did, he would relieve them of their winnings.

Marty had followed them all around town, many times. He'd made frequent, secret visits to their house. In the past four weeks, Marty had learned a great deal about the Richardsons.

He knew they had an electric fence, but he had a plan to deal with the electric fence. He knew they had a dog, but he had a plan to deal with the dog. He knew they had a burglar alarm, but he had a plan to deal with the burglar alarm. He knew they had a safe, but he had a plan to deal with the safe. He even had a way to deal with the Richardsons themselves, if they woke up during the robbery. Marty had a gun, and would use it if he had to.

Marty had planned every tiny detail.

All Marty needed was for the Richardsons to win big, and that night, it happened. Mrs. Richardson hit the Double Diamond Jackpot—a cool half a million dollars.

The Richardsons celebrated, cheering and laughing. The casino manager came by to congratulate them both. The couple left with two satchels full of cash, accompanied by two armed guards.

Marty followed.

The Richardsons lived exactly 6.3 miles away from the riverboat. They always took the same route, but just to be sure they didn't deviate from their routine, Marty kept them in sight. He tailed them up to their estate and parked across the street. Once the Richardsons were through their electric fence, the armed guards waved farewell and drove away.

Which left Marty alone to do his work.

He kept his tools in a large satchel under his seat. After setting the parking brake, he grabbed the bag and exited his vehicle through the rear door.

The electrified gate crackled in the night air. From the bag, Marty removed some heavy rubber gloves and galoshes. Rubber didn't conduct electricity, and Marty climbed over the fence safely.

The mansion stood three stories high, boasting dozens of rooms. Marty located the five bullhorns attached to the outside of the building. Any unauthorized person trying to get in through a door or window would trigger these sirens. He filled each bullhorn with a can of aerosol insulating foam—the kind homeowners use in their attics to reduce drafts. The foam filled every crack and crevice, quickly hardening into a solid material. The sirens would still go off, but they wouldn't be any louder than a whisper.

With the alarm system beaten, Marty located the living room window and pushed a plumber's plunger onto the surface. Using a diamond edged tool, he cut around the plunger until he could remove the glass.

When he had a hole in the window, he took a thermos from his bag and shook out a ball of raw hamburger.

Scruffy, the Richardson's harmless but noisy pug, came running into the room. Before the dog could begin barking, Marty stuck his hand through the hole in the window, holding the hamburger. Mixed in with the meat were sleeping pills.

The dog gobbled up the treat, then stared at Marty, waiting for more. Marty gave the dog a rawhide bone. Scruffy chewed for five full minutes, then closed his eyes and began to snore harmlessly.

Marty felt for the latch and opened the window. He listened closely for the Richardsons, hearing a TV in another part of the house.

The safe, Marty knew from his many reconnaissance visits, was behind a large painted portrait of Mrs. Richardson. Marty crept up to it in the darkness, removing a cordless drill and a feather pillow from his bag. Unzipping the pillow, he placed the drill inside until just the large bit protruded, and then began drilling the safe, the sound muffled by the feathers.

He'd barely begun when the lights suddenly switched on. Marty spun around, reaching for his pistol, but decided against it when he saw the room was filled with cops.

Marty dropped the drill and raised his hands.

"How did you get here so fast?" Marty asked. "My plan was perfect!"

The lead detective answered. "The casino helped the Richardsons set up the phoney slot machine payoff tonight, to lure you here. We've been waiting for you for over an hour. You made one very big mistake."

What was Marty's mistake?

* * *

SOLUTION: Marty didn't own a car, so every time he followed the Richardsons and parked near their house, it was using his work vehicle...a school bus. The Richardsons spotted it easily, and knew something was going on because there are no school buses that run at night.

Piece Of Cake

This is the Mini Mystery that Woman's World finally bought. I still have no idea why they preferred this one over the other three. It's actually my least favorite.

Some folks will do anything to win...

The Bitsy Farmer Rocky Mountain Cake Bake-Off had played host to many wonderful desserts over the past ten years, but this was the first time it played host to a criminal.

Bitsy stared at the five finalists and frowned. When she began the contest a decade ago, it was to help new chefs. But things had gotten ugly. Really ugly.

Bitsy's skills in the kitchen had given rise to a multi-million dollar cake-mix company. Always the innovator, Bitsy used the Rocky Mountain Cake Bake-Off to encourage amateur cooks. The winner received ten thousand dollars, plus her recipe would be sold through Bitsy's company. But never before had Bitsy been faced with this dilemma.

An anonymous phone caller had informed Bitsy that one of the remaining contestants was planning to sabotage her competitors. Not only was that unfair, but the scandal could hurt the integrity of the event—an integrity Bitsy had spent years building.

Bitsy knew she had to figure out who the villain was, before the competition was ruined.

She walked over to Contestant #1, Suzi Snow. The elderly Ms. Snow reminded Bitsy of her grandmother; hair up in a gray bun and always smiling.

"Hello, Ms. Snow. What are you baking for us today?"

Ms. Snow grinned, showing off super-white dentures.

"My famous angel food cake, with a fresh raspberry glaze. I have a secret ingredient, passed down through six generations."

"What is it?" Bitsy asked, curious.

Ms. Snow winked. "I'll only share it if I win."

Bitsy wished her luck, and walked through the kitchen studio over to Contestant #2, Maureen Hamilton. Maureen was Bitsy's age, but shorter and perpetually scowling. She looked to be in a mood when Bitsy approached.

"The altitude is murderous," Maureen moaned. "It will be a miracle if this chocolate cake turns out. Plus I don't think this oven is calibrated correctly. I don't want to lose because of faulty equipment."

"I'll send a technician over to check it out," Bitsy said. She spoke into her walkie-talkie and asked someone to come by.

Maureen frowned and kept mixing.

Contestant #3 was Maria Espinoza. She'd brought her teenaged daughter with to assist, which the rules allowed. Both wore white latex gloves, which was definitely sanitary, but somewhat unusual.

"This will be the best angel food cake you've ever eaten," Maria beamed.

Bitsy noticed that Maria's daughter was opening a package of raspberries.

"Are you making a raspberry glaze?" she asked.

"Yes. I know that other lady is making a similar cake, but mine will be better. You'll see."

Bitsy bid her good baking and moved on the Contestant #4, Holly Doolittle. Holly was opening up packages of cream cheese, and Bitsy noted that her counter top was covered with graham cracker crumbs.

"Bitsy! I'm so excited to meet you! You're my idol!"

"Thank you," Bitsy said, a little embarrassed.

"I only hope my cake is half as good as one yours. You've got the be the best baker in all of Colorado. Boy, I just love you!"

Bitsy endured a hug, then moved along to the final contestant, Georgia Peters.

"Ms. Peters, I..."

"Shhh!" Georgia put a finger in front of her lips. "The first layer of my quadruple golden layer cake is in the oven. With this elevation, I can't take any chances."

"Sorry," Bitsy whispered, somewhat mollified. "Good luck."

"I don't need luck," Georgia whispered back. "This cake will win for sure."

Bitsy's walkie-talkie squawked. Georgia shot Bitsy an evil look at the intrusive sound, and Bitsy hurried away.

"What is it?" she asked into the radio.

"We found something." It was Niki James, Bitsy's assistant. "You'd better come and look."

"Where are you?"

"In the hospitality suite.

Bitsy flew through the kitchen, down the hallway, and to the suite. When she arrived, Niki was as pale as cake flour.

"It was under the sofa, in a plain paper bag."

She pointed to the table, and Bitsy gasped when she saw a gun laying next to a bowl of chips.

"When I became your assistant, I never knew I'd have to deal with anything more dangerous than a spatula," Niki said. "Who would bring a gun to a bake-off?"

"Did you touch it?" Bitsy asked.

Niki nodded. "I didn't know what was inside, so I reached in."

"No name on the bag?"

"It's just a regular paper lunch sack," Niki said.

"How about on the gun?"

"I didn't look close enough."

Bitsy thought out loud. "How long has the hospitality suite been open?"

"It's been open all night. I know for a fact that every contestant has been in here, some several times."

Bitsy rubbed her temples. She couldn't believe that one of the women she'd just met would commit murder just to win.

"Should we call the police?" Niki asked.

"Yes. We'll have to cancel the bake-off."

"The negative publicity will be devastating."

"I know. But there's nothing—"

Bitsy's voice trailed off when her eyes locked on the gun. There was something unusual about it. She crept closer to get a better look.

"This isn't a regular gun," she said. "Look at the writing on the side."

Niki came over and read the word engraved into the stock.

"Starter pistol? What's that?"

"It's used for races. It doesn't fire real bullets. Only makes a loud noise."

As the words left Bitsy's mouth, she smiled.

"Call security. I know who the saboteur is."

Who is the saboteur, and how did Bitsy know?

* * *

SOLUTION: Bitsy believed Holly Doolittle had brought the starter gun. A loud noise, especially at the high altitude in the Colorado Rockies, would cause flour-based cakes to collapse. Holly was making a cheesecake, which would be unharmed by the loud bang, ensuring a win. Holly had bragged about her plan to her next door neighbor, who placed the anonymous call to Bitsy.

Animal Attraction

After I sold Piece of Cake, I figured I had a new market that would take everything I wrote. I was wrong. After buying my previous story, Woman's World gonged this one. My hat's off to Encyclopedia Brown, because this isn't as easy as it looks.

Only obscure knowledge will lead to a killer...

The First Annual Spokane Zoologist Convention ended on a very sour note...a murder.

To make matters even worse, no one knew who the dead man was.

"I'm sure he's a registered zoologist," said the convention organizer, Dr. Myrna Simmons, who claimed she recognized the deceased from the day before. "I checked him in at the reception table. I remember searching for his name tag. But for the life of me. I can't recall his name. The poor man."

The victim was a handsome forty-something male, wearing a blue suit and a red tie. His wallet was missing. A cheese knife pierced his back—it had apparently been taken from the hors d'oeuvres table. A napkin was wrapped around its handle, preventing the killer from leaving fingerprints.

The body had been found lying face-first on the coatroom floor. One of the convention attendees had gone to hang up her jacket, and almost tripped over him. Immediately afterward, the police had been called, and the banquet hall sealed. No one was allowed to leave without permission from the authorities.

Detective Robbie Walker personally checked the alibi of every person in attendance, and was left with four remaining suspects. During the course of his investigation, Walker cross-referenced the guest list and discovered that there was one person too many in the banquet hall. Walker deduced that this convention crasher was the murderer, and he'd taken the dead man's name tag in an attempt to blend into the crowd and escape.

None of the four suspects had any form of picture ID on them, and each was unable to confirm his identity.

Walked needed to figure out who the imposter was.

He approached the first man, an elderly fellow with a bushy white beard who claimed to be Dr. Jordan McDermott.

"Dr. McDermott, what types of animals do you specialize in?"

"I study the duck-billed platypus," McDermott said, a bit too cheerfully considering the morbid circumstances. "Its fur is among the softest in the world. It lays eggs, and after they hatch it nurses its young. The male platypus is also poisonous. Quite an amazing animal."

Walker was skeptical. "Is all of that true?" he asked the others.

They each shrugged.

"Zoology has so many specialties," said Dr. Apu Patel, a tall, thin man with penetrating brown eyes. "It's impossible to know everything about everything."

"What do you specialize in, Dr. Patel?"

"Elephants. They can smell water from three miles away. And an elephant is the only animal that cannot jump."

"Really?"

"It's true. Did you know that African elephants only have four teeth?"

"I did not know that," Walker admitted. It sounded very suspicious.

"That's nothing," said Dr. Harry Reinsdorff, a fat man with thick, round glasses. "I'm a marine biologist, and I'm studying why sharks don't get cancer. Did you know that sharks can smell a drop of blood in the water from five miles away? And besides the five senses humans have, they also have an extra sense called the Line of Lorenzo, which lets them detect electrical fields in the water."

Walker felt a headache coming on. He didn't know if any of these outrageous facts were true or false.

"How about you?" he asked Dr. Mark Kessler. "What do you specialize in?"

"I unashamedly admit that I study cockroaches," Kessler said. His bulging eyes and brown suit made him look sort of like a cockroach himself. "They're really fascinating creatures. Their blood is white, not red. They can hold their breath underwater for more than ten minutes. And did you know a cockroach can live up to two weeks with its head removed?"

"Yuck," Walker said. The other suspects echoed the sentiment.

"Let's go over your stories again. Dr. McDermott," Walker said, turning to the platypus specialist, "Where were you when the body was discovered?"

"In the bathroom," McDermott said. "I wasn't feeling very well. Too many libations last night. I tried a drink called a rusty nail. Vile stuff."

"How about you, Dr. Patel?" Walker asked the pachyderm professor.

"I was on my cell phone, checking my voice mail. I'd gotten a message from the San Diego Zoo. Apparently one of their elephants has elephant pox."

"And you, Dr. Reinsdorff?"

"I was also on the phone, confirming my reservation tonight at an expensive Japanese sushi restaurant that serves sea cucumbers. They can be poisonous, unless you remove the brain at the center."

Walker said, "Yuck," again, and then asked, "How about you, Dr.

Kessler?"

"I'm afraid I was just staring out the window, doing nothing at all. I'm not a very sociable person."

Walker had no idea what to ask next, but fortunately Dr. Myrna Simmons, the convention organizer, came hurrying over.

"Detective Walker! I've got that book you wanted."

She handed him a copy of The Complete Encyclopedia of Animals. Walker thanked her, excused himself, and went into the other room for some fact-checking.

He returned ten minutes later, a broad grin on his face. With dramatic flourish, he pointed at one of the suspects.

"I've discovered that you are lying. I'm afraid you'll have to come downtown with me to answer some more questions."

Which of the suspects was lying?

* * *

SOLUTION: The so-called shark expert. Walker discovered that sharks do in fact get cancer, that they can only smell blood in the water from a quarter mile away (not five miles), and that the sense that detects electricity is called the ampullae of Lorenzini, not the Line of Lorenzo. He also discovered that sea cucumbers don't have brains, therefore their brains could not be poisonous, and the man must have been lying about his sushi restaurant reservations. Incredibly, all of the other facts strange animal facts were true. The imposter soon confessed that he had snuck into the convention and murdered Dr. Reinsdorff for having an affair with his wife.

Urgent Reply Needed

Another Amazon.com short, this one in response to the email spam we all get, seemingly all the time. I've remained undecided if the last page hurts the story or helps it, and I've cut the ending many times. Here it is uncut.

When Conroy saw the message in his INBOX, he smiled.

URGENT REPLY NEEDED!!!

Allow me sir to introduce myself. My name is Dr. William Reingold, executor to the estate of Phillip Percy Jefferson III, former CEO of...

According to the email, Dr. Reingold had 17 million dollars that he was required to distribute to Jefferson's heirs, and a detailed genealogy search had turned up Conroy.

Conroy considered his luck. Just last week, a diplomat from Nigeria had emailed him requesting assistance to help distribute 42 million dollars in charity funds, and a month prior he was contacted by an auditor general from Venezuela with 24 million in a secret arms account and a lawyer from India trying to locate the relatives of a billionaire who died in a tragic plane crash.

He'd also recently become a finalist in the Acculotto International lottery in Madrid, which wanted to give him a share of a 30 million euro prize.

Conroy hadn't even bought a lottery ticket.

"Wonderful thing, the Internet," he mused.

"Playing computer solitaire again?" Ryan, from the cubicle to his right, spoke over the flimsy partition.

"Email. If I just give this fellow my bank account number, he'll wire 9 million dollars into my account."

Ryan laughed. "Spam. I got that one too."

Conroy darkened. "Did you reply?"

"Of course not. Who would reply to those things?"

"Who indeed?" Conroy thought. Then he hunched over his keyboard.

Dear Dr. Reingold, I'm very interested in discussing this with you further...

* * *

The warehouse where Dr. Reingold had scheduled their meeting was located in Elk Grove Village, a forty minute drive from Conroy's home in Elgin. The late hour troubled Conroy. Midnight. If Conroy hadn't needed the money so badly, he never would have agreed to it. Insurance barely covered half of his mother's nursing home costs, and since his layoff he'd only been able to find temp data entry work at nine dollars an hour—not even enough for one person to live on.

Conroy pulled his BMW into the warehouse driveway, his stomach fluttering. This was an industrial section of town, the area deserted after hours. Conroy wondered how often the police patrolled the area.

He switched on his interior light and reread the email he'd printed out.

Park in front and enter the red door on the side of the building.

Conroy stuffed the note into his jacket and peered at the warehouse. His headlights illuminated a sidewalk, which led to the building's west side. A few seconds of fumbling through his jacket pocket produced a roll of antacids. He chewed four, the chalky taste clinging to the inside of his dry throat.

"I don't like this at all," he whispered to himself.

Then he killed the engine and got out of the car.

The sidewalk was invisible in the dark, but Conroy moved slowly toward the warehouse until he felt it underfoot. He followed the perimeter of the building around the side, and saw a dim light above a red doorway, a hundred feet ahead.

The walk seemed to take an eternity. When he finally put his hand on the cold knob, his knees were shaking.

The door opened with a creak.

"Hello?"

Conroy peeked his head inside, almost crying out when he felt the steel barrel touch his temple.

"Hello, Mr. Conroy."

He dared not turn his head, instead peering sideways to see the thin, rat-faced man with the .38. His light complexion was pocked with acne scars, and he wore too much aftershave. Standing behind him was another, larger man, holding a baseball bat.

Conroy couldn't keep the tremor out of his voice when he said, "Where's Dr. Reingold?"

The man snickered, his laugh high-pitched and effeminate.

"Idiot. I'm Dr. Reingold."

He didn't look very much like a doctor at all.

"You bring your bank account number?"

"No, I—"

Dr. Reingold grabbed Conroy by the ear and tugged him into the room, a small office lit with a single bare bulb hanging from the ceiling.

"I told you to bring that number! Can't you follow instructions?"

Conroy didn't see the blow coming. One moment he was on two feet, the next he was flat on his back, his head vibrating with pain, his world completely dark.

"I can't find his wallet."

A different voice. Probably the big guy.

"No wallet. No check book. What a loser."

A jingle of keys.

"A Beemer. That's worth a few grand. Wasn't a total waste of time."

"In his email, he said he was rich."

"Could have been lying." There was a cold laugh. "Internet is filled with liars."

A gun cocking, close to Conroy's head.

"So let's waste him and—"

"I have money," Conroy croaked.

He managed to open his eyes, unable to focus but sensing the two men staring down at him.

Dr. Reingold nudged him with his foot. "What did you say, buddy?"

"I have a coin collection. Worth over fifty thousand dollars."

"Where is it?"

"At my house."

"Where's your house?"

"Please don't kill me."

Dr. Reingold leaned down, scowling at Conroy. "I'll do worse than kill you if you don't tell me where your house is."

Conroy cursed his own stupidity. He doubted he'd live through this.

"In Elgin. It's in a safe."

"Marty, find a pencil on that desk."

Conroy tried to touch his throbbing head, but Dr. Reingold kicked his hand away.

"The safe combination is tricky. Even if I gave it to you, you probably couldn't open in."

Dr. Reingold tapped the gun against his own cheek, apparently thinking.

"You live alone?"

"Yes."

"Any dogs? Guns? Nasty surprises?"

Conroy's eyes teared up. "No."

Dr. Reingold grinned. "Well then, Mr. Conroy, let's go see this coin collection of yours."

* * *

Conroy sat wedged between the two thugs. The big one, Marty, drove. Dr. Reingold kept the .38 pressed into Conroy's ribs, hard enough to bruise.

This wasn't supposed to happen, Conroy thought. This should have ended in a bank account deposit, not in my death.

He pictured his poor mother, who would be sent to a State nursing home if the checks stopped coming. Filthy living conditions. Nurses who stole jewelry and medication. Sexual abuse.

Conroy pushed the images out of his mind, focusing on the problem at hand.

"This it?" Marty asked.

Dr. Reingold gave Conroy's sore ribs a jab.

"Next house, on the end."

"Nice neighborhood. Real quiet. Bet you can put the TV volume all the way up, neighbors don't complain."

Conroy didn't answer.

Marty pulled the BMW into the driveway, parking next to the garage. Dr. Reingold tugged Conroy out of the car and shoved him up to the front door.

"Move it. We gotta another sucker to meet later tonight."

Conroy's hands were shaking so badly he could barely get his key into the lock. He took a deep breath before he turned the knob.

"I'd better go in first," he said, quickly pulling the door open. His house was dark, quiet.

"Easy there, speedy." Dr. Reingold had Conroy's ear again. "You're a little too eager to get inside. I think I'd better..."

The bear trap closed around Dr. Reingold's leg with a sound that was part clang, part squish. He screamed falsetto, dropping the gun and prying at the trap with both hands.

Conroy reached for the pistol, swinging it around at Marty, who watched the whole scene slack-jawed. He shot the large man four times in the chest, then raised the gun and cracked it alongside Dr. Reingold's head, silencing the screams.

* * *

Conroy was shoveling the last bit of dirt atop the grave when Dr. Reingold woke up.

"Good morning," Conroy said, wiping a sleeve across his sweaty brow.

Dr. Reingold's eyes were wide with terror, and he struggled against the chair he'd been bound to.

"You can't get away, Dr. Reingold. The knots are too tight."

"What the hell is going on?"

"You don't remember? You and your associate lured me to a warehouse in Elk Grove, using a fake email story. Right now you're in my basement."

"Where's Marty?" Dr. Reingold said, his voice creaking.

"He's right here." Conroy patted the fresh mound. "Next to him is Mr. Bekhi Kogan, a highly dubious Nigerian diplomat. One mound over is Sr. Domingo, who spoke no Spanish, though he was supposedly a Venezuelan auditor general. The third grave is Zakir Mehmood, who had a distinct Chicago accent, even though he claimed to be from Pakistan. Behind him is a lottery commissioner from Madrid, I forget his name. Began with an L, I think."

Conroy set the shovel on the table, next to the pliers and the filet knife.

"Spammers. All of them. They all promised me riches. Just like you did, Dr. Reingold. All they wanted in return was my bank account number. Speaking of which..."

Conroy picked up the filet knife, and held it against the bound man's ear.

"...why don't you tell me your account number, Dr. Reingold?"

Dr. Reingold began to sob.

"Who...who are you?"

"I'm your most dreaded enemy, Dr. Reingold." Conroy grinned, his eyes sparkling. "I'm a spam killer."

Conroy pushed the knife forward and Dr. Reingold began to scream.

* * *

All in all, a pretty decent take. Dr. Reingold's bank account contained over seventeen thousand dollars. He'd had a little trouble remembering his routing number, but Conroy was good at helping people remember things.

Next time, he'd do things differently. He hadn't expected an Internet swindler to have a partner. Or a weapon. The ones he'd dealt with previously had been con artists, not hardened criminals.

Well, live and learn. In the future, he'd be more prepared.

After a quick shower, Conroy visited his favorite all night diner for some meatloaf and a slice of cherry pie. Late night grave digging made a man hungry.

"How are you, Mr. Conroy?"

The regular waitress, Dora, was in mid coffee pour when she sneezed, spilling some onto the table.

"Sorry about that."

Conroy grimaced.

"Sounds like you have a cold."

Dora sniffled. "Yeah. Bad one too."

"Shouldn't you be home, resting?"

"Can't. Need the money."

"I'm sorry to hear that."

Dora sneezed again, not even bothering to cover her mouth. "You want the usual?"

Conroy thought it over, then made his decision.

"Not today. I just remembered something I have to do."

Conroy left the restaurant. Instead of climbing into his car, he walked around back and waited in the alley for Dora's shift to end. His hunger had been replaced by a hunger of a different kind.

He fingered the .38 in his pocket, pleased with his newfound sense of purpose.

I'm giving myself an upgrade, he mused.

From now on, he would be Conroy Version 2.0—Spam Killer and Virus Eliminator.

Blaine's Deal

Before I owned a computer, I had WebTV, which was an Internet browser that hooked up to the television. I found some online writing groups, and would regularly type stories to post for critiques. This was the first story I ever put on the world wide web.

They shoot cheaters at The Nile.

Blaine lost his mentor that way, a counter named Roarke. Didn't even have a chance to get ahead before the eye in the sky locked on, videotaping skills that took years to master. Then it was burly men and a room without windows. One between the eyes, tossed out with the trash.

Poor bastard deserved better.

Blaine pushed back the worry. He was dressed like a tourist, from his sandals to his Nile Casino T-shirt. Made sure to spill some beer from the paper cup down his chin when he took a sip. Sat by a loud slot machine called Pyramids and plunked in quarters, trying to look angry when he lost. Ugly American. Probably had a job in the auto industry.

When the coins ran out, he frowned, scratched himself, and made a show of looking around. He'd had an eye on a particular Blackjack dealer for the last two hours. Surfer guy, looked like a tan version of the Hulk, too young to have been in the business long.

Blaine wandered over to the table, pretended to think it over, then sat down and fished some cash out of his shorts. Three hundred to start.

He took it slow. Six deck shoe, sixteen tens per deck. Too many to keep track of mentally. But no need to. Every counter had his tally method.

Roarke had been one of the best. Subtle. See a ten, adjust the elbow. Ace, move the foot. Depending on his body position, Roarke knew if the shoe was heavy or light with face cards.

But the silver globes in the ceiling caught him just an hour into his game. Roarke was found a few days later in an alley, the offending foot and elbow smashed. Back of his head was missing, and no one bothered to look for it.

Blaine was a counter as well, but his tally couldn't be seen by the cameras. No tapping feet or odd posture. Pit boss could be taking a dump on his shoulder, wouldn't notice a thing.

He bet small, safe. Won a few, lost a few. Turned more cash into chips and bided time until he got a nice, fat shoe. Then it was payday.

Thirty minutes. Twelve thousand dollars.

He lost a grand, on purpose, before tipping the Hulk a hundred bucks and calling it quits for the night.

Blaine walked out of the casino happy, not needing to fake that particular emotion. He'd be off this tropic isle tomorrow. Back to his wife, laden with money. A memorable and profitable trip.

The goons grabbed him in the parking lot. Nile Security. Guys with scars who were paid to give them.

"What the hell's going on?"

No answer. They dragged Blaine back inside. Past the crowd. Down a hall. To a room without windows.

Panic stitched through his veins. He fought to stay in character. Hackles and indignation.

"I'm calling the police! I'm an American!"

The door slammed. A bare bulb hung from the ceiling, casting harsh shadows. The pit boss forced Blaine to his knees. Big guy, a walrus in Armani, breath like rotten meat.

"We shoot card counters here."

"What are you talking about? I won the money fair!"

The blow knocked Blaine off his feet. Concrete was sticky under his palms. Old stains.

"Camera caught it. Under the table."

The blood in Blaine's mouth contrasted sharply with his blanched face. The pit boss reached down, pulled at Blaine's shorts, his underwear.

Blaine stared down between his naked legs. The abacus was along his thigh, taped to the right of his testicles.

The pit boss ripped it off, a thousand curly hairs screaming.

"This belong in your shorts?"

"How did that get there?" Blaine tried for confused. "I swear, I borrowed this underwear. I have no idea how that got on me."

His explanation was met with a kick in the head. Blaine kissed the mottled floor, his vision a carousel. He flashed back to Roarke's funeral, closed casket, the promise he made. "I'll beat the Nile for you, old buddy."

Should have stuck with Vegas.

The pit boss dug a hand inside his sport coat. "Never saw a guy count cards with his dick before. Man with your talent, should have gone into porno."

The gun was cool against Blaine's temple.

"No one cheats the Nile."

Blaine's wife cried for seven weeks straight when she learned of his death.

Light Drizzle

The title, and much of the plot, is a nod to my friend Barry Eisler and his John Rain series. But this is also a satire of the entire hitman sub-genre, where tough guy assassins with exotic pasts follow strict codes and kill in bizarre ways with common, everyday objects to get the job done.

The mark knelt next to a garbage can, two hands unsuccessfully trying to plug nine holes in his face, neck, and upper body. A gambler, late in his payments, with one second-chance too many. I didn't have all of the details.

Rule #1: Don't make it personal.

Knowing too much made it personal.

He dropped onto his face and spent a minute imitating a lawn sprinkler—a lawn sprinkler that sprayed blood and cried for his mama. I kept my distance.

Rule #8: Don't get all icky with the victim's fluids.

When all movement ceased, I moved in and planted the killing corkscrew in his left hand. In his right, I placed a bottle of 1997 Claude Chonion Merlot. His death would look like an unfortunate uncorking accident.

Rule #2: Make it look natural.

I ditched the latex gloves in the Dumpster and spun on my heels, practically bumping into the bum entering the mouth of the alley. Ragged clothes. A strong smell of urine. Wide eyes.

I reached into the inner pocket of his trench coat, tugged out another pair of latex gloves.

Rule #3: No witnesses.

"Who're you?" the bum asked.

"I'm John," I lied.

Rule #19: Never give your real name.

My real name was Bob. Bob Drizzle. I'm half Japanese. The other half is also Japanese. I also have a bit of Irish in me, which accounts for my red hair. Plus some Serbo-Croatian, a touch of Samoan, a dab of Nordic, a sprinkling of Cheyenne, and some Masi from my mother's side.

But I blend invisibly into all cultures, where I ply my unique trade. I'm a paid assassin. A paid assassin who kills people for money.

I gave the bum a sad frown and said, "Sorry, buddy."

The gloves didn't go on easy—the previous pair had left my hands sweaty, and my palms fought with the rubber. The bum watched the struggle, his stance unsteady. I considered going back to the dead gambler and retrieving the corkscrew, to make the scene look like a fight for Merlot gone deadly.

Instead, I pulled out a pocketful of skinny balloons.

"I'm unemployed," the bum said.

I shoved the multicolored mélange of latex into his filthy mouth, and while he sputtered and choked I blew up a pink one and expertly twisted it into a horsey. I dropped it by his twitching corpse. Street person dies making balloon animals. We've all seen it on the news many times.

I tugged off the gloves, balled them up inside out, and shot the three pointer at the open can.

Missed.

"What's going on?"

A man. Joe Busybody, sticking his nose in other people's business, watching from the sidewalk. Linebacker body, gone soft with age.

I reached for another pair of gloves. "Sir, this is police business. Would you like to give a statement?"

The guy backpedaled.

"You're no cop."

I didn't bother with the second glove. I removed the aluminum mallet from my holster. That, along with a little seasoning salt and the pork chop I kept in my shoe, would make his death mimic a meat tenderizing gone wrong.

But before I had a chance to tartare his ass, he took off.

I keep in shape.

Rule #13: Stay fit.

Any self-respecting hitman worth his contract fee has to workout these days. Marks were becoming more and more health conscious. Sometimes they ran. Sometimes they refused to die. Sometimes they even had the gall to fight back.

I do Pilates, and have one of those abdominal exercisers they sell on late night television. I bought it at a thrift store, with cash.

Rule #22: Don't leave a paper trail.

The witness had a head start, but I quickly closed the distance. When the guy glanced, wide-eyed, over his shoulder, I was able to smash the mallet on his forehead.

See ya. Wouldn't wanna be ya.

The mark stumbled, and I had to leap over the falling body. I skidded to a stop on thick rubber soles.

Rule #26: Shoes should be silent and have good traction, and good arch support.

I took a moment to scan the street. No one seemed to be watching.

I played Emeril on the mark's face, then put the mallet in his right hand and the pork chop in his left.

I was sprinkling on the Mrs. Dash when I heard something behind me.

My head snapped up at the sound, and I peered over my shoulder. The number 332 commuter bus had stopped at my curb. Right next to the big sign that said BUS STOP.

I cursed under my breath for breaking Rule #86: Don't kill anyone where people are likely to congregate, like bus stops.

I stared. A handful of riders, noses pressed to window glass, stared back.

The bus driver, a heavy-set woman wearing a White Sox hat, scrambled to close the bus door.

But I was fast. In three steps I'd mounted the stairs and withdrawn a can of oven cleaner from my holster. Nasty stuff, oven cleaner. The label is crammed full of warnings. The bus driver stared at the can and got wide-eyed.

"Drive," I told her.

She drove.

I faced the terrified group of riders. Two were children. Three were elderly. One was a nun with an eye patch.

Rule #7: No sympathy.

I snapped on another latex glove.

After counting them twice, I came up with nine people total. Just enough for a soccer team.

Perfect.

I removed the uninflated ball and the bicycle pump from my holster. Soccer games got rowdy. Casualties were common.

After screwing some cleats into the bottoms of my thick, rubber soled shoes, I spent a good ten minutes stomping on the group. The nun was especially tough. But I had training. I was a fuscia belt in Jin Dog Doo, the ancient Japanese art of killing a man using only your hands and feet and edged weapons and blunt weapons and common household appliances and guns.

Eventually, even the nun succumbed. Some torn goal netting and a discarded ref's whistle completed the illusion. Only one last thing left to do.

"Stop the bus!" I yelled at the driver.

The driver didn't stop. She accelerated.

Rule #89: Don't attract attention.

This bus was attracting more than its share. Besides speeding, the driver had just run a red light, prompting honks and screeching brakes from cross-town traffic.

This simple hit had become a bit more complicated than I'd anticipated.

"Slow down!" I ordered the driver.

My command went unheeded. I took a Chilean Sea Bass out of my holster. It used to be called the Pantagonian Toothfish, but some savvy marketers changed its name and it's currently the hottest fish on the five star menus of the world. So hot, that overfishing has brought the Chilean Sea Bass/Pantagonian Toothfish to the brink of extinction.

Beating the driver to death with the fish would look somewhat...well...fishy. At first. But when I planted a deboning knife and a few slices of lemon in her pockets, the cops would get the picture. Just another endangered species taking revenge.

I walked up to the front of the bus and tried to recall if "The Complete Amateur's Guide to Contract Killing" had a rule about whacking a driver while you were a passenger. Nothing sprang to mind.

Still, it didn't seem like a wise idea. I tried another tactic.

"Stop the bus, and I'll let you go."

That was Rule #17: Lie to the mark to put her at ease.

Or was that Rule #18?

I reached for the cheat card that came with the book, folded up in my pants pocket.

Rule #18: Lie to the mark. Rule #17: Get in and out as quickly as possible.

I'd sure blown that rule to hell.

I shook the thought out of my head, recalling Rule #25: Stay focused.

I put the crib sheet back in my pocket and poked the driver in the hat with the bass.

"Stop the bus, and you'll live. I give you my word."

I grinned.

Rule #241: Disarm them with a smile.

The driver hit the brakes, catapulting me forward. I bounced off the front window and into her back. The Sea Bass—my weapon—went flying, which broke Rule #98 and Rule #104 and possibly Rule #206.

Dazed, I sat up, watching as the driver shoved open the door and ran off, screaming.

I did a quick search for the Toothfish, but couldn't find it amid the soccer massacre. I'd have to leave it behind, a blatant disregard for Rule #47. Luckily, the fish had been wiped clean of prints (Rule #11) and was unregistered (Rule #12) so it wouldn't lead back to me.

Now for the driver.

I sprang from the bus and saw her beelining for Comiskey Park, where the White Sox played baseball. There was the usual activity around the stadium; fans, hotdog vendors, people selling programs, and no one seemed to pay any attention to me or the screaming fat lady.

The South Side of Chicago; where screaming fat ladies are commonplace.

Doubling my efforts, I managed to catch up with her just as she reached the ticket counter. I took a 1/10,000th scale replica of the Washington Monument out of my holster and pressed the pointy end to her back. She was about to become another sightseeing souvenir victim. But before I got ram the monolith home, the ticket attendant caught my eye from behind the thick bullet proof glass.

I had a hunch the glass was also souvenir proof, and I couldn't kill the bus driver with someone staring straight into my eyes, practically salivating to be a witness for the prosecution.

So I did the only thing I could in that situation. I whispered to the woman to keep quiet, and then smiled at the attendant.

"Two for the cheap seats," I said.

I paid, then walked arm in arm with the driver through the bustling crowd. The picture presented to me was disheartening. People were everywhere.

There was no private corner to drag the woman into. No secluded nooks. The bathrooms had lines out the door. Every square foot of space was crammed to capacity.

How do you kill a person in a crowded space without anyone seeing you?

I closed my eyes, trying to remember if this situation ever came up in the book. Rule #90? No, that had to do with airplanes. Rule #312? No, that was for killing a mark in a rain forest.

At times like this, I really wished I'd kept my job at the grocery store. Or bought that other book, "The Complete Amateur's Guide to Kidnapping and Extortion."

"Let me go or I'll scream," the bus driver said over the pipe organ music.

"If you scream, I'll kill you," I answered.

A classic stalemate. It happened to me once before, in the Har Dong peninsula, on the isle of Meenee Peepee, in the city of Tini Dik. I was at a hotel (I recall it being the Itsee Wang), and came upon a gorgeous Mossad agent named Desdemona, who I managed to manipulate by engaging in massive quantities of athletic sex with her. Later, when I sobered up, I realized I'd been duped. Rather than a beautiful double agent from Israel,

Desdemona had actually been just a large pile of dirty towels.

I had no idea what that had to do with anything, or how it could help me now.

No other options open, the bus driver and I made our way to the seats. They were in Section 542, way up in the nosebleed part of the stadium.

Even that section was full, fans packed shoulder to shoulder. We stepped on several toes and spilled a few beers wading through the crowd.

"These seats suck," said the bus driver.

I told her to shut up.

To keep her quiet, I decided to appeal to her inner overeater, and bought two red hots from a hawking vendor.

She took both of them.

Then we settled in to watch the game.

It was the bottom of the fifth, Sox down two runs.

I chose to make my move at the seventh inning stretch. By then, all of the drunken fans around us would get up to relieve their bladders, and I'd be able to off the bus driver and slip into the stream of moving bodies. Then I could...

The next thing I knew, the bus driver was shoving a hot dog with the works into my face, trying to blind me.

"Help!" she screamed, at the same time trying to get her big ass out of the stadium seat.

First one cheek popped free, then the other, and then her big butt was out and shaking in my face.

I wiped ketchup out of my eyes and looked around.

No one paid any attention to the bus driver. Someone behind us even yelled "Down in front!"

I stood and wrapped an arm around her fat shoulders, under the pretense of helping her back to her seat.

Then I jammed the souvenir monument into her throat. Hard. Six or seven times.

An eerie silence settled over the crowd. Then the stadium exploded in screams.

I looked onto the field, wondering if there had just been a spectacular play.

The game had stopped. Instead of baseball players, I saw myself on the Jumbotron monitor, forty feet high, the bloody Washington Monument in my hand.

Oops.

I did a quick scan of the ball park. Thirty, maybe thirty-five thousand people.

This was going to be tough.

I reached into my holster for the roll of fabric softener and the Perry Como LP, and got started.

Don't Press That Button!

A Practical Buyer's Guide to James Bond's Gadgets

Written for the essay collection James Bond in the 21st Century. I had a lot of fun with this, being a Bond fan for practically my whole life. Plus, it gave me the opportunity to simply string jokes together, rather than deal with a plot or characters.

If your first exposure to James Bond happened before the age of nine, you probably fell in love with the series for one reason: The Gadgets.

The women were hot, but you wouldn't care about that for a few more years. James Bond was tough and could fight, but so could those short guys on UHF's Samurai Saturday, and they had the added appeal of speaking without their lips matching their words. Global politics, espionage, and undercover infiltrations still aren't interesting, years later.

No, the thing that made your pre-pubescent brain scream with unrestrained joy was all the cool stuff Bond picked up in Q Section. You wanted the grappling hook pistol, and the pen filled with acid, and the laser watch, and the hand-held suction cups for climbing walls, and the wrist dart gun, and the rappelling cummerbund—even though you had no idea what a cummerbund was.

But now that you're all grown up, do the gadgets still have the same appeal? Do you still wish you could run to the nearest Wal-Mart and buy an electric razor that can deliver a close shave plus sweep your room for electronic listening devices?

This practical guide will look at some of best of Bond's gadgets, and offer valuable buying advice to those interested in plunking down their hard earned dollars for spy gear.

* * *

GADGET - False bottom briefcase which holds a magnetic mine, used by Bond in Octopussy.

USES - Protecting and transporting papers, blowing things up.

COOLNESS - Hidden compartments are always cool. So are mines.

REALITY - These already exist, in a wide variety of colors and payloads.

DO YOU WANT IT? - Yes you do. Think about how memorable your next corporate meeting will be if you're carrying one of these.

SAFETY TIP - Don't try to bring it through airport security.

* * *

GADGET - Snorkel that looks like a seagull, used by Bond in Goldfinger.

PRACTICAL USES - Fool your friends at the pool, see other seagulls up close, collect change from the bottom of public fountains.

COOLNESS - Uncool. The crocodile submarine in Octopussy has many more applications. In fact, so does simple SCUBA gear. Q Section was apparently hitting the NyQuil when they thought this up.

REALITY - Possible to manufacture, but tough to market, depending on where you put your lips.

DO YOU WANT IT? - Not really, except to amuse yourself while drinking too much.

HYGIENE TIP - Boil the bird after every use.

* * *

GADGET - Ski pole that fires a rocket, used in Octopussy.

USES - Improve your slalom time, blow up your friends, roast a chicken really fast.

COOLNESS - Very cool.

REALITY - Single use wouldn't be practical, it would be too heavy, and it might go off too soon (many men have this problem, and it's nothing to be embarrassed about.)

DO YOU WANT IT? - Yes, but you should be careful—tucking high explosives under your arm while speeding 70mph downhill isn't for anyone under the age of 14.

SAFETY TIP - Practice on the bunny slope before you take it down that black diamond run.

* * *

GADGET - Aston Martin DB5 sports car, used by Bond in Goldfinger and Thunderball.

USES - The ultimate road rage machine/babe magnet. Oil slick sprayer, smoke screens, tire slashing blades, machine guns, and an ejector seat for when your blind date turns out to be a bore.

COOLNESS - This is one pimped out ride.

REALITY - You could probably pay to have this car custom made, but it would cost a lot of money, and you wouldn't be allowed to drive it anywhere, except maybe in Texas.

DO YOU WANT IT? - Hell, yeah. Rush hour would never be the same.

BUYING TIP - At the dealer, don't be afraid to haggle. And don't get suckered into buying the undercarriage rust protection.

* * *

GADGET - Stick-on third nipple, used by Bond in The Man With The Golden Gun.

USES - For those many times in life when you just need a third nipple.

COOLNESS - At first glance, not very cool. But once you consider the possibilities, the coolness factor rises, much more so than the fake fingerprints Bond used in Diamonds Are Forever.

REALITY - Hollywood SPFX guys make these all the time, and you can too with some plaster for an impression cast, and some foam latex.

HINT: Shave your chest first.

DO YOU WANT IT? - Yes. Put them on sofas, on jewelry, on windows, on fruit, and all over yourself before that visit to the public pool.

SAFETY TIP - Don't use super glue.

* * *

GADGET - Little Nellie portable gyrocopter with rocket launchers, machine guns, flamethrower, and heat seeking-missiles. Used by Bond in You Only Live Twice.

USES - Fly around, impress the ladies, drop stuff on people.

COOLNESS - Uber-cool. Smaller than a helicopter. Not nearly as expensive to use as the Bell-Trexton rocket pack Bond used in Thunderball, but with a lot more firepower.

REALITY - Available on Ebay for under 20k, but without the weaponry. (Weaponry is available separately on Ebay.)

DO YOU WANT IT? - Of course you want it. Just think about all the stuff you could drop on people.

TIP - From three hundred feet, a small honeydew melon can cripple a man.

* * *

GADGET - Wrist watch with plastic explosive and detonator, used by Bond in Moonraker.

USES - Blow stuff up, threaten to blow stuff up.

COOLNESS - Cool. Blowing stuff up never gets old.

REALITY - Possible, and cheap to make. But you'd have to buy refills all the time. They always get you on the refills.

DO YOU WANT IT? - Yes. Excuse me, what time is it? It's time to blow stuff up! Let's start with that stupid seagull snorkel.

SAFETY TIP - Don't play with all the dials until you've read the instructions.

* * *

GADGET - Keys that open 90% of the world's locks, used by Bond in The Living Daylights.

USES - Unlimited. Steal cars. Rob banks. Take the change from parking meters. Shop after hours. And never pay for a vending machine again.

COOLNESS - Opening stuff up: Cool. Walking around like a janitor with a big key ring: Uncool.

REALITY - Master keys exist, and can be found on the Internet. So can lock picks. So can lawyers, which you'll need after you get caught opening up other people's locks.

DO YOU WANT IT? - No. You'd probably just lose them.

SAFETY TIP - Don't keep these in your back pocket while ice skating. Or your front pocket.

* * *

GADGET - Surfboard with concealed explosives, combat knife, and mini computer, used by Bond in Die Another Day.

USES - Hang ten, then kill seven.

COOLNESS - Super cool. You can shred that gnarly barrel, and at the same time Google what the hell that means.

REALITY - It's possible to produce, but be careful you don't wax your mini-computer.

DO YOU WANT IT? - Of course. But instead of weapons and electronics, you can fill your board with soda and snacks (that you got for free at the vending machine.)

SAFETY TIP - Make sure the combat knife is properly secured before you hit the waves, or you'll be hanging nine.

* * *

GADGET - X-Ray eyeglasses, used by Bond in The World Is Not Enough.

USES - Seeing though things like playing cards, safes, walls, doors, and clothing (to look for concealed weapons and stick-on third nipples.)

COOLNESS - Perhaps Bond's coolest gadget. It would sure make everyday life a lot more interesting.

REALITY - If you ever sent away for a pair of these in the back of a comic book, you know they don't work, but what did you expect for $2.95? Your mother told you they wouldn't work, didn't she? Real versions may exist, but they probably cost big bucks. And cause cancer.

DO YOU WANT IT? - Sure you do. Just don't take them to family reunions. Or retirement homes.

COMFORT TIP - Wear baggy pants.

* * *

GADGET - Underwater manta ray cloak, used by Bond in License To Kill.

USES - Pretend you're a manta ray, get close to other manta rays, get sexually assaulted by a manta ray.

COOLNESS - Not cool, unless you have a secret thing for manta rays.

REALITY - Can be made in real life, but for God's sake why?

DO YOU WANT IT? - Only if you're really lonely. You might also consider getting the seagull snorkel as well, and you can pretend you're a ray chasing a seagull. You can play that one for hours and hours.

BUYING TIP - If you spend more than $30 for this, you're a real moron.

* * *

GADGET - Lotus Esprit sports car that turns into a submarine, complete with mines, missiles, underwater ink jets, and self-destruct mechanism, that Bond used in The Spy Who Loved Me and Moonraker.

USES - Never take the ferry again, drive into swimming pool to fetch the quarters Grandpa throws in there.

COOLNESS - A hot car, and a hot submersible, all in one. Plus rockets.

REALITY - Boat cars do exist in real life, but they're actually dorky looking, and driven by people who can't get dates.

DO YOU WANT IT? - You know you do. But when purchasing options, go for an Alpine stereo and Bose speakers instead of a self-destruct button—it's more practical.

UNDERWATER TIP – If you drive over a starfish and cut it in half, it will grow into two new starfishes, both of them very pissed off at you.

* * *

GADGET - Dinner jacket which turns into a black sniper's outfit, used by Bond in The Living Daylights.

USES - When black tie events become boring.

COOLNESS - Cooler than the light blue tux with the ruffle shirt which turns into an adult diaper, but not by much.

REALITY - They already have these for rent at Gingiss. You'll need two forms of ID, and there's a mandatory 14 day waiting period.

DO YOU WANT IT? - You don't want to admit it, but yes you do. But then, you never had much taste in clothing.

FASHION TIP - Belts are okay, but the trendy sniper prefers suspenders.

* * *

GADGET - Cigarette lighter grenade, used by Bond in Tomorrow Never Dies.

USES - No smoking means no smoking.

COOLNESS - Anything that blows up is cool (see plastic explosive watch.)

REALITY - You can put explosives into anything; lighters, bottles, cans, small animals, etc.

DO YOU WANT IT? - Absolutely. Think about taking it to a heavy metal concert when the power ballad is playing.

SAFETY TIP - Don't get it confused with your real lighter because you might accidentally throw your real lighter at the bad guys and they'll say, "Why'd you throw a lighter at us, stupid? Are we supposed to be scared?" Also, you might blow your face off.

* * *

GADGET - Piton gun with retractable wire, used by Bond in Diamonds Are Forever and Goldeneye.

USES – Climb up buildings and rock faces, retrieve the remote control without getting up from the couch.

COOLNESS - Climbing, swinging, and shooting things are all cool.

REALITY - Wouldn't actually be strong enough to hold a man's weight, but you could have fun letting your buddies try it out.

DO YOU WANT IT? - Yes. It's like being Spiderman, but without the webby discharge.

SAFETY TIP - Don't point it at your own face, or at family members, unless you're trying to climb them.

* * *

GADGET - Exploding talcum powder tear gas, used by Bond in From Russia With Love.

USES - Personal hygiene, making enemies cry.

COOLNESS - Talc isn't very cool. Neither is tear gas. But it does explode, which counts for something.

REALITY - It might already exist. It might not. Who cares?

DO YOU WANT IT? - No. You make your significant other cry all the time without gas, and no one uses talc anymore.

SAFETY TIP - Wear a gas mask before applying to your underarms.

* * *

GADGET - Magnetic watch with circular saw, used by Bond in Live And Let Die.

USES - Cutting through rope tied around your wrists, finding screws you dropped on the carpeting.

COOLNESS - Having your watch face spin around really fast is cool. Cutting off your own hand at the wrist is uncool.

REALITY - Buy a chainsaw that tells time instead. It's cheaper and more effective.

DO YOU WANT IT? - No. If you want a cool Bond timepiece, get the plastic explosive watch. Or the laser bean watch from Tomorrow Never Dies. Or the grappling hook watch from The World Is Not Enough. Or the ticker tape message watch from The Spy Who Loved Me. Or the digital radio watch from For Your Eyes Only. Or even the Geiger counter watch from Thunderball—you can't have too many Geiger counters around the house.

SAFETY TIP - Careful you don't lose any fingers when you reset for different time zones.

* * *

Remember: You're never too old to play with toys. Especially explosive, potentially deadly, extremely expensive toys. Just think about how envious your friends and family will be when they see you driving around in your sporty new BMW 750 iL with the electrified door handles, bulletproof glass, re-inflating tires, and rear nail ejectors.

Go ahead. Think about it. Because that's as close as you'll ever get to owning one, spy-boy.

Now go boil your seagull snorkel—that thing is riddled with germs.

Piranha Pool

A story about being a writer. It's humorous, but there is a lot of truth behind the jokes.

"What do you think?"

I was a cup, waiting to be filled with praise. Instead I got silence. She sat there, my pages in her hands, staring at a point over my shoulder.

"How about that ending?" I prodded. "Weren't your surprised?"

Miranda clucked her tongue. "I guessed the ending."

"You did?"

"Yeah. And I really don't think you need the first few paragraphs."

"Hold on a sec." I motioned time-out with my hands. "The first paragraphs set the scene."

"Sorry—I didn't think you needed them."

I looked away, then back at her. My friend, wife, companion for eight years.

"Did you like anything?"

"Joe, you're a wonderful writer. But this story—I think you were just trying too hard." She brightened. "I thought the middle part was funny."

My eyes narrowed. "When the character died?"

"Yeah. It was cute how you did that."

"That wasn't supposed to be funny."

"Oh."

There was a ticking sound. The hands of my watch. Miranda tried on a smile.

"I like the title."

Great. I remembered how much I loved her, and somehow found the strength to thank her for her opinion. Just because we were man and wife didn't mean we had to agree on everything.

This particular piece didn't speak to her, but that was probably a matter of taste. I was certain that others would view it differently.

* * *

"It stinks."

"Excuse me?"

Gerald pinched his nostrils closed. "The story stinks, Joe. Sorry, but it isn't your best."

"What about the surprise ending?"

"Saw it coming."

"You did?"

"It was obvious."

I took the story from my brother's hands and paid too much attention to lining up the sheets of paper.

"You probably guessed it because you know me too well."

"I guessed it because it was cliché. The middle part was kind of funny, though. What did Miranda think of it?"

"She loved it."

"Well, there you go. My opinion probably means nothing, then. I liked that other story you did. The one about the otters."

"I wrote that in second grade."

"Yeah, that was a good one."

I looked at my bare wrist. "Damn, I gotta run, Gerald. Thanks for the input."

"It's a good title, Joe. Maybe you can write a different story using the same title."

* * *

"Wow. Great story."

"You liked it?"

"Loved it."

The relief was better than a foot massage.

"How about the ending?"

"Terrific."

"What was your favorite part?"

My mother's smile faltered for a split second. "Oh—there were so many."

Mr. Dubious took over my body. "Mom...?"

"The middle part. I have to say that was my favorite. Very funny."

So much for my relief.

"You thought the death scene was funny?"

Caught in the lie, her demeanor cracked.

"No, not that. But there were some other funny parts."

"What parts were funny, Mom?"

"Well...you had some pretty funny typos."

I rubbed my eyes. "Did you like anything?"

"Joe, I'm your mother. Everything you do is precious to me."

"How about the title?"

Mom shook her head sadly.

"Not even the title?"

"Joe, I'm not a good judge of fiction. You should ask your wife or your brother. I'm sure they'll love it.

* * *

"Poopy."

I stared at my four-year-old, a child who is captivated by his own toes.

"Why is it poopy?"

"You should have Spider Man in it."

"I don't want Spider Man in it."

My son looked at me, serious. "Spider Man can climb walls."

"I know he can. But let's talk about Daddy's story. Did you think it was sad when the character died?"

"Does Spider Man tie people up and suck their blood?"

"What?"

"Spiders tie up bugs and suck their blood."

I sighed and looked at Fluffy, the family cat.

Why the hell not?

* * *

"Fluffy, dammit, get back in this house!"

But the feline had beat a retreat only two pages into the narrative. Gone to tree, sitting ten feet out of reach in the crook of an elm branch.

"I'm serious, Fluffy."

He stared back down at me with indifferent eyes and then began to groom.

"Fine. Count the days until you get tuna again, cat."

I smoothed out the wrinkled edges of the manuscript and went back to my desk.

A few clicks of the mouse later and I was online. Surely Usenet had fiction forums. Without too much difficulty, I located an amateur fiction newsgroup and posted my tome proudly. Let the compliments commence...

* * *

"Joe? What is that sticking out of out computer monitor? Is that a hammer?"

"It slipped."

"You attacked the computer with a hammer? What were you thinking?"

I gave Miranda malice wrapped in a fake grin. "I don't want to talk about it, honey. It's still under warranty."

"I don't think a hammer in the screen is covered by the warranty."

"Miranda..."

"What's wrong with you? Does this have anything to do with that stupid story?"

I stood up, deaf. The story was clenched in my left hand. "I'm going out. I'll be back later."

* * *

"So, what did you think?"

The wino held out a filthy hand. "Do I get my five dollars now?"

"First you have to tell me if you liked it."

He brought the paper bag to his lips, took a pull off the unseen bottle.

"It was..."

"Yes?"

"It was wonderful."

His eyes went dreamy, beatific.

I beamed. "Wonderful?"

He hic-cupped. "The loveliest thing I ever heard."

Who would have thought it? I didn't normally endow people who smelled like urine with good taste, but here was an obvious exception.

"What was your favorite part?"

"The chicken."

I stared at my pages, confused.

"Chicken? There's no chicken in this story."

"I ate chicken in Cleveland. Cooked so tender, it fell off the bone. You gonna give me my five bucks?"

Great—he was a lunatic. You can't get an honest opinion from a lunatic. I turned to walk away.

He grabbed my arm. "Man, you owe me five bucks! I stood here listening to that garbage, I want my money!"

I decided, right then, that I'd rather be disemboweled than give this guy five bucks.

I pulled free and hit the street in a sprint. Shouldn't take long to lose him. He was drunk and disheveled and—

"Gimme my damn money!"

—right behind me. For a guy wearing at least four layers of clothing, he could run like the wind. I cut through an alley and hurdled a cluster of garbage cans.

"I listened to that whole crappy story!"

The bum was closing in. I could hear his mismatched shoes slapping the pavement only a few steps back. Just my luck—I'd given a reading to an Olympic sprinter fallen on hard times.

Another turn, between two apartments, into the back parking lot. Dead end.

"Gotcha." The bum grinned, gray teeth winking through a scraggly beard. He gestured with his hand—give it to me.

I sucked in air and nodded submission, my hand producing my wallet.

He shook his head. "All of it."

"You said five bucks."

"I'm gonna need a month's worth of booze, to get that lousy story out of my head."

I left the parking lot forty bucks lighter.

* * *

I stared at the page. My story. My child. Why couldn't anyone else see the symbolism? The imagery? This story was perfect! From first word to last, a marvel of narrative genius! What the hell was wrong with the world, was it—

Hmm. Actually, I could probably change this part, here, to make it stronger. And this sentence could be tightened. And perhaps that paragraph is a bit wordy. Where's my pencil?

* * *

"Wow, Joe. It doesn't even seem like the same story."

I grinned at my wife. "I took everyone's suggestions into account, and did a little self-editing."

"A little? You practically changed every line. Even the characters are different."

"I kept the title, though."

Miranda nodded, handing back the papers. I could see her searching her thoughts for the right compliment.

I gave her some help. "So it's tighter?"

"Oh, yes. Much tighter."

"Is the death still funny?"

"Not funny at all. Very somber."

I sighed, letting out the tension. "So it's a lot better."

Miranda winced. "Actually, I thought the other version was better."

* * *

"See that?" I held my painting in front of my son, keeping it out of reach because the acrylic hadn't dried it. "Daddy made a picture of Spider Man."

My son squinted at my artwork. "It's poopy."

* * *

"Joe, you've been staring inside the fridge for ten minutes."

"I want to make a sandwich," I told my wife.

"What are you waiting for?"

"I doubt my ability."

"Joe—it's a slice of ham and two pieces of bread."

I frowned. "I'm having some competency issues."

"Didn't Darren like your cow painting?"

"That wasn't a cow. It was Spider Man."

Miranda rubbed my back. "Go sit down, honey. I'll make you a sandwich."

* * *

"Miranda! Come here! What is this?"

She stared at the kitchen table.

"It looks like you've made a big letter A out of pretzel sticks."

"Damn right!"

"Joe—are you okay?"

"I'm fine. Want to see me make a B?"

"I'm calling Dr. Hubbard."

* * *

"Many people have feelings of inadequacy. It's natural."

The shrink was old, bespeckled. His gray goatee pointed at me when he talked.

"This is more than inadequacy, Doc. I'm questioning every move I make. I feel totally incompetent."

"All because of one little story?"

"That's how it started."

"May I see it?"

Without getting up off the couch I pulled the crumpled story out of my pants pocket and handed it over. As he read, I could feel body go numb. Ice cold, unfeeling. One more heartless comment couldn't hurt me. I was immune to criticism.

"This is pretty good."

I sat up and spun towards him. "Excuse me?"

He held up a finger, still reading. When he finished the last page, he handed back the story and smiled.

"I liked it."

"Really?"

"Yes. Really."

"You aren't just saying that because I'm paying you three hundred dollars an hour?"

"Really, Joe. I thought it was a nice, touching story. Good structure. Well-defined characters. Interesting subtext. I'd actually like to have a copy to pass around the office."

I sprang to my feet, my blood replaced by helium. "Well, sure, no problem, you can have this copy, absolutely, it's all yours."

"Would you sign it for me?"

Were there clouds above nine?

"Of course. Here, I'll borrow your pen."

"You know," Doc Hubbard said as I scrawled my name on the top margin, "I'm a bit of a writer myself."

"Really?" I added 'To Doc' above my name, and then underlined it.

"Perhaps you'd like to read one of my stories?"

"Sure," I told him, drawing a large circle around my signature. "Be happy to help you with it."

Doc grinned, then opened up his desk drawer. He held out some paper. "Go ahead. Off the clock."

I smiled and accepted his story, pleased to be valued for my opinion.

It was bad. Real bad.

"So? What did you think?"

"Well, Doc, it's interesting."

"Yes. Yes. Go on."

"Um, very few typos."

His grin lost some wattage.

"How about the ending?"

"Actually, I, uh, saw it coming."

The grin was gone now.

"Should have figured," he mumbled.

"What was that?"

"How can you recognize talent, when you have none yourself?"

"But you said..."

"I lied. I said it for three hundos and hour. I've read aspirin bottles with more entertainment value than your stupid story."

"How can you..."

"I'm sorry," Doc Hubbard offered a placid smile. "Our time is up."

* * *

"Joe?"

"Hmm?"

"Were you ever planning on going back to work?"

I glanced at Miranda and scratched at my stubble. "I haven't given it much thought."

"You've been lying in bed for three weeks."

"Hmm."

"Work called. I told them you were still sick. They want a doctor's note, or you're going to be fired."

"Bummer."

Miranda's eyes went teary, and she walked off.

* * *

"We're leaving."

I stared at my wife and son over the pile of cellophane wrappers cluttering my bed.

"Leaving where?"

"Leaving you, Joe. You're not the man I married. I've been talking to a lawyer."

She handed me a sheaf of papers. The word DIVORCE was on the header. I gave them a token look-through.

"This is terrible," I concluded. "Poor sentence structure, too much legalese, look at this typo..."

But they were already gone.

* * *

My story was in front of me, on the table, next to a picture of my family.

I was done dwelling. I'd had enough.

The gun went into my mouth and I pulled the trigger, my last sensation a tremendous BOOM coupled with a sense of perfect relief.

* * *

The pitchfork jabbed me in the ass.

"Hey!"

"Keep moving."

I stared out across the inferno, Satan's minions tormenting the damned as they slaved away.

"This room is for rapists. Any rapists in the group?"

Two guys in line with me raised their hands. The devil opened the door for them, and they were seized by a huge goat-like creature and thrust into a cauldron of boiling oil.

"Next room, adulterers."

Four more of my group went in. I winced when the whips began to swing.

"Bad writers. This room here, bad writers."

No one moved.

"That's you, Joe."

I was prodded in, my bowels jelly. But rather than hideous tortures, I found myself in a large classroom, stretching back as far as I could see. People of all races, creeds, and dress sat at undersized desks, rows and rows going off into infinity.

"Hello, Joe." The teacher had a pig snout and tusks, her hair done up in a bun and her pointy tail raised behind her like a question mark.

"What is all this?"

"This is eternity, Joe. Who would like to critique Joe's story first?"

Three million hands went up.

"Who are these people?" I asked.

"Murderers. As punishment for their sins, they were forced to listen to your story. Several times, in fact."

"My story is their torture?"

"Well, I have read it aloud several times. There used to be twice as many people in the room, but a few million elected to go to the boiling oil chamber rather than hear it again."

I shut my eyes. When I opened them, I was still there.

"And I have to listen to their opinions for eternity?"

"Every thirty years you get a one week vacation in the piranha pool."

The teacher made me stand in front of the classroom, and the critiques began.

I counted the days until the piranha pool.

A Newbie's Guide to Thrillerfest

Written for a special edition of the magazine Crimespree, which was given away for free at the first Thrillerfest convention. A variation on this essay also appeared in a special Love Is Murder issue for that conference, using different names and tweaking some of the jokes.

Every year there are dozens of writing conferences. If you're a fan of mysteries and thrillers, 2006 brings you Love is Murder in Chicago, Sleuthfest in Ft. Lauderdale, Bouchercon in Madison, Left Coast Crime in Bristol, Men of Mystery in Los Angeles, Magna Cum Murder in Muncie, and a slew of others, many of which suck.

The best conference of them all is undoubtedly Thrillerfest, presented by the International Thriller Writers. In one short year, the upstart ITW has grown to become the writing organization with the longest website URL: www.internationalthrillerwriters.org.

What can you expect when you attend Thrillerfest? How can you make sure you get your money's worth? Will you have a chance to corner ITW Co-President David Morrell and ask him to blurb your new manuscript, The Speech Impediment Murderererererer? (Answer: Yes. Uncle Davy loves this. The best time to approach him is while he's eating, or in the bathroom.)

Reading and memorizing this carefully compiled article will fully prepare you for anything this conference has to offer. It might even save your life.

REGISTRATION - If possible, buy your conference pass in advance. Bring proof of your registration to the event (a Paypal receipt, a copy of the letter saying you've been confirmed, your hard drive) because there's a 90% chance your registration was lost, and the people running the conference will have no idea who you are. A much easier, and cheaper, tactic is to simply buy a nametag and a black marker. Stick it on your chest when no one is looking, and you're in.

THE HOTEL - If possible, stay at the hotel. After the days' events are through, there are always exclusive parties where you can get free food and drink and meet cool people. You won't get invited to these parties, but you can hang out in the hallway with your ear to the door, and listen to JA Konrath make a fool of himself. Actually, you probably won't need to put your ear to the door to hear that. JA's pretty loud.

WHAT TO WEAR - The fashionable conference-goer wears business casual. Comfortable shoes are a must, because you'll be walking a lot. A book bag is a great accessory. Not only can it hold books, but also an emergency fifth of vodka (do you really want to pay $9 for a martini at the hotel bar?)

AUTHOR SIGHTING - Imagine it: You're in the lobby, putting the cap back on your vodka, and suddenly James Rollins appears out of nowhere. Do you just run up to him, squealing like a schoolgirl, and beg him to sign your paperback copy of Map of Bones that you've read 36 times, the last time aloud to your pet parakeet that you named Sigma?

The answer: NO! Jim is a bigshot author, and they all hate signing paperbacks. Go to the bookroom and buy a hardcover first edition. When you approach him, make sure it's on your hands and knees, because you are not worthy. Address him as "Mr. Rollins" or "Sir" or "Your Highness." And NEVER make direct eye contact. He's far too important to look at you.

In contrast, if you spot James O. Born, feel free to bring him your paperback ex-library copy of Shock Wave. Born will be thrilled to sign that. He'll also sign other authors' books, cocktail napkins, food products, and basically anything but the check.

PANELS - If you're an author, you need to speak on a panel. But it's too late to sign up for one now, bonehead. They've already printed the programs. If you are on a panel, there's only one important rule to follow: Make sure you're on a panel with Barry Eisler. Barry is the one with the gaggle of drooling women following him around, hoping he'll suddenly keel over so they'll get to administer CPR. Don't expect anyone to remember a single thing you've said when you're on a panel with Barry, but at least you'll be speaking to a packed room.

FOOD - Conference food is usually barely edible, but it's expensive to compensate. That's why all of the popular authors usually go out to eat at the trendiest restaurant in the area. It's very easy to get invited to one of these exciting outings, where industry gossips flows fast and loose, and Barry often takes his shirt off and dances the lambada—the dance of love. If you want to go along, all you have to do is write a NYT Bestseller. If you haven't done that, then you're stuck with the hotel food. Be sure to try the potato salad. Is that potato salad? It might be rice pudding. Or lamb. Or a big dish of pus.

ITINERARY - There are many things to see at a conference, and often you'll be tortured by the dilemma of two good panels happening at the same time, with no clue which to attend. The answer is easy. Attend both of them. Authors love seeing scores of people leave the room while they are talking—they believe they're being so effective, the crowd is rushing out to buy their book. Try to do this five or six times per hour, and make sure you open and close the doors loudly. Also, take that extra time between panels to talk on your cell phone. If your conversation carries on into the panel room—it's okay. His Majesty Rollins will forgive you.

WHERE ARE THE AUTHORS? - You've been trying desperately to get F. Paul Wilson's autograph, but he's been missing in action for two days. Where is he? He's in the hotel bar. In fact, all of the authors are in the hotel bar. If you want to chat in depth with your favorite thriller writer, arrive early while they're still coherent. In Paul's case, I challenge you to figure out when that it.

THE BOOKROOM - This is the most important room in the whole conference. Here, you'll find all of the books by all of the authors in attendance, expect for the one book you truly want to buy. They'll be out of that one. But don't worry, there will be plenty of pristine, unsold, unread copies of Bloody Mary by JA Konrath. Plenty of them.

BARGAIN HUNTER TIP - All the paperbacks in the bookroom are free if you simply rip off the cover beforehand! Don't be bashful—the booksellers love it!

ETIQUETTE - It's during one of the delicious buffet-style meals. You've got your plate piled high with something that might be meat in gravy, or it might be a cobbler, and you're searching for a place to eat. While walking around the room, you see an empty chair between Tess Gerritsen and ITW Co-President Gayle Lynds. Do you dare ask to sit there? In a word, NO! They are huge mega bestsellers and that seat belongs to someone a lot more important than you are. Go sit by Jon and Ruth Jordan, who publish this magazine. Always plenty of chairs around them. The surrounding tables are usually free too.

PAID ADVERTISEMENT – Buy the anthology Thriller – Stories To Keep You Up All Night, an ITW collection featuring stories by superstar mega-bestselling authors such as JA Konrath, and others.

ATTENDEES - Conferences are a great place to meet new people who share common interests. They're also a great place to get abducted by some weirdo and killed with a blowtorch. Wise convention goers avoid talking to anyone else, at all times. Try to keep some kind of weapon on you. They sell $59 letter openers in the hotel gift shop, right next to the $42 tee shirts and the $12 bottled water. If you're an author, save the receipt—it's deductible.

Or try carrying around a plate piled high with that stuff they served at lunch—the stuff in the gravy. That way, if someone tries to assault you, you can say, "Stop it! I'm eating!"

AWARDS - At most conferences, the writers like to congratulate themselves by giving each other awards. They usually do this over a nine course meal that takes eleven hours, and a cash bar that charges so much for a Budweiser you'll need to put it on lay-away. In an effort to distinguish itself from the many other conventions and organizations that do this sort of thing, the ITW decided to do this as well.

The star-studded gala begins at 7pm on Saturday, and ends sometime on Thursday morning. When the event has concluded, be sure to congratulate the lucky winners. It's also a lot of fun to go up to the losers and congratulate them for winning, and then pretend to be confused when they tell you they've actually lost. Do this two or three times to the same loser. They'll start to find it funny, eventually.

SIGNINGS – There will be many scheduled signing times, where dozens of authors all sit in the same room and greet the hundreds of fans waiting in line for Lee Child. If you're in Lee's very long line, remember that to keep things moving quickly you aren't allowed to say more than two words to him, and he'll only have time to sign an "L." A lower case "L." Lee's a very busy man.

Lee Goldberg, on the other hand, will have plenty of time to sign his full name. Plenty of time. If you so desire, he'll even sign it using the time-intensive, hand-lettered art of calligraphy. Don't be afraid to ask. He has plenty of time.

SUNDAY – This is the day where everyone sleeps in and/or catches their flight home, and panel attendance is traditionally low. By some dramatic conference oversight, 9am on Sunday is when JA Konrath has his scheduled panel. He's not sure how this happened. Perhaps he pissed someone off somehow, unlikely as that may sound. But he urges you to attend this panel, on the super-exciting topic of writing for female characters. Never saw that hot-button topic at a convention before, have you? There will be some other high caliber authors on this panel, probably, and JA is bringing some butterscotch schnapps to put in the audience's coffee. Get your lazy butt out of bed and be there. He'll be entertaining. Promise.

CONCLUSION - Remember, if you want to have a memorable conference, responsibility rests squarely on one person's shoulders—the person running the conference. Be sure to complain about every little thing, at any given time, even if it's something they can't fix such as, "The carpet is too soft" or "F. Paul Wilson touched me inappropriately" or "I hear voices in my head." Demand a refund. Threaten to contact an attorney. And above all, remember to have fun.

Inspector Oxnard

A humorous take on the many detectives in crime fiction who are able to glance at a crime scene and brilliantly deduce everything that happened. I wrote this for an anthology, but they rejected it. Too Monty Python-ish, they said.

Special Investigations Inspector J. Gerald Oxnard arrives on the scene moments after the crime has been committed. The usual entourage of detectives from the SI Division of New Bastwick's Police Department accompanies him.

I'm the newly appointed member of this crack investigating team, a reward for my exemplary grades at the Police Academy. It's just my luck that my first case is a murder.

The portly Inspector kneels beside the cooling body of a man in his late twenties. After several minutes of intense scrutiny, he nods and clears his throat, prompting one of the nearby detectives to help him to his feet.

"He was killed by a lion," Inspector Oxnard says. "I'm thoroughly convinced."

The room absorbs the declaration, mulling and silent.

"But...Inspector," I say, "How did a lion get up to Room 715 of the

Vandenburg Hotel without anyone seeing it?"

Inspector Oxnard puts a thin and elegantly manicured hand up to his mustache and rolls the waxy end.

"A disguise," he says.

"A disguise?" I ask.

"Of course. Perhaps a long overcoat and some dark glasses. Haven't you ever seen a lion walk on his hind legs at the circus?"

Several of the detectives standing around sound their approval. One writes it down in his note pad.

"But what about the knife?" I ask.

"The knife?" Inspector Oxnard shoots back, eyes sharp and accusing.

"In the deceased's back." I say.

There's a moment of chin-scratching silence.

"Don't lions have an opposable thumb?" Detective Jenkins asks.

"No, you're thinking of monkeys," Detective Coursey says.

"But isn't a lion kind of like a big orange monkey with sharp teeth?" Detective Rumstead asks.

There are several nods of agreement. Inspector Oxnard runs a hand through his gray hair, which is slicked back with mint-smelling gel, and wipes his palm on Detective Coursey's blazer.

"It had to be a lion with a knife," the Inspector says, "wearing an overcoat and dark glasses. Put out an All Points Bulletin, and check to see if a circus is in town."

"But Inspector," I say, "there's no sign of forced entry. How did the lion get into the room?"

"Simple. He had a key."

"Why would he have a key?" I ask.

The silence that follows is steeped in apprehension. After a full minute, Inspector Oxnard makes a self-satisfied yelping sound and thrusts his finger skyward in apparent revelation, poking Detective Graves in the eye.

"The deceased was having an affair with the lion! Thus, the lion had a duplicate key!"

Excited applause sweeps through the group. Inspector Oxnard draws on his pipe, but it does little good because the bowl is upside down, the tobacco speckling his shoes.

"Did the lion prefer the company of men?" Detective Struber says.

"Perhaps," Inspector Oxnard says. "Or perhaps it was...a lioness!"

Several 'ahs' are heard. Someone pipes in, "Of course! The lioness is the one that does the hunting!"

"But what about motive?" I ask, my Police Academy training coming out. "What was the motive?"

"Hunger," the Inspector says. He nods smartly to himself.

"But the body is intact."

"Excuse me?"

"None of it has been eaten!" I say.

"That makes no difference. Maybe the lioness was scared away before she could finish, or perhaps she simply lost her appetite."

"I sometimes have terrible gas, and can't eat at all," Detective Gilbert says.

Nods of acquiescence all around, and several discussions of gas pains ensue.

"But where are the paw prints?" someone shrieks. "Where is the fur? Where is the spoor? Where is the damn reason that this was done by a lion and not a human being?"

Everyone stares at me, and I realize I've been the one shrieking.

Inspector Oxnard frowns and gives me a patronizing pat on the head.

"I know you're only a novice, so I can understand why you cannot grasp all of the subtle intricacies of a murder investigation. But in time, Detective Cornhead, you'll begin to catch on."

"My name is Richards, Inspector. Detective Richards."

"Nothing to be ashamed of." Inspector Oxnard slaps my shoulder. "We were all young once."

Detective Oldendorff runs through the door and trips over the body. He picks himself up, urgency overriding embarrassment.

"There's been another robbery!" he says. "The First New Bastwick Bank!"

Inspector Oxnard thrusts out his lower lip and nods.

"It sounds like that blind panda has struck again. Come, gentlemen!"

Inspector Oxnard gracefully exits the room, his entourage filing behind him like ducklings. I stare at the body for a moment, and then follow.

This police work is a lot harder than I thought.

ONE NIgHT ONLy

A farce, very much in James Thurber territory. I've always want to write a straight humor novel, but there isn't any market for it.

Frank stood beneath the mismatched letters on the marquee and frowned.

ONE NIgHT ONLy, it proclaimed.

That was still one night too many.

Ahead of him in line, another poor dope with an equally unhappy face was being tugged towards the ticket booth by his significant other.

"He's supposed to be brilliant. Like Marcel Marceau, only he talks," the wife/girlfriend was saying.

The man was having none of it, and neither was Frank. He stared at his own pack leader, his wife Wendy, mushing him forward on the Forced Culture Iditarod. She noted his frown and hugged his arm.

"Stop moping. It'll be fun."

"It's the playoffs."

"It's our anniversary."

"We have another one next year."

Wendy gave him The Look, and he backed down. He glanced at his

Seiko, wishing he had a watch like Elroy on The Jetsons, with a mini TV screen. It was ten after nine. Halftime would be almost over, and it was the pivotal fifth game in the Eastern Conference Finals, the score tied 48-48.

Frank had managed to catch the other four pivotal games, but this one was really pivotal. If the Bulls won, it meant there would only be seven more pivotal games left in the playoffs.

They reached the ticket counter, and Frank noted several divots in the thick glass. Probably made by some other poor bastard forced here by his wife. Tried to shoot his way out, Frank guessed.

He could relate.

His mind wrapped around the fantasy of pulling out an M-16 and taking hostages to avoid seeing the show, but he lost the image when he noted how many twenty dollar bills his wife was setting in the money tray.

"This costs how much?!?"

"It's an exclusive engagement," the cashier said. "Alexandro Mulchahey is only in town for one night."

"And what does he do for this kind of money? Take the whole audience out for dinner in his Rolls Royce?"

Wendy gave him The Elbow. But Frank wasn't finished yet.

"Maybe you folks will finally be able to afford some more capital letters for the marquee."

Now Frank received The Love Handle Pinch; Wendy's fingernails dug into his flab and twisted. He yelped and his wife tugged him aside.

"You're embarrassing me," she said through a forced smile.

"I'm having chest pains. Do you know how many Bulls tickets we could have bought with all that money?"

"If you don't start pretending to have a good time, I'm going to invite GrandMama over for the weekend."

He clammed up. Wendy's grandmother was 160 years old and mean as spit. Her mind had made its grand exit sometime during the Reagan years, and she labored under the delusion that Frank was Rudolph Hess. The last time she visited, GrandMama called the police seven times and demanded they arrest Frank for crimes against humanity.

Plus, she smelled like pee.

Wendy led him into the lobby, and began to point out architecture.

"Ooo, look at the columns."

"Ooo, look at the vaulted ceiling."

"Ooo, look at the mosaic tile. Have you ever seen anything so intricate?"

"Yeah, yeah. Beautiful."

The theater was nice, but it was no Circus Circus. While his wife gaped at the carved railing on the grand staircase, Frank's attention was captivated by a little boy sitting alone near the coat check.

The boy had a Sony Watchman.

"Did you want a drink, dear?"

Wendy smiled at him. "A glass of wine would be wonderful."

Frank got in line—a line that would take him right past the little boy and his portable TV. He made sure Wendy was preoccupied staring at a poster before he made his move.

"Hey, kid! Nice TV. Can you turn on the Bulls Game real fast? Channel 9."

The kid looked up at him, squinting through thick glasses.

"I don't like the Bulls."

"Come on, I just want to check the score." Frank winked, then fished five bucks out of his pocket. "I'll give you five bucks."

"Mom!" The child's voice cut through the lobby like a siren. "An old fat man wants to steal my TV!"

Frank turned away, shielding his face. The bartender gave him the evil eye.

“Merlot,” Frank said, throwing down the five.

The bartender raised an eyebrow and told him the price of the wine.

“It’s how much?!?”

“Frank, dear...” Wendy was tugging at him as he pulled out more money.

“Hold on, hon. I think I just bought you the last Merlot on earth.” Frank watched the bartender pour. “And it’s in a plastic cup.”

“I want to get a program.”

Frank’s wife led him past the little boy, who held up his Watchman and stuck out his tongue. The little snot was watching the Bulls. Frank squinted but couldn’t make out the score.

They got in line for the programs and Frank momentarily forgot about basketball when he saw the prices.

“For a program?!? Don’t they come free with the show?”

“That’s a Playbill, Frank.”

“What’s the difference?”

The difference, apparently, was forty bucks.

“Do they have a layaway?”

“They have sweatshirts, too, Frank. Would you like one?”

“I don’t want to have to get a second job.”

“Your birthday is coming up.”

Wendy grinned at him. Frank couldn’t tell if she was joking or not. He forked over the money for a program, and then they walked to the mezzanine and an usher took their tickets.

“Row A, seats 14 and 15.”

“Front row center,” his wife beamed. “Happy Anniversary, Frank.”

She kissed his cheek. Then she began pointing out more architecture.

“Look at the balconies.”

“Look at the stage.”

“Look at the plasterwork. Have you ever seen anything so beautiful?”

"Yeah, yeah. Beautiful."

The usher showed them their seats and Frank frowned.

"I thought we were front row."

"This is the front row, sir."

"How about all those guys in front of us?"

"That's the orchestra pit, sir."

They took their seats, which were actually pretty nice. Plush red velvet, roomy and comfortable. Too bad they didn't have seats like this at the United Center, where the Bulls played.

Wendy handed him a Playbill, and Frank squinted at the cover. A man in period clothing stared back at him.

"Who is this guy, anyway? Alexandro Mulchahey?"

"He's the famous Irish soliloquist."

"One of those guys who talks with a dummy on his lap?"

"He's a dramatic actor, Frank. He does Shakespearean sonnets."

Frank slumped in his chair. This was worse than he'd thought. When Wendy nagged him about this night, during a pivotal regular season game a few months back, he hadn't heard her mention Shakespeare.

"And this guy's famous?"

"He's the hottest thing in Europe right now. He's in all the papers."

Frank folded his arms. "If he was in all the papers, I would have heard about him."

"He wasn't in the sports section."

Frank frowned. The most pivotal basketball game of the century was playing right now, and Frank was stuck here watching some fruit in tights talk fancy for three hours.

Maybe he could fake a heart attack. Those ambulance guys have radios. They could tune into the game...

Some people needed to get to their seats, and Frank and Wendy had to stand up to let them by.

It was the kid with the Watchman! He stuck his tongue out at Frank as he passed, and then sat three seats away from them, his TV still tuned to the Bulls game.

Frank glanced at Wendy. She was absorbed in her program, gaping at big, color photos of Alexandro, who appeared to be in the throes of agony or ecstasy or a massive bowel movement.

"Look at how passionate he is," Wendy beamed.

"Or constipated," Frank muttered. He turned to look at the kid. The little boy held up the Watchman so Frank could see the game. The screen was tiny, but there was a score in the corner that Frank could almost make out. He leaned closer, straining his eyes.

The little snot switched the channel to Tom and Jerry.

"Goddamn little..."

There was a moaning sound in front of them.

"Orchestra is warming up." Wendy bounced in her seat like an anxious schoolgirl. "It's going to start soon."

The little boy whispered something to his father, and they both got up. Once again Frank and Wendy had to stand. Frank fought the urge to strangle the little monkey as he sashayed past.

The father took the kid by the hand up the aisle.

"Wendy, I have to go to the bathroom."

"The show's about to start."

"It's an emergency." Frank made his Emergency face.

"Hurry back."

Frank stood up and followed the boy into the lobby. As he guessed, his father led him into the bathroom.

The kid's father was standing by the sink, checking out his hair from three different angles.

"I just joined Hair Club for Men," he told Frank.

"Looks good," Frank told him. It looked like a beaver had died on the man's head.

"Can you see the weave?"

"Hmm? No. Seamless."

Frank eyed the stalls. Only one door was closed. Had to be the kid.

He walked into the nearby stall and closed the door. Removing twenty dollars from his wallet, he slipped the bill under the partition

"Psst. Kid. Twenty bucks if you can give it to me for an hour."

There was no answer. Frank added another bill to the offer.

"How about forty?"

The voice that came from the stall was far to low to belong to a child.

"I normally don't swing that way, man. But for sixty, I'll rock your world."

Frank hurried out of the bathroom and into the lobby. The kid and his dad were going back into the theater.

"Hey! Buddy!"

Several people in the crowd turned to stare at him. He pushed through and caught up with Hair Weave and his kid.

"You think I could check out the game on your son's TV?"

"The game?" Hair Weave scratched his roots.

"Bulls game. Playoffs."

"Clarence, let this man see your TV for a second."

"Batteries are dead."

Clarence switched on the Watchman and nothing happened. He smiled. Malicious little bastard.

"Did you see the score?"

"Yeah–fifty-four to sixty-eight."

"Who was winning?"

"Sixty-eight."

"Come on Clarence, Mommy's waiting."

Clarence stuck out his tongue and followed his father down the aisle.

Frank felt as if his head were about to blow apart. He almost began crying.

"Are you okay, sir?"

An usher, red vest and bow tie, no more than eighteen. Frank grabbed his arms.

"Is there a TV anywhere in this place?"

The boy scrunched his eyebrows. "TV? No. I don't think so."

"How about a radio? It's the Eastern Conference Finals. I have to know the score."

"Sorry. There's a TV in the dressing room, but..."

Frank lit up. "There's one in Evander Mulrooney's room?"

"You mean Alexandro Mulchahey?"

"I went to school with Evander, in Italy."

"Mr. Mulchahey is Irish."

Frank clapped the usher on the shoulder, grinning broadly.

"I should stop in, say hello to the old hound dog. Where's his dressing room?"

"I don't think..."

Frank held the forty dollars under the kid's nose.

"Just tell me where it is."

The usher sniffed the money, then nodded. He led Frank through an unmarked door and down a winding hallway that had none of the frill and pizzazz of the lobby. It barely had ample light.

The hall finally ended at a door to the backstage. Frank half expected to see a jungle of sandbags and painted backdrops, but instead it was very orderly. There were several people milling about, but none of them paid Frank any attention.

"He's the third room on the right. Don't tell him I let you in. I'll lose my job."

Frank didn't bother thanking him. He ran to the door, flinging it open, seeing Evander Fitzrooney sitting in a make-up chair.

The soliloquist turned to him, venom in his eyes.

"I don't allow visitors before a performance! Get out!"

Frank ignored the actor, scanning the room, searching frantically for the...

"Television!"

Frank ran to it, arms outstretched, and Evander stood up and punched Frank square in the nose.

* * *

"How many times can I say I'm sorry?"

Wendy stared at Frank through the bars. She didn't seem sympathetic.

"I've decided to let you spend the night in jail, Frank. Maybe it will help you prioritize your life."

"Wendy...please. I need you to bail me out. The game has to be almost over, and I gave my last forty bucks to that pimply usher."

Wendy darkened, then turned on her heels and walked out.

"Wendy! Will you at least find out the score for me? Please!"

After Wendy left, Frank slumped down on the metal bench, alone. Every second seemed to last an hour. Every minute was an eternity. Are the Bulls winning? Will they move on to the finals? What was the score?

Never a religious man, Frank silently begged the Lord to please send someone to give Frank the score.

When Frank finished the prayer and opened his eyes, he was confronted with a wondrous sight.

The cops were bringing in a man–a large, burly man–wearing a Bulls jersey.

"Is the game over?"

The man squinted at Frank. “Yeah, it’s over. Most amazing ending I’ve ever seen. It’ll be talked about for decades to come.”

“Who won? Who won?”

The door closed, and the cops went away. The burly man looked Frank over, top to bottom.

“You a Bulls fan?”

Frank began to jump up and down.

“Yes, dammit! Who won the game?”

The man smiled. It was an ugly thing.

“How much is it worth to you to know?”

“Name your price. I don’t have any money on me, but I’ll get it to you. My word is good.”

Burly Guy licked his lips. “Don’t want no money.”

“What is it you want, then?”

Fifteen minutes later, Frank learned a valuable lesson: If you dedicate your life to sports, you’ll only get hurt in the end.

An Archaeologist's Story

Written for a college anthropology course, as a final project. The Woody Allen influence is obvious. I've always liked this story, but no one ever expressed any interest in publishing it, even though it made the rounds.

DAY 1 – 2:47pm

The funding has come through! As I write this, I am in a plane heading to the Bahamas, on a grant from the University of Sheboygan. With me are my colleagues Dr. Myra Bird and Dr. Jerome Sloan.

I'm thrilled, though my excitement was somewhat dampened when I had some trouble getting my excavation tools through airport security. Jerome's sly joke that I wasn't really an archaeologist, but rather a homicidal maniac, prompted them to conduct an embarrassing and somewhat uncomfortable body-cavity search.

I'm grateful the airport security gentlemen had small hands.

As for the site, none of us knows what to expect. Sure, there have been stories of fossilized Homo erectus skulls just lying on the beach, waiting to be picked up, but archaeological rumors are plentiful. I still remember traveling to the Antarctic six years ago, because of the discovery of what seemed to be an Australopithecus boise tooth, but instead turned out to be just a small white rock. I sorely miss those three toes I lost to frostbite.

But this site seems like the real thing. The authenticated femur of a Homo habilus was found by a vacationing family in a small cave. Evidently, the children were acting up, and the father had grabbed something lying next to him to beat them with. It turned out to be the fossil in question. Luckily, it remained intact, even though the father used it.

I also believe the children have gotten out of intensive care.

Myra, Jerome and I have been waiting a week now for the go ahead to investigate. My bag was long ago packed and waiting for the word, leaving me pretty much without anything to wear for the last week.

But now we were finally on our way.

Jerome just tapped me on the shoulder, smiling. He is also obviously thrilled about this trip. No, he just wants my martini. I give it to him. I am so high right now I do not need alcohol. This package of peanuts is fine.

DAY 1 – 9:35pm

What a horrible flight! Jerome threw up on the stewardess, who then refused to acknowledge us for the rest of the trip. We didn't even get served our dinner, which as far as I could make out was some kind of meat in brown sauce. When we got to the airport, Customs confiscated Jerome's suitcase, which was filled with liquor. Both Myra and I are appalled at the lack of professionalism on our colleague's part, and we attempted to confront him and express our disappointment.

Unfortunately, he was unconscious.

We managed to get him to the hotel by strapping him to the hood of our taxi, but they charged us fare for three just the same.

The hotel we are staying at is very cheap, and we all must share a room due to budgetary constraints. Myra and I propped Jerome up on the sink, then discussed where we would sleep, there being only one bed. I was willing to be adult about it and share the bed with her, half and half. She agreed, and now I must sleep on the underside of the mattress.

Myra is very sharp, so sharp in fact that I once cut myself shaking her hand. But she has really sexy bone structure, and her teeth are exquisite. I long to run my hands over her illium and ischium, but realize such thoughts are dangerous, as I must work closely with her. Nothing must jeopardize our excavation.

I can barely wait to start work tomorrow.

DAY 2 – 5:43am

I am awakened in the morning by Jerome retching. The sound was disturbing enough, but the fact that he was retching on me made it impossible to sleep any longer. After a shower, I dressed and went down to the lobby and waited for my colleagues to join me. Myra arrived a few minutes later, without Jerome. When I inquired about him, she told me he was sick and going to stay in bed for the day. I wanted to protest, but realized he probably wouldn't be much help to us anyway, and would only throw up on anything we might find.

We called a cab and took it to the sight. My mind was giddy with anticipation. I could tell Myra was nervous too, because she bit off all her nails and spit them in my face (a cute habit she has.)

When we arrived, it was exactly as I had expected; a clearing in the tropical forest of about eighty square yards. On the edge of it was a rock formation that held a small cave. Myra had brought her camera, and she began to take pictures of the area. Then she gave the camera to me, and asked me to take some pictures of her posing on the rocks.

After shooting three rolls of film, we broke out our equipment and began our excavation. Armed with a flashlight, a horse hair brush, and a small pick, we entered the cave. Myra clutched my arm, afraid of being attacked by vampire bats. Every so often I would flash my light at the ceiling and yell “A bat!” just for fun.

I soon quit, as Myra would slap me repeatedly in the face when she discovered there was no real danger.

A quick inspection of the cave showed no real evidence of primitive man. Though we were unduly excited about seeing something on the wall, which just turned out to be a spray painted picture of a man’s genitalia, with “Eat me Jonny” written beside it. Primitive as it may be, it wasn’t what we were looking for.

After examining the cave, we went to inspect the area where the femur was found, twenty feet east of the opening. The ground was hard clay, and we discovered the impression of where the discovered femur bone had been lying. Using our picks, we dug roughly six inches down for a square yard of the area encompassing the impression, but got nothing for our efforts except a large pile of clay.

By then it was late afternoon, and we chose to break for lunch. Unfortunately, neither of us had brought anything to eat. But this was a tropical jungle, and there were many edible roots and tubers growing around us. I also noted that several of the rocks were slate, and if need be we could knock off a Mousterian point using the Levallois technique and go hunting for rodents.

Myra, however, wanted a burger and fries, so we had to go back to the hotel.

DAY 2 – 1:46pm

Upon finishing lunch, it was our intention to report our progress to Jerome, then return to the sight. But to our surprise Jerome was not in the room. We begin searching the hotel, and I find him sitting by the pool in a chaise lounge, sipping a Mai-Tai.

I am shocked at his conduct, and threaten to tell our superiors of his insubordination. He flips me the bird.

I find Myra peeking in the Men's room, and tell her of Jerome's attitude. She agrees we should file a report recommending he be dismissed, or at least have his suave safari hat taken away. Then we take a cab back to the sight.

While I continued to excavate the area where the fossil was found, Myra decided to start in another area, closer to the mouth of the cave. It is hard, laborious work, but it is made more bearable by Myra, who sings operettas while she digs.

Four hours into it, I discover something. Rather than get Myra excited over what may be just a rock, I bit off a small portion of my lower lip to keep from yelling with joy. As I dig around it I realize it was smart that I waited, for my discovery was nothing but a long, thin stone. Or perhaps a petrified snake. Either way, it wasn't important.

The sun begins to set, and we know we must go. We aren't discouraged, as neither of us expected to find anything on the first day, but we are a little disappointed. When we get back to the hotel, Jerome is watching "Emmanuelle in Egypt" on pay-per-view, eating what appears to be his third room service filet mignon. He apologizes profusely about earlier, and promises to accompany us tomorrow. We reluctantly forgive him, and Myra lets him sleep next to her that night.

I must sleep on a small wooden chair.

It doesn't bother me, for I have slept in far worse places. Like Detroit. Or that time I was in Cairo, and slept on a bed of camel dung. To this day, I still attract more than the average amount of flies.

DAY 3 – 7:30am

I awake to the sound of gagging. I then realize that it was me, as Jerome stuffed a small gourd into my mouth as a joke.

He is really beginning to irritate me.

Jerome and Myra had gotten up earlier, so there is no time to change or take a shower, as they are on their way to the sight. I am already in the cab when I realize I am still wearing my Snoopy pajamas.

Myra reassures me not to worry, as the sight is secluded, and they are pretty nice pajamas. Then she takes several pictures, while she and Jerome laugh hysterically. I haven't been so embarrassed since I interned with Leakey, and mislabeled a gracile Australopithecine skull fragment for robust, completely forgetting to take into account the sagittal crest.

I smile politely, and jokingly tell them both to go to hell. We do not talk until we reach the sight. When we get there, Jerome is impressed with our progress. He agrees we should keep at what we are doing, and he'll start work further in the cave. I like this idea, as it keeps Jerome away from me.

Several hours later, I again come upon what appears to be fossil material. But this time it is more definite. I call Myra over, and we begin to dig it out together. It turns out to be a parietal bone, intact! I am so excited I kiss Myra. She surprises me by passionately responding. She then goes into the cave to give the news to Jerome, whom she finds is sleeping. He becomes very excited, and clutches the bone tightly, yelling, "Mine! All mine!"

In the meantime, I excavate the area further, and soon uncover an occipital bone. It begins to get dark, but the prospect of finding a complete skull prompts me to go on. Then I realize my colleagues have already left, and I must walk the seven miles back to the hotel, as I have no cab fare in my pajamas.

DAY 3 – 11:22pm

I make it to the hotel, my feet raw and bloody, and my occipital bone clutched firmly in hand. To my disgust, Myra and Jerome are in bed. Naked. Also in bed with them are several gourds. This sickens me, and I go to the bathroom to clean my feet. I will never eat gourds again.

DAY 4 – 6:45am

A loud banging on the bathroom door wakes me up. I had fallen asleep on the sink. I open the door and it is Myra, who holds out the parietal bone and demands I examine it. I tell her it is an average Homo erectus parietal. Then she tells me the curvature is too extreme for erectus, yet too round for habilus. I examine my occipital, and then agree. It is possible we may have found the link between the two! It is possible we have found a new species!

In her excitement, Myra kisses me again. I resist at first, after what she did with Jerome, but soon respond to her advances and begin pressing against her body. She falls over backwards, and pulls me down with her. It is then, when we are on the floor, fornicating like animals, that Jerome walks in with the camera. He takes several pictures before I realize what is happening. All the time Myra is laughing and smiling. I finally pull away and hide in the bathroom, humiliated.

Jerome knocks an undetermined time later, and tells me I must give credit for the find to him, or he is sending the pictures to "National Geographic". I am shocked, and cannot speak. He rants on and on, about how he'll call the new species Homo jerome, and how it will make him rich and famous beyond his wildest dreams. I begin to cry.

Myra busts in and takes a picture of this.

DAY 4 – 12:54 pm

I am now convinced, after sitting in the bathroom and thinking about it all morning, that Jerome must die. Myra too. I cannot be humiliated in front of the scientific world. Nor can I let the credit for such an important discovery go to someone else. The answer is murder.

I go to Hertz and rent a large SUV. My plan is simple. I will run them over. Then back over them five or six times to make sure they are dead. I park the car behind a palm tree in front of the hotel, then wait for them to come back from the sight. Thoughts of being featured on The Discovery Channel fuel my thirst for vengeance.

The second they step out of the cab, they're pancakes.

DAY 4 – 8:45pm

Myra and Jerome finally return to the hotel. My fingers sweat as I turn the ignition key, and the engine roars to life like a prehistoric beast–perhaps an Indricotherium transsouralicum, or a Doedicurus with a slight cold.

Myra wraps her arms around Jerome and kisses him lovingly, as they both stand innocently on the curb, waiting to be flattened.

I put the car into gear, and slam the accelerator to the floor. My mind is racing, but I foresee everything in slow motion: the look of shock on Jerome's face when he sees me coming at him, the scream Myra will barely have a chance to let out, the crushed, bleeding mess of bone and sinew that was once my colleagues.

I drive past them and keep on going. I cannot bring myself to do it.

I am not a killer. I am an archaeologist.

Who cares if I don't get credit for this find? There will be other excavations. I will find other fossils. There is a big wide world out there, covered in dirt. Somewhere there is bound to be other extraordinary discoveries, and I will be there to make them. I and I alone will go down in history as the man who revolutionized archaeology, even if it takes me the rest of my life. I will bounce back!

Nah...too much work.

I turn the car around and level Jerome and Myra in mid-kiss.

Homo jerome my ass.

After they were flattened, I hit Reverse and backed up over their bodies. Twice.

If only Leakey could see me now.

Could Stephanie Plum Really Get Car Insurance?

I have a dirty little secret. Even though my books are compared to Janet Evanovich's, I'd never read her until after writing Rusty Nail. I was invited into an essay collection about Evanovich's character, called Perfectly Plum, so I read all the books back-to-back, then contributed this piece.

By my count, Stephanie Plum has been involved in the loss or destruction of twelve vehicles at the time of this writing, which is 8:55am, Eastern Time. But, in all fairness, I'm not very good at counting. Plus, I listened to two of the books on abridged audio, which is known for cutting incidental bits from novels, such as characterization and plot.

Since I had nothing better to do today, other than to donate my kidney to that sick guy who paid me fifty thousand dollars, I decided to find out if, in the real world, could Ms. Plum get insured?

Let's take a moment to look at the phrase "in the real world."

Have you taken a moment? Good. Let's move on.

Since Stephanie Plum is a fictitious character, who lives in a fictitious place called Trenton, New Jersey, she isn't expected to completely conform to all aspects of reality, such as car insurance, or gravity. Since I knew that this task before me would involve a great deal of painstaking research and determination, I immediately went to work. After work, I went to a movie. Then, a nap.

Discouraged by my lack of progress, I called my neighbor Shelby, who knows a lot of stuff, such as why bottled water costs the same as bottled iced tea, even though it doesn't have all the stuff in it that tea has. Such as tea. Quote Shelby:

"Stephanie who?"

The story would end there, except that I have a lot more to tell.

My next course of action was to take my phone off the hook, because I kept getting obnoxious messages along the lines of, "Where's that kidney?" and "You have to get to the hospital immediately!" and "He's dead."

Then I went to the Pleasant Happy Valley Assisted Living Facility (Now with 14% Less Elderly Abuse) to meet with renowned Stephanie Plum Scholar Murray Christmas. That's his real name, and though it may seem odd, it isn't nearly as odd as is sister's name, Groundhog Day. Murray attempted to be cooperative, but being a hundred and three years old, he'd forgotten much of the minutiae, such as his own name. After much patience, and some help from his nurse to understand his drooling wheezes, I got nowhere. So I have no idea why I'm telling you this.

But when the nurse left, I looked through his personal effects, and got a real nice gold watch.

This opens up a large topic for serious discussion, which I am merely going to skip.

After pawning the watch, I pulled out my trusty phone book and began calling insurance companies. After eight calls that went nowhere, I decided I needed a better plan than giggling and making fart sounds when someone answered. So I decided to try talking.

Here are some of the conversations I had. My name has been changed to protect me.

CALL NUMBER ONE

ME: Do you sell car insurance?

INSURANCE MAN #1: Yes.

ME: My name is Julie Pear, and I'm not a fictitious character. I played a hand in destroying twelve cars in my last thirteen books. Will you insure me?

INSURANCE MAN #1: I need more information.

ME: I like the color red, and dogs.

INSURANCE MAN #1: I meant about your driving background.

ME: I also like Rob Schneider movies.

INSURANCE MAN #1: I'm sorry, we can't insure you.

CALL NUMBER TWO

ME: Hello?

INSURANCE MAN #2: Can I help you?

ME: My last four cars have exploded, but it wasn't my fault. Can you insure me?

INSURANCE MAN #2: How did these cars explode?

ME: definition of explosion

INSURANCE MAN #2: Well, you're welcome to come in and we can give you a quote.

ME: How about I give you a quote instead? How about, "This was no boating accident!"

INSURANCE MAN #2: Excuse me?

ME: That was from Jaws. I loved that movie. I still get scared taking baths.

INSURANCE MAN #2: You're an idiot.

CALL NUMBER THREE

INSURANCE MAN #3: Making rude noises like that is very immature. (Pause) I know you're still there. I can here you giggling.

CALL NUMBER FOUR

ME: I want a large thin crust, sausage and extra cheese.

PIZZA GUY: That will be fourteen ninety five.

After all of this hard work, I only knew one thing for certain: if Stephanie Plum were a pound of bacon, she'd sure be a clever one. I'd pay a lot of money to see a talking pound of bacon in high heels. A lot of money.

The next thing on my to do list, after a good scratch, was attend an insurance convention. The convention brought many to tears, due to a chemical leak that gave most attendees second degree burns.

Quote Harold Barnicky, one of the attendees: "Those little crackers they had, the ones with the spinach and cheese—mmmm-mmmmmmmm!"

Personally, I preferred the three bean casserole, which was inappropriately named because I counted at least a dozen beans, and counting isn't my strong suit.

But none of this effort brought me any closer to the end of this essay.

Undaunted, superfluous, and proselytical, I decided to try a more direct approach, because even though I'm a writer, I've always wanted to direct.

So I wrote an impassioned, persuasive letter to the largest auto insurer next to my house. The letter brilliantly detailed the whole sordid tale, and was perhaps the greatest thing I've ever written on a cocktail napkin. Without permission, here is the company's reply:

We CARE Auto Insurance

WE INSURE EVERYONE!™

8866 Haknort Lane

CHICAGO, IL 60610

(847) 555 - AUTO

To: Margaret Apples

Re: Recent Insurance Inquiry

Ms. Apples–

When my father began We Care Auto Insurance 64 years ago, he had a grand dream: To supply auto insurance to everyone who needed it, regardless of their driving record or accident history. He wanted to be the insurance company for the common man--the senior citizens with senility issues, the veterans missing important limbs, the narcoleptics, the mentally retarded, the unrepentant alcoholics.

Father believed everyone--even those with heroin habits and cataracts the size of dinner plates--deserved to be insured. For more than six decades, We Care Auto Insurance carried on this proud tradition.

We have insured drivers with organic brain damage of such severity they couldn't count past four. We have insured drivers with quadriplegia, who drove using a suck-and-blow straw. We have insured the legally blind, the morbidly obese, the legally dead, and Mr. Chimpo the Driving Baboon. We've even insured several Kennedys.

Now, for the first time in our history, We Care Auto Insurance must turn down an application.

Yours.

While the law doesn't require us to provide an explanation for the reason you aren't being allowed into the We Care Auto Insurance family, I've chosen to write this letter to make something perfectly clear: We are not to blame, Ms. Apples. You are.

While reviewing insurance applications, we compile statistics from several sources, which allows us to come up with monthly rates and deductible figures. When feeding your information into our computer database, our network promptly froze.

We haven't been able to reboot it.

According to our information, you've been responsible for destroying more cars than any single driver in North America, and possibly South America as well.

You've destroyed more cars than Carzilla, the giant robotic crane that tours with monster truck shows and eats cars.

In layperson's terms; you've destroyed a huge fucking butt-load of cars.

There have been so many, I'm guessing you've lost track of them all. Allow me to refresh your memory.

After your Miata was repossessed (which seems to be the only nice car you've ever owned) you played a hand in the explosion of a Jeep owned by a Detective Gepetto of the Trenton Police Department. This, unfortunately, was not the last automobile casualty Detective Gepetto suffered at your hands.

Your next vehicle, a Jeep, was stolen. You'll be pleased to know that a VIN search has recently located it, in a scrap yard in Muncie, Indiana. The odometer reading was well over 220,000 miles. Having escaped you, this Jeep led a full and possibly interesting life, without explosions, though your insurance company still had to foot the bill for it nonetheless.

The blue Nissan truck you acquired shortly thereafter soon went to the big parking lot in the sky after being blown up with a rocket launcher. I must admit, I had to read the claim report three times before the phrase rocket launcher sunk in. I've insured several CIA operatives, a movie stuntman named Jimmy Rocket who specialized in pyrotechnics, and a scientist who actually worked for a rocket company (I believe they called him a rocket scientist) but none of them ever lost a vehicle to a rocket, missile, or any comparable exploding projectile.

Your replacement car, a Honda CRX, was soaked in gasoline and burned. My record search was unable to turn up the name of the perpetrator, but might I suggest it was one of your previous insurance agents? That wouldn't surprise me.

Your name came up in several claims made by a company cryptically called Sexy Cuban Man. The claims included an exploded Porsche and a stolen BWM. Not content with that, you somehow also managed to burn down a funeral home. Did you get confused in the dark and mistake it for a car somehow?

A Honda Civic, registered to you, was torched, and a Honda CRV registered to you was totaled, and then set ablaze. Why you bought another Honda is beyond my mental capacity, but you did, and it was promptly burned, along with another Sexy Cuban Man vehicle, by—and this is in your own words—a giant rabbit. Was Jimmy Stewart anywhere in the vicinity, pray tell? Or did this rabbit happen to have a basket of brightly colored eggs?

Your next vehicle, a Ford Escape, didn't escape at all. Again it was burned. Perhaps car insurance isn't what you need. Perhaps you simply need a car made of asbestos. Or a Sherman Tank.

Your next victim, a Saturn, was bombed. So was an SUV belonging to the unfortunate Joe Morelli. You also had a hand in the recent explosion of a Ford Escalade.

Records show you just purchased a Mini Cooper. Such an adorable car. I've included it in my nightly prayers.

While the first few explosions might be written off as coincidence, or even bad luck, somewhere around the tenth destroyed vehicle a little light came on inside my head. I finally understood that no one could be this unlucky. There was only one possible explanation.

You're sick in the head.

The psychiatric community calls your specific mental illness Munchausen's by Proxy. A parent, usually the mother, purposely makes her children sick so she can bask in the attention and sympathy of others.

I've decided that this is what you're doing, only with vehicles. Rather than feeding little Molly peanut butter and bleach sandwiches, you've been deliberately destroying your own cars. All because you crave attention.

But your warped scheme to put the spotlight upon yourself isn't without casualties. I'm not speaking of your helpless automotive victims. I'm speaking of my wonderful company.

Writing this letter fills me with sadness, Ms. Apples, for

you have destroyed my father's dream. For the first time in our history, we are rejecting an applicant. This comes at a great moral cost, and a great financial cost as well.

Because of you, we have been forced to change our trademarked slogan, We Insure Everyone! Do you have any idea how much letterhead we have with that slogan on it? A warehouse full. And unless we hire someone (perhaps an immigrant, or a homeless person) to cross out the slogan on each individual sheet of paper, it is now land-fill bound.

Ditto our business cards. Our refrigerator magnets. Our full color calendars we give to our loyal customers every holiday season. The large and numerous interstate billboards. And our catchy TV commercials, which feature the jingle written by none other than Mr. Paul Williams, naturally called, "We Insure Everyone."

What will out new slogan be? I'm not sure. There are several in the running. They include: "We Insure Practically Everyone," "We Really Want to Insure Everyone," and "We Insure Everyone But Margaret Apples." I also like the slogan, "Why Can't You Be in the Next Car You Blow Up or At the Very Least Get a Job at the Button Factory," but that has too many words to fit on a business card.

You have crippled us, Ms. Apples. Crippled us worse than many of the people we insure, including the guy with the prosthetic pelvis and the woman born without arms who must steer with her face.

I hope you're happy.

As a public service to the world, I'm sending copies of this letter to every insurance agent in the United States.

Hopefully, this will end your reign of terror.

If it takes every cent of my money, every single one of my vast resources, I'll see to it that you never insure another vehicle again. When I get done with you, you won't be able to put on roller skates without the Feds breathing down your neck.

Whew. There. I feel a lot better now.

And though we aren't able to insure you, Ms. Apples, I do hope you pass our name along to any friends or relatives of yours who are seeking auto insurance.

Sincerely,
Milton McGlade

So there you have it. Based on the minutes of hard work I've devoted to this topic, Stephanie Plum would not be able to get car insurance.

In conclusion, if I had only ten words to end this essay, I'd have a really hard time thinking of them. Now if you'll excuse me, I've got a kidney to sell on eBay.

Cozies or Hardboiled?

How to Tell the Difference

A fluff piece for Crimespree magazine. I got a big kick out of writing this.

Mystery is a broad genre, encompassing thrillers, crime novels, whodunnits, capers, historicals, and police procedurals. Two of its most bi-polar brethren are the tea-cozy, as typified by Agatha Christie, and hardboiled noir, best portrayed by Mickey Spillaine.

But with the constant re-catagorizing and re-inventing of sub-genres, how can you, the reader, tell the difference?

Fear no more! Here is a definitive set of criteria to determine if that potential bookstore purchase The Winnipeg Watersports Caper is about a gentleman boat thief, or a serial killer with an overactive bladder.

* * *

If the book has an elderly character that solves crimes in her spare time, it is a cozy.

If the book has an elderly character that gets shot seven times in the face and then raped, it is hardboiled.

* * *

If the protagonist drinks herbal tea, and eats scones, it is a cozy.

If the protagonist drinks whiskey, and makes other people eat their teeth, it is hardboiled.

* * *

If a cat, dog, or other cute domestic animal helps solve the crime, it is a cozy.

If a cat, dog, or other cute domestic animal is set on fire, it is hardboiled.

* * *

If the book has a character named Agnes, Dorothy, or Smythe, it is a cozy.

If the book has a character named Hammer, Crotch, or Dickface, it is hardboiled.

* * *

If the murder scene involves antiques, it is cozy.

If the murder scene involves entrails, it is hardboiled.

* * *

If the hero does any sort of knitting, crafting, or pet-sitting, it is a cozy.

If the hero does any sort of maiming, beating, or humping, it is hardboiled.

* * *

If the sidekick is a good natured curmudgeon who collects stamps, it is a cozy.

If the sidekick is a good natured psychopath who collects ears, it is hardboiled.

* * *

If the book contains recipes, crossword puzzles, or cross-stitching patterns, it is a cozy.

If the book contains ass-fucking, it is hardboiled.

* * *

If cookie crumbs on a Persian rug lead to the villain, it is a cozy.

If semen stains on a stab wound lead to the villain, it is hardboiled.

* * *

If any characters say, "Oh my!" it is a cozy.

If any characters say, "Jesus Goddamn Fucking Christ!" it is hardboiled.

* * *

If the murder weapon is a fast-acting poison, it is a cozy.

If the murder weapon is a slow-acting blowtorch, it is hardboiled.

* * *

If the main character has a colorful hat that is filled with fruit and flowers, it is a cozy.

If the main character has a colorful vocabulary that is filled with racial slurs and invectives, it is hardboiled.

* * *

And finally, if the author picture looks like your grandmother—beware...it could be either.

The Addiction

Another humor story about what it's like to be a writer. Like Piranha Pool, this is semi-autobiographical, and pretty much anyone who has ever tried to write for a living can relate to the narrator.

The first time I ever saw it was at a party.

College. Dorm. Walls constructed of Budweiser cases. Every door open, the hallways and rooms crammed with people, six different rock tunes competing for dominance.

Rituals of the young and innocent—and the not so innocent, I found out that night.

I had to give back the beer I'd rented, popped into the first empty room I could find.

He was sitting in the corner, hunched over, oblivious to me.

Curiosity made me forget about my bladder. What was he doing, huddled in the dim light? What unpleasant drug would keep him here, alone and oblivious, when a floor thumping party was kicking outside his door?

"Hey, man, what's up?"

A quick turn, guilty face, covering something up with his hands.

"Nothing. Go away."

"What are you hiding there?"

His eyes were wide, full of secret shame. The shame of masturbation, of cooking heroin needles, of snatching money from Mom's purse.

Then I saw it all—the computer, the notebook full of scrawls, the outline...

"You're writing fiction!"

The guilt melted off his face, leaving it shopworn and heavy.

"Leave me alone. I have to finish this chapter."

"How can you be writing with a party going on?"

He smiled, so subtle that it might have been my beer goggles.

"Have you ever done it?"

"Me?" I tried to laugh, but it sounded fake. "I mean, when I was a kid, you know, drawing pictures and stuff, I used to make up stories..."

"How about lately?"

"Naw. Nothing stronger than an occasional essay."

"You want to try it?"

I took a step back. All of the sudden my bladder became an emergency again.

"No, man..."

The guy stood up. His eyes were as bright as his computer screen.

"You should try it. You'll like it."

"I'm cool. Really."

He smiled, for sure this time, all crooked teeth and condescension.

"You'll be back."

I hurried out of the room.

* * *

The clock blinked 3:07am. I couldn't sleep.

To the left of my bed, my computer.

My mind wouldn't shut off. I kept thinking of the party. Of that guy.

Not me. I wasn't going to go down that path. Sitting alone in my room when everyone else was partying. I wasn't like that.

My computer waited. Patient.

Maybe I should turn it on, make sure it was running okay. Test a few applications.

I crept out of bed.

Everything seemed fine. I should check MS Word, though. Sometimes there are problems.

A look to the side. My roommate was asleep.

What's the big deal, anyway? I could write just one little short short short story. It wouldn't hurt anyone.

I could write it in the dark.

No one would ever know.

One little story.

* * *

"Party over at Keenan Hall. You coming?"

"Hmm? Uh, no. Busy."

"Homework?"

"Uh, yeah. Homework."

"That sucks. I'll drink a few for you."

"Sure."

I got back to plotting.

* * *

I raised a fist to knock, dropped it, raised it again.

What's the big deal? He probably wasn't in anyway.

One tiny tap, the middle knuckle, barely even audible.

"It's open."

The room was dark, warm. It smelled of old sweat and desperation.

He was at his desk, as I guessed he'd be. Hunched over his computer. The clackety clack of his fingers on the keyboard was comforting.

"I need...I need to borrow a Thesaurus."

His eyes darted over to me, focusing. Then came the condescending smile.

"I knew you'd be back. What are you working on?"

"It, uh, takes place in the future, after we've colonized Jupiter."

"It's impossible to colonize Jupiter. The entire planet is made out of gas."

"In 2572 we discover a solid core beneath the gas..."

I spit out the rest of my concept, so fast my lips kept tripping over one another.

"Sounds interesting. You bring a sample to read?"

How did he know? I dug the disk out of my back pocket.

* * *

I knew it was coming. Short stories weren't enough anymore. The novella seemed hefty at the time, but now those twenty thousand words are sparse and amateurish.

I was ready. I knew I was. I had a great idea, bursting with conflict, and the two main characters were already living in my head, jawing off at each other with dialog that begged to be on paper.

All I lacked was time.

"Hi, Mom. How's Dad? I'm dropping out of college."

I couldn't make much sense of her reply; it was mostly screaming. When my father came on the phone, he demanded to know the reason. Was I in trouble? Was it a girl? Drugs?

"I need the time off to write my novel."

I hadn't ever heard my father cry before.

I don't need understanding. Certainly not sympathy. The orgiastic delight that comes from constructing a perfect paragraph makes up for my crummy apartment and low-paying job at the Food Mart. They let me use the register tape for my notes, and I get a twenty percent discount on instant coffee.

Reality is tenuous, but that's a good sign. It means I'm focused on the book. I'm not really talking to myself. I'm talking to my characters. You see the difference?

Sometimes I need to take days off, like for that problem I had with Chapter 26. But I worked through it. The book is more important than food, anyway. Who needs to eat?

* * *

The tears were magic, and the sob was more beautiful than any emotion ever felt by anyone who ever lived.

Helium had replaced the blood in my veins. My hands trembled.

I typed The End and swore I heard the Voice of God.

* * *

The alley is cold. I stuff my sweatshirt with newspaper and hunch down by a dumpster, my CD-ROM clutched in a filthy hand that I can barely recognize as my own.

It is my third week on the street. I've made some friends, like Squeaky, who is sitting next to me.

"They locked me out. Sold my stuff to pay the back rent. Even my computer."

Squeaky squeaks. I offer him an empty Dorito bag, and he scurries inside, looking for crumbs. I don't mind him being distracted. He's heard the story before.

"I've still got my novel, though." The CD isn't very shiny anymore, and it has a crack that I pray hasn't hurt the data.

"Best thing I've ever done in my life, Squeaky old pal. Wouldn't change a damn thing about the path I chose."

It starts to rain. I stare at the CD, at my reflection in it. My beard is coming in nicely. It gives me sort of a Hemingway look.

"Did I tell you about the Intervention, Squeaky? Right before I got kicked out. My parents, my brother, the chaplain, and some guy from WA. Tried to get me to quit writing. Follow some stupid 12 step program."

I still feel a twang of guilt, remembering my mother's pleas.

"They wanted me to admit I had a problem. But they don't understand. Writing isn't an addiction. It's a way of life. Like being a rat. Could you stop being a rat, just because your family wanted you to?"

Squeaky didn't answer. The rain was really coming down now.

"I have to write. I don't have a choice. It's who I am."

The CD in my hand got warm to the touch, glowing with an inner spirit that I knew for sure isn't just my imagination. It's worth something. Even if it never sells. Even if I'm the only one who ever reads it.

It validates me.

"I'm no one trick pony, either. I won't rest on my laurels. I've got more books in me."

I pull out my collection of gum wrappers and sort them out, chapter by chapter.

After reading what I wrote that morning, I take my stubby pencil from my shirt pocket and start where I left off.

After all—writer's have to write.

It's what we do.

Weigh to Go

A Personal Essay on Health Clubs

Once upon a time I wanted to write a humor column like Dave Barry. I quickly learned that only Dave Barry was allowed to write humor columns, and newspapers weren't looking for anyone else. This was penned during college, and then tweaked to put on my website.

I was watching "The 20 Minute Workout," sitting back in my easy chair and eating a box of Twinkies. The blonde aerobics instructor (at least I think she was blonde, for I was having trouble seeing over my stomach) was chirping away about how eating healthy and exercising were the keys to a better you, while doing thigh lifts that made me exhausted just looking at her.

Among other health conscious things, she said that if you are truly satisfied with your body, you should be able to stand naked in front of a mirror and like what you see. I accepted the challenge, and after finishing the Twinkies and two bowls of Frosted Sugar-O's Cereal (now with 30% more corn syrup), I disrobed and went straight to the full length mirror.

Much to my dismay, I looked like a giant sack of potatoes with a penis. This did nothing for my self-esteem, and I dove into a Piggo Size Jay's Potato Chips and didn't stop until I hit cellophane.

It was not until later that I realized most of my problems, such as not understanding my income tax return, were directly linked to my overweightedness. I decided at that moment to start a strict regimen of diet and exercise, but soon just limited it to exercise, not wanting to give up my favorite meal, beer and Snickers Bars.

The thing I had to do, as told to me by countless celebrities on TV who can't get work elsewhere, was join a health club. I went to a popular one nearby, housed in a building the size of Rhode Island. Inside was like stepping into The Jetsons: chrome...mirrors...flashing lights...techno music...a running track lined with spongy foam...rows and rows of exercise machines, as far as the eye could see...Elroy, walking Astro...

I was greeted at the door by a very muscular guy who'd been packed into a Spandex outfit so tightly I could see individual corpuscles pumping through his veins. His name was G.

"How do you spell that?" I asked.

"With a G."

"Do you have a last name?"

"It's just G."

"So on your birth certificate..."

"Enough about me." G grinned big, making his neck muscles ping out. "Let's talk about you."

G herded me through a throng of beautiful people, telling each in turn that he was in a meeting and couldn't be disturbed even if Madonna called with a Pilates emergency. We went into his office, which was decorated with pictures of G with his shirt off and smiling, G with his shirt off and scowling, and G with his shirt off and looking apprehensive, probably wondering where he'd left his shirt.

G handed me a bottled water from his personal mini-refrigerator and sat me at his desk. He remained standing.

"It's a good thing you came today, Mr. Konrath, because you're about five beats away from a major myocardial infarction. If you don't join our club right now, I'll ask you to sign this waiver to absolve us of responsibility when you walk out this door and your ventricles explode."

"I actually just had my heart checked, and..."

"Plus, you're so disgustingly fat, no one will ever love you."

"My wife says..."

"Hey, Joanie and Brenda, come in here and meet my new best friend, Mr. Konrath." G motioned for two attractive young women standing in the hall to come in and smile at me. "Don't you think he'd benefit from our programs?"

"I'd love to get him in one of my Prancercize classes," Brenda said, licking her lips. "I'll help you take off that disgusting, icky fat."

Joanie put her head to my chest. "I hear his pulmonary artery crying out like a sick kitty."

"You truly are a disgusting man, Mr. Konrath," G said. "I suggest the Super-Duper Extra Special Presidential Package. That will give you access to all of the club's facilities."

He handed me a color brochure filled with pictures of smiling, healthy people. The Super-Duper Extra Special Presidential Package monthly dues were slightly more than what I earned in a month, but I would have full access to everything, including unlimited use of their one racquetball court, should I ever decide to take up racquetball.

"Sign it and we'll be your friends forever," Joanie said.

"Sign it or you'll get sick and die alone," Brenda said.

G put a hand on my shoulder and squeezed. Hard. "I don't want to sugar coat this—"

"If you did, I'd probably eat it."

"—but if you don't sign this contract you'll be the biggest wuss-boy I've ever met."

I stared at G and had a momentary delusion that I, too, might be able to look like someone stuck a tube up my ass and inflated me. Sure, his shoulders were so broad that he probably needed help wiping his own ass, but he looked damn good without a shirt.

"Sign," they chanted. "Sign. Sign. Sign..."

I signed, and left the club feeling cheerful about my new commitment to get in shape. The pounds would soon begin to drop off, I was sure. They had to, because I no longer had any money for food.

When I shared the good news with my wife, she was equally excited.

"It cost how much?!?"

"Don't think of it in terms of costs," I said, repeating what G had told me, "think of it in terms of benefits."

"You tell the kids they can't go to college because their father spent all of our savings."

"College is overrated. You don't really learn anything useful. Trade schools—that's where it's at these days. You see that one on TV, teaches you how to repair air conditioners?"

My wife shook her head. "You've got issues, Joe. In fact, you've got a whole damn subscription."

"Why don't you come down to the club, check it out? G said there's a discount for spouses."

"Are you saying I'm fat?"

"I'm saying that your support hose isn't hiding your little pouch like it used to when we were dating."

My wife smiled. She was obviously coming around.

"How long is this stupid contract for?" she asked.

"Three years."

"That's how long you're going without sex. Enjoy the couch."

The couch was close to the refrigerator, so it wasn't too bad.

During my fourth week as an Extra Super Special Guy Member, G called me up.

"Mr. Konrath, you joined a month ago. When are you going to come down and start working out?"

"I can't now, G. I'm waiting for a pizza."

"Come on, Mr. Konrath. Joining was just the first step. Now you've got to start coming in. I'll blend you a fifteen dollar kelp smoothie, personally train you on the equipment for sixty dollars an hour, and give you a nice thirty dollar rub down afterwards."

"I thought all of that was included in my Jumbo Deluxo Mega Membership."

"Did you read the fine print?"

"It was in a different language."

"Don't let money keep you from being the best Mr. Konrath that you can be, Mr. Konrath. Come in today and you can take my Jazz Kwon Do class for half price."

"What do you drive, G?"

"A Mercedes. And my payment is due."

G was right. I'd made the commitment to get in shape. It was time to put up or shut up. Even my wife, after having our lawyer try unsuccessfully to break the heath club contract, had begun encouraging me to go.

"You wasted all that money!" she'd say, encouragingly. "Put down the cheese wheel, get off your lazy ass, and go work out!"

But, truth be told, I was scared. I knew if I went to the club I'd be surrounded by beautiful people, and I would be alienated and my self-esteem would sink even lower.

My plan was to get in shape before I went to the club. It could happen. I lost four pounds just last week, though I found it later, in my upper thighs.

"G, I feel too uncomfortable to come in. Can we do this over the phone?"

"There's nothing to be ashamed of, Mr. Konrath. There are plenty of fat, ugly people who come here every day. You'll fit right in."

"If they come there every day why are they still fat and ugly?"

"You're disappointing me, Mr. Konrath."

"Sorry, G. I'll drop by later today."

"Great! See you then."

"Are you mad at me, G?"

"No. Not this time."

"Thanks. Bye."

I hung up the phone, happy about recommitting myself to getting into shape. Twenty minutes later I was in the health club parking lot, finishing the last of my pizza. G greeted me warmly, pumping my hand like I was a lat machine. He was bigger than I remembered. I bet he had more definition than Webster's Unabridged.

Well, come on, all the jokes can't be good.

"How's my bestest buddy, Mr. Konrath?"

"Hungry. How about that smoothie?"

"Sure thing. You bring your Visa?"

"My wife took it. But I found some change in the couch."

G led me to the juice bar, and spent five minutes measuring out assorted powders into a stainless steel blender.

"The base is macrobiotic organic yogurt," he told me. "Low fat and sugar free."

"What flavor?"

"Plain."

"Sounds good. Can you add a few scoops of those chocolate chips?"

After the smoothie, G and I hit the equipment. Almost immediately I knew we were going to have problems. First of all, he wanted me to start a program he called "weight training." From what I gathered, this involved picking up weights, and lifting them up and down. G gave me a preview, grabbing a barbell the size of a Cadillac (when they still made them big), and curling it up to his chest several times. I very politely told G that he was out of his freaking mind if he thought I was going to do that. You couldn't pay me to do that. I certainly wasn't go to pay them to let me.

G let out a friendly laugh and then threw me a weight belt and told me to get started while he went to the juice bar for a creatine shake. "For a boost of energy," he said.

"Put in some of those mini marshmallows," I told him. "And some ham."

While I waited for my energy boost, I sat on an exercise bike, content with watching a girl in a string bikini do leg presses. She had a body that could make a priest give up choir boys. When G came back I was sweating like a pig.

"How are we doing, Mr. Konrath?"

"Great, G. I'm glad I signed up."

"Let's not overdo it your first day. Time for your rubdown."

While G rubbed my achy muscles for three dollars a minute, I had to admit that this health club thing was a good idea after all. Sure, I had to take out a second mortgage to pay for it, but seeing that girl do those leg presses gave my heart a workout it hadn't had in years.

And later that night, I actually got in a few minutes of strenuous exercise. With my wife, while thinking of the leg-press girl.

I was so quiet I didn't even wake her up.

BIO

J.A. Konrath is the author of seven novels in the Jack Daniels series, along with dozens of short stories. The eighth, STIRRED, will be available in 2011.

Under the name Jack Kilborn, he wrote the horror novels AFRAID, ENDURANCE, TRAPPED, SERIAL UNCUT (written with Blake Crouch) and DRACULAS (written with Blake Crouch, Jeff Strand, and F. Paul Wilson.)

Under the name Joe Kimball, he wrote two novels in the TIMECASTER sci-fi series which feature Jack Daniels's grandson as the hero, and Harry McGlade III.

Visit Joe at www.JAKonrath.com.

BIBLIOGRAPHY

The Jack Daniels Novels

Shot of Tequila
Whiskey Sour
Bloody Mary
Rusty Nail
Dirty Martini
Fuzzy Navel
Cherry Bomb
Shaken
Stirred

In the Jack Daniels Universe

Jack Daniels Stories (Collected Stories)
Truck Stop
Suckers by JA Konrath and Jeff Strand
Planter's Punch by JA Konrath and Tom Schreck
Serial Uncut by Blake Crouch and JA Konrath
Floaters by JA Konrath and Henry Perez
Killers Uncut by Blake Crouch and JA Konrath
Banana Hammock - A Harry McGlade Adventure

As Jack Kilborn

Afraid
Trapped
Endurance
Draculas by J.A. Konrath, Blake Crouch, Jeff Strand, and F. Paul Wilson
Horror Stories (Collected Stories)

Other Work

Origin
The List
Disturb
55 Proof (Short Story Omnibus)
Crime Stories (Collected Stories)
Dumb Jokes & Vulgar Poems

As Joe Kimball

Timecaster
Timecaster Supersymmetry

Made in the USA
Lexington, KY
11 December 2011